What Reviewer's Say About Jane Fletcher's Books

The Celaeno Series

"...captivating, well-written stories in the fantasy genre that are built around women's struggles against themselves, one another, society, and nature." – *WomanSpace Magazine*

"In *Rangers at Roadsend* Fletcher not only gives us powerful characters, but she surprises us with an unexpected ending to the murder conspiracy plot, pushing the story in one direction only to have that direction reversed more than once. This is one thrill ride the reader will not want to get off." – Independent Gay Writer

"...compelling narrative, plot twists, intense action sequences, vivid scenery..." – *Midwest Book Review*

"*The Walls of Westernfort*, is not only a highly engaging and fast-paced adventure novel, it provides the reader with an interesting framework for examining the same questions of loyalty, faith, family and love." – *Midwest Book Review*

"*The Walls of Westernfort* is...a true delight. Bold, well-developed characters hold your interest from the beginning and keep you turning the pages. The main plot twists and turns until the very end. The sub-plot involves likeable women who seem destined not to be together." – *MegaScene*

The Lyremouth Chronicles

"*The Exile and the Sorcerer* is a mesmerizing read, a tour-de-force packed with adventure, ordeals, complex twists and turns, and the internal introspection of appealing characters. The author writes effortlessly, handling the size and scope of the book with ease. Not since the fantasy works of Elizabeth Moon and Lynn Flewelling have I been so thoroughly engrossed in a tale. This is knockout fiction, tantalizingly told, and beautifully packaged." – *Midwest Book Review*

T0162091

Dynasty of Rogues

by

Jane Fletcher

2007

DYNASTY OF ROGUES

ISBN 1-933110-71-6
ISBN 978-1-933110-71-4

This Trade Paperback Is Published By
Bold Strokes Books, Inc.,
New York, USA

First Edition, March 2007

Credits
Editors: Cindy Cresap and Stacia Seaman
Production Design: J. Barre Greystone
Cover Image: Tobias Brenner (http://www.tobiasbrenner.de/)
Cover Design: J. Barre Greystone

By the Author

Acknowledgments

Once again, Cindy Cresap was the most constructively supportive editor that any writer could wish for, even though (aside from the editing process) she stubbornly refuses to tell me how far a block is.

Having finally been fortunate enough to meet Stacia Seaman in real life, I now know that not only is she a whiz at spotting dangling modifiers, but she also recognises a good Scotch when she meets it.

As ever, Radclyffe and the whole BSB team were both friendly and professional, giving me the warm, confident feeling of knowing that all I needed to worry about was the writing, since everything that needed to be done was covered, in-hand and on schedule.

I would like to thank Tobi for the cover art and Mary for help with horses in general and their hooves in particular. Also Jo for her critical appraisal, with and without accompanying gestures.

DEDICATION

To Paul and Brent
brother and brother-in-law
honest men at last

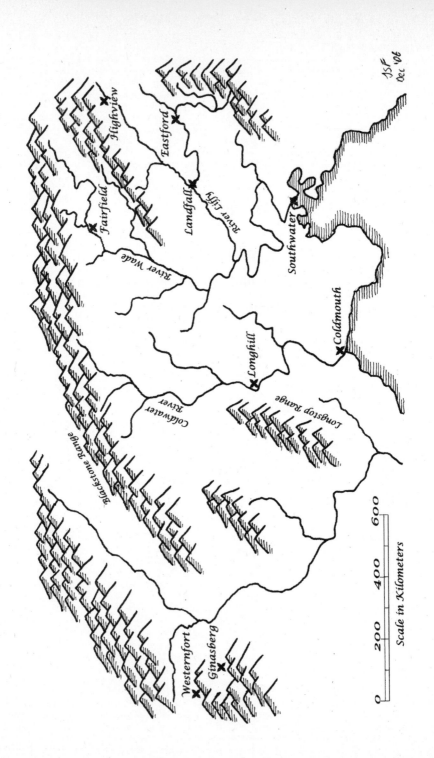

Scale in Kilometers

PART ONE

Against The World

23 February 561

Chapter One—The Troublemaker

Leading Ranger Rikako Sadiq could no longer feel her toes. Her fingers were not faring much better. The icy north wind was the problem, stealing the heat from her. The miserable weather was even less enjoyable than might normally be the case since she was standing on the most exposed spot the sergeant could find. As a lookout position it was a questionable choice. As a place anyone would pick for loafing around on a cold day, it was a complete non-starter.

Admittedly, the top of the rocks offered an impressive view. On the hillside above, fir trees swept over the contours in a blanket of green. A hundred meters away downhill, the forest ended in a straggling line, where farmers had cleared land for crops and animal pasture. The canyon holding the heretic stronghold of Ginasberg was a wide crack running along the edge of the fields.

Riki slapped her arms around her sides and yawned. The morning was dragging. Standing lookout would not be so bad if there were something to look out for. Terminal boredom had set in hours before. Her only entertainment was tapping out rhythms as she stamped life back into her feet, and even this had become too painful to be any fun.

The wind shifted, sneaking under her jacket with cold fingers, pinching at her stomach. Riki tried to seal the gap and looked down enviously at the logging camp beneath the rocks. The workers were out of the wind. They were also moving around, which would keep them warm. Best of all, they had something to do, and people to talk to while they did it. The new mine shaft needed more timber to shore it up, and a group of miners had been sent from Ginasberg to get it.

Sentry duty was supposedly in case of danger approaching, and the rocks overhanging the camp were ideal for this—as long as the danger approached by swinging through the treetops. However, if whatever it was tried walking along at ground level, it would be completely hidden from view. Fortunately, with winter barely over, there was no risk of Guards being so far from their Homelands.

Although nothing had been said, Riki was sure the real reason she had been made to stand on lookout was that the sergeant thought she had untied Corporal Lopez's horse so it had strayed. Nothing could be proved, so the sergeant had settled for unofficial retribution in the form of freezing Riki's tits off on pointless sentry duty. Riki grimaced as she thought about it. The reason nothing could be proved was that she had not done it. Lopez had been sloppy about taking care of her horse. If Riki had wanted to play a trick, she would have been far more imaginative.

As she stood there, Riki was studiously trying not to think about what those more imaginative things might be, in case she came up with something too tempting to be ignored. She was in enough trouble as it was.

Cheers from the miners recalled Riki's attention. A young woman was lurching into the logging camp, carrying a large metal pot that swung back and forth in an awkward off-beat to her steps. Riki frowned, recognizing the new arrival as Beth. The pot would contain lunch, brought from Ginasberg, half a kilometer away. Hot food, either soup or stew, would be very welcome, but this description did not apply to Beth, and the feeling was mutual. What chance was there that Beth would put her responsibilities as waitress before personal animosity?

Beth deposited the pot on a tree stump and shrugged a pack off her back. From it, she pulled bowls and bread. The miners left their ropes, saws, and axes and gathered around. After receiving their share, several sat on felled tree trunks to eat. Everyone appeared happy. Laughter rang out. Beth glanced up at Riki a couple of times but showed no sign of bringing her food.

Riki sighed and settled her eyes on the distance, trying to appear unconcerned. Of course, personal animosity would win every time with Beth. How silly to even pose the question. Probably Beth was hoping for Riki to call out so that she could make a point of ignoring her. Riki would not give her the satisfaction. Eventually Beth would have to bring food up to the rocks, and Riki knew there was nothing she could do to make it happen any quicker.

Fifteen minutes passed, and the miners had taken second helpings, before Beth trudged into the forest. A few minutes later, she appeared on the uphill side of the rocks, where they emerged from the covering of soil.

"I've brought you your lunch." Beth's manner could only be described as sneering.

"Oh, that's really kind of you."

Riki made sure her own tone and expression suggested nothing other than cheerful sincerity, as if Beth had done her a favor. She fixed her smile before examining what Beth had brought. As Riki had feared, the bowl was half full of cold, watery dregs. The bread was clearly the most overbaked portion Beth could find.

Beth watched her smugly. "I'm sorry, there wasn't much left."

Riki just nodded and chewed off a mouthful of bread, as if noticing nothing wrong, and was rewarded by seeing Beth's smirk falter.

"I'm afraid that bit's burnt."

"It's fine. I like a decent crust."

"I gave the miners more because they're working, and you're just standing around up here doing nothing." Beth was now digging, trying to provoke a reaction.

"Oh yes, sure. I wasn't hungry anyway."

The lies were worth it for the expression of pique that displaced the last of Beth's taunting smile. She glowered in silence while Riki drained the bowl and handed it back.

"Thanks. That was great."

Beth snatched the bowl and stomped away. Riki waited until the surly young woman was gone before letting her shoulders slump. Winding Beth up by refusing to rise to the bait was the most fun Riki had felt all day, but Beth was far too predictable to be a challenge. Hot food would have been better, because now, after a morning of being cold, miserable, and bored, all that lay ahead for Riki was an afternoon of being cold, miserable, bored, and hungry.

Why did Beth have to be so petty? It was six years since Riki had broken her arm, and it had been an accident, a childhood fight that had ended in a fall. Anyway, Beth had started it.

However, Riki had gotten the blame. She had always gotten the blame. Riki sighed and kicked a loose pebble. It bounced away down the rocks and into the undergrowth clinging to the hillside below. To be fair, she generally was the one responsible, but not that time. She certainly had not been a bully, as Beth claimed. Even though Riki had been fourteen at the time, and Beth only twelve, Beth had been the taller by a clear ten centimeters.

At one meter fifty-five, Riki was still small and lightly built, but her agility and wiry muscles meant that she could easily hold her own, although she was now far too mature for childish scuffles and similar mischief. Riki's lips set in a line. How long would it take everyone to notice that she had grown out of her adolescent troublemaking? She still got blamed for far more than she was guilty of—as with Lopez's straying horse.

Down in the camp, the miners-cum-lumberjacks returned to their work, all except for Faye, who remained by the stew pot, talking to Beth. From her vantage point, Riki considered them cynically. It was no secret that Beth had her sights set on the young miner. Even Riki had heard the gossip, and she was always last for the rumor mill.

Maybe Beth volunteered to bring the food in hope of talking to the object of her desire, and inexplicably, Faye was not running away—quite the opposite. Was Beth about to land her catch? The body language certainly suggested it was a possibility. The two were edging closer as they chatted.

Riki pursed her lips thoughtfully. Trying to be objective, she guessed that Beth was sort of pretty in a bland, brain dead, bitch from hell type of way. Perhaps that was what Faye went for. Riki's expression changed to a wry grin, with more than a touch of self-mockery. She could hardly claim any sort of expertise on the matter.

Beth pulled off her wool cap and lay it on the tree stump beside the stew pot, and then tossed her head coyly, so her hair bounced around her face. Riki snorted in derision. Beth could not even flirt imaginatively, although Faye did not seem to mind. Presumably Beth's imagination was not the source of attraction. Faye put her hand on Beth's arm and leaned forward to whisper into her ear. The pair giggled like three-year-olds, glanced at the other miners, and then, arm in arm, slipped away into the woods.

On the other side of the clearing, everyone else was busy. Riki shook her head in scornful bemusement. Why had no one complained about Faye shirking work? They certainly had noticed. Riki was too far away to hear what was said, but from the gestures passing between the group, they appeared to be mainly amused. Even the forewoman had a tolerant smile. All the irritation and discomfort of the morning returned to Riki in a wave of bitterness. In no way would she be allowed to get away with it.

Riki's stomach rumbled. She stared at the discarded cap, unable to keep the scowl from her face. How nice to be warm enough to take your hat off, for whatever reason. Riki's eyes turned to the stew pot beside it. Was it really empty as Beth claimed? A sudden idea bounced into Riki's head. Immediately, she tried to clamp down on it. Stamping her feet, she turned away, but the thought had taken hold.

Riki attempted to push back the knowledge that she was cold and hungry, being punished for something she had not done. She tried to forget the smug sneer on Beth's face. But then her stomach rumbled again, and she gave in. The temptation was far too strong to withstand.

The miners were all occupied with sawing and splitting a huge fir into manageable lengths of timber. Riki gave them one last look, judging their likely positions for the next few minutes, and then hopped down from the rocks. Her feet landed silently in the soft carpet of pine needles.

The light undergrowth beneath the trees was mainly snagweed and rock holly, although the first shoots of lemon vine were breaking through the soil. Riki crept down the hillside. Her small, agile build was ideal for sneaking. She had always been good at passing unnoticed, and childhood hikes with her gene mother had given her an empathy with the wilderness.

The miners' voices got louder as Riki approached. The mundane comments made it clear that her absence from lookout had not been noticed. Riki grinned as she ducked past the last few trees and reached the edge of the clearing. From the shelter of a knotted clump of snagweed, she peered out. The tree stump bearing the stew pot and Beth's hat was only two meters away. The miners were all hard at work on the opposite side of camp. Nobody was looking around, and her Ranger's green uniform should blend into the background. Keeping low, Riki scuttled to the tree stump.

As she had thought, a good two centimeters of stew remained at the bottom of the pot. The food was now congealed, but Riki could see more than three times as much meat and vegetables sitting there wasted as had been in the bowl she had received. Beth must have deliberately strained the liquid she gave to Riki.

The ladle was hanging on the side of the pot. Riki picked it up in one hand and Beth's hat in the other. With a cheery cook's flourish, she deposited a good dollop of cold stew in the hat, squashed it around to ensure that the wool was nicely coated, and then carefully put the hat back exactly where it had been. Riki hung the ladle over the rim and snuck back into the undergrowth.

Crouched beneath the snagweed, Riki paused to consider the scene. A niggling doubt about the wisdom of her actions surfaced, but it was too late now. And just how much trouble would she get into? Would Beth even make a complaint, since it might mean owning up to her own spite? Once she had thought about it, she would probably keep quiet, although she was going to create a bit of noise at first, when she put the hat back on.

At the thought, Riki's grin returned. Any comeback was going to be worth it. Quite apart from the anticipated amusement, the activity had warmed her up. Riki's grin got still wider as she began her stealthy return to the lookout rocks.

A scream ripped through the forest, long and high, slicing the cold air.

Riki leapt from her crouch, moving into the open. Across the clearing, some miners had instinctively ducked for cover. Others were jerking their heads left and right, trying to work out where the sound came from. The more alert were scrabbling for their axes. Riki did not wait for them. She raced around the camp, toward the source of the scream, and dived back into the forest.

Another scream sounded, quieter but more desperate than the first.

Riki sped between the trees, plowing heedlessly through the barriers of snagweed and rock holly. Her feet skidded on the soft ground. After twenty meters, Riki hurdled over a fallen tree and joined a forest trail marked by two fresh sets of footprints. Riki sprinted along the track. The path led downhill, toward the sound of water. Ahead, the undergrowth was thinning out. Riki rounded one last thicket of rock holly and burst onto the open banks of a stream.

Ten meters from where she emerged, Beth lay on the ground. Poised over her was a mountain cat, pinning her down. The animal's dappled rump was toward Riki. Its tail switched back and forth like a whip. Beth's heels were scrabbling in the mud between its rear legs in a pointless attempt to squirm away. Her arm was across her face and blood was staining the torn sleeve of her jacket.

Riki ripped her sword from its scabbard and charged forward, shouting. The cat barely responded, just the faintest flick of its ears. Its attention was fixed on the woman under its paws. Open jaws lunged down at Beth's throat, knocking her arm aside.

Riki's sword arced through the air. She did not have the time to get in close for a clean, killing thrust. The blade only made glancing contact with the cat's tail, barely drawing blood, but that was enough to divert the animal away from Beth. The cat whirled round. Riki leapt back and brought her sword to the guard position.

For a moment, the two stared at each other. The cat snarled, but its eyes were hooded and its stance unsteady. The animal must be fresh from hibernation and still groggy. However, it would also be ravenous from the winter fast and therefore very dangerous.

The cat pounced, claws outstretched, striking for Riki's head. She ducked aside but one of the cat's paws clamped on her right shoulder. The thick reinforced leather of Riki's jacket prevented the claws from piercing deeply enough to cause serious injury, but the weight dragged her to her knees. The cat's saber fangs raked toward Riki's face, but the paw locked on her shoulder meant the cat's chest was exposed. Riki thrust her sword deep into its body. The animal spun away, yowling, almost wrenching the sword from Riki's grip.

Riki managed to keep hold of the hilt and pull her sword free, ready to strike again, but there was no need. The wound was fatal. Already the cat's rump was sagging to one side as its rear legs lost their strength. Its head flung back in a last roar, and then its shoulders crumpled. The dying animal collapsed onto Beth, who screamed again.

Riki scrambled to her feet. The cat twitched a few times and then lay still. Beth carried on screaming.

Running footsteps sounded, both ahead and behind. Looking up, Riki saw Faye splashing through the stream and scrabbling to Beth's side. Where had the miner been? There had been no sign of her when Riki arrived. Clearly Faye had found a place to run and hide, safeguarding her own skin.

The feet behind were getting closer. Riki looked over her shoulder and saw three miners arrive, hefting axes. At the sight of the dead cat they slowed and lowered their weapons. After a moment of shuffling hesitation, they went to assist Faye in extricating Beth from beneath the carcass. Riki was about to help, but she felt stinging in her shoulder. Her leather jacket had not fully protected her from the claws. The wound was not major, although she suspected the liquid trickling down her arm was blood.

Gingerly, Riki knelt and wiped her sword clean on a patch of grass, then resheathed it. When she stood up, the situation was getting calmer. Beth had thankfully stopped screaming and was standing, wrapped in Faye's arms. The other miners were gathered around supportively.

More footsteps and shouts announced the arrival of the remaining miners. In the lead was the forewoman. The fear on her face faded at the sight of everyone standing, limbs and life intact, but in an instant her expression changed again to one of fury. Shaking with rage, she stormed over and grabbed Riki's uninjured shoulder.

"Why the fuck weren't you on lookout?"

❖

"How many more last chances does she get?"

"It wasn't deliberate."

"She wandered away from sentry duty by accident?" Lieutenant Aisha O'Neil's voice dripped sarcasm. She stomped into her office.

Kavita Sadiq was not about to give up so easily. She followed the commander of the Rangers at Ginasberg into the room, closed the door, and then slumped unbidden on a chair beside the desk. As a civilian, she did not need to meet military protocol. Beyond this, her on/off relationship with Ash O'Neil made any formality unnecessary. Kavita rubbed her forehead, hoping to ease her tension. How many of those offs had been due to friction over her unruly daughter?

"Faye and Beth were as much to blame. They shouldn't have wandered into the woods on their own."

Ash threw herself into her chair and glared across the desk. "The other two aren't Rangers. They're civilians who're free to wander wherever they want."

"Even if Riki had stayed on lookout, they'd have been out of her sight."

"That's not the point."

"But—"

"No buts. She was on guard duty and she left her post for no good reason. That's a court-martial offense."

Kavita rested her head in her hands, thinking of all the other times she had been in that office, making excuses for Riki. What more could she say? What more did she need to say? Ash knew the situation, and knew Kavita's feelings of guilt that prompted her to plead Riki's case.

As a child, Riki had been a handful, as befitting the youngest in a family with three older sisters to spoil her. Maybe she had been given her own way too much, but she had never been out of control. Riki had been no worse than any other high-spirited girl, back when Kavita had lived with her partner, Eli Diaz, in their home at Highview.

But then Kavita had been denounced as heretic, and there was no time for her to think things out. Her other birth daughter, Sue, had been twenty-two and newly settled with a partner. Eli's two birth daughters, Bron and Jan, were eighteen and twenty-seven respectively. All of them were old enough to make up their own minds, and none were implicated in the heresy. Kavita had left them behind when she fled via the heretic network, into the Wildlands. Only twelve-year-old Riki had been still a child and still her responsibility.

Kavita bit her lip, thinking of her former partner, Riki's gene mother. Riki and Eli had been so close. Kavita had watched their bond strengthen as her own relationship with Eli had crumbled. In her heart, Kavita knew that Riki would have been happier with her gene mother. At the core of Kavita's guilt lay doubts about how much her action had been motivated by jealousy. Had she taken Riki as a way of hitting back at her ex-partner?

"It's my fault."

Ash snorted. "How are you to blame for your daughter deserting her post?"

"I should never have brought her here. I should have left her at Highview with Eli. When the Guards came for me, I panicked. I grabbed Riki and fled. I should have thought."

"You were her birth mother. She belonged with you." Ash sounded bored. The argument was an old one that they had long ago kicked over to the point of tedium.

"But Riki never asked to become a heretic."

"Is she? I thought she still worshiped Celaeno. That's what she keeps telling people."

"She never asked to come here," Kavita amended.

"Nor have any of the other kids brought here. But they don't go around like hell on legs." Ash's voice softened. "You're not to blame for everything Rikako does."

Yet Kavita knew she was responsible. When she had first heard the heretics' claims that the Goddess Celaeno was no more than misremembered folktales of a ship that had brought people from another planet, she had been intrigued. It made sense of some things that had long puzzled her. Why had she not left it at that? Why had she felt compelled to seek out the truth and find all the answers? And if she had to indulge her curiosity, why had she not waited until Riki was grown, so the consequences would affect no one else?

Joining the heretics would never have been without pain—Kavita missed her other daughters and granddaughters desperately—but she had been able to settle in. Back in Highview, Kavita had been a building forewoman. When she and Riki arrived in the Wildlands, the township at Ginasberg was newly founded and Kavita's experience had been put to use, constructing the town's defenses. She now worked as the chief engineer in the mines. Kavita might even have been happy in a relationship with Ash, comforting after the turmoil with Eli, had it not been for her disruptive daughter.

Riki had reacted to the family breakup with increasingly troublesome behavior. At first she had limited herself to bouts of quarrelling, sullenness, and disobedience. Then she had started causing mayhem outside the home. The fights with other children had been followed by petty theft and vandalism. In a community as small as Ginasberg, Riki had become notorious.

Kavita's only hope had been that as Riki got older, she would start to understand and learn to deal with her anger and pain in a mature way. The hopes had met with limited success. In the last few years, Riki's behavior had improved, but the mother-daughter relationship was showing no sign of healing.

The general consensus in town was that Riki needed discipline, and with her reputation, job prospects were limited. There was no chance of her following Kavita into engineering. In temperament and interests, Riki took after Eli, a fur trapper. Math, geology, and mechanics bored her. She was happiest in the wilderness, using the skills she had learned from her gene mother.

In a rare moment of contrition, Riki had let herself be talked into joining the Rangers. Kavita had needed to exert even more pressure getting Ash to accept her, and it still had not worked out. Riki was no longer raising hell in town, but rules and regulations were never going to sit well with her. Membership in the Rangers was an invitation for trouble—one more thing for Kavita to feel guilty about.

"She's been so much better these last few years. But people remember the fuss she caused in the past and won't give her credit for making an effort now."

"Fuss! Can I mark that down as understatement of the day?"

"Whatever. She's changed, but people won't give her a chance."

"I've given her plenty of chances, as you know. She deserted her post. Now. This morning. Not some time in the past."

"I agree she shouldn't have done it. But everyone's acting like she's committed some terrible crime, and nobody's praising her for killing the cat and saving Beth's life."

Ash sucked in a deep breath. "You're right. People haven't gotten around to being angry about this morning. They're still angry about the five counts of theft, eleven counts of vandalism, four counts of drunk and disorderly, the first when she was only thirteen, and one count of arson. She played truant from school so much it's amazing she can read and write."

"The arson was an accident, so she..." Kavita's voice died. Whether or not it was intentional was fairly irrelevant. Riki should not have been playing with fire in a hay barn.

"And that list doesn't include all the things aimed directly at you that you hushed up."

Kavita could feel the tears forming. "It was all aimed at me. All of it. Riki was just trying to punish me for splitting up the family."

Ash sighed. "If you'd stayed in the Homelands, the Guards would have had you tried and executed. You weren't to blame. You had no choice."

"But Riki was just a child who was hurting. You can't expect her to understand."

"She isn't a child anymore. She's twenty."

"And she isn't getting into the same sort of trouble. That list you just gave, the theft and the vandalism and the rest. None of it happened in the last few years. But people always look for the worst in her. Leaving her post today. It was just mucking around."

"But she was mucking around on duty. And it isn't the first time.

She still treats the rules as if they're an optional exercise. I will not put up with that in the Rangers."

"But she—"

Ash cut her off, sounding resigned rather than angry. "I'm responsible for the security of Ginasberg. Her actions were unacceptable. I can't afford to have someone like her under my command. It was her last chance and she's blown it."

"So what are you going to do?"

"I'm tempted to tie her up and dump her on the Homelands borders for the Guards to deal with."

"You're not serious."

Ash left her chair and walked to the window. Kavita stared at her back, waiting for Ash to give judgment. She caught her lip between her teeth, fighting back tears. She could make one last emotional appeal, playing on what remained of the affection between them. But their relationship had suffered enough because of Riki. Ash had always tried to be fair and did not deserve to be pressured by the forlorn remains of their relationship.

Three minutes passed in silence before Ash sighed and turned back. "Okay. One very last chance. She gets a fresh start, somewhere that people won't start out by hating the sight of her."

❖

Riki marched into Lieutenant O'Neil's office and snapped to attention: "Ma'am."

O'Neil remained seated on the other side of the desk. The glare she gave Riki could have stripped paint off woodwork.

Riki kept her own eyes on the wall while she worked at keeping her expression under control. She was in trouble again. It was not fair or rational, but letting her anger show would not help.

The whole thing was a joke. If she had stayed at her post, she would not have seen the cat and she would have had farther to run when Beth screamed, which would have meant getting there too late. Instead of the pointless sentry duty, she should have been patrolling the perimeter of the camp. Then she might have spotted the cat before it attacked anyone. Yet nobody was criticizing the sergeant for giving inane orders that had put the safety of the miners at risk.

The embroidered badges on Riki's jacket sleeves felt heavy. They carried the single bar of a leading ranger. Normally, when someone entered the Rangers, it took two years to complete probation and get the automatic promotion. Riki had taken over three, and she had the nasty feeling that she was about to go back to private again. She hoped nothing worse would follow.

O'Neil got to her feet and stalked around the desk. She stopped to one side, standing so close that Riki could feel the lieutenant's breath on her cheek.

"Okay, Ranger. This is your chance to tell me your side of it. Why you weren't at your post?"

"No reason, ma'am."

"That's not a bloody answer," O'Neil barked. "What were you doing?"

"I...ah..." Riki restrained the urge to sigh. She was sure that O'Neil was not really interested in the details, but she might as well say it. "I was pouring cold stew into Beth's hat, ma'am."

"Why?"

"I was angry about the portion of food she had given me for lunch, ma'am. I wanted to get back at her."

O'Neil turned away sharply and paced around Riki, circling like a predator sizing up its next meal. Her footsteps sounded slow, heavy, and ominous. At last, she came to a stop in front of her desk. Her eyes bored into Riki.

"Your mucking about nearly got Beth killed. Is that enough getting back at her for you? Or do you want to have a go at breaking her arm again?"

Riki clenched her jaw shut. Her mucking about was what had saved Beth's life, and O'Neil was quite experienced enough to know it.

"Answer me!" O'Neil shouted.

"No, ma'am."

"You're supposed to be a Ranger, not a kid on a frigging picnic. Do you know the difference?"

"Yes, ma'am."

"Really? I'm surprised, because I'd never guess it from the way you act. In over forty years, you are the most pathetically irresponsible excuse for a soldier I've ever seen. I wouldn't trust you to watch over a dung heap. I certainly can't trust you to defend the town. You're a fucking liability from the moment you wake up in the morning. It's all one big game to you, isn't it?"

"No, ma'am."

"I think it is. And I'm not putting up with it anymore. You're out of my command."

The first ripples of concern awoke. Things were going worse than Riki had feared. What happened to a Ranger who was flung out of the service? Would she be allowed to stay in Ginasberg? Or would she be exiled back to the Homelands, to take her chance with the Guards and the Sisterhood?

O'Neil spun away and stormed back to her chair, although she did not sit. She leaned forward, resting her knuckles on the desk. "I ought to kick you out of the Rangers altogether, but I'm going to give you one last chance. A fresh start. I'm transferring you to Westernfort. You'll join one of the squadrons based there. And if you screw up again, it won't be me who deals with it. Captain Coppelli will be the one who works out what to damned well do with you."

CHAPTER TWO—BACK ON THE OUTSIDE

Riki checked her horse's water for the third time, adjusted her saddle on its stand, twitched the harness so it hung a little straighter from the hook, and then scratched her horse's nose. None of these activities was necessary, just a way of putting off the impending encounter. Riki pouted, deriding herself. She had been in trouble enough times before and it never used to bother her. Why was she hesitant now? Had she lost her nerve? Or was it that Westernfort and Captain Coppelli were unknown entities?

Regardless, dawdling in the stable was a waste of time. She might as well get it over with. Maybe Captain Coppelli would have some amusing personal quirks that she could laugh about afterward. Most people did. It was just a question of learning how to set them off. After a final pat of her horse's neck, Riki shouldered her pack and marched into the bright afternoon sunlight.

At the doorway, she paused and considered the view. A soaring line of cliffs ran away east and west, fading into the distance. The only break in the sheer rock face was where the mouth of a hanging valley emerged midway down. This was the entrance to Westernfort. The only way in was a narrow path, cut into the cliff. The opening to the high valley was further protected by a stone wall along its bottom. A stream cascaded through a culvert at one side of the gate and fell in a single glittering drop to the plain below.

The disorderly collection of barns and animal shelters were clustered around the start of the pathway up. They were light structures that could be abandoned and rebuilt, should the Guards attack. Riki shifted the pack on her shoulder and set off, threading her way between the rough timber structures and avoiding spots where the ground had been churned to thick mud by countless hooves.

Westernfort lay five days north of Ginasberg, on the rim of the high escarpment overlooking the plains around a winding river. Like the other heretic stronghold, its location had been chosen for its defensive capabilities. In the case of Westernfort, these had already been tested. Thirteen years before, the Guards had attempted to storm the site. The cairn raised over the bodies of the fallen was the only reminder of the battle.

The ascending path, when Riki got to it, was a meter and a half in width, allowing no more than two women to walk side by side, and all the way, attackers would be exposed and vulnerable, at the mercy of archers above. As she climbed, Riki craned her neck, studying the wall hanging over her. The stone blocks continued the sheer line of the cliff, allowing no foothold for attackers. The open gate was solid, with insufficient room in front to maneuver a battering ram.

Rangers stood sentry on the wall. Riki could hear their voices. They would have marked her since her arrival at the stable. Riki spared a glance for the cairn on the valley floor and grimaced. She did not envy the Guards who had been sent to attack Westernfort.

From the top of the pathway, Riki had a clear view over the broad floodplain below. Herds of sheep and cows were grazing on the water meadows while pigs rutted through the mud. Loose pine groves crowned the tops of scattered tumuli. Sunlight sparkled on loops in the river. Several kilometers away, another parallel escarpment rose on the northern edge of the plain, and beyond it, the serried ranks of mountains faded into the distance. Spray from the waterfall misted past. Riki spent a moment longer, taking in the panorama, then she turned and marched through the gateway.

On the other side of the wall, Riki found herself at the entrance to a valley surrounded by mountains, a kilometer wide at its broadest and several kilometers long. This valley held forests and farmlands, and also the town of Westernfort itself. It was the older and larger of the heretic settlements, with close to a thousand inhabitants. Riki and her mother had lived there briefly after they fled the Homelands, but she had not been back since they moved to Ginasberg.

Faced with the unfamiliar layout, Riki hesitated, wondering where to go next. However, the sentries were not going to let an unrecognized face slip by unchallenged. A woman with a sergeant's badge on her sleeve trotted down a flight of stairs inside the wall.

"Do you need help?" Despite a frown at the sight of a stranger dressed in a Ranger uniform, the words were delivered in a friendly fashion.

"Ah, yes, ma'am. Leading Ranger Sadiq, from Ginasberg. I have a letter from Lieutenant O'Neil. Where can I find Captain Coppelli?"

The information sufficed and the frown changed to a welcoming smile. "She should be in the headquarters." The sergeant pointed to a group of brick buildings on the edge of the town. "If you go there, someone will escort you to her."

"Thank you, ma'am."

As Riki marched along the road, an unexpected feeling of tension in her stomach grew. Whatever O'Neil had written about in the letter was unlikely to be flattering, and Riki was not looking forward to the forthcoming meeting. Would Captain Coppelli really give her a clean start, rather than decide that further disciplinary action was needed?

Riki slapped her leg with the palm of her hand. Did it matter? Riki knew that she would not keep out of trouble for long. Nor did she want to. Life was too short to waste, busting your ass about senseless regulations. Yet with each new incident, Riki was finding it harder to shrug off the ensuing reprimand and punishment. Was it because she was older? Or was it just that she no longer deliberately sought the notoriety? Now the notoriety came hunting her.

Within minutes of reaching the buildings, Riki had found an orderly and passed on her request to meet Captain Coppelli. She also handed over the sealed letter from O'Neil. On balance, Riki felt she would rather not be present when it was read.

The orderly nodded, took the letter, and directed Riki to a stool in a corner. Riki sat down to wait, reminding herself of all the reasons why she did not care about how the meeting went.

❖

Captain Coppelli was in her early fifties. Her hair was cropped short, soldier style, and graying at the temples. She had a solid, muscular build. Her eyes were sharp, radiating a fierce intelligence. Laughter lines creased around her mouth, although no trace of a smile was currently visible. She tossed O'Neil's letter onto the desk and fixed a withering gaze on Riki. "That is the most dismal report I've ever read about any Ranger. You're a disgrace to your uniform. Are you proud of your record?"

Riki stood to attention a few feet away. "No, ma'am."

"You're lucky I trust Lieutenant O'Neil's judgment better than I trust my own. Because if it was my call, you'd be on a trip back to the Homelands, with a warning that if ever you were seen west of the Blackstone Mountains again, you'd be shot on sight. We've got enough problems with the Sisterhood and the Guards. We don't need shitheads like you stirring up trouble in our midst."

Coppelli paced to within an arm's length of Riki. She jerked her thumb back over her shoulder, indicating the desk. "That's not the first report I've read about you. You've been nothing but trouble since the day you arrived. Is it five or six times you've been found guilty of theft?"

"Five times, ma'am." Riki knew there was no point adding that the last time had been three years ago, when she had taken a bag of apples from the stores and used them for target practice.

"Yet for some reason, O'Neil thinks you should get one more chance. So okay. You get your chance. But if you step a millimeter out of line, you'll be out of the Rangers, out of Westernfort, and lucky if you've still got your skin intact. Do you understand me?"

"Yes, ma'am."

Coppelli marched to the door of her office. She called to the orderly outside, "Can you tell Geraldine Baptiste I want to see her. I've got a new recruit for her patrol." She returned her attention to Riki. "You'll be in 2B Patrol. Sergeant Baptiste is short of a woman. If you cause her trouble, you'll regret it. And while we're waiting for her to get here..."

Captain Coppelli went behind her desk and removed the trail knife from the service belt hanging there, then came to Riki's side. With the tip of the knife she unpicked the stitching that attached the badge of rank to Riki's jacket sleeve. Once the corner was loose enough to provide a grip, she ripped it off and then went to Riki's other arm.

Riki stood stock still, outwardly impassive, although her guts were churning. The demotion was expected. She had thought she was prepared for it. She was wrong. The rank of leading ranger had been hers for less than two months. Getting there had taken so long, and already she was busted to private again. Riki pressed her lips together tightly, summoning anger as a defense. She was used to everyone thinking of her as bad. That she could live with. Incompetent was another matter.

It was unfair. If she had stayed at her post and Beth had been killed, would they still have found some way to make it her fault? Who were they going to blame for everything back in Ginasberg, now that she was gone? Was it worth suggesting that Coppelli invent a new rank for her of squadron scapegoat? Perhaps the badge should be an ass with a target on it and the words "Kick here."

Coppelli dropped the two badges, with their single bar, on top of O'Neil's letter. "When Sergeant Baptiste has finished showing you around, your first task is to get some new blank badges and sew them on your uniform, Private Sadiq."

"Yes, ma'am."

A knock sounded on the door.

"Enter," Coppelli called out.

The woman who came in was about thirty-five, square-faced and square-shouldered. She snapped to attention. "You wanted to see me, ma'am."

"Bad news, I'm afraid, Sergeant Baptiste. I've got a new recruit for your patrol."

Out of the corner of her eye, Riki saw the sergeant's expression shift to confusion.

"Ma'am?"

"I know you're short-handed, but I don't think Private Sadiq is going to be an asset to your patrol. I'm sorry, but someone has to have her. She's been sent here from Ginasberg because Lieutenant O'Neil is sick of the sight of her. I'd tell you to keep a strict eye on her, but I think you need to keep two, and maybe a guard dog as well. At the first sign of trouble, let me know, because I'm just itching for an excuse to kick her out of Westernfort."

Sergeant Baptiste drew in a sharp breath. "Yes, ma'am."

Captain Coppelli stood in front of Riki one more time. "Okay, Sadiq. You've heard the briefing I've given your sergeant. No secrets. No excuses. You know where you stand. And if you want to keep standing in the Rangers, you get your ass into line."

"Yes, ma'am."

"Dismissed." Coppelli turned away. "And sorry again, Gerry."

❖

Dusk was falling as they left the headquarters building. A chill wind gusted between the houses. Across Westernfort, lanterns were being lit. Laurel, the smaller of the two moons, was three-quarters full over the mountains to the east of town. Baptiste led the way around the outskirts of Westernfort in silence, but several times Riki caught the sergeant sending unfavorable scowls in her direction.

So much for the clean start. The words slunk bitterly through Riki's head. However, it was not quite as bad as Ginasberg. She would not be liked or trusted, but nobody would have any real personal hatred toward her. *And it might take as long as three days before they all get to feel that way about me.*

Riki knew that the Rangers at Westernfort were formed into six patrols, each with eight women. These would include a sergeant and a corporal. She also thought that the patrols were divided into two rotations, so presumably 2B was the middle patrol in the second rotation. She could ask Baptiste, although she doubted if a display of enthusiasm for the job would be the slightest help in counteracting Captain Coppelli's introduction.

Their route ended at a long building that had the unmistakable air of a barrack block. When Baptiste opened the door, light and heat spilled out. Riki took a second to gather herself and then followed the sergeant in to meet her new patrol comrades. How would Baptiste portray her arrival? Not that it mattered much. Everyone would see the cut stitching on her shoulders, learn her rank was private, and work out for themselves that she was recently demoted.

The room Riki entered had the traditional barracks layout. In three corners were double bunks; in the fourth was a single bunk for the corporal. The door at one end would lead to the sergeant's room. Lockers took up the remaining wall space. The building would be as much a spiritual home for the women as anything. Many would also have a family home in town, with parents or partner. However, the barrack room symbolized the tight bonding of the patrol. In a crisis, the women would literally depend on each other for their lives.

Currently, all the remaining patrol members were there. Four sat playing cards on the corporal's bunk, while two more were chatting by the iron stove.

"We've got a new patrol member." Baptiste claimed everyone's attention. "She's transferred here from Ginasberg. She's Private Sadiq.

Private..." She turned to Riki, clearly wanting her first name.

"Rikako Sadiq. Riki." She tacked on the shortened version of her name for good measure, although her mother was the only one who ever used it now.

"Right. Well, it's too late to sort out everything tonight. Dinner's soon. We'll get you settled in tomorrow." Baptiste pointed to the lower bunk opposite the card players. "That's the free bed. And the second locker from the right is yours. I'll just introduce you to everyone."

The card players scrambled off the bed and formed an uneven line, joined by the two from the stove. Riki ran her eyes along the row. The women of the patrol looked to be a fairly typical cross section of Rangers, until Riki got to the last in the line.

She was of average height, lightly built, in her early twenties; certainly no more than a couple of years older than Riki. Her face was finely formed, with firm lips, a small nose, and large eyes—a face that would have earned a second look from anyone. However, what caught Riki's attention was the badge on her shoulder, which held the twin bars of a corporal.

How did anyone get to be corporal so young? Riki turned her head slightly so that she could just catch sight of a trailing thread where her leading ranger badge had been ripped off. Not only was she back at private, but she was going to be saying, "Yes, ma'am. No, ma'am," to someone the same age as herself.

Sergeant Baptiste worked her way down the line, naming each Ranger in turn. She reached the end of the row. "And this is Corporal Tanya Coppelli."

Riki fought to control her expression as she muttered a quick "ma'am," but now it all made sense. *That* was how you got promoted so quickly.

"Right. Dinnertime. We don't want to be late at the mess." Baptiste addressed the room.

With the sergeant in the lead, the patrol filed out of the barrack room. Riki opened the door of the locker she had been told was hers, threw her pack in, and then hurried to catch up. She ended up at the rear, walking beside a woman whose name she thought she remembered.

"It was Stevenson, right? Loke Stevenson?"

The woman looked down at Riki. Something about her expression made it clear that this was not just a question of height. She must have been in her early thirties, tall and thin, with a gaunt face. Her hair was longer than normal for a Ranger, enough to reveal a tendency to frizz. Eventually she condescended to give a half nod of acknowledgement

"Yes, Leading Ranger Stevenson. And Loke. Short for Lokelani."

"Right."

They walked in silence for a few more steps. Then Riki indicated the woman in front and dropped her voice so she would not be overheard. "The corporal. Tanya Coppelli. She has to be some relation of the captain's."

"Her daughter."

"Oh."

Riki chewed her lip and glanced again at Loke. The leading ranger had to be at least ten years older than Tanya Coppelli. Surely it must rankle to be overstepped like that, with such blatant favoritism.

"Easy to get promoted when your mother's the captain." Riki made her voice a conspiratorial whisper.

"Chip Coppelli would never be biased."

"Oh, I'm sure." Riki made no attempt to keep the scorn from her voice.

The only response was a sharp glare.

Riki rolled her eyes. Judging by Loke's reaction, the captain had her absolute trust and loyalty. Loke also felt enough affection to refer to her commanding officer by nickname. However, Riki could not stop herself from saying derisively, "And you reckon Tanya deserves to be corporal? It's not that someone wanted to please her mom? Her name didn't help just a little bit?"

"You don't—" Loke broke off sharply and increased her pace. She slowed only when she had drawn level with the woman in question. Riki saw Loke duck her head and whisper something to Tanya, who glanced back, offended anger plain on her face. Clearly Loke had just repeated the doubts cast on her fitness for her rank.

Riki could not believe it. *Just my luck. I pick the patrol ass kisser to talk to.*

Tanya opened her mouth as if she was about to speak, but then turned away and continued walking beside Loke. Riki tagged on alone at the rear, considering their backs and wondering which of the two she disliked the more.

❖

"Private Sadiq." Baptiste summoned Riki straight after breakfast the next morning.

The sergeant was standing by the door to the barrack room. Riki hastened to join her. "Yes, ma'am?"

"I want you assessed to see what you're good at." *If anything.* Baptiste's tone and expression made the last two words as clear as if they had been spoken. "We've got two new applicants for the Rangers. Corporal Coppelli is going to be testing them today to see if they're up to standard. I've told her to check you out at the same time. Get your full kit and meet her by the gates in ten minutes."

"Yes, ma'am."

Riki hurried away, making sure her face revealed no dissent, but alone in the barrack room she stood, hands on hips, glaring at the door to her locker. She was being treated worse than a raw recruit—put on a par with a couple of wide-eyed kids. Demeaning did not begin to describe it. And just how competent was Tanya-frigging-Coppelli to judge her abilities anyway?

Riki grabbed her equipment, then slammed the locker door to vent some of her indignation and stomped out of the room. She was prepared to bet that she knew far more about being a Ranger than the captain's damned daughter.

❖

Two sets of hoofprints scuffed through the leaf litter, becoming clearer atop a slight mound where the wind had blown the loose covering away. The sandy soil held the clear imprint of the animals' feet.

Tanya called the small group to gather round. "Right. What can you tell me from these tracks?"

"They're spadehorns," one of the sixteen-year-old applicants piped up.

Riki kept her eyes on her feet, working to hide her grin. Not that the girl was wrong, but she sounded so pleased with herself. What other animal could have made the huge tracks? An adult spadehorn was two meters high at the shoulder and nearly four meters long.

"What else can you tell me?" Tanya asked.

"One's bigger than the other, and the only time you get spadehorns together are mothers and their babies. So this must be what these are." The youngster sounded less sure of herself.

"Timing? Any idea of when these were made?"

"Um...they're fairly fresh, but we haven't seen the animals." The girl looked around to emphasize her point. "So they probably came through yesterday sometime."

"Anything else?"

The teenagers exchanged nervous looks. Both were clearly desperate to impress. Riki could almost see the cogs going round in their heads as they tried to think of anything intelligent to say. She yawned and looked back to Westernfort several kilometers away. The appraisal was proving every bit as tedious as she had feared, and Tanya was being decidedly patronizing. Admittedly, anyone might have a hard time taking the two applicants seriously, but Tanya was making it plain that she considered Riki to be no different.

"Private Sadiq. What should you do if there's a mother spadehorn around, with offspring?" Tanya asked, possibly noticing Riki's wandering attention.

"If?" Riki said it as a question. "You should go very carefully and make sure you don't end up between them. Spadehorns are normally no problem, but the mothers get very protective. One of them charging you is nasty."

"Very good. Right. We'll move on." Tanya's tone and smile were reminiscent of someone talking to a baby making slow progress at potty training.

"Before we go, ma'am," Riki spoke up. She'd had enough of being treated like an idiot. "I wonder if you can tell us what you'd make of the tracks. Just for reference."

Tanya shot a quizzical glance at her and then frowned at the ground. "Like Jackson said. A mother spadehorn with offspring. I'd put the time at a few hours ago, around dawn."

"Really?" Riki let a pointed edge creep into her tone and she received a sharper stare from Tanya in response.

"Is there something you want to add?"

Riki pursed her lips and shook her head with blatant insincerity. "No, ma'am."

"Come on, Private Sadiq. Let's have your thoughts." Tanya's tone was now challenging.

Riki shrugged, crouched by the tracks, and pointed. "It's not a mother and offspring. Look here. The bigger animal. The front hoof marks are deeper than the back. It's got a lot of weight on its shoulders. That's a sign of a male. The prints are more even for the other one." Riki estimated the size with her fist. "I'd say it was a young female. Three years old. Probably coming into season for the first time this spring."

She took a pinch of soil from the edge of one hoofprint and rubbed it between finger and thumb. "The dew has soaked in, so the female came through well before dawn, and the edges are starting to crumble, so the time was about yesterday sunset. The male was a short while after. Its tracks are always on top. It's following, and I can guess what it has on its mind. It would only be dangerous if you were another male spadehorn."

Riki stood up and brushed the soil off her hands. "At least, ma'am, that's what I'd have made of it. But you're the corporal, and I'm sure you were right."

While Riki had been speaking, Tanya's expression had shifted between surprise and awkwardness, but with the final gibe it changed again to anger. The silence was broken by a faint snigger from one of the teenagers, quickly smothered. A noticeable flush darkened Tanya's cheeks and her eyes narrowed. Riki fought to keep any trace of smugness from her face, but it felt good to have shown up the captain's daughter.

Tanya's lips compressed in a thin line and she drew a sharp breath. "So. You're a wilderness expert?"

"Not really. But my gene mother was a fur trapper." Riki shrugged. "I picked up a few things from her."

❖

The arrow thudded into the straw target, no more that a hand's span from the center. Riki lowered her bow, smiling. She could not have picked a better time to turn in one of her best displays at archery. The score was close to her all-time record, and far better than anything the teenagers had managed.

Tanya stood to one side, marking down the results. Her face showed neither approval nor surprise. "Okay, Private Sadiq. That will do. We're finished here. Go and collect the arrows."

Riki felt a flare of anger. *Do?*

"What was my score, ma'am?" Riki knew the answer, but wanted to hear Tanya confirm it.

"Four hundred and six. It's acceptable." Tanya's tone was neutral. She started to walk away.

Riki looked at her feet while composing her features. Two hundred and fifty was the standard for archery in the Rangers. Anything over four hundred should count as excellent, and even on a bad day, Riki scored well above average. Early training in hunting had given her that.

Riki lifted her head and addressed Tanya's back. "I'm sure it's nowhere close to what you could do, ma'am."

Tanya looked back sharply. For a moment she met Riki's eyes, acknowledging the challenge, but then merely tilted her head, as if agreeing. "Maybe. But my archery skills aren't what we're here to assess."

"Well, before we go, perhaps you'd like to give us a display, ma'am. Just so we know what sort of level is expected."

Tanya's eyes narrowed in anger. "Two hundred and fifty is the regulation standard. Which you should know. You've passed. You don't need a display from me."

"But it would be nice, ma'am. Since I know you could do so much better than me." Riki kept her tone innocent.

Off to one side, the teenagers stood uneasily, clearly sensing the confrontation underlying the words. Tanya made as if to walk away again and Riki felt a glow of triumph. The overrated corporal could not match her score and knew it. But then, Tanya turned back abruptly and held out her hand for Riki's bow.

"Let me borrow that."

Caught by surprise, Riki was slow to respond. Tanya all but snatched the bow from Riki's hands, then pulled six arrows from a quiver on the rack, stuck them through her belt and went to stand at the mark.

Once her surprise had faded, Riki stood back, arms crossed. She was delighted to have drawn Tanya into a direct contest and eager to see how well she would do. And Tanya would have to do very well indeed to justify the dismissal of a four hundred plus score as merely *acceptable*.

Tanya's back was toward Riki, her face visible only in oblique profile. The archer's pose emphasized her slim, well-balanced build.

Riki's gaze ran over her in appraisal. There was no denying that the packaging was nicely put together, but looks were not at issue. The grin on Riki's face widened.

Without bothering to fit a bracer to her arm, Tanya nocked the first arrow and raised the bow. In rapid succession, she put all six arrows into the center of the target. Riki felt the smile freeze on her face. Her best shooting had been made to look feeble.

Tanya lowered the bow but remained in position for a few seconds, staring at the target, then she turned and dropped the bow back in Riki's hands.

Tanya's eyes again met Riki's, but this time with a sardonic glint. "My gene mother is the best archer in Westernfort. I've picked up a few things from her."

❖

Riki pushed open the tavern door and strolled in, happy to leave the miserable rain outside. The atmosphere in the taproom was lively. A fire burned in the hearth, adding to the lantern light. The twin scents of beer and wood smoke filled the room. Voices made a constant hubbub, overlain by the occasional laugh. Riki made her way to the bar and ordered beer.

With her drink in her hand, Riki faced the room and looked for somewhere to sit. The tavern was busy, but there were still plenty of options. After four days in Westernfort, Riki was starting to recognize faces, but there was no one she could call a friend. Then she saw three of her patrol comrades around a busy table at the side of the room.

Riki took a half step before spotting Tanya there as well. *Of course, she would be with them*, Riki derided herself. She had already discovered that Tanya was well liked and an essential part of any social gathering.

Riki slunk off to a space in a dark corner. As she crossed the room she caught snatches of a dozen conversations, some flippant, some intense, reflecting the daily patterns in the lives of the townsfolk. The tavern was the heart of the community.

Once settled, with her tankard on the table before her, Riki stared at the group Tanya was with. Apart from Rangers, several other women were present. The smiles told of friendly gossip and good humor, a band of friends relaxing after work and enjoying each other's company.

Riki's gaze shifted away and fixed on her drink. She'd had no friends in Ginasberg. Few children her age had lived there, and most wanted nothing to do with the town's bad girl. The few who were not scared off by her reputation had been forbidden to associate with her by their parents, especially after Beth's arm had been broken.

Westernfort had been her chance to make a new start, to put it all behind her. Riki's lips tightened in a line. As if that could be possible with her unerring instinct for a foul up. Again she looked at Tanya, who was laughing and chatting. Tanya was good looking, and easy in company. She had a wide circle of friends, a loving family, and her mother was captain. She was clearly the center of attention. And Riki was back on the outside again.

CHAPTER THREE—THE NEW CORPORAL

Tanya put down her drink before she spilled any and then continued laughing with the rest. The saga of Dani's lost glove was getting sillier by the minute, aided by various interjections from around the table.

"So who do you think had a hand in it?"

"She doesn't think it was a hand. That's what's so worrying."

Tanya leaned forward, about to add her own comment, when she caught sight of Private Rikako Sadiq on the other side of the tavern. The new addition to the patrol was doing nothing, just sitting alone, staring somberly at her tankard, but the sight was enough to put a dent in Tanya's happy mood. The twinge of irritation was followed swiftly by even less comfortable emotions. Tanya turned back to her friends, but her thoughts stayed with Rikako.

The initial antagonism between them was not fading. If anything, the reverse was happening, but it should not be an issue. No rule said that everyone in a patrol had to like each other. Tanya knew all she had to do was be fair and ensure that patrol morale was not affected. All Rikako had to do was obey orders. Yet it did not feel so simple.

Niggling self-doubts picked at Tanya's thoughts. Her promotion had been little more than a month before. Twenty-two was young to become a corporal. Everyone assured her that she deserved the rank, and it had nothing to do with her mother. But in her own heart, Tanya was unconvinced. Perhaps there had been no direct manipulation, but were people expecting her to become a second Chip Coppelli? And did the force behind her hostility to Rikako come from hearing her own fears voiced aloud?

Tanya chewed her lip. Maybe she had let the taunts get under her skin, but Rikako Sadiq had clearly taken an instant dislike to her and seemed intent on stirring up ill will between them. It might become a serious problem. Gerry Baptiste had briefed Tanya on the new recruit's record. Tanya was amazed she had been allowed to join the Rangers in the first place, let alone remain. On past performance, Rikako might well do something stupid and potentially dangerous.

Should she discuss the matter with her mothers? They were both Rangers, with experience of command. They must have dealt with troublesome subordinates in the past. Maybe they could offer advice. Tanya pushed the idea aside. If she was to justify her rank, she could not go running to Mommy every time she had a problem. She had accepted the promotion. She had to do the job.

Tanya took a mouthful of beer and tried to force her mind back onto the tale of Dani's glove.

❖

Sergeant Baptiste strode into the barrack room. "Okay. We've got our orders."

Lunch had just finished, and archery practice was scheduled for that afternoon. Riki had been taking her bow from her locker. She glanced over her shoulder. Around the room, the Rangers stopped their preparations and looked expectantly at the sergeant, waiting for her to continue. Riki put her bow back and shut the locker door.

"We've been put on the southern marches. The weather is looking good and the snow has gone from the passes. We leave at dawn tomorrow. You've got this afternoon to ready your kit. Inspection is a half hour before sunset, in the stable. Any questions?"

There were none. The announcement had been expected for days. Everyone knew the rotation was due to go out, watching for trouble from the guards and meeting any heretics who were fleeing the Homelands. They would be away for four months. The only question had been over which section of the Wildlands 2B Patrol would cover.

Baptiste nodded. "Get to it."

The Rangers made a general move outside, heading along the path to the lower valley. Riki followed at the rear, but after a few dozen meters, her footsteps slowed and then stopped. Her kit was in good order. It was a lesson from her gene mother. You never knew when a crisis might hit, and alone in the wilds, nobody would come to your aid. Your equipment was what could save your life and you kept it in nothing less than perfect condition.

Riki knew her routine maintenance was better than for most others in the patrol. Maybe they needed half a day to get ready. She did not.

Riki turned toward the kitchens. A family of moggies lived there, and the mother had just given birth. By the time she returned, the litter of young would no longer be kittens. Riki wanted to say good-bye before she left.

❖

The tawny colored kitten pounced on the straw, missed, tripped, and rolled into one of the others. It then decided that its sibling's tail was more fun and chewed that instead. Riki laughed and tapped the second kitten on its rump with the straw, thus claiming the attention of both. They scrabbled after the lure. A third kitten joined in, but this one ignored the straw and went straight for Riki's hand.

Riki pried its small teeth off her fingers. Luckily, the saber fangs were not yet grown and had not broken her skin. She grasped the small body around the ribs and lifted it up level with her face. The kitten chirped at her.

"You don't want to bite me. It would make you ill."

The kitten chirped again and tried to reach her nose. Riki put it back with its siblings. The mother was lazing nearby. It yawned, revealing the adult fangs that certainly would break human skin. However, the older moggy was wise enough not to try. Riki reached over and scratched its head.

The moggies were small versions of mountain cats, and as with their bigger relatives, humans were poisonous to them. The cat that attacked Beth could not have eaten her, but it was straight out of hibernation, groggy and starving. It must have pounced on the first moving thing it saw. Unfortunately for all, this happened to be Beth. Usually the animals' sense of smell warned them off. A healthy cat only attacked women or farm animals when provoked. No doubt it would have realized its mistake, but only after Beth was dead.

Animals could be divided into two mutually poisonous groups. Apart from the lethal effect of eating anything from the other group, the main distinction was that one group reproduced by the interaction of males and females, and the other was exclusively female and reproduced by the healer sense—the psychic ability possessed by some women. In the case of farm stock this took the form of cloning. For humans, the skills of an imprinter were needed.

In the Homelands temples, the Sisters taught that the reason for the two distinct groups had to do with souls. According to their doctrine, all unique creatures had souls. Imprinters, by the sanctified power of the Goddess Celaeno, were blessed sufficiently with the healer sense to step inside the DNA of a cloned embryonic cell and imprint new sequences, taken from the mother's partner. Thus, humans were unique and had souls that went to Celaeno after the body died. Since it would be sacrilege to eat anything with a soul, farm animals were simply cloned, requiring a far lesser degree of ability with the healer sense.

However, the cloners could not get near to wild animals, nor were there enough to cover all the wilderness, so these animals had been given a non-divine method of procreation. However, the combining of male and female DNA meant that each individual was genetically unique. To remove the temptation of eating something with a soul, the Goddess had made wild animals poisonous to humans.

Riki fixed her eyes on the moggies. The trouble was, when you looked at it with the benefit of the heretics' skepticism, the Sisters' explanation made no sense. There was no reason for male moggies; anyone could touch them, cloners included. Riki stroked the mother again. And what was the point of cloned livestock being poisonous to the cats? Why were predators allowed to eat other wild animals, including their souls? Yet if it was okay for snow lions to eat fenbucks, why was it wrong for dogs?

The heretics' explanation had fewer holes. The heretics claimed that humans and all their livestock had originally come from another planet. This world was thus alien to their biology. Much of the vegetation was edible for the imported animals (although not all; spadehorns and fenbucks happily grazed on plants that would poison cows or sheep) but the complex animal chemistry of each group contained elements that were deadly to the other.

Furthermore, the heretics claimed that the off-world species had also originally had two sexes, but the males had been unable to survive on the alien planet. The healer sense had been engineered into people so that they could continue to reproduce without need of two sexes. According to the heretics, the colonists were able to do this because they possessed such astoundingly advanced science that it allowed them to redesign life forms—a science that had now been lost.

As a final sacrilege, the heretics said that the Goddess Celaeno herself was no more than misremembered folktales of the ship the colonists had built, using their science, to carry them between the stars.

Riki frowned. Since arriving in Ginasberg, she had made a point of maintaining the worship of Celaeno, but she was no longer sure if she truly believed. She had blamed the heretics for destroying her home and had decided that she would have nothing to do with their ideas. Refusing to give credence to the beliefs had also been one more thing she could argue with her mother about—not that there had ever been a shortage of topics.

The memory made Riki's frown deepen. Now that they were no longer living in the same town, it was easy to see how many of her words and actions had been prompted by a desire to upset her mother. It was immature and definitely not a good way to plan out her life.

Maybe she should make a start by reconsidering her ideas about Celaeno, because the heretics' version of things explained the moggies very nicely. According to the heretics, moggies were an indigenous species that had been domesticated so they could catch the vermin that would otherwise infest the grain stores. They had to be a native species so they would not be poisoned by what they caught, and therefore they had males.

Riki looked at the male moggy, and for a moment toyed with the idea of human males. How would they look? And what would it feel like to meet one? Riki thought about the spadehorn tracks, the male pursuing the female. When out with her gene mother she had seen various examples of wild animals' mating behavior. It was always dependent on the time of year, and scent generally played a large part.

So, supposing there had once been human males. Presumably, once a year, women would have come into season. The males would have tracked them down by smell and then fought battles with all the rival males who turned up. The women would be driven into a frenzy of lust by the combination of their biological clocks and the scent of the victorious male and would consent to being mated with.

Riki caught her lip in her teeth, chuckling, part amused, part bewildered. Well, if that was how it used to be, she could not help feeling that the current way of doing things was an improvement. A long-term relationship based on love and friendship seemed far better. And as a courtship technique, Riki would choose chatting over sniffing any day—or would, if anyone was willing to chat with her. She sighed. Her prospects of finding romance were showing no sign of improvement, and if having a friendly conversation was the crucial first step, then the outlook was not good.

Riki picked up another straw, about to tease the kittens again, when she noticed that the sun had dropped behind the mountain peaks. She had spent longer with the moggies than she had intended, and would need to run to the stables. Riki gave one last stroke to the mother moggy and set off, thankful that her kit needed only laying out and a quick brush-over to be ready for inspection.

❖

Tanya put down the wax and picked up the brush. Someone obscuring the light made her look up. A Ranger from another patrol stood in the open doorway.

"Message from Sergeant Baptiste, ma'am. She's been held up and can't make the inspection. She wants you to do it."

"Fine. Tell her I'll report to her later."

The Ranger nodded and jogged off. Tanya checked the sun's position and then looked back down the length of the building.

"Did you hear that? You've got me checking your kit. Ten minutes to go."

A range of assenting noises drifted back. Tanya grinned and then felt her smile freeze. Rikako Sadiq was now in the stable, working at her stall. Tanya had not seen her enter but knew that she had not come down with the rest of them. Tanya had noticed her slinking off after they got their orders and had been watching for her arrival. She did not know how Rikako had snuck in unseen, but it could not have been long ago. In no way had she left herself enough time to adequately prepare. Tanya took a deep breath. Well, soon she would see what sort of state Rikako's kit was in.

"Okay, time's up. Inspection." Tanya called out a few minutes later.

All along the stable was a last-second scuffling as the women got into position. Tanya began her check down the row, examining the field gear arranged beside each of them in turn. Everything was well prepared, as she expected, but then she reached Rikako, the fifth in line.

To a first glance, Rikako's gear looked in good order. Tanya was sure the impression was purely superficial. She bent down and lifted the flap on the saddle. To her surprise, the leather underneath was as clean and polished as the rest. The stitching was sound and even showed signs of recent repair work. Despite Tanya's best efforts, she could find no faults. When she got to Rikako's service belt, she pulled out the trail knife. The blade was sharp, with no trace of muck trapped by the hilt.

Tanya's lips tightened. Galling though it was to admit, Rikako's gear was in perfect condition. How had she managed it? Tanya moved on to the horse. The animal was well groomed. Tanya lifted a front hoof. The frog was unclogged, but the edge of the hoof was overgrown and flaking.

Tanya let the hoof drop and faced Rikako. "Private Sadiq. Why have your horse's hooves not been trimmed?"

"I didn't think it was necessary yet, ma'am."

"Come here."

Tanya waited until Rikako was beside her and lifted the hoof again. She ran her thumb over the rough edge. "You think that doesn't need trimming?"

Rikako's expression remained defiant. "It's getting to the stage where you'd think about it. But the hooves are sound and could go for another ten days easily."

"Sergeant Baptiste ordered you to get your kit ready. The time for everything was this afternoon. There's absolutely no excuse for anything being left undone."

"It's only—"

Tanya cut her off. "This is not a debate. You were given the order to come down here and get your kit ready. You didn't come down here and your kit isn't ready. A lame horse risks the safety of the whole patrol. You disobeyed a direct order. That's a disciplinary offense."

"If you say so, ma'am."

Tanya was furious, but kept her tone low and brisk. "I do say so. I'll be reporting it to Sergeant Baptiste. In the meantime, I want you to reclean all your gear and get your horse's hooves in acceptable condition. Do you understand me?"

"Yes, ma'am." Rikako's face was impassive, except for an insolent pout.

"You'll be hearing more about this."

Tanya moved on to the last member of the patrol.

❖

Riki lifted the horse's hoof and braced it in her lap. She placed the rasp against the edge, ready to start filing, but then took it away again. Her hands were shaking with anger. If she tried to file the hooves now she would most likely make a mess of it, which was the surest way to send the horse lame.

She let the hoof drop and leaned against the animal's flank, breathing deeply. Riki knew she had been victimized. She had seen Tanya check her way down the line. The bitch had spent three times as long on Riki's kit as anyone else's, examining in detail things she had not even glanced at on the other Rangers' equipment.

Tanya had been looking for something to pick on. Of course she had found it. If she had checked the rest of the patrol's kit so stringently, she would have found far worse faults. The hooves were a close judgment call. Riki knew that if she had not spent so much time with the moggies she would have filed them, but their state was far from critical. To make a disciplinary offense of it was bitterly unfair.

Riki took another deep breath. She had to calm down before she filed the hooves. More than anything, she owed it to her horse. A brisk walk might help. Riki put down the rasp and stomped to the door. Dusk was advancing, as gloom seeping over the lowlands.

"Where are you going?" Tanya was watching from the end of the stable.

"I want to get some hoof oil from the stores, ma'am. To rub in."

Tanya glared at her in the lantern light, but then nodded. "Don't be long. I'll be waiting for you."

Riki marched off toward the path up to the gates.

❖

Stars glinted over the mountains. The last glow of the sunset had faded and Private Sadiq had still not returned. As each minute trickled by, Tanya's anger grew. The ill-disciplined lout was blatantly disobeying orders again, without any regard for being caught. The flagrant nerve left Tanya astounded. This would be the last time. Rikako Sadiq would be out of the Rangers before sunset tomorrow, if Tanya got any say in it.

A disturbance caught her attention. Someone was running toward her. Thinking it might be Rikako, finally returning, Tanya stepped forward to meet her, but the runner proved to be another Ranger.

"Fire in the military stores. All hands needed at once." The Ranger ran on without saying more. Nor was anything required.

Tanya extinguished the lanterns in the stables—the last thing anyone wanted was a second fire to contend with—and raced toward the path. But as she ran, a nasty thought crept into her mind. Rikako had gone to the stores, clearly angry, and now they were on fire. Would she have started it deliberately? According to her record, she had done it once before. Tanya pushed the idea aside. Rikako had been a young teenager then. Surely she was no longer so immature or malicious.

In the upper valley, people were converging on the blazing building. The breeze whipped smoke and sparks around the central yard. Flames erupted through the open door, twisting and snapping against the darkening sky. The fire lit a scene of hectic activity. Three separate groups were apparent. Rangers and younger women were actively trying to beat back the flames. Older women were forming a chain, passing buckets of water to the firefighters. A third group were empting the adjacent barn, in case the fire spread.

Tanya was about to join the firefighters when a fresh group of Rangers arrived, coming from the direction of town. In the lead was Rikako. Where had she been? And what had she been doing? However, now was not the time for questions. Tanya marched over, intending to direct Sadiq to the barn and make sure she did not abscond again.

Only when she got close did Tanya notice the soot smudge on Rikako's forehead and the burn on the back of her hand. Rikako had made it look as if she had just arrived at the scene, yet the evidence showed that she had already been close to the fire. Tanya's suspicions returned with sickening force, but the investigation would have to wait until tomorrow. Dealing with the fire came first. Meanwhile, she had to make sure that Rikako was where she could do no more harm.

"Sadiq. Get over and join the chain." That seemed safe, with a woman on either side and nothing to do but pass buckets back and forth.

Rikako glanced toward the line of elderly women. "I think I'd be more use elsewhere."

"I don't care what you think. I gave an order. Do it."

Defiantly, Rikako met her eyes for a second but then marched off to join the chain. Tanya watched her go. The situation was serious, and way beyond the scope of what she could deal with. This was something she could quite justifiably turn over to her mother.

Tanya hurried to join the other Rangers, tackling the heart of the blaze.

❖

The fire was out. Two-thirds of the roof was gone but the walls still stood. Nothing inside would be salvageable. Damp, smoldering heaps, dragged from the building, were off to one side.

Totally exhausted, Tanya sank to her knees and watched pale wisps of smoke trail away in the moonlight. Her eyes felt as if they had been cooked. Her face and hands stung where sparks had landed. Shoulders, legs, and arms ached from the bones out. She drew a deep breath and started to get back to her feet. A passing Ranger lent a hand.

"Bit of a mess." The Ranger stated the obvious.

Tanya shrugged an agreement. "Does anyone know how it started?"

"Not me." The Ranger wandered off.

Tanya looked around. Her mother had arrived shortly after Tanya herself and had taken charge. When the chaos had been at its peak, Chip Coppelli's voice shouting commands had been a solid anchor. Something in the captain's tone had instilled the certainty that she knew both what was happening and what to do about it. The firefighters had followed her orders with confidence. Now the captain was making the rounds, offering words of praise and support, even cracking jokes.

Tanya could see the effect her mother had on the women she spoke to. They stood straighter, looking less tired and dejected. Laughter broke out. With Chip Coppelli there to lead them, the women acted ready to tackle a dozen more fires. Tanya felt a fresh set of doubts creep into her thoughts. What chance was there that she could ever fulfill the same role? Were people expecting it of her? And would they count her as a failure if she was never anything more than a halfway decent sergeant?

Tanya's jaw tightened as she forced her mind onto issues that she needed to deal with, rather than fears that lay outside her control. She was exhausted and wanted only to crawl off to her bed, but first she ought to talk to her mother and pass on her suspicions about Private Sadiq's role in the fire.

Tanya's gaze traveled on, seeking out the troublemaker. The elderly women who had been in the chain were huddling to gossip. Rikako was not with them. Nor was she standing with the other exhausted firefighters. Then Tanya spotted her, in the middle of the crew by the winch and pulley that had been used to clear the upper floor of the adjacent barn. The flames had not spread, and now they were returning stock to the barn, the only people still working in the yard.

Rikako was clearly an established member of the team and had been working there for some time. She had not stayed in the chain. Yet again, she had broken a direct order. Tanya was at the limit, both of her stamina and her patience. The sight of Rikako's open defiance tipped Tanya over the edge. No Ranger should dare act like that.

Too tired to bother with caution, Tanya stormed over. "What the hell do you think you're doing? Why weren't you on the water chain?"

Rikako turned around. Her face was smeared with sweat and soot. Her eyes matched the dazed exhaustion of those around her until sudden anger fired them back to full alertness. "I'm obeying orders, ma'am." The harsh tone made the last word sound like an insult.

"Not mine, you're not."

"No. Your mother's. She outranks you and she put me on the winch."

"Like hell she did." Tanya was not ready to believe any excuse the bitch came out with.

"Don't take my fucking word on it, then. Ask her. Maybe I imagined her ripping me a new asshole for hiding with the old women. Like I was too scared to go near the frigging fire."

"And you'd know all about the fire, wouldn't you? You need to think up some damned good excuses."

"What I know is that you and your damned mother need to sort out your game plan. 'Cause I'm sick of being fucking kicked around."

They were standing toe to toe, but their voices were loud enough to turn heads around the yard. Tanya realized that she was making a very undisciplined scene. No officer should let herself get dragged into a shouting match with a subordinate.

She dropped her voice. "We'll sort this out tomorrow. And I've got a good idea of how the fire started. You can kiss your ass good-bye."

Tanya started to walk away. As she did so, a sudden movement sounded behind her and a blow struck the back of her head, sending her staggering. She spun around to see Rikako with her arm still outstretched. Tanya did not need to see more. The evening of mounting anger exploded in white-hot fury. She threw herself forward, fists clenched.

Rikako barely had time to respond. She ducked away, but not quickly enough. Tanya's first punch connected with the side of her head. Tanya pressed forward, moving in for a second attack, aimed at her opponent's ribs. Rikako managed to block this and countered with a blow of her own, but she was out of position and it did no more than glance off Tanya's shoulder. Then Rikako's heel clipped a bystander and she stumbled. Her arms shot out for balance, leaving her open. Tanya's next punch connected squarely, and Rikako crashed to the ground.

Hands landed on Tanya's shoulders, pulling her back and restraining her, but it was unnecessary. Her head cleared and she became aware of the people surrounding her and their voices. Tanya was appalled at herself. She had just completely lost control. Brawling in public was no way for an officer to act, but Rikako had provoked her beyond bearing.

Tanya shook herself free of the restraining hands, but made no other movement. She glared down at her opponent, who was still sprawled on the ground, although starting to rise. A fresh disturbance sounded and the crowd parted. Captain Coppelli stalked through, with an expression that made any thunderstorm look mild.

Tanya felt her heart sink. More than anything else, brawling in public was no way for her mother's daughter to act.

❖

Tanya marched into the office and snapped to attention. The captain shifted back in her chair and subjected her to a critical scrutiny. As the seconds drew out, Tanya felt her pulse rate rise and the ice in her stomach solidify. She kept her eyes on the wall.

At last, Captain Coppelli rested her elbows on the table and said, "Would you like to explain to me exactly what you thought you were doing by fighting with Private Sadiq last night?"

The words were neutral, although the tone made them sound like a threat. However, Tanya had her answer ready. "I accused her of deliberately starting the fire in the stores, ma'am, and she attacked me."

The captain's face went through a range of expressions, of which confusion was the most easily identified. "What reason did you have to make that accusation?"

Tanya took a deep breath while she gathered her thoughts and then launched into her story, including her suspicions.

Captain Coppelli listened in silence, giving nothing away until Tanya had finished, and then she said, "Would you like to hear how the fire really started?"

"Ma'am?" The response was not what Tanya had expected, and none of the implications were good.

"When Private Sadiq arrived at the stores, Lieutenant Weinberg was checking the roof brace with the aid of a carpenter. They needed someone to hold the bottom of the ladder while Weinberg stood back to get a view and give directions. Weinberg commandeered Sadiq's services for this. It should only have taken a few minutes, but the carpenter engaged in some unwise acrobatics and fell, smashing an oil lantern and breaking her leg. The lantern was what started the fire. Private Sadiq was in no way to blame. She and Weinberg carried the carpenter to safety, which was when she got the burn on her hand. Weinberg then dispatched Sadiq to raise the alarm. I subsequently sent Sadiq to summon help from the town and barracks. Hence she returned to the stores from that direction, leading the people she had been instructed to find."

Throughout her recounting of events, the captain's tone was terse, not hiding her anger. Tanya felt sick. She was stupid to have jumped to conclusions, and yet Rikako had started the fight.

"She hit me first."

"Not according to the witnesses. The sound of your squabbling attracted quite an audience. Someone was so taken up with the spectacle that she failed to keep a good hold on the winch rope. It swung free and you got in its way. Private Sadiq actually tried to catch it before it struck you."

Tanya closed her eyes in disbelief. She was not only stupid, she was completely in the wrong. Rikako was the hero who had rescued the carpenter from the fire, and furthermore, she had been obeying orders as given by superior officers throughout the incident. Tanya struggled to keep her head from sinking. There was nothing she could say.

The captain however, was not tongue-tied. "You're an officer in the Rangers, not a child in the playground. If you can't control yourself, you stand no chance of controlling anyone else. Regardless of provocation, officers do not strike their subordinates. Brawling is not the way to enforce patrol discipline. Because of the circumstances, I'll let you off this one time, but if anything like this happens again, you will be joining Sadiq with the rank of private. Due to the fire, 2B Patrol will not be leaving Westernfort for another three days. Until you leave, while off duty, you are confined to barracks. Dismissed."

Tanya turned to go. As she reached the door the captain spoke again. "I'm very disappointed in you."

Tanya again closed her eyes, this time to hold back the tears. Up until then, it had been Captain Coppelli speaking. That last line had been from her mother, and it cut like nothing else could have. Tanya left the office and stood for a while outside, gathering her composure and thinking about just how much she hated Rikako Sadiq.

❖

Riki lay on her back, staring at the slats of the bunk above. If she rolled her head to one side, she would be able to see Tanya, who was over on her own bed—not that she had any wish to do this. If it was not bad enough being confined to barracks, Riki had to endure her company. Of course, they were not talking, but just knowing she was there was an ordeal.

Riki raised her hand to gently prod the sore spot on her face, a reminder of where Tanya had punched her. So far, she had received only the most grudging of apologies for the assault and none for the accusations that underlay it. On top of this, Captain Coppelli had fined her for not trimming her horse's hooves when Sergeant Baptiste ordered the gear preparation. Added to her demotion, it meant that she was now in a state of negative salary. Riki suspected that the only reason she had not been thrown out of the Rangers, as previously threatened, was because of Tanya's involvement in the affair.

When she thought about it all, Riki's main regret was for the insufficient words at her disposal to express just how much she hated Tanya Coppelli.

CHAPTER FOUR—ON PATROL

The air smelled clean with the warmth of wet earth and the acidic tang of yellow cedar. The ground between the massive tree trunks was soft and red from the remains of last year's fall of leaves, with coils of lemon vine bursting through wherever the sun's light pierced the canopy. The only sound other than the chattering of birds and the rush of the nearby river was the dull thump of the horses' hooves.

The land rolled in gentle folds, cut with streams. On the left it fell away more sharply toward the river. The four Rangers rode in single file through the forest. Tanya was in front, leading half of the patrol. The remaining members were farther up the hillside with Gerry Baptiste.

After the trek across the wilderness, the patrol had reached the region twelve days before. Now they were on their circuit, watching for signs of Guards invading the wilderness and checking the secret rendezvous sites for heretics who had fled the Homelands and needed an escort to the safety of Westernfort.

Patrolling the wilderness was what Tanya loved about being a Ranger, and she felt at peace with the world, or as much at peace as she could be with Rikako Sadiq riding two places behind her.

Tanya's mouth pulled down at the corners. She would like to forget about the disruptive private and enjoy the bright spring morning, but Rikako was hard to ignore. Even her smile was irritating, although fortunately there had been no more direct confrontations between them since leaving Westernfort.

"Wait. Stop your horses." As if in answer to Tanya's thoughts, Rikako broke the silence.

One of the other Rangers spoke up. "What's—"

"Hush." Rikako held up her hand assertively while looking down toward the river.

Tanya felt a flicker of anger even as she reined in her horse. She was the corporal. A private should not be the one issuing orders. Against this, the previous month had shown that Rikako had a seemingly supernatural ability to read the Wildlands. She would have been a great asset to the patrol if she were not such a pain in the ass. Regardless, it would be stupid to ignore what she said. Tanya waited patiently until Private Sadiq would consent to share with them whatever it was that she had noticed.

Rikako turned to face her. "Something's upsetting the skirrales on the other side of the river. That's the third troop to sound off."

Skirrales were active, tree-living nut eaters, about thirty centimeters in length and black in color except for the distinctive white stripe down their backs. They lived in large family troops. Their high-pitched yips were a common sound throughout both Wildlands and Homelands.

"Could it be a tree rat?"

Rikako shook her head. "Nope. Whatever's upsetting them isn't keeping pace with us, but still moving at a fair rate. When I heard the first troop, they were a short way ahead, and we've just overtaken them. A tree rat won't travel that fast for more than fifty meters."

"So what do you think it is?"

"Something with enough sense of purpose to travel in a straight line for two kilometers."

Tanya frowned. Only one candidate met that criterion, leaving just the question "friend or foe?" She raised her fingers to her mouth and gave the birdsong code signal meaning *Halt investigating* to the other half of the patrol.

Down the hillside, water glinted between the tree trunks some way off, but nothing of the other bank could be seen. Tanya slipped from her saddle and stole cautiously down to the river. Soon, the ground became squelchy underfoot. Heavy reed beds lined the bank, obscuring her vision. The barrier was too wide for parting it to be possible, quite aside from the risk that such an action would be visible on the other bank.

Tanya looked up. The trees growing here were smaller and lighter than those farther up the hillside. She grabbed a branch just above head height and pulled herself up. From that position she was high enough to have a clear view across the river.

The opposite bank was identical to the one she was on. Nothing was moving. Then suddenly a flash of red between the trees caught Tanya's eye, a bright brilliant red that belonged to no animal or plant. Tanya recognized it immediately. It was the color of a Guard's uniform. She concentrated on the spot where she had caught the brief sighting.

Just to the right was a break in the trees. A second later, women dressed in red and gold appeared there on horseback. Tanya caught a glimpse before the rider disappeared again, but behind came a line of her comrades. Two abreast, the Guards rode through the forest. The column had to contain at least fifty of the pious warriors.

Tanya remained motionless until the last had passed, grateful that her own green and gray uniform would not be so conspicuous—not that the Guards were showing any sign of being on the lookout for danger—then she dropped to the ground and trotted back to where the other Rangers were waiting.

Tanya hopped up into her saddle and looked at the expectant faces. "We've got company."

❖

Both moons were in the sky. Their cool blue radiance contrasted with the red flickering of the campfire. Tanya sat beside the burning logs, grateful for the warmth against the night chill. Four other members of the patrol were with her, sitting around in a circle. The remaining three were on sentry and scouting duties. Some way off, the horses were grazing.

The camp was set amid the rocky upland. The poor soil would not support the towering yellow cedars. Consequently, long grass and ferns covered the open ground, and brushwood filled the hollows. The Rangers' camp was in a clear spot at the bottom of one such dip. The upland location had three advantages over the forest. There was grazing for the horses, the lookouts had good visibility to spot danger, and the bushes shielded the campfire that would otherwise have shone out like a beacon.

A whistled signal from one of the lookouts announced the scout's return. Tanya turned toward the sound. At the edge of the firelight, the line of bushes was silent and motionless, except for a slight wavering in the breeze. And then Rikako stepped through them into the open.

Tanya shook her head, with more than a touch of admiration. As a Ranger, Tanya thought she had pretty good wilderness skills, but she had not heard Rikako's approach nor seen anything that would have alerted her. Rikako might have dropped from the sky for all the disturbance she had made passing through the dense brushwood—which was why Gerry Baptiste had picked her to be the scout, regardless of what doubts might be held about Rikako's general fitness as a Ranger.

Rikako joined the group around the fire.

"Are they settled?" Gerry asked.

"Yup. They're not going anywhere."

"Any sign they'll be sending out patrols?"

"No, they've got a ring of sentries, but that's it."

Gerry nodded and signaled for the two lookouts to join them for the briefing. Once everyone was together, she gestured to Rikako. "Okay. What's the score?"

"There's sixty-two of them. Looks like a major in command, though I couldn't get close enough to check her badge. They have ten packhorses, so unless they've worked out what plants they can eat out here, they won't have enough supplies for more than another twenty days, especially seeing as how two horses were carrying just the major's tent. Added to some bits of conversation I overheard, I think it's a routine training hike."

"What did you hear?"

"Nothing of note. Two of them were going for a piss. They exchanged confidences that it was their first time in the wilderness. One said she wasn't afraid because Celaeno would look after them. The other agreed and said if the impious could live here without aid from the Goddess, then it would be a piece of cake for them." Rikako grinned. "I'm paraphrasing a bit there."

Gerry frowned. "You must have been inside their sentry cordon to hear that."

"Oh yes. If you can call it a cordon. They seem to think sentry duty means standing so still that they're always staring at the same spot. They don't even move their eyeballs."

"I told you not to take unnecessary risks."

Rikako shrugged. "No risk. You'd have to dance naked through the camp to alert their sentries."

Tanya bit her lip to conceal her smile. Rikako clearly had been taking unnecessary risks, but Tanya could not help being impressed, despite herself.

Gerry's frown grew, but she apparently decided to let it go. Her expression became thoughtful. "I agree, a wilderness training expedition would be the most likely reason for them being here. They don't have the numbers or supplies to cause any trouble. We'll keep a loose tail on them. If others show up, or they join with a baggage train, we'll send word to the captain. And if a small group go off on their own, maybe we'll get the chance to see how much protection the Goddess really gives to her faithful. We don't want them to start thinking they can wander through our territory at will."

The sergeant's eyes ran around the ring of faces. "We need them under constant surveillance. We'll run the patrol in shifts, half on duty, half off. Two Rangers on foot will keep within sight of the Guards. With the speed they move, that shouldn't be a problem. Two more will hang back about a kilometer. Close enough to exchange signals. They'll have the horses and will provide rotation support and messengers, if needed. The half of the patrol that's off duty will keep well away. If it's training, they most likely won't be going in a straight line."

"With the Guards' sense of direction, they couldn't if they wanted to," someone interjected.

"Maybe. But it'll mean there won't be much catching up to do at shift changeover. At night we can go down to a pair of lookouts." Gerry looked across to Tanya. "Do you want to take first or second shift?"

"Either."

"Right. Second shift. You'll have Loke, Sasha, and Rikako with you. My half will do the first overnight watch. You're on at dawn."

The Rangers dispersed; those designated to watch the Guards headed off, while the rest went to their bedrolls. As she lay down, Tanya's attention was caught briefly by Rikako on the other side of the campfire, also getting ready to sleep. The woman had unquestionable talents that could be so useful to the patrol. She could also be a liability, taking risks for the fun of it. She was undisciplined, unfriendly, and overconfident.

Tanya rolled over and closed her eyes. As she did so, the thought came to her that maybe the charge of overconfidence was unfair. She could not deny that Rikako Sadiq was very good at what she did.

❖

Five days later, the weather had turned and rain clouds replaced the sunshine. Riki took satisfaction from knowing that the Guards were enjoying it far less than she was. Quite apart from their inexperience in living out of doors, their uniforms had been designed to look impressive when standing duty in the temples, rather than for survival in the wilds. Presumably someone had decided that the Goddess would be offended if they changed to anything more practical.

Judging by the increasing desperation of the shouted commands, the major was just as unhappy as her troops and would probably call the entire exercise to an early halt. Riki hoped so, and not just because the excitement of tracking the Guards had worn off. When she was on duty, Riki found that she was spending far more time than she liked paired with Loke Stevenson.

In the late afternoon they were working together again, keeping the column of Guards in sight. They were close enough to hear when the order to stop was called for the third time since lunch.

"Do you reckon the major wants a break to wring out her cloak again?" Riki asked.

Loke did no more than grunt in reply. She raised her hand to her mouth and sent the birdsong whistle for *Halt* to Tanya and Sasha, who were providing backup a kilometer to the rear.

Riki looked at her companion. Of all the patrol, Loke was the most consistently hostile. Even Tanya acted in a coolly professional manner. Loke, though, refused to make any sort of concession in the interests of patrol unity. However, Riki had noticed the way she watched Tanya, and suspected it was because Leading Ranger Stevenson was interested in a rather non-military form of unity with the corporal. Maybe Loke was hoping that a conspicuous display of ignoring anyone who had slighted Tanya would win some reciprocal attention.

The Guards had been following a river along the bottom of a valley. Riki and Loke's path had shadowed them farther up the hillside. Without horses, the trees presented no obstacle, and the firm ground meant they had not even needed to jog to keep up. They found a good vantage point and settled down to watch what the Guards would do next.

The drizzle had finally stopped, although the wind knocked drips off the branches overhead. The Guards dismounted and formed up in an open space in the loop of the river. Riki sneered. The Guards spent a quite astounding amount of time standing in straight lines. The major addressed them for a short while before they dispersed and began pulling packs off their horses.

"Looks like they're stopping for the day," Loke said.

Riki considered the gray sky. Even with the sun obscured she could make a fair guess of the time. "It's a bit early, even for them."

"The major must be really pissed off." Loke's tone implied that she was too.

After a few minutes, a dozen Guards left the camp in a group and started to climb the hillside on foot.

"I wonder where they're off to," Riki said.

"Don't know. I'll follow them and see."

"Wouldn't it be better if I did that?"

Loke gave Riki a surly look and said, "No. You stay here and watch the main group."

"But—"

"No. I'm the leading ranger. I've got the experience. You stay here."

Without more debate, Loke slipped off through the forest. Riki watched her go. Leading ranger outranked private, but not by much. On past experience, neither the sergeant nor the corporal would have pretended that their rank made them better suited to tracking and scouting. Both had shown trust in Riki's abilities.

The thought struck Riki that the real benefit of having Loke Stevenson in the patrol was she made Tanya Coppelli look good.

❖

"It's not too slippery here."

"Do we need to bear left more?"

"This gully's going in the right direction."

Loke could not restrain her expression of contempt. As if the Guards were not making enough noise by their passage, they were giving a running commentary as they went. A blind idiot could have tailed them. Yet Rikako-fucking-Sadiq acted like she was the only woman in the patrol who could follow a track.

The lower reaches of the valley were largely free of undergrowth, and the bright Guards' uniforms made them easy to spot between the huge trunks of the yellow cedars. Loke kept well to the side of the flashes of red and gold. She did not want to risk running into the backs of stragglers.

As they got higher, the character of the trees changed and hagwood firs started to appear. The undergrowth also thickened, which caused the Guards yet more trouble. Loke moved in a little closer.

"We're blocked in here."

"I think there's a way through on the left."

The Guards were moving away from her. Loke followed after, keeping ducked beneath the height of the bushes. Suddenly she realized that the voices were getting nearer again. The Guards were doubling back. Furthermore, a couple had looped around downhill, trapping her. A knotted mass of border weed formed a solid hedge at her back, cutting off any quick escape route. Loke dropped to the ground and rolled underneath it, wrapping her green cloak around her. Her clothes acquired a fair coating of mud and dead leaves—unpleasant, even though it would aid her camouflage.

Through the web of stems she saw the red and gold uniforms get closer. The Guards stopped fifteen meters from where she lay.

"Over here," the major called out, summoning the scattered members of her band.

Loke studied the assembled Guards. Their uniforms held so much gold braid and emblems that it had to be the expedition's entire officers cadre.

"There's no route up, ma'am," one of them said.

"You've got swords. Hack your way through."

Judging by the expressions, this was a novel idea to the officers. Hesitantly at first, they put the plan into action. Within five minutes they had cleared a path through the border weed and were continuing up the hillside. Not one had glanced in Loke's direction.

Once their voices were fading, Loke rolled from her hiding spot, grinning partly with relief and partly from amusement at the Guards. There was no need to cut a route through border weed—the springy lacework of stems was so soft you could simply roll over it. Only the noise it created had stopped her doing it when they cornered her. Loke followed the Guards' trail, but now keeping well back.

The vegetation continued to get lower and denser. Eventually the trees thinned out and ended in a ragged fringe. The top of the hill was covered in waist-high brushwood, mainly honey bramble and dover fern. Only a few isolated hagwood firs broke through this matting, their trunks knotted and twisted from exposure to the wind. A hundred meters away, an outcrop of rocks crested the top of the ridge. The fist of gray granite stood some five meters high. The Guards were huddled in conversation by its base.

Loke studied them from the cover of a tall patch of honey bramble. Why had all the officers come to such a remote location to talk? What were they saying that they did not want their subordinates to overhear? Rikako had bragged about getting close enough to eavesdrop on some Guards. Loke's lips twisted in a sneer. If the arrogant little shit could do it, so could she. Loke dropped to a low crouch and started working her way closer.

She was just getting within earshot when the Guards broke from their debate. Loke grimaced in frustration. What had they been talking about? However, rather than return down the hill, the Guards' attention turned to the rocks. After a few seconds of shuffling around, one of them began to climb. The obvious explanation was to use the rocks as a viewpoint.

Loke shrank under the deepest cover she could find. Even so, from up high, her position might be visible. To her relief, though, once the Guard reached the top of the rocks, it became clear that her interest was purely to the east, on the other side of the hill.

"Can you see it?" the major called out.

"Um…um. Yes, ma'am. Yes, I can." The Guard's voice went from uncertainty to elation.

"How far?"

"A day, maybe."

"The Goddess be praised. Do we need to cross this hill?"

The Guard turned north. "No, ma'am. If we follow the route we're on, we'll join up with another valley that will lead us there."

"Well done. You can come down."

The Guard scrambled from the rocks and re-joined her comrades. The group had barged their way through the dover fern, tramping the fronds into the mud. They now returned by the same route, traveling in single file and passing within a dozen meters of Loke. As they went by, she heard the major say, "We'll make an early camp and set off at first light tomorrow. Our food will last till we get there."

"It's been tight going."

"The Goddess would not desert us."

"The women will be happy to come off half rations."

Their voices faded away. Loke chewed her lip, thoughtfully. The Guards were almost out of food—so much for Rikako's estimate that they had enough for twenty days. Although, on second thought, Loke considered that nobody knew how long the Guards had been in the wilderness before they were spotted.

She looked at the granite outcrop. What had the Guards been trying to find? And why had so many officers come to look for it? From what she had overheard, it sounded like a supply dump, or maybe a rendezvous point with a better provisioned detachment—the very things Gerry Baptiste said to watch out for. Loke had to learn more before she reported back. Maybe if it was an unmanned supply dump, the Rangers would be able to raid it before the Guards arrived.

Loke waited until the Guards were well gone before approaching the rocks. Quickly, she scrambled up to where the observer had stood. The trees on the eastern side of the hill grew taller and closer to the summit, obscuring the view. Was this why the observer had needed to climb up? The mist and low cloud also made for poor visibility.

The eastern horizon was filled with a line of high hills that Loke recognized as the Longstop Range, the last barrier before reaching the Homelands. Between the Longstops and where Loke stood was a flat region, about twenty kilometers wide, containing trees and absolutely nothing else.

Loke shook her head in confusion. Apart from the absence of a flag or other marker, the observer had given the distance as a day's travel, which made no sense. Even if you counted that the Guards would only cover thirty kilometers a day, and allowing for the long route around the top of the valley, this would put them at the pass over the Longstops, and out of view from the rock. What had the Guard been looking for? And what had she seen?

Loke turned to look back at where she had been hiding in the undergrowth, trying to assess the observer's exact line of sight, when a flash of red at the edge of the woods alerted her. The Guards were returning.

Loke dropped flat so she would not be skylined. If they came all the way back, surely the Guards would still not want to climb the rocks again. But if they did, where would she hide? The bare granite offered no cover. Carefully Loke slid to the edge, on the side away from the

Guards. She looked down. On this side, the drop was over six meters, and the ground was littered with loose boulders. She did not want to jump, but did she have the time to climb down? Did she need to?

The Guards were now close enough to hear their voices. The major's was the loudest, clearly angry. "Patel, you go up and check this time. Take Rivelle with you. We can't afford to wander around out here any longer. Once we're over the range we've three days' ride before we get back to civilization. Make sure you are absolutely certain this time. The pass is between a ridge rising in three steps on one side, and a higher hill with a sheer face on the north."

"I'm sorry, ma'am. I thought that was what I saw before."

"For the love of the Goddess. *Thought* is not good enough."

Loke looked around frantically. They were going to climb up again and she was trapped. She slipped over the edge and began to feel her way down. The rock face was more difficult on this side, with an awkward overhang, and already Loke could hear the sounds of climbing on the other side. She would have liked to get to the ground and find cover quickly, but she was out of time. The guards were standing on top, and all Loke could do was hug herself tight to the rocks where she was, praying that the Guards would not come close to the edge—praying that they would not look down.

The two Guards spoke together quietly. "That's the pass, sure enough."

"I don't know why the major wanted to come back. Burstein said she saw it."

"Kaur's rattled. So far the women have accepted the story that half rations are part of wilderness training. They won't believe it if they start dropping from starvation. And it wouldn't look good on her record."

"And if they knew that Major Kaur has lost the map..."

The other gave a soft laugh and then raised her voice. "Yes, ma'am. It's the pass that'll take us home."

Loke rested her forehead on the rocks in disbelief, which changed to mockery aimed partly at herself. Of course. The Guards were lost and simply looking for the way home. Only the officers had come up the hill, because only they could be trusted with the knowledge that the major needed both hands to find her own ass in the dark.

Loke looked up. The Guards had not gotten close to the edge, and now they were going down. She drew an easier breath.

"Hey. What—"

"Ma'am, it's a—"

Sudden loud shouts made Loke jerk her head right. A group of three Guards had wandered around the rocks and spotted her. Loke had to act quickly. She kicked away from the granite, hoping that she would land safely. Unluckily, her foot hit on a boulder at an oblique angle, which threw her sideways and wrenched her ankle. Loke crashed to the ground.

For a moment, she lay dazed, but the sounds of the Guards were close, and getting closer. Fear surged through her, giving her the impetus to shove herself to her feet and start running. The pain in her ankle was forgotten. If only she could get to the cover of the trees, surely she would be able to lose the incompetent Guards. More sounds told of others joining the pursuit, but she did not look back. Her attention was on the line of trees, downhill.

Loke charged through a patch of soft ferns. Her foot snagged on a dead branch, and she stumbled into a patch of honey bramble. The scratches she hardly noticed, but the thorns latched onto her clothes. Desperately she fought to tear herself loose. To the sound of ripping material, she pulled free and continued running.

The footsteps behind were nearing, and then a heavy weight landed on her back, throwing her to the ground again, and driving the breath from her body. Her face was pressed into the mud. Hands grabbed her shoulders, and a voice called out, "Ma'am, I've got her."

Loke struggled, but more Guards were arriving. Her arms were caught and pulled behind her, and then she was hauled to her knees. The point of a blade touched her throat. Loke looked at the ring of Guards surrounding her. More arrived. Someone tied her hands and removed her sword and trail knife. Excited half sentences leaped from Guard to Guard.

"She was just hanging there listening..."

"How long do you think..."

"How many more..."

The circle parted and the major arrived—Major Kaur, the Guards had called her. The voices fell silent. The major stared at Loke for several seconds and then turned to her subordinates. "This is what I've been telling you. We probably picked them up ages ago. You never know they're there until they attack, which is why you can't afford to take chances. That's why you never go wandering around on your own. Always make sure there are at least ten of you in any group." Kaur's eyes returned to Loke. "It's all too easy to underestimate these heretics. They're at home in the Wildlands like savages."

"Um...ma'am." One of the other Guards spoke up. "Maybe she could guide us back. Since they know the region so well."

Major Kaur gave a dismissive snort. "She'd lie and send us chasing in circles. You couldn't believe a word she said. When we get her to Landfall, the Intelligence Corps will wring the truth out of her, if she knows anything worth hearing."

A raw panic gripped Loke. Death she could have faced, but not being taken alive to the Intelligence Corps prison in Landfall. The remnants of her courage shattered. Everyone knew about the interrogation techniques they used. Her thoughts jumped wildly, desperate, barely rational.

"Please. Let me go. I'll make a trade." Loke hardly knew what she was saying.

"Guards do not trade with those who defy the Goddess. She has delivered you into our hands. We will not disregard her gift."

"But I can give you—"

"You can give me nothing. Everything you know will be extracted by the Intelligence Corps. There's nothing of value in your pitiful existence, apart from a few clues that might speed our task of cleansing the world of your heresy."

"I...I..." Loke's mind was drowning in panic. One idea drifted past, a straw to cling to. "The captain's daughter. Our captain. Captain Coppelli. Her daughter is in our patrol. If I help you to catch her, let me go. She's a corporal, she knows more than me. And she'll have overheard her mother speaking. She'll know more to tell you. Please. Let me go."

"You'd sell out one of you own comrades?"

"Yes...please," Loke begged. The walls of the Corps dungeon seemed to solidify around her. She could feel tears in her eyes as she stared up at Kaur.

At first there was little of comfort, but then a more thoughtful look settled on the major's face. She fixed a critical gaze on Loke. "And just how would you propose doing that?"

CHAPTER FIVE—BETRAYAL

Tanya pulled her cloak tighter around her shoulders and shivered. The rain had stopped, but hanging around was making her cold. Of the various roles in monitoring the Guards, rotation backup was the one she liked the least. She could not relax, but equally, she could not see the Guards, so she had no idea what was going on. The last whistled signal from the contacts had been over half an hour earlier.

"They've been stopped a long time. Do you think the Guards are making camp for the night?" Sasha Li asked.

Tanya looked at the gray sky. "A bit early. But they probably don't have much idea themselves, the way they've been dithering back and forth the last few days."

"I know what you mean. I've seen Guards before, wandering aimlessly in circles. I hadn't realized they needed special training on how to do it."

Tanya grinned. At that moment a fresh whistled signal from the contacts sounded through the forest. *Request officer presence.*

After sharing a quick worried glance with Sasha, Tanya signaled back. *Question. Danger.*

No. Request officer presence.

The signal was coming from the hilltop, rather than the valley where the Guards had been.

Tanya looked at Sasha again and shrugged. "Oh, well. Hopefully it will be something interesting."

"And not just Rikako being a jerk."

Tanya shared a last grin and set off on foot in the direction of the signal.

Although sunset was another two hours away, the forest was gloomy beneath the overcast sky. The breeze through the branches sent bursts of drips splattering down. The air felt heavy and slick. As she got higher, the trees thinned out and the light improved. At one point, she stopped to signal, *Where are you?* and received a locating whistle in reply.

Tanya reached the open hilltop, largely devoid of trees. Only a thick matting of grass, bramble, and ferns covered the ground. An outcrop of granite marked the summit, a hundred meters away. Standing alone at the base was Loke Stevenson.

Loke had clearly been looking out for Tanya and beckoned her over urgently as soon as she appeared. Tanya wove her way between the waist-high ground cover, wondering what was going on and where Rikako was. When she was halfway to the rocks she met up with more tracks through the dover fern. Clear in the mud was the imprint of Guards' boots. By the look of it, at least ten had passed that way.

"Guards have been up here?" she called to Loke.

"They were. They've gone now. But I've got to show you this."

Tanya cast about the hilltop, confused as to what might be of interest. Nothing out of the ordinary was visible. Then from the corner of her eye, she thought she caught a glimpse of a bush moving, and maybe a sliver of bright red peeking through beneath the fronds. However, when she looked back it had gone. Tanya shook her head and trotted onto the rocks. Loke would hardly be lounging around in the open if Guards were anywhere close at hand.

Loke stood at the side of the outcrop, leaning against the vertical rock face. As Tanya got close, she saw that Loke's clothes were mud-stained. A graze marked her cheek. Despite her casual pose, she was tense. Her eyes were downcast, and her hands were clenched in a tight double fist. Yet only when Tanya stopped two meters away did she realize that something was wrong—seriously wrong. Both Loke's sword and trail knife were missing.

Loke looked up and met her eyes. "I'm sorry."

Tanya had no more than a second to puzzle over the words. A Guard major stepped from behind the rocks, her sword tip touching Loke's ribs. Tanya leapt back, turning, ready to run.

Across the hilltop, the undergrowth burst upward as a dozen Guards emerged from cover, surrounding her. Tanya froze and then backed toward the rocks. She ripped her sword from its scabbard. The odds were hopeless, but she would go down fighting. Around the rocks, the Guards were closing in. Tanya looked toward Loke, partly in amazement, partly in appeal.

Loke seemed lost in a daze of remorse, but then a new firmer expression crossed her face. In a sharp burst of movement, she elbowed the Guard major in the stomach and dived out of reach of the sword. The major was clearly caught out by the sudden maneuver and reeled backward. Loke slid into place by Tanya's side.

Irrationally relieved that she would not die alone, Tanya fumbled at her belt for her trail knife to pass over. She was unprepared for the hand that clenched around her right wrist, immobilizing her sword, and then the second hand that swung into her face as a fist. The blow cracked her head back on the rocks. A sharp wrench dragged her to her knees and loosened her sword from her grip. It fell to the soft earth with a thud.

Dazed and bewildered, Tanya's eyes fixed on her attacker's feet, a pair of Ranger's boots. And then the Guards were upon her, knocking her flat. Her thoughts struggled to catch up with her eyes, but at last the knowledge sank in that her initial assailant had been Loke Stevenson.

By the time Tanya's head had cleared, both from the blow and the shock, her hands were tied behind her. She was dragged to her feet. Wetness covered her lower face, sticky and salty to taste. The punch to the face had given her a nosebleed. She could feel the blood dripping off her chin.

"There. I did it. I did what I said. Now you have to let me go." Loke was babbling.

The major walked forward, massaging her stomach where Loke had struck her. "You attacked me. That wasn't in our agreement."

"If I hadn't, you'd never have taken her alive."

"Maybe." The major stood in front of Tanya. "I am Major Kaur of the 16th Company of Temple Guards, and you are Tanya Coppelli. Daughter to the self-styled Captain Coppelli, leader of the ragtag mob that call themselves Rangers among the heretics."

Tanya said nothing. She glared over the major's shoulder at Loke, unable to credit the depth of the betrayal.

"Won't you even answer to your name?" the major jeered.

Tanya looked at her. "I am Corporal Tanya Coppelli of 2B Patrol of the Westernfort Rangers. I will tell you nothing else."

"Maybe you won't tell me, but you will tell someone. I can

guarantee that. The Intelligence Corps in Landfall are good at getting answers."

"She's the captain's daughter, all right. You can take my word on it."

Major Kaur sneered at Loke with clear contempt. "I wouldn't dream of taking your word on anything. None of you heretics have the first idea of honor. No Guard would betray her comrade as you've just done."

"Why, Loke?" Tanya could restrain herself no longer. She needed answers. "What are you getting from this?"

Loke would not meet her eyes. "They caught me. I said I'd help them catch you if they let me go. I'm sorry. I couldn't face—" She broke off, breathing harshly. "I told them that your mother was captain. That you'd be more valuable than me. I'm sorry."

"When I put on this uniform, I become just another Ranger. You don't know the first thing about my mother if you think she'd make a single concession on my behalf that she wouldn't make for any other Ranger."

Loke shrugged awkwardly. "It's up to the Guards now. I'm done with Westernfort. I'm getting a pardon. I'm going back to the Homelands."

Major Kaur swung to face her. "Whatever gave you that idea?"

"You did. You swore you'd let me go and give me a pardon if I helped you capture Tanya. And you're a Guard. You always keep your word."

"I swore I'd let you go free, here and now. And a pardon for spying on me today. I'm sorry if you think I implied it, but I promised nothing about your sins in the past."

Loke looked dumbstruck. "So what do I do?" she blurted.

"You go back to Westernfort and carry on as before." Major Kaur smiled. "This has really been a most useful exchange. Not only do we have the leader's daughter as hostage, but we also have an agent inside the heretic stronghold who'll do exactly as she's told."

"What will you want me to do?"

"I think that it's time for another assault on Westernfort. You'll make sure that the gate is opened when we attack. When Westernfort falls, then you'll get your full pardon."

"I won't be able t—"

"Otherwise your Captain Coppelli will find out exactly how her daughter became a prisoner."

Loke fell silent, but from the blankness in her eyes, she was panicking. "But everyone will have heard me signal. They'll know I called her into the trap."

"That's not my problem."

"You said you want me as an agent inside Westernfort. I can't do that if I'm dead."

Major Kaur stared at her disdainfully. "They heard one of your rabble signals. Is there any way to be sure which one of you it was?"

"No, apart from knowing who was where and who could have signaled."

"Then I suggest you find somebody in a suitable position to frame."

❖

Riki yawned and leaned against a tree. The absence of activity among the Guards was startling. About a third of them were engaged in a prayer meeting, which was their main hobby when not standing in straight lines, but even this looked to be half-hearted. The sentries were less alert than normal—if that was possible. Riki pursed her lips. The whole camp had the air of demoralized troops lacking guidance from officers.

A soft noise made Riki slip into cover, but the person who appeared a few seconds later was Loke. Riki waited for her to pass, then stepped out behind her and coughed. She made no attempt to hide her grin when Loke jerked around, startled and angry.

"Where are the Guards?" Riki asked.

"They're on their way back."

Riki was about to ask what they had been doing but was diverted by the sight of a raw graze on Loke's cheek, and her cloak torn and splattered with mud. Obviously, Loke had been in some sort of trouble.

"What happened to you?"

"None of your business."

"Was it anything to do with what you wanted to talk to Tanya about?" Riki had heard Loke's signals a while earlier.

"I said it's none of your business."

Riki's grin broadened. Judging by Loke's excessively sharp tone, whatever had happened was too embarrassing for her to want to reveal.

"Fell down somewhere? Did you need Tanya to pull you out?"

Loke merely glared and fumbled at her waist. "I've dropped one of my gloves. Go and get it for me."

"What!" Riki's amusement turned to outrage.

"You heard me."

"I'm not your errand girl."

"No. You're a private and I'm a leading ranger. And I'm telling you what to do."

"I don't know where your glove is."

"I took them off in the open at the top of the hill, where the trees end. You're supposed to be so good at tracking, I'm sure you'll be able to find it."

Riki was tempted to tell Loke just where she could stick her glove, but it would probably be breaking some frigging regulation.

"Right," Riki snapped and turned away. Arguing was pointless.

"And run. The Guards might move off as soon as the others return. I don't want to be waiting for you."

"Then you should have taken better care of your gloves."

"I didn't ask your opinion. Leave your cloak here. You'll go quicker without it."

Riki stripped off her cloak and tossed it at Loke. In truth, after an hour of watching the Guards do nothing, a run up the hill and back was not such an unattractive idea. Loke bossing her around was what pissed Riki off. There was no doubt about it—Loke definitely made Tanya look like a wonderful human being. The patrol corporal would never be such a total asshole.

Riki jogged between the tree trunks. At one point, she heard the returning Guards in the distance, but they were some way off and she saw no warning red through the trees. At the top of the hill she reached the open space Loke had spoken of. Riki started to track around the perimeter, looking for the glove or for traces of Loke being there.

Soon she found the line of boot marks made by the Guards, cutting through the vegetation toward a granite outcrop at the summit. Nearby was a lighter single track made by a Ranger. Riki followed this route. The wet ground was soft and muddy. Riki was midway to the rocks when she saw the lost glove, lying in the center of a well-scuffed patch of ground. She was tempted to tread it further into the mud, but it was a childish impulse, of the sort that generally got her into more trouble than it was worth.

Riki retrieved the glove and trotted down through the forest. By the time she got back to Loke, the Guards were clearly setting up camp for the night. Already the major's tent had been erected. It was immediately apparent that the atmosphere among the Guards had changed. Now, they appeared excited and alert.

Riki handed over the glove and gestured to the Guards. "What's got into them?"

"Who knows?" Loke grunted the reply. "Here's your cloak back."

The second Riki took the cloak, she knew something was wrong. Most of the mud had been scraped or brushed off, but even in the poor light, the torn corner was a clear giveaway.

"Hey. This isn't my cloak. It's yours."

"I don't know what you're talking about."

"You've switched cloaks."

"No I haven't."

Riki glared at Loke in furious disbelief. This time she had gone way too far. The cloaks were nominally identical standard issue. Rangers were responsible for maintaining their own uniform, and making good any loss or damage. Maybe Loke was hoping that she could avoid being docked pay to replace her torn cloak.

Only common sense restrained Riki from physically grabbing her own cloak back. She did not want to get into a fight. Regardless of whether she won, she was sure that nobody would believe her story. And it was not necessary. Presumably, Loke had called Tanya in response to whatever difficulty she had got into. In that case Tanya would have seen the state of Loke's uniform and would have no trouble sorting out which cloak belonged to whom.

Riki directed another contemptuous scowl at Loke and pulled the torn cloak around her shoulders without further protest. When they got back to camp that evening, Riki would formally appeal to the corporal to get the matter resolved. Tanya Coppelli might be a stuck-up, overrated idiot, but she would not let a subordinate be swindled so blatantly, regardless of her personal feelings about the victim.

❖

Riki had been back for about ten minutes when she again heard someone approaching through the woods, but this time the rustle of footsteps was accompanied with the chirped whistle of a Ranger identifying her location. The arrival was expected. Tanya and Sasha were due to take over the watch rota, while Riki and Loke went back to stay with the horses.

However, when the backup arrived, it consisted solely of Sasha. She in turn seemed just as surprised to see only two other Rangers waiting for her.

"Where's Tanya?"

"Why isn't she with you?" Riki asked.

"She never came back. I thought she must be staying up here."

"Where did she say she was going?" Loke directed her question at Riki.

"When?"

"After she left you."

Riki frowned. "When?"

"When you called her."

"I didn't call her. You did."

"No, I didn't. And what did you want to talk to her about? You never said."

"I..." Riki's gaze shifted between the other two. Both looked as confused as she felt. "It was you, up the hill who called her. I was down here, watching the Guards."

"What? You weren't—" Loke broke off. "Oh, it can be sorted out later. We need to let Gerry know that Tanya's missing." The look Loke shot at Sasha was the exasperated indignation of an adult catching a child in a tiresome and potentially dangerous prank. "Are you okay watching the Guards on your own? They look to have set camp for the night."

"Yep. I'll be fine." Sasha's response was directed to Loke.

Riki noted the brief eye contact the leading rangers shared that made it quite obvious whose version Sasha was more inclined to believe. It was not fair, but hardly surprising. Riki said nothing more until she and Loke were on their way back to the horses and out of

Sasha's earshot. Maybe Loke would tell the truth, without an audience to sway.

"What game are you playing? You were the one who called Tanya."

However, Loke merely sneered in her direction and marched on. When they reached the horses, a kilometer from the Guards, Loke untied one and pulled it around, ready to mount. Only then did she speak. "Stay here and mind the other horses. I'm going to tell the sergeant."

"And make sure you get to tell your lies first? Not fucking likely. I'm coming too." Riki was losing her temper.

Loke swung into her saddle and leaned down. "You stay here. If you come along, I'll tell Gerry that you disobeyed orders and left Sasha unsupported, which won't be a good start for you. Don't worry. You'll get plenty of chance to tell your side."

She wheeled around and rode off. Riki untied her own horse, preparing to follow, but then stopped and stood, trying to work out what to do for the best.

Loke was pulling some weird trick. But what? She must know that as soon as they found Tanya it would all get sorted—which could only mean that Loke did not think Tanya was going to be found in a fit state to reveal the truth.

Riki's guts clenched and her hands went cold. Murder was a hell of a big leap to make, but if that was what Loke was trying to cover up, she would fail. If Tanya was dead, it would mean a full public trial with all the evidence presented. It would take more than one Ranger's word against another to swing a conviction, even if one of the Rangers was a troublemaker with well publicized hostility to the victim.

Riki chewed her lip and stared both ways through the forest—the direction Loke had gone, and the route Tanya would have taken to the hilltop. She did not like Tanya, but her dislike was nowhere near severe enough to wish her serious harm. But was she dead? Or injured? Or in need of help? Riki almost started to run and find her.

Common sense returned in a wave. Riki stopped and shook her head. She had to be misreading the signs. There had to be some other explanation. The idea of murder was melodramatic and absurd. Loke had no reason to kill Tanya. She was simply being her typical stupid asshole self.

Before long, the sound of horses announced Loke's return, bringing the rest of the patrol with her.

Gerry Baptiste jumped down from her horse. "Private Sadiq. Where were you when you called Corporal Coppelli?"

Riki noted the use of rank and last name—something that had fallen into disuse in the wilderness, but she did not need the hint to know that things were serious. "I didn't call her, ma'am. It was Leading Ranger Stevenson."

Loke joined them. "That's what I told you she'd say."

"Because it's the truth. Stevenson left me watching the main body of the Guards while she followed a small group that went uphill. I heard her signal from there. She came back about half an hour later. I haven't seen Corporal Coppelli since the switchover this afternoon."

Gerry scowled at her. "We seem to have two different versions. But it can wait. We need to find Corporal Coppelli. Presumably she'll know which of you she met with. At least you agree that she was called to the hilltop."

Riki glanced at the sky. The clouds were breaking up, allowing a little more light through, but there was still less than half an hour of decent visibility before dusk. She appreciated the need to hurry, not least because she wanted her own chance to read any tracks that might have been left.

One Ranger was left minding the horses and the remaining five set off through the forest. Twice Riki spotted footmarks that clearly had been made by Tanya earlier. Gerry only nodded when she pointed them out.

After ten minutes, they reached the open hilltop. The sergeant now took the lead, looking out for any sign of what had happened there. They soon reached the Guards' pathway through the ferns, and then the spot where Loke's glove had lain. Gerry raised her hand, making the group halt. She crouched by the mud.

"Private Sadiq. You say you stayed downhill, and Stevenson followed the Guards up here alone?"

"Yes, ma'am."

"Well, I'm thinking that this print was made by a Ranger's boot, and it looks a little small to be either Leading Ranger Stevenson or Corporal Coppelli."

"Er...yes, ma'am. Stevenson sent me up here after she returned, to collect a glove she'd dropped. That would be when I made the footprint."

Loke gave a contemptuous snort. "Do you need me to deny that, ma'am?"

Riki shot an angry glance at her and advanced to Gerry Baptiste's shoulder. "If you look, ma'am, my footmarks are on top of the Guards'. I was here after they'd all gone."

"But no proof of how long after. And I hardly thought that you'd have been walking along together, holding their hands."

The sergeant continued leading the way toward the granite outcrop at the summit. Once they got there, the signs of much activity were clear. Snapped branches and crushed leaves showed where someone had fallen into a clump of honey bramble. Guards' boots had trampled the weaker ferns flat. It looked as if at least a dozen of them had been milling around for some time, but the marks were too confused for any coherent story to be drawn.

Riki spotted more Ranger footprints in the mud. "There. Those are too big for my feet. That would be Leading Ranger Stevenson."

"Or Corporal Coppelli," someone said.

"Sergeant." One of the Rangers called Gerry over. She was crouched by the base of the rocks. "This is blood. And there. A handprint in the mud. Someone was lying on the ground here, bleeding from a head wound."

Riki was aware that two Rangers had moved in behind her. They were not going to seize her yet, but they were manifestly getting ready to do so on the word from the sergeant.

"Ma'am. It was nothing to do with me. I never came this close to the rocks."

The sergeant rose and stood before Riki, appraising her. Gerry's expression was angry and worried, but a shade of uncertainty remained. Her eyes bored into Riki. "You're sure you've no idea what went on here?"

"Yes, ma'am. I nev—"

"Sergeant. Over here." Loke was standing by a trampled honey bramble. "Someone left something behind."

Gerry marched over and carefully reached in between the thorns. Gently she teased out a triangle of green material.

In an instant, Riki realized what the material was, and how it would be interpreted. "This isn't my cloak, ma'am. Loke made a switch when she sent me for the glove."

Gerry said nothing but stalked back and reached for the edge of the cloak that Riki was wearing. She pulled it up, revealing to all the numerous small tears in the fabric, clearly the result of something very similar to bramble thorns, and most definite of all, the missing corner. Gerry placed the section she had taken from the bush into the gap.

"Are you sure you've been nowhere near these rocks?" Her tone made it clear she thought it a rhetorical question.

"Yes, ma'am. This isn't my cloak. Loke switched it with me."

"I don't be—" Gerry broke off sharply and pulled another section of the cloak up, tilting it to catch the last of the evening light. Even in the gloom, the splattering of blood was unmistakable. Gerry let the cloth drop from her hand and nodded to the two Rangers behind Riki, who now grabbed her arms.

Riki could see that all Gerry's doubt had gone. The fury and outrage ripped through. "What did you do to her?"

Everyone was now staring at Riki, so she was the only one to see, over the sergeant's shoulder, the expression of smug triumph that crossed Loke Stevenson's face.

❖

Riki inched across so that she sat more fully in the patch of early morning sunlight. With her hands and feet bound, she could not move around to keep herself warm. Sasha Li, standing guard, eyed her suspiciously but said nothing.

Riki gazed bitterly at the rope around her wrists and then across the camp to Loke, who was standing and talking to Gerry Baptiste in a voice too low to be overheard. At the sight of her sickeningly earnest expression, Riki's shoulders slumped. She could not believe how slow she had been. Why had she not challenged Loke over the switched cloak? Why had she agreed to find the supposedly lost glove? Why had she let Loke go alone to give the first report?

Or as a last resort, why had she not added the evidence up, so that she could have given her explanation as soon as the sergeant and the others arrived and before her footprint and the piece of ripped cloak had been found? Her story would have sounded far more convincing if it had not been pulled from her as each new incriminating scrap of fabricated evidence was found.

Two Rangers rode into the camp and leapt from their saddles. "Ma'am. The Guards have broken camp and moved out. And—" The Ranger broke off and looked at her companion, as if seeking support.

"And?"

"They have Tanya...Corporal Coppelli, prisoner. She's alive."

Riki let her head drop into her bound hands, unable to restrain the groan. From the sounds around the camp, others were reacting to the news in a similar fashion. Captured alive by the Guards was worse than dead, and there was no hope of a rescue. Even if they sent a messenger off with spare horses to use in relay, and riding the animals into the ground, the news would not get to Westernfort for at least twelve days. By the time Captain Coppelli could assemble a large enough force of Rangers to tackle the Guards and bring them out this far east, well over a month would have passed. No matter how much the Guards might dither around, they would surely be back in the Homelands long before then.

"Was she badly injured?"

"We couldn't tell, ma'am. But they left this nailed to a tree."

Riki looked up. The speaker was holding up a sealed letter.

"On the outside it says, *To Captain Coppelli, concerning your daughter.*"

Sergeant Baptiste strode across the camp, reached down, and grabbed Riki's jacket, close to her throat. She jerked Riki's face to within a few centimeters of her own. "So it wasn't some sort of accident. The Guards didn't just ambush the pair of you. You fucking called her into a trap and you told the Guards who she was as well."

"No. I didn't. I—"

The sergeant raised her free hand in a fist. Riki tuned her head aside. She had no way to duck the blow, but then the grip on her jacket relaxed.

"You fucking pile of shit." The voice was a snarl of contempt. "I knew you hated her, but I never thought you'd pull something like this. I'd like to gut you here and now. But I'm going to do something much worse. I'm going to take you back to Westernfort for Captain Coppelli to deal with. I just hope she lets me watch whatever she decides to do to you."

CHAPTER SIX—FRAMED

Riki's denials ended in a grunt as Captain Coppelli's fist pounded into her stomach. Coppelli's other hand was twisted into the collar of Riki's shirt, holding her steady and providing extra purchase, but the third punch was hard enough to unbalance the stool Riki sat on. With her hands tied behind her, and her ankles bound together, she was unable to break her fall. Riki and the stool hit the ground hard. The impact jarred every bone, adding to the burning spikes in her stomach. Her cheek cracked against the stone floor and she tasted blood from a bitten tongue

Coppelli grabbed another fistful of Riki's shirt and hauled her into a sitting position. "Why did you do it?"

"I didn't do—"

The backhand swipe sent Riki crashing to the ground again. She lay where she landed, trying to suck enough air into her lungs to clear her head, but every movement of her rib cage provoked fresh darts of pain.

They were in the cellar of the council building in Westernfort. The small room had no windows. Its only light came from two oil lanterns and its only furniture was a desk and a bookshelf full of ledgers. A wooden flight of stairs in the corner led up to the ground floor. A doorway in the wall opposite gave access to a corridor with storerooms leading off. One of these rooms had doubled as a jail cell, where Riki had been dumped after arriving in Westernfort two hours earlier, and from which she had just been dragged for an interview with Captain Coppelli.

Gerry Baptiste, Sasha Li, and Loke Stevenson had provided her escort for the journey to Westernfort and would also be acting as witnesses in her trial. However, Captain Coppelli had clearly heard their evidence and already made up her mind.

"Why did you do it?"

A rough shove from a boot rolled Riki onto her back. She looked up at the woman towering over her. Every muscle in Coppelli's body was knotted with tension. Her fists clenched and unclenched. Her face held an expression of crazed fury, demonic in the lamplight. She was not going to hear a word Riki said that did not fit with what she already believed.

Riki gave up. What was the point of telling the truth when it would only get her a worse beating? She carefully drew a shallow breath and said, "I hated her."

"Just that?"

Riki closed her eyes. Was a confession not enough? Did Coppelli want imagination as well?

"There has to be more!" Coppelli shouted.

Riki flexed her stomach muscles; the hot stabs had dulled to a general burning. Breathing was getting easier. She scrabbled among her thoughts for something to say, because it was clear that the captain was not going to give up until Riki had said what she wanted to hear.

"I was angry she outranked me. She was better at archery than me. Never bought me a drink. She insulted my new haircut. Her horse was prettier than mine." Riki knew that she was getting inane, but what else could she say? "Her nose was too small. I couldn't—"

A savage kick stopped Riki's flow of words. More followed. She tried to roll away, to protect her body from the battering, but there was no way to avoid the succession of blows. Each one triggered a fireball explosion in muscle and bone. Riki heard her own voice whimpering, groaning, and screaming. The echoes filled the basement room, punctuated by the thud of impacts, but it all felt distant. Everything else was irrelevant behind the wall of pain and panic.

The back of Riki's head cracked on something hard. Her body dissolved into water. Sparks swam in the darkness. Her thoughts drifted away with the echoes, and for a while there was peace, but then the sounds flowed back. Riki found herself still lying on the floor in the cellar, but the kicking had stopped.

A new voice was speaking. "Chip, I understand. Believe me, I understand. But it won't help Tanya, and when you come to look back on this, you won't be proud of yourself for beating a prisoner to death."

"I...she...that little shit. She's not even sorry. She—" Coppelli's words stumbled to a halt and were replaced by sobs.

"Chip. I'm sorry. I'm so sorry. But we'll do this the right way."

Riki stayed motionless, struggling to restrain any sound that might draw attention to herself, but cautiously, she opened her eyes a slit.

The only other person present in the cellar was Kimberly Ramon, the elected leader of the heretics. Riki knew that Ramon had been a Ranger and that she and the captain were close friends of many years standing. So far, Ramon had played no part, but now she had clearly decided to intervene. She had her arms around Coppelli, holding her while she cried.

"Tanya should've..." Again Coppelli's words were lost in sobs.

Ramon rubbed her back. "Oh, Chip. This is tough. I wish I could say something to help."

Coppelli's arms tightened around her friend and for a while she just cried, but eventually her sobs subsided and she pulled back. "You do help. Just being here."

"I still feel useless."

"If you weren't here, I'd—" Coppelli drew another deep breath and moved away, wiping her eyes. She scowled in Riki's direction. "I want to rip her to pieces. But you're right. It won't help. She's not worth feeling guilty about afterward."

Coppelli leaned back against the wall, pressing the sides of her head with both hands.

Ramon watched her for a while, and then asked, "How's Katryn taken the news?"

"On the face of it, better than me. She's busy being strong for our other kids. She's not asking any questions. I think she's blocking a lot out. But we both know, in Landfall, the Intelligence Corps will—" Coppelli broke off again and she fixed her eyes on the ceiling, clearly struggling to maintain her newfound composure.

"I know. It's what they'd do to any of us," Ramon spoke softly. "And I know it's a trite thing to say, but Tanya knew the risks. It was her choice to become a Ranger. And she'll continue to do her duty, as well as she can, for as long as she can."

"I know. But the Guards know she's my daughter, which might make them take a bit more care with her, and not in a good way." Coppelli's tone was battling to stay even.

"I heard the Guards left a letter for you. Was that one of the threats in it?"

"It was nothing."

"Nothing?"

"Nothing I'm going to give any thought to."

"Would you like me to give it some thought on your behalf?"

"No."

Ramon studied her friend. "Now you've got me wondering what it could have said."

Coppelli groaned and turned her face away. "They offered to swap Tanya for Lynn."

"Ah."

"I don't want you to even pretend you're giving a split second of thought to it, because I haven't."

"I wouldn't be your friend if I didn't."

"And you wouldn't be our leader if you did. That Tanya's my daughter and Lynn's your partner is irrelevant. Tanya's just another Ranger. Lynn's our only Imprinter. She's far more important to us. And the Guards know it."

"Yep." Ramon sounded regretful. "Actually, most of the split second thought I gave was to do with the offer only being intended to create divisions here."

"Exactly. Which is why I don't want Lynn or Katryn to know."

"I don't think Lynn would do anything stupid."

"But she'd feel guilty. Anyway, I bet the Guards wouldn't give Tanya back. They'd find some loophole to break their word while pretending they hadn't." Coppelli's face crumpled again. "There's nothing we can do. Tanya's gone. I just wish she'd died cleanly."

Coppelli pushed herself away from the wall. Riki forced herself not to react as the boots stopped, scant centimeters from her face, hoping the captain would not take one last kick if her victim was already unconscious.

"We'll have our trial tomorrow. And then we'll string this bitch up by her neck. I wished I'd had her dumped on the border the first day she set foot in Westernfort. It was what I wanted to do. But I was the one who put her in Tanya's patrol. I set all this up."

"Hindsight is the bitch. You can't blame yourself for not knowing the future."

"How many times do you think I'll need to tell myself that before I believe it?"

"Come on. Let's go. Katryn will need you."

"And promise you won't tell Lynn about the letter?"

"Yes."

Riki heard the sound of feet on the wooden stairs.

"I'll get someone to throw Sadiq back in the storeroom and stand guard. I know that even doing it properly won't help much, but I'm so looking forward to watching her swing tomorrow."

❖

The straw-stuffed mattress on the ground was the only item in the cell. Riki eased herself around on it, trying to lie more comfortably— not easy with her hands tied behind her back. Her bruises were sore and stiffening, and her head ached, but nothing appeared broken. The narrow room was in complete darkness. Riki was sure that it was after nightfall, although she had no way to check. She had missed seeing her last sunset.

Persuading anyone of her innocence on the next day was a hopeless task. To be fair, with the way Loke had set her up, Riki could not blame them. She doubted that she would believe her own story if she were hearing it from someone else. Her situation was not helped by Tanya's popularity. At the moment, people were more interested in revenge than justice. Everyone knew she and Tanya hated each other. In addition to providing Riki with a motive, although a weak one, it meant that she was an especially fitting target on which the town could take out its grief.

Apart from Loke's testimony, the only evidence against Riki was the incriminating footprints and the torn cloak, but it would be enough. Loke had judged her ploy with the lost glove well. Not only had it resulted in the false clues, but it had taken Riki away while the Guards returned to camp. If she had seen that they held Tanya as a prisoner, Riki would have been more alert and might not have sleepwalked into the frame-up so blindly.

Riki turned her face to the ceiling, staring up, though she could see nothing in the darkness. One of the offices overhead would be used as the courtroom tomorrow. From there she would be taken out to the town square and hung from a gibbet. At least she would get to see the open sky one more time.

The sound of a key in the lock made Riki tense and look down. A thin line of light shone through the gap beneath the door. Who was coming to see her now? And were they also interested in some impromptu pre-trial retribution?

The door swung open. Riki was temporarily blinded by the lantern shining directly into her eyes. She averted her head, while listening for footsteps. Just one pair of feet. Whoever it was had come alone. This was not a good sign. One person could inflict as much damage as a mob, and there would be no calmer heads calling for restraint.

The lantern was put down in front of Riki's face and then whoever had entered the room knelt behind her. Riki's bound hands were pulled back, straining her shoulders. Riki clenched her jaw, bracing herself, but to her surprise, the only thing she felt was the rope being loosened. Riki looked over her shoulder. The lamplight showed Loke, frowning in concentration as she worked on the knots.

"What?" Riki was bewildered.

Loke glanced up. "Look. I'm sorry about all this. I didn't mean it to go so far. I didn't mean Tanya to get caught. I'm sorry. I...I can't just let you hang, when I know—" She ducked her head and returned to the rope.

"You're going to tell the truth?"

"No, I can't. It wasn't my fault, but Captain Coppelli won't believe it. She's going to want to hang someone. If not you, then me. But I'm giving you a chance to escape."

"Doesn't sound like much."

"It's the best I can do for you."

The rope fell away and Loke moved to Riki's ankles. Riki rolled over and gently rubbed the chafed spots on her wrists, then flexed her hands to get the circulation back. As she did this, her thoughts bounded ahead.

"Why did you give Tanya to the Guards?"

"The Guards cornered me and caught me by the rocks. They said they'd take me back to Landfall for the Intelligence Corps to play with unless I helped them catch somebody more important. Tanya was the only person around who'd count. I hoped when she arrived we'd be able to sort something out and escape, but the Guards had everything covered."

"You mean you sold Tanya out to save your own skin?"

"No. It wasn't like that."

Riki was not convinced, but getting the truth out of Loke would take more time and coercion than she had access to. The last knot loosened, and Loke stood up. Riki also got carefully to her feet, with her hands braced on the walls. She tried not to wince as her bruises complained.

"Okay. So you've untied me. Now what?"

Loke licked her lips. "I'm the only one on jail watch down here, and there's just a couple of clerks in the office upstairs. When I leave here I'll go and chat to them, which will be your chance to sneak out. Just give me two minutes, and then you're on your own. If anyone sees you escaping, I won't help. I've done my bit for you."

Riki made a show of massaging and flexing her knees. The first thing was to get a bit more time to work with. She did not trust Loke or the offer to create a diversion. "Can you make it ten minutes? I've been tied up for ages. I'll stand a better chance if I get my legs working properly before I try moving."

"All right. Ten minutes." Loke nodded and picked up the lantern. At the doorway she paused and glanced back. "Sorry, again. And good luck."

"Thanks."

Riki listened to Loke's footsteps departing down the corridor, and then the sound of the door at the end opening and closing. She shook her head scornfully. Just how gullible did Loke think she was? Okay, she had been played for a fool once, but she was not going to be caught out again so easily. Riki was sure that she was reading the signs right.

Tomorrow, at the trial, she would get the chance to tell her version of events, clearly and in full. Of course, nobody would believe her. She would be found guilty and executed. But in a month or two, when everyone had calmed down a little, surely a few folk might start to wonder why a Ranger skilled in bushcraft had left her footprints behind so carelessly. Some would come to realize that it really had been just Loke's word against hers.

The rethink probably would not be enough for a retrial, or a posthumous pardon, but it would have people looking slightly more suspiciously at Loke. When you considered what she was like, it would be amazing if Loke did not have her full share of enemies, eager to believe the worst of her. This was why she did not want Riki to stand up and lay out the whole story for everyone to hear. And for her part, Riki was not greatly interested in anything that might happen posthumously.

Riki crept into the passageway, alert for signs of a trap. The door at the end was outlined by lantern light from the room beyond. Riki caught her lip in her teeth. She was prepared to stake her life that Loke was waiting there, sword drawn, ready to cut down the escaping prisoner, who would thus never get her chance in court.

Riki had ten minutes to find another way out of the cellar.

The room she had been locked in was halfway down the corridor. It was too dark to tell how many other doors there were, but the reduced risk of Loke hearing was as good a reason as any to start with those farther away from the exit.

The first door Riki tried opened easily, but touch revealed that the room contained only crates and barrels, stacked floor to ceiling. The second door was locked, and forcing it would be too noisy for anything other than a last resort. Riki crossed to the other side of the corridor and began working her way back,

As soon as she opened the next door, Riki saw the faint glimmer of moonlight in a far corner. Moving carefully so as not to bang into anything and knock it over, Riki edged past piles of sacks. The air was full of dust and the scent of grain. The ground felt gritty underfoot. Many farmers paid their taxes in goods rather than coin; this presumably was where their payments were stored.

Soon Riki was directly under the source of the moonlight. She grinned. A trapdoor. She guessed that the room extended beneath the street outside. The trapdoor allowed farmers to deposit their goods without having to lug the sacks and barrels through the council building. The moonlight was squeezing in through the crack by the hinges. It would be too faint to be seen were it not for the otherwise total darkness.

The ceiling was just low enough for Riki to reach. She ran her hands around the edge of the trapdoor. It was locked, of course. Otherwise the cellar would not be a secure place to keep a prisoner. The key was probably in the room with Loke. Riki examined the lock mechanism.

Even working by touch, she recognized the type immediately. One advantage of her youthful misdemeanors was a familiarity with such things. Although the lock was big and heavy, as if hoping to impress by its size, it would be easy to pick—but not with bare hands. Riki needed a metal spike, and time was running short.

Riki slipped across to the room opposite, the first one she had tried. People were always careless when opening crates and rarely tidied up afterward. Riki knelt and ran her hands over the floor. In under ten seconds she found what she wanted, a discarded nail. In fact, she found several. Riki selected the straightest two and returned to the trapdoor.

The lock surrendered without a fight, but Riki was still nowhere near tall enough to push open the trapdoor. Possibly there was a ladder or removable ramp somewhere nearby, but Riki did not have time to hunt for it in the dark. Instead, she assembled a pile of grain sacks and then clambered on top. Riki placed her hands on the underside of the trapdoor, but then paused, listening for movement above. She thought she could hear faint voices, but no footsteps.

Cautiously, she raised the trapdoor a few centimeters and peered out. No more than twenty meters away, a group of women were huddled in conversation—undoubtedly discussing the next day's trial. Riki chewed her lip. With gossip like that, they could be nattering away for hours, and she could not afford to wait until they went. Not that the gossipers were showing any sign of being on the lookout for escaping prisoners. Their heads were clustered close together, and fortunately, the spot where Riki was emerging was in deep shadow.

Even so, she did not want to throw the trapdoor fully open. Apart from the extreme visibility of such an action, it would fall back with a crash. Far safer to squeeze herself out through a gap, although this was not without pain. The heavy wooden boards raked her back, even through her clothes, but worse was where her bruised stomach was dragged over the metal frame around the opening. Riki clenched her teeth, ignoring the protest of her battered body. Once she was nearly clear, she caught hold of the trapdoor, pulled her feet free, and then lowered it back into place. Throughout all this, the group of women did not miss a beat of their intense debate.

Riki took a deep breath. She was out, but far from being safely away. She reckoned that Loke would give her the full ten minutes and a bit more, then search the entire cellar, before panicking for a while and finally raising the alarm. At most, Riki had half an hour to get out of Westernfort. After that, she would have a long trek across the wilderness, pursued by every Ranger at Captain Coppelli's command, before she could reach the relative safety of the Sisters' Homelands. She was going to need supplies and horses, and she did not have time for stealth. Her only hope lay with speed and nerve.

At the moment, nobody would expect her to be walking brazenly across the town. So that was what she was going to do. Riki shoved herself to her feet and set off at a crisp march, quick, but nothing that would attract attention. Only one moon was in the sky—Hardie at a shade off full. As far as she could, Riki kept it at her back, so her face was in shadow, and adjusted her route to keep as far from others as she could without making the avoidance too conspicuous.

The streets of Westernfort were quiet. Nobody gave a second glance to the woman in Ranger uniform marching across town. Most folk were in groups, walking slowly and talking together. The few loners were striding along purposefully, probably in search of home and someone to discuss the news with. Riki was just one more.

Soon she reached the patrol barracks. This was the most critical moment. If anyone was inside, they would not fail to spot and recognize her, but opening the door cautiously and peering round the edge would be too blatantly furtive. Riki glanced at the moon, judging the time. Three of the patrol were still out in the Wildlands. Loke was in the cellar. With luck, Gerry Baptiste would be making the most of the chance to catch up with her family, and Sasha would be in the tavern, telling everybody how evil Private Sadiq had handed Tanya over to the Guards. Surely nobody would be in the barracks.

Riki pushed the door open and stepped inside. As she had hoped, the room was empty. The only light was the dim red glow from the stove. Nobody lay on the bunks. Riki hurried to her locker and pulled out her pack. Then she went to the next one. Now was not the time to worry about stealing from your comrades. At the thought, Riki gave a sarcastic grin. When had that scrap of ethics entered her conscience?

Within a few minutes, she had everything she needed. A new cloak was wrapped around her shoulders and a broad-brimmed Rangers' hat was pulled low over her face. A sword and trail knife hung at her side.

Riki carefully hoisted the full pack over her shoulder, trying not to strain her damaged muscles, and turned to leave. At the door she stopped for a last look around, checking off her mental inventory for anything she had overlooked. The corporal's single bunk caught her attention. Tanya would never again sleep there.

"I'm sorry. I wish I could have stuck the bitch for you. I didn't have the chance. I—"

Riki was surprised at the unexpected surge of emotion that choked her throat. They had not liked each other. Their relationship had started off on the wrong foot and gone downhill from there, but it had not all been Tanya's fault. She was, in Riki's estimation, no worse than any other officer, and regardless, no Ranger should be sold out by her supposed comrade and handed over to the Guards. Loke deserved to pay, but there was nothing Riki could do. She wished things were different, that she could let Tanya know her outrage over Loke's treachery and take revenge on behalf of them both. For once, they were on the same side. Riki's jaw clenched. Wishing was pointless. She gave a small formal nod of solidarity to Tanya's bunk and returned to the night.

The gate guarding the path down to the stables was less than half a kilometer away; five minutes' walk. How much longer did she have? Riki set off, wishing she could run without attracting attention. However, the adrenaline was kicking in and she felt a grin settling on her lips.

At last, the wall rose before her. Riki could see Rangers on duty, silhouetted against the backdrop of stars over Westernfort. Torches burned on either side of the gate. When she passed them, she would not have the benefit of shadow for concealment. Riki was sure that the sentries had seen her approach, but if their suspicions were not aroused, they would not watch her every step. She shifted the pack as if to settle it more comfortably on her shoulder, while incidentally obscuring slightly more of her face, and raised a hand in greeting.

"Evening, all." Riki kept on marching, fighting not to limp from her bruises.

"You going?"

"Just dropping this off." She was under the gate and still walking.

"See you soon, then."

"Right."

Now, Riki was on the path down and the torches were behind her. She heard soft voices from the sentries.

"Who was that?"

"I thought it was Julie."

"Oh."

Each step down the pathway felt like a new barrier passed. Riki raised her eyes to the moon. Well over twenty minutes had elapsed since Loke left her in the cellar. By Riki's reckoning, she had only a few minutes more before the alarm was raised, but now she was ahead of any pursuit with nothing left to block her way. She was not yet safe, but the feeling of triumph was growing.

Riki reached the lowland, and still no shouts sounded from the wall. The patrol stable was less than twenty meters away. Riki crossed the space, expecting chaos to erupt from the upper valley at any moment. She reached the door, pulled it open, and stepped inside. The warm smell of animals and hay enveloped her. Now at last, she could run.

Riki raced to her horse. She grabbed the saddle and flung it over its back, and then ducked to grab the girth strap. Never had her hands performed the task quicker. The pain of her injuries was forgotten. Within minutes, her horse was ready.

Riki turned to the stall next door. Taking Loke's horse was not much by way of reprisal for her crimes, but Riki liked the thought of annoying her. She slipped a halter over the horse's head, and tied the loose rein to her own saddle. A second mount to swap with would increase her speed dramatically, as well as providing insurance should one go lame.

Riki led the horses to the door and paused. Still no shouts broke the quiet night air. Was Loke being even slower at raising the alarm than expected? Or was she playing the innocent, now that she had discovered that her scheme was not going to plan this time? Maybe she hoped to cover her own involvement. At that moment, was Loke looking for a way to fix the blame on the Ranger who took watch after her? It was the way her mind worked.

Riki paused, wondering if she might even have until breakfast the next day before the pursuit started, but then shook her head. Maybe. Maybe not. She should not rely on it. The sentries would see her ride off with two horses. It would alert them that something was wrong, but they would know that soon enough. Speed had served her so far and would serve her again. If she could get clear of Westernfort and into the wilderness, then she could slow down.

Riki smiled and looked up. Hardie shone overhead, bright enough to see by, and small Laurel was rising in the east. She led the horses into the open and swung up into the saddle. Another five kilometers and she would be clear of the animal pasture. Then she would see if any other Ranger could match her in bushcraft.

Laughter bubbled in Riki's throat. She dug her heels into her horse's flank and urged it into a canter.

❖

Eighteen days later, Riki stood on the northern foothills of the Longstop Range. She had made good time, pushing the horses in the effort to stay ahead of any messengers from Westernfort. She was now close to the point where Tanya had been captured, and in the region patrolled by Coppelli's Rangers. Slipping by would be easier if they did not know they were supposed to be looking for her.

Riki pursed her lips. In truth, she was sure enough of her abilities to think that she would have no problems anyway. She even toyed with the idea of finding a patrol, letting them know she was there, and then giving them the slip, just so they would know she had the edge on them. But it was not a sensible idea. She had seen quite enough trouble for one month. Now was the time to play it safe. Riki grinned at her own expense. Avoiding unnecessary risk? Maybe she was finally starting to grow up. People had been telling her to do it for long enough.

From where she stood, Riki could see the land ahead flattening out into the plains around the Coldwater River, still four days' ride away. Somewhere between the Longstops and the Coldwater, the Wildlands ended and the Sisters' Homelands began, although no map would show the line.

The Sisters claimed divinely sanctified dominion over all the planet and would consider it blasphemy to concede control anywhere to the heretics. They would never draw a line on a map to show where their power ended. For their part, the heretics were not bothered with claiming land and concentrated merely on keeping the Guards away from their settlements.

Riki looked back. She had never wanted to join the heretics and had never been happy with them. Now she was leaving their Wildlands for good. Would she get on any better in the Homelands? Surely she would be able to make a life for herself. The risk of Guards arresting her as a heretic was small. After all, she had never fully renounced her belief in Celaeno. When she left, she had been only twelve. Who now would recognize her with certainty?

Riki's expression softened. Of course, there were some people she wanted to recognize her—her sisters and her gene mother. She could reclaim the family she had never wanted to leave. Riki urged her horse forward, wondering why the idea did not make her quite as happy as it should.

PART TWO

Games With The Matriarch

CHAPTER SEVEN—OPENING GAMBITS

Tanya stood and braced her shoulder against the wooden slats of the prison wagon so that she could see out through the bars above the driver's head. Sitting on the bench opposite, both Guards from the Intelligence Corps sneered but made no move to stop her. For additional support, she rested her knee on the bench and clung to the iron ring that was riveted to the wagon frame. The short length of chain between the ring and the manacles on her wrists swung against the wooden side with each pothole-induced lurch.

However, the shaking was getting less. The sound of the wheels had also changed. The road was improving and had gone from rutted earth to cobblestones. At the moment, these were poorly maintained, chipped, and cracked, but it marked the change from country to town. They had reached the city of Landfall. This would undoubtedly be Tanya's only chance to see the place where her birth mother had been born and had grown up. Relatives still lived here. It would most likely also be her last chance to see the open sky. She did not want to miss it.

After her capture, Major Kaur had needed ten days of increasingly desperate meandering to get her troops out of the Wildlands and to the Homelands town of Longhill. As far as she could judge, Tanya had spent a month in an underground cell at the Guards' fort on the outskirts of town, waiting for the Intelligence Corps to take charge of her. The four corps members who had turned up with the enclosed prison wagon had then taken the best part of another month to cover the 800 kilometers between Longhill and Landfall.

Loke Stevenson had turned her over to the Guards at the beginning of May. It was now mid-July and the wagon was arriving at Landfall at the end of a long, hot afternoon. The enclosed caboose was a meter and a half wide and two meters long. The temperature inside was baking, and unlike the Guards, Tanya did not get to take turns sitting outside with the driver. As she stood looking out, the breeze through the bars was wonderfully cool, drying the sweat on her face, although her clothes still stuck to her. Tanya tried not to remind herself that her conditions of imprisonment were about to get far worse. Since the moment of her capture, she had known what awaited her in Landfall. Giving in to fear would do no good.

Landfall was the biggest city in the world. Seeing the great capital was a dream that Tanya had never expected to realize. She had been born at Westernfort, and had no more than touched the borders of the Homelands while on patrol, but she had heard stories from her mothers and from other heretics. The current circumstances were material for nightmares rather than dreams, but she should not let panic ruin her chance to fulfill this one last wish.

Landfall was home to the Coppellis, one of the most powerful merchant families. According to her mother, they owned a third of the city and controlled the rest. An unwillingness to be drawn into the corrupt political maneuvering had driven a young Chip Coppelli to run away from home and enlist with the militia. She had then advanced to the Rangers, the branch of the Homelands military who patrolled the borders of the Sisters' territory, battling wild animals and bandits. Chip had been a member of the elite force for over ten years before her entire squadron had deserted to join the heretics at Westernfort.

Through the bars, Tanya could see down the length of a long, empty street. On either side were single-story huts. The roofs were red tiles, although many were cracked or missing. Plaster on the walls was flaking so that the timber frames beneath were exposed in places. Weeds grew along the edges of the road and the breeze carried the stench of decaying waste.

At first, Tanya assumed these buildings were abandoned, or animal shelters. The sounds of squabbling chickens aided this impression, but then she saw girls playing in the alleys between, and old women sitting in doorways. A few able-bodied adults were working on vegetable plots to the rear. Tanya was shocked to realize that these were family homes. Nobody at Westernfort lived in such squalor.

At the end of the street, the wagon turned onto another road. The buildings here were bigger and in better repair. The weeds had gone. A steady drone of voices had been rising for a while. Tanya did not know when she had first noticed it, but now the occasional shout caught her attention. The road turned a bend and a bridge stood before them.

On her journey across the Homelands, Tanya had seen longer bridges but never one so wide. Four wagons abreast could have crossed it, were it not for the crowds packing it out. The road had joined another busier one, and the cobbles were overflowing with horses, wagons, and pedestrians.

Tanya felt herself flinch at the hubbub. Fewer than one thousand people lived at Westernfort, and maybe nine-tenths would congregate in the town square for big events. This was the most Tanya had ever seen gathered together. Yet there looked to be at least as many people trying to cross the river at once on an ordinary Landfall afternoon.

The wagon fought its way onto the bridge, to the accompaniment of the driver shouting threats to clear the way. Tanya tore her eyes from the surrounding mob. The clear view over the river allowed her to gauge the scale of the city. On the other side, roofs filled the skyline, rising even higher and higher, in rank upon rank.

Hanging above them all was a huge dome—the great temple of Celaeno. In the ideology of the Sisters it stood on the exact point where the Blessed Himoti, greatest of the Elder-Ones, had been sent into the world by the Goddess. In the understanding of the heretics, it was somewhere close to the spot chosen for landfall by a group of stranded colonists from a malfunctioning spaceship.

Once the wagon reached the opposite bank, the press of bodies eased as people dispersed through the network of streets, but if anything, the noise got louder. Women, girls, and crones were everywhere, talking, calling, even singing. Wheels and hooves pounded the cobblestones. The clanks, rattles, and thumps of tradeswomen echoed from shop doorways. Above it all were the cries of street traders, hawking their wares. The traditional words were familiar—traders in Westernfort used the same patters, but never had Tanya heard so many competing for attention at the same time. The buildings were now three stories high or more. Tanya pressed her face against the grill, trying to see the tops. The street was wide enough for six wagons.

A hint of panic coiled in Tanya's gut. All these faces, and not a single one she recognized. She had not known every woman in Westernfort by name, but few were not familiar by sight. She knew their families, their jobs, their friends. They had been there since the day she was born. But here were strangers—thousands and thousands of strangers.

The fear grew. The crowds were pressing in. Tanya heard them banging against the side of the wagon and rubbing against it as they squeezed by. She wanted to shrink away from the bars, to hide, but she forced herself to stay in place. Yes, it was frightening. It was also something she had wanted to see. She would not run from this last experience before she was taken into the Intelligence Corps prison.

The wagon halted briefly before swinging sharply to the left. Tanya caught a glimpse of a wide gateway as they went through, with Guards standing sentry in their bright red uniforms. Immediately, the noise began to fade. This was a military compound. Tanya recognized barracks and stables. The only women in view were Guards, marching silently about their business.

The wagon crossed an open parade ground, passed under a low arch into a small courtyard, and stopped. The whole frame shook as the driver and other Guard jumped down. A low murmur of voices was followed by the key in the lock and then the caboose door at the rear swung open. The two Guards opposite left and another entered, with a key to release Tanya from her manacles.

Tanya stood surrounded by Guards in the courtyard. Celaeno's temple was so close that she was literally in its shadow—the temple built in honor of a Goddess in whose name she was about to be tortured and killed. Tanya turned her eyes away and instead studied the sky overhead, which was clear and blue. It might be the last beautiful thing she ever saw. She had only a few seconds before the Guards pulled her away.

Once inside, they immediately turned through another door and down a spiral staircase. The Guard in the lead had a lantern. Shadows surged over the rough-cut stonework as they descended. At the bottom a corridor led away left and right. A firm hand in her back propelled Tanya along, past a row of heavy doors. Tanya thought she heard sobbing from behind one. Eventually the Guard ahead pulled a door open and those behind shoved her through. The door slammed shut and the familiar clank of a key turning in a lock sounded. The faint light under the door faded with the departing footsteps, leaving only darkness and silence.

Tanya felt her way around. The cell was about two meters square with a pisspot in the corner and a bunk on one wall. She sat and leaned back against the cold stone. It was very peaceful after the heat, noise, and chaos of the Landfall streets, but Tanya knew her feeling of relief was misplaced. She was in the worst place that any heretic could be— the Intelligence Corps dungeon.

❖

"How many armed fighters are there in Westernfort?"

Tanya said nothing.

The Intelligence Corps captain paced slowly around the chair. Tanya resisted the urge to turn her head to follow. With her hands tied to the armrests, she could have had only limited success. Instead she kept focused on the wall in front. The footsteps paused behind her. Tanya felt the back of her neck prickling, imagining the captain's eyes on her. Apart from the captain, two other Guards were in the room, but so far they had said and done nothing, other than escort Tanya from her cell and bind her to the chair.

The room was underground and lit by oil lamps. Was it part of the game not to let the prisoners see the sky? Was it intended to disorientate or demoralize? Tanya tried not to let it affect her, yet she could not stop herself from wondering what was going on in the world above. Was it day or night, raining or dry? Was anyone thinking about her?

She was sure that she had been in the dungeon for a few days. In that time, she had been interrogated three times, twice in her cell and once in another room. On all occasions the questioning had been routine and dull, devoid of threat. This time was different. The eyes of the Guards held an expectant tension. The room was different too, empty apart from the chair that Tanya was on and a bench against one wall with a long wooden crate on top. The flagstones of the floor were stained brown—a color Tanya recognized as dried blood.

Eventually, the captain continued pacing and returned to her position in front of Tanya. She leaned back and rested against the wall, looking casual and relaxed, apart from the coldness in her eyes.

Unlike the rest of the Guards, the Intelligence Corps were not zealous about their appearance. The captain's hair was unkempt and shoulder length. Of course, much of their work was carried out undercover. A proper short military cut would be too conspicuous.

Equally, their uniforms were something they put on only when in their headquarters. It was not the defining mark of their calling. The captain's red tunic was stained along the cuffs and the lacing was loose at her neck.

"How many armed fighters are there in Westernfort?" The captain repeated her question. After a minute of silence, she continued. "I know your mother styles herself as Captain Coppelli and is the bandit chief for the thugs in your heretic strongholds. I know you claim the rank of corporal for yourself, trying to pretend that you can be considered a Ranger. I also know you are going to tell me everything you know, or have seen, or have overheard your mother say. And though you may not believe it, I really would prefer if you told me what I want to know now, without forcing me to hurt you."

Tanya pressed her lips together.

The captain stood up straighter, nodded to her two subordinates, and then clasped her hands together and bowed her head:

> *Devine Celaeno, we implore that you look down upon us and guide us. We ask for your blessing and your absolution. Keep all malice and base cruelty from our hearts. Know that ever we seek only to follow your will. Give us the resolve not to flinch from what we must do in your name. We ask your forgiveness for this lost daughter...*

Tanya closed her eyes, wishing that she could also close her ears and cut out the insane prayers as the Guards wrapped their justification for what they were about to do in their warped piety.

The captain fell silent. Tanya opened her eyes, fighting to control her breathing and not to start whimpering in fear. One of the Guards went to the crate on the table and released the catches on the top. The side folded down to reveal an interior lined with knives, spikes, pliers, and clamps. Tanya looked away, but it would not help. Nothing was going to help her now.

The Guard who had opened the crate walked around the chair and knelt at the side. The other one stood behind Tanya. She felt the woman's knuckles in her back as the Guard braced the chair steady. The kneeling Guard pressed a hand down on the back of Tanya's, forcing

her fingers out flat against the armrest. Tanya looked down. The Guard was holding a fine spike, the size of a needle. She touched the point to Tanya's index finger, just beneath the nail.

"How many armed fighters are there in Westernfort?"

Tanya looked back and met the captain's eyes. She could feel her pulse racing. Her stomach was clamped in knots. Her throat was taut and dry, but she managed to rasp out, "Fifty-seven."

The captain smiled.

"Or was it seventy-five?" Tanya went on. "No, it was fifty...or fifteen. Maybe it was one hundred and fifteen." Tanya pressed back in the chair, forcing her voice to remain steady, forcing her lungs to obey her, forcing her eyes to hold the captain's, unblinking. "You can make me talk. I know you can. But you can't make me stick to the truth. More fool you, if you believe a word I say."

The captain's smile changed to a scowl. She snapped out, "Go ahead, Sergeant."

A sharp tearing pain ripped up Tanya's hand as, millimeter by millimeter, the Guard pushed the needle under her fingernail. Tanya clamped her jaw shut, holding back the urge to scream. She would give in, sooner or later, she knew, but it was important to her self-respect to hold out for as long as possible. Her ankles were bound to the chair legs, but her heels rammed against the ground. The Guard behind her grunted, holding the chair from tipping.

At last the pain stopped getting worse and the pressure on her hand relaxed a little. Tanya's eyes were scrunched shut. She did not want to look down and see. The pain shot up her arm, flaring at knuckle and wrist. Lightning rippled through her palm. Her finger was on fire. Despite all her effort, high-pitched cries were escaping through the fence of her teeth.

"Another, ma'am? Or shall I continue with this one?" the kneeling Guard asked.

"Another."

Tanya felt the tip of a second needle touch her middle finger. Again pain exploded in her hand.

A knock sounded on the door.

"What is it?" the captain shouted impatiently.

The sound of the door opening was followed by whispering. Tanya opened her eyes. The world swam before her. Focusing was impossible, beyond noting that a new Guard had entered and was whispering urgently in the captain's ear.

"What? Now?" The captain's tone held frustration.

The Guard leaned forward and whispered some more.

"But I..." The captain's shoulders slumped and she sighed. "Oh well. If that's it." She looked at the other Guards. "We're finishing for now. Take her back."

It's a game they're playing with me. The words shot through Tanya's head even as she screamed when the needles were plucked from beneath her fingernails. The captain gave a final scowl and stomped out of the room, followed by the messenger.

Without another word, the two remaining Guards untied Tanya's wrists and ankles and hauled her to her feet. They marched her down the corridor and back to her cell, where they locked her in and left.

Tanya sat alone in the darkness, cradling her hand and fighting with herself. She must not relax. She must not feel reprieved, because they would come back again—in three days, or three hours, or three seconds. The Guards could take as much time as they wanted. It was all a game, but Tanya knew, with absolute certainty, they would come for her again.

❖

All too soon, Tanya heard the key turn again in the lock. The pointless urge to hide in a corner almost overwhelmed her, followed by the dread that, before long, any self-control would desert her. She would pathetically try to hide and be dragged from the cell screaming like an infant. She pressed her uninjured hand against her forehead, holding back tears. Whether she broke today, or in a year's time, nobody who might care would ever get to hear. It was no longer about living up to her mother's reputation or impressing her friends. Only enemies were here and all that was left to keep her going was her pride.

Light streamed in from a lantern in the corridor, dazzling after the dark. Two Guards in silhouette entered the cell. "On your feet and turn around."

Tanya obeyed, standing beside her bunk. She felt the cold metal of manacles snap around her wrists, and then a hand on her shoulder steered her from the room. With every step, the panic knotting her guts grew worse. Halfway down the corridor, the Guard ahead ducked through a doorway. The unmistakable sound of feet climbing stairs followed.

Tanya stumbled after, bewildered. Were they really taking her back to the surface? Would she see the sky again? Was this some new trick? Tanya dared not let herself hope. However, they emerged into the open air. Tanya rolled her head back, staring up. Overhead were soft strands of pink—sunset. The world smelled clean, free of the stench of blood, piss, and fear. A shove sent her staggering forward, forcing her to look where she was going.

A small group of Guards stood waiting in the courtyard. Presumably, they were Intelligence Corps, yet unlike the rest, their uniforms were immaculate. The one in the center had so many gold stars on her badge that she had to be the colonel. She was in her fifties, of average height, average weight, average looks. Her overall appearance was so unremarkable that she might easily go unnoticed, except for her contemptuous expression, belonging to someone who clearly expected everyone else to jump at her command.

The colonel's eyes ran over Tanya disapprovingly. She scowled. "You could have cleaned her up a bit."

"I'm sorry, ma'am. My orders didn't say."

"Well, there isn't time now. We'll have to take her as she is."

Two Guards from the colonel's escort positioned themselves at Tanya's shoulders. Two more stood behind her. A touch set her again marching forward, under the archway and across the parade ground. On three sides lay the barrack blocks that Tanya had seen on her arrival. The bulk of Celaeno's temple was directly ahead, on the other side of a high wall. By the time they were halfway across the parade ground, Tanya realized that they were heading for a small gate into the temple grounds.

The moment they had passed through, Tanya was aware of a change in atmosphere. The air felt heavier and stiller. A rich spicy scent wafted around. Incense, Tanya guessed it to be. The party climbed a flight of stairs and entered the temple itself. Tanya had a brief impression of a huge dim cavern, lit by hundreds of candles, and then they turned off, through hanging drapes, where six uniformed Guards stood sentry.

At last they entered an audience chamber. Only the colonel and one other senior Guard accompanied Tanya. Awaiting them were three white-robed and masked figures. These were Sisters, the priestesses of the Goddess. The fine gauze masks over their lower face made them indistinguishable, or should have, but it was clear that the Colonel and her comrade recognized the one in the middle. They snapped to attention with a crisp deference that left no doubt of the Sister's importance.

Just one other person was present, an elderly civilian of eighty or more years. Her hair was pulled back in a white bun at the back of her head. Her clothes were clearly expensive, with bold colors and satin sheen. Rings on her fingers glittered in the candlelight. Her face was set in an expression of calm authority, as if she was used to giving orders and having them obeyed. Her eyes fixed curiously on Tanya.

"This is her?" the central Sister asked.

"Yes, my lady," the colonel replied.

The Sister turned to the civilian. "Is there anything you wish to ask her?"

"I'd like to have her identity confirmed first."

"Of course."

One Sister walked sedately to a rear doorway and left. Nothing was said until she returned a few minutes later, leading a woman dressed in plain blue tunic and leggings. Even though Tanya had never seen the clothing before, she had heard it described often enough to recognize. The woman was an Imprinter, someone so talented with the healer sense that she could step inside a cell, read the DNA, and imprint new patterns on it. They were the ones who created new life in women's wombs, blending the birth mothers' genes with that of their partners.

In the Homelands, Imprinters were revered as the chosen of the Goddess, the conduits through which the Goddess's blessing was given in each new daughter. They were kept sequestered from all harm in the temple, cared for by the Sisterhood and their holy warriors, the Guards.

In Westernfort, there was Lynn, a friend of her parents, who spoke of life in the temple as a form of slavery, from which she had been rescued, who denied any sort of divinity in herself and lived a normal life, with partner and children—something forbidden to Imprinters in the Homelands. Around the room, the faces not hidden behind masks revealed awe as they watched the woman in blue, but Tanya, remembering all she had heard from Lynn, could view the Imprinter with nothing but pity.

The senior Sister spoke. "Imprinter, I wonder if you could confirm the degree of relatedness between the prisoner and Madam Coppelli."

In reflex, Tanya's head jerked toward the elderly civilian, clearly the other person referred to. Coppelli? Before Tanya could consider the implications, a light tap on her arm claimed her attention.

The Imprinter was a middle-aged woman with a tired, worn expression. "May I take your hand?"

"Um..." Tanya half turned, indicating her wrists.

"Take them off," the senior sister ordered.

The colonel's subordinate darted forward, and after a moment of fumbling, removed the manacles. The Imprinter lay her hand over Tanya's and closed her eyes for several minutes, then she moved to the elderly civilian and repeated the process. At last, she turned back to the senior Sister.

"They are close blood kin."

"How close?"

"Most likely granddaughter and grandmother. Aunt and niece is possible, although the age gap makes it unlikely. Certainly no relationship more distant."

"Thank you."

The senior Sister gave a nod of dismissal and the Imprinter left the room.

Once the door had closed, the colonel cleared her throat. "We're grateful for the confirmation of the prisoner's identity. But this is delaying her interrogation. I'd ask that we be allowed to return her to the prison forthwith."

The elderly civilian—Tanya's grandmother, if the Imprinter was to be believed—frowned sharply. "I don't think one of your cells is an appropriate place for her."

"I would remind you, Madam Coppelli, that she's a heretic."

"And I would remind you, Colonel Zelenski, that she's my granddaughter."

Tanya watched the colonel exchange angry looks with the other officer before returning to the attack.

"I'd have thought you'd rather have your family shame hidden from the eyes of the pious. It's not something you've trumpeted in the past."

"Just because I chose not to announce on the streets that my youngest daughter's a heretic doesn't mean I'm happy for my grand-daughter to rot in an underground cell."

Colonel Zelenski appealed to the senior Sister. "Chief Consultant, surely you're not prepared to allow this?"

The Sister's title came as no surprise to Tanya. Who else could summon the Intelligence Corps Colonel to appear with a prisoner? Chief Consultant Bakara was the thirty-third to hold the title, in line from Himoti, the first Chief Consultant. Even in Westernfort Bakara's name was known. She was the leader of the Sisterhood, and thus ruler of the Homelands. All Guards were sworn to uphold her authority, both in matters of religion and government.

"I'd like to hear what Madam Coppelli is proposing before I make up my mind."

Tanya's grandmother smiled in gratitude. "Thank you. Of course, I'm not suggesting that she's set free, but I think she should be held here, in the temple, under the care of the Sisterhood. I'd point out that, though she's a heretic, it's not by her choice. She was born in the wilderness and has never had the benefit of proper instruction. She should be given the chance to embrace the true faith."

"That's ridiculous," Zelenski said. "She has valuable information, and only the Corps are trained in suitable interrogation techniques."

"You mean torture," Tanya's grandmother countered.

"Call it what you will. It's necessary."

"I'd dispute that. From what I've heard, your techniques are very good at getting confessions and very poor at anything else. You can make someone say whatever you want. Which means they end up telling you exactly what you want to hear, regardless of whether it's the truth. How many times have you got into a mess because you've forced someone to tell you a reassuring lie?"

"I don't thi—"

"Please." The Chief Consultant held up her hand, cutting off Zelenski. She turned to Tanya's grandmother. "Bringing an innocent to the worship of the Goddess is a virtuous goal, but we have standard procedures and I'm not sure we should make an exception in her case."

"I'd remind you of the services I've performed for you in the past. Is this so much to ask?"

The words were delivered in a calm, even tone, but Tanya could feel the nuances underlying them. Her grandmother was clearly exerting pressure. *Threat* was too strong a word, but it was obvious to her, and anyone with ears, that her grandmother and Chief Consultant Bakara had shared history and shared secrets.

"I..." Bakara hesitated. "Maybe you're right."

"My lady, I protest." Zelenski was losing the debate and her tone revealed that she knew it. "You don't have the resources."

"We have secure rooms in the temple."

"But—"

"If you're so concerned, I'll keep her under constant surveillance. Guards will be on duty outside her room and I'll have a Sister watch over her."

The final exchanges were lost on Tanya as she scrambled to adjust to the idea that she would not be returning to the dungeon. Before she knew it, she was being led from the audience chamber, in the company of two Sisters and four Guards.

It's a trick. The words jumped into her head. *It's to make you think you're safe, so you'll crack when they get the needles out again. Don't believe it. Don't trust anyone.*

Tanya was still repeating the mantra to herself when they arrived in a long room, high in a tower. Sunset was over, but the sky was still light enough to see the bars across the window. The furniture was austere, a narrow bed and a table with two chairs. The walls and floor were bare, but compared to the underground cell, it was bliss.

The Guards remained outside, but one Sister followed Tanya in and took up position on a seat just inside the door. Her grandmother also entered the room. She placed a hand on Tanya's arm and led her to the table under the window. They sat on opposite sides. If they spoke softly, the Sister was now too far away to overhear what was said, but quite able to see should anything be passed over.

"You'd have to be an exceptionally dense member of my family if you haven't worked out that I'm Piety's mother." The old woman's lips twitched in a smile. "Except I doubt she ever uses the name. I believe she prefers to be called Chip."

Tanya nodded, thinking rapidly. Her mother's real name was common knowledge in Westernfort, although only the suicidal would dare use it. The name Piety was probably in the official enlistment records with the Homelands Militia, but how widely known in Landfall would the nickname be? That the woman across the table knew it was more convincing than the scene with the Imprinter, although this did not mean Tanya dare let herself think she was truly safe.

"Yes, she does. I'm her oldest daughter, Tanya."

"I'm pleased to meet you. I'm Isabel Coppelli." Again she smiled. "You can call me Grandma Izzy if you wish."

"Oh, right. Thank you for, um...rescuing me from the Corps."

"I acted as soon as I found out they had you. I hope it was in time to spare you too much unpleasantness."

"Things were just starting to get nasty." Tanya kept her hands under the table, but she got the feeling that her grandmother had already seen the blood under her nails. "How did you know I was here?"

"The Corps is not the only organization in Landfall with spies. And I like to think that mine are all the more effective for not being hampered by dogma."

"Why did you help me?" Tanya glanced at the Sister by the door and dropped her voice still lower. "You're not a heretic too, are you?"

"I'm a faithful daughter of the Goddess, as long as it doesn't impact on my profit or my family. I think this makes me a pragmatist." Isabel smiled. "How much do you know of your mother's history here in Landfall?"

"I know the two of you didn't get on. She ran away to join the Militia when she was seventeen."

"I see diplomacy still runs in the family. *Didn't get on* is a tactful way to put it. I tried to force her to be what I wanted her to be, and she insisted on being herself. She was my youngest daughter and the only one who dared defy me. I'm now old and wise enough to know this makes her the only one who could possibly take my place. And someone has to. I'm eighty-eight and I won't live forever."

"I don't think..." Tanya was unsure where the conversation was going.

"Oh, I know I've lost my chance with your mother. I'm trying not to make the same mistake with the next generation." Isabel's expression became earnest, with a hint of sadness. "I drove Piety...Chip out, and I've had thirty-five years to regret it. I'm going to do everything in my power to help you, partly because I owe it to your mother, but mainly because you're a Coppelli. And nobody pushes a Coppelli around."

CHAPTER EIGHT—THE PLAYERS ASSEMBLE

R iki had visited Landfall twice as a child, staying with an aunt who lived on the south side of the city. The memories of playing in the street with her cousins and visiting the great temple were clear in her mind. A small square had been nearby, with a statue of a mounted rider. With this to work on, Riki was sure she could find her aunt's home again, although she had no idea whether her relatives still lived there, and she had other, safer leads to pursue first.

Her route, down a wide street lined with shops, took her toward the center of the city. The midday sounds, sights, and smells of Landfall washed over her like an avalanche, the vibrant anarchy that she remembered. Riki loved the wilderness, the beauty of mountains and forests, yet the city had a mad energy, a sense that anything was possible, that at any moment, some new opportunity might open before her. Riki was sure it would get tiring after a while and she would long for solitude and silence, but for the moment, she was enjoying the buzz that made her feel in some way more alive than normal.

As soon as she reached the Homelands, Riki had acquired some nondescript clothing while the owners were not looking. Once dressed so as not to draw attention, she had sold the two horses and bought an old pony. She had covered the distance to Landfall at a steady rate, staying at the cheapest lodgings. The money from the horses was holding out well and would last her to Highview and beyond. However, she did not want to go all the way to the far side of the Homelands, only to find out that her gene mother no longer lived there.

Jan, her oldest sister, had moved to Landfall with her partner several years before Riki and her birth mother fled. She had been a member of the Merchants' Guild and worked as a clerk at their guildhall. Even though Jan might also have moved on, as a Guild member, her whereabouts would be known, and a matter of public record. All Riki had to do was ask, and the guildhall was certainly easy to find.

Riki halted her pony outside the ornate façade and tied its reins. A broad flight of polished steps led up to an entrance with the words *Merchants' Guildhall* engraved above. Deep stone mullioned windows on either side were glazed with expensive clear white glass, rather than common green. A row of carved gargoyles looked down from the rooftop. The Merchants' Guild was wealthy and wanted to make sure everyone knew it.

Riki stopped just inside the doorway and looked around for somebody who could give directions. Several candidates were in sight. Riki was working out who best to approach, but it was not necessary. Her uncertainty attracted notice and a woman bustled over—a scribe, Riki guessed from her ink-stained fingers.

"Can I help you?"

"I hope so. I'm passing through Landfall and I thought I'd look up my cousin who used to work here some years back. Her name's Jan Diaz. I don't know if she's still here."

The scribe smiled. "Yes, she is. She'll be working, but I'm sure she can spare a few moments. Who shall I say it is?"

"Tina. Tina Diaz."

Riki gave the name of a cousin. Her own was not wise to toss around casually. Most likely, the clerk would not recognize it and would know nothing of the sister who had joined the heretics, but there was no point taking the risk. Jan might be confused, especially if Tina was still living in Landfall, but she would put it down to a garbled message. Regardless, she was unlikely to refuse to see Tina—unless they'd had some major falling-out while Riki had been in the Wildlands.

The scribe returned in a few minutes. "She can see you. I'll show you to her office."

"Has she got her own office now?"

"Oh yes. She got promoted to head of archives two years ago."

Riki smiled. A private meeting would make things easier. The scribe led her down a short flight of stairs and rapped helpfully on a door. She then smiled again at Riki and left.

"Enter," a voice called out.

Riki pushed the door open and stepped inside. Jan was alone, sitting at a desk by the window. She was older than Riki remembered, and heavier, although that was only to be expected for someone now in her mid-thirties. Her face held a look of mild confusion that changed to surprise.

"I'm sorry. I thought Liz said you were my cousin Tina."

"That's what I told her to say."

"But you're not... Who are you?"

Riki moved closer. "Don't you recognize me?"

"No. I don't think I..." Jan's voice died. "By the Goddess! Riki?"

Riki nodded.

"What are you doing here?"

"Coming home."

"But you...you haven't told anyone who you are, have you? If the Guards—"

"No. That's why I told your clerk I was Tina."

Jan sank back in her chair and smiled weakly. "Right."

Suddenly Jan's face split in a huge grin. She launched herself from her chair and flung her arms around Riki. "Oh, little sis. It's good to see you. I've been wondering and worrying about you and Mama Kav."

"I've missed you. I've missed all of you." Riki laughed and returned the hug, slapping Jan's back. She felt tears welling in her eyes. "And I want to hear all the news. Have you made me an auntie again? How about Sue and Bron?"

"Six times over, between us." Jan stepped back, holding Riki at arm's length. Her expression shifted from joy to astonishment and back. "How long can you stay in Landfall?"

"As long as you'll have me."

Jan took a deep breath. "Great. We've a lot of catching up to do. But not here. If I give you my address, do you think you can find it?"

"If you throw in a few directions as well."

Jan swung around and stretched across her desk, taking a pen from its stand and pulling a scrap of paper toward her. She dipped the pen in an inkwell.

"Okay. Here you go. Fia's birth mother lives with us. She'll be there and will let you in if you show her this and tell her..." Jan paused, biting her lip. "She's met Tina, so we can't use her. Um...tell her you're my cousin's daughter, Vanda Sadiq. You remember her?"

"She not around?"

"Haven't heard from her in years. It should be safe."

Riki took the note and nodded. "Fine. I'll see you there tonight."

Jan reached out and rubbed Riki's head, a familiar gesture from their childhood. Riki felt her throat constricting and tears again in her eyes.

"Sure thing, little sis. I'll try to get home early. I'm so pleased to see you. I want all the news."

❖

Jan and her partner, Fia, lived in a modest three-story townhouse in a quiet area of the city, with their three daughters and Fia's elderly mother. The home was snug, noisy, and affectionate. Only Fia was let in on the secret of Riki's true identity. The children were too young to trust their discretion, and the old woman was a little too devout in her beliefs to confide in. Even so, she was unlikely to have informed to the Guards—not with her own daughter implicated—but it would have placed an unnecessary strain on her conscience, and she was a sweet, soppy old soul who nobody wanted to upset.

The children were happy to bounce over any new relative. Riki played with them until their bedtime. The grandmother went next, followed shortly by Fia, who worked in the market and would be making an early start in the morning.

With the house at peace, the two sisters sat at the kitchen table, sharing a pot of tea. The walls around them were lined with overflowing shelves. Light from the candle on the table reflected on copper pans hanging over the stove. The long summer's day was over and the window shutters were closed. Sounds from the city outside were muted. Now they could talk without inhibition.

Jan leaned forward, resting her elbows on the table. "So why have you returned? Weren't you happy with the heretics?"

"Not really." Riki wrinkled her nose. "And then I got blamed for something I hadn't done. But I couldn't prove it. So I legged it."

"You've left Mama Kav alone?"

Riki shrugged. "I didn't have a choice. But she's not totally alone."

Jan smiled. "She's found a new partner?"

"Sort of."

"And she knows you're innocent?"

"I don't know. We didn't get a chance to talk. I hope so, but..." Riki shrugged and stared into her tea.

She had not been thinking about her mother, but that was to block out uncomfortable images. How had her mother taken the news? Had she been upset? Riki pursed her lips. Stupid question. Of course her mother had been distraught, grief-struck, and frantic. Riki knew how many times she had deliberately tried to hurt her mother. She now regretted it and wished she could have the chance to say she was sorry. But most of all, she would like her mother to know that this time she was innocent and had not been trying to cause trouble. Her mother might be the only one in the Wildlands who would believe Riki when she denied betraying Tanya. Too late to wish she had given a better return on her mother's unconditional love.

"I'm pleased she's found someone new." Jan's voice recalled her to the kitchen.

Riki took a sip of tea. She did not want to talk about Westernfort any more than she could help—certainly not with so many other topics she would rather discuss. "How about Mama Eli? Has she found someone?"

"I don't know and I don't care."

The harsh tone caught Riki by surprise. "You're not in contact with her?"

"No."

"How about Sue and Bron?"

"They won't have anything to do with her either."

"Why?"

Jan sighed and leaned back. "You were too young to get involved back then. You were shielded from most of what went on, but I guess you're old enough now. So, the short answer. Mama Eli was an evil, two-timing bitch."

"But...she was..." Riki was bewildered.

"I got most of the story secondhand from Bron. Fia and I were here in Landfall for the last few years, and Sue had just moved in with Penny. But Bron was still living at home and she kept us both up to date with what was going on." Jan pursed her lips. "Did you know about Mama Eli and her string of tarts?"

"No."

"I found out when I was fourteen. I was skipping school with some friends. We snuck back home, and I saw Mama Eli with another woman. They were"—Jan grimaced—"I'll spare you the details. Let's say they weren't just having a quiet chat."

"Did Mama Kav know?"

"I think she must have, deep down, though mostly she acted like she didn't. But I'm sure she had suspicions. Sometimes, you'd see the hurt on her face. And once I knew what to look for, it wasn't hard to spot when Mama Eli was on to a new woman. I told Sue about it, but Bron worked it out for herself."

"No one told me."

"You were too young. And you and Mama Eli were really close. I mean, I'm her birth daughter and I never had the sort of bond with her that you did. She always showed you her best side and behaved when you were around."

Riki put her elbows on the table and rested her head on her hands. The revelations were the last thing she had expected, and impossible to reconcile with the home she remembered. She had been twelve when the family had split up. Had she really been that immature back then, for the truth to be so completely hidden from her?

Riki lifted her head. "Did Mama Kav ever find out?"

"Yes. Because Mama Eli told her all about it. A couple of months before you had to run, Mama Eli started a new affair, but this one got way more serious that the rest. Mama Eli totally lost her head. The week before you fled, she finally got it out in the open and told Mama Kav she was going to leave her and go off with this new tart."

"I don't remember this."

"You wouldn't. You were the baby of the family, and everyone was protecting you. Mama Eli waited until you were staying overnight with Sue, so she and Mama Kav could scream the house down without upsetting you. But Bron was there and heard it all."

"So Mama Kav took me and left? Was the heretic thing just an excuse?"

The grimace on Jan's face got even more sour. "The Guards were coming, sure enough." Jan met Riki's eyes. "You were the problem. I think maybe you were why Mama Eli stuck around so long to start with. She was fine about leaving Mama Kav, but she wouldn't leave you. But with this new woman, she was torn, because if our mothers split up, you'd go with your birth mother, not her."

Anticipating what would come next, Riki felt a cold hand squeeze her stomach.

Jan continued. "Mama Eli knew about Mama Kav tinkering with the heretics. I don't think she gave a flying fuck about the beliefs. What she saw was a way to hang on to you. She was the one who informed on Mama Kav. She told the Guards. Luckily Bron found out and was able to warn Mama Kav and give her the chance to escape before the Guards arrived."

Riki slumped back and stared at the ceiling. She felt as if her past had been stolen from her, that her memories had been smashed and poisoned. She was shocked, horrified, but was she surprised? Riki remembered Mama Eli guiding her through the undergrowth, playing football with her, tickling her, telling her stories. She had loved Mama Eli with a child's unquestioning trust. But considering her with a critical adult eye? Mama Eli had been devious, a rule breaker, unreliable, and if something was not fun then she was not interested in it. Riki swallowed. In fact, Mama Eli was a lot like her.

Riki's thoughts returned to Jan's story. "Did Bron tell Mama Kav who had turned her in?"

"No. She kept the details from her. To be honest, there wasn't time for big explanations. And she thought that Mama Kav had enough to deal with, without knowing that her partner of thirty years was trying to murder her."

"Murder?"

"That's the way we see it. Just because her murder weapon was the Guards and the law doesn't make it any better than if she'd tried to stick a knife in her. That's why we've had nothing to do with her since the day you went. Bron moved in with Sue and Penny that very night. She went back once to pick up her things, but that's been it. Mama Eli wrote to me twice. I burned the letters, unopened. She wanted Mama Kav dead so she'd get custody of you."

Riki stared down at the tabletop, struggling to come to terms with a new wave of guilt. Tears blurred her vision. "I didn't...it's not..."

Jan reached across and grabbed her hand. She rubbed her thumb over Riki's knuckles. "You mustn't blame yourself. It wasn't your fault. You were just a kid."

❖

Riki sat curled in a window seat on the top floor of her sister's house, staring down on the street below with unfocused eyes. The day had been spent thinking about Jan's disclosures of the previous night, and none of the places her thoughts had taken her had been good.

Jan had said she was not to blame for the family breakup, but how much guilt should she carry for everything that had followed? Riki thought about the mother she had worshipped and the mother she had blamed. How could she have been so stupid as to get them round the wrong way? And what could she do about it now?

Riki's eyes turned to the west. She wanted to see her birth mother again, to say she was sorry for everything she had done, and to say that, through it all, no matter how it might have seemed, she had loved her. Riki wiped her eyes on her sleeve again. Crying was something else she had done a lot of that day.

What could she do? If she returned to Westernfort she would be arrested, tried, and hanged. In her current frame of mind, this did not seem too much of an issue, but it would not do Mama Kav any good. Maybe Jan and the others could collect up letters for Riki to take with her. Surely she would be allowed to hand them over. Would Mama Kav feel that getting childish notes and drawings from the granddaughters she had never seen was enough of a repayment for the grief Riki had caused her over the years?

Of course, the letter Riki really wanted was one from Tanya Coppelli, saying something like, *Rikako Sadiq is innocent. It was all that frigging bitch Lokelani Stevenson.* Riki's gaze shifted to the temple. The huge dome loomed over the rooftops. Was Tanya also currently in Landfall, imprisoned in the Guards' compound beside the temple? Not that it made any difference. The Intelligence Corps would hardly be allowing visitors.

Riki's thoughts drifted on. Tanya was somebody else who she would like to talk with and see if they could improve their relationship. They were due some bonding over mutual hatred of Loke Stevenson. Unless it turned into another competition over who hated the bitch more, in which case Riki would concede. Loke's schemes would have killed them both, but in her case they had failed, and it was a clean death in a hangman's noose. Riki's expression hardened. There was no hope of them meeting again, and thinking of the Corps' reputation, Riki hoped, for Tanya's sake, that she was already dead.

The sound of the street door opening below was followed by delighted squeals from her nieces. Jan must be home from work. Riki sighed. She really should go down and be sociable. Yet she was not in the mood for anything much other than brooding.

Footsteps on the stairs made her look back. Jan strolled into the room, a smile of greeting on her face.

"Hi. How's your day been?"

"Okay." This was not strictly true. Riki shrugged. "I've had a lot on my mind." She shifted around on the seat to allow more space for her sister to slip onto.

Jan examined her red eyes for a few seconds, then reached out and squeezed her shoulder. "I guess you have. I've had a long time to get used to the idea that one of my mothers is a frigging heap of shit."

"Yup." Riki did not want to say more. She turned her face back to the window.

Jan watched in silence for a while. "The guildhall's been buzzing with rumors today."

"Really? What about?" Riki asked listlessly.

"One of your heretics. Is there someone in Westernfort named Coppelli? Been there about twenty-five years?"

"Captain Coppelli? The commander of the Rangers?"

"Could be her. Is she Old Lady Coppelli's daughter?"

"Who's Old Lady Coppelli?"

Jan laughed. "Oh, you are out of touch with the way of things in Landfall. The Coppellis are the richest, most important, powerful bunch of rogues in the city. They run the Merchants' Guild, and just about everything else. They've got hooks in every game in town. And the old lady, Isabel Coppelli, is at the center of it all."

Riki faced Jan, her interest kindled. "So what's the rumor?"

"Well, there's long been stories about one of Isabel's daughters. How she disappeared and became a heretic. The stories now are that she'd been captured by the Guards and brought back to Landfall."

"The captain? I doubt it. She was safe in Westernfort when I left. I think your sources have got it wrong. The captain's daughter, Tanya, was the one captured." Riki pulled a wry pout. "She might be this Isabel's granddaughter. I told you I was blamed for something I didn't do. It was about Tanya's capture. Someone framed me as the one who'd handed her over to the Guards."

"But it wasn't you, was it?"

"Of course not."

"That's a relief. It's one thing being a heretic and upsetting the Sisters and the Guards, but you don't fuck around with the Coppellis." Jan was smiling as she spoke, but Riki got the feeling that she was not entirely joking.

"So, is there any news about what's happened to Tanya?"

"Yes, that's what I was coming to. It's what the rumors have been about. Apparently, the old lady marched in and got the Chief Consultant to order the Intelligence Corps to release her daughter, or granddaughter, from their prison and had her locked up in the temple instead."

"But could she do that? Can anybody make the Sisterhood do what she tells them to?"

"If anyone can, it's Isabel Coppelli."

❖

The Coppelli mansion made the Merchants' Guildhall look shoddy. Riki stood in the street staring up at the four-story edifice. A high iron railing and gateway sealed off the gravel forecourt from the street. Twin ramps swept around and up from there to the colonnaded front door.

Riki pushed on the gate. To her surprise it was unlocked, although on more thought, who would dare to enter, uninvited? She paused, looking left and right, while wondering whether it might be better to hunt for a tradesman's entrance. But she wanted to see Isabel Coppelli. This was the quickest way to find someone qualified to deal with her request.

The main door was carved from dark wood, and so highly polished that Riki could see her reflection in it. The knocker was a huge brass affair. Dismissing any doubts, Riki rapped it twice sharply. Within seconds the door was opened by a heavily built woman with large fists. Her eyes ran over Riki, sizing her up.

"Can I help you?" She delivered the words with surprising courtesy. From the woman's looks, she would be better suited to spitting out threats.

"I'd like to speak to Madam Isabel Coppelli, if I may."

The doorman again subjected Riki to a once-over and then stood back. "Come inside to wait. Who shall I say you are?"

Riki slipped into the entrance hall. "She won't know my name. But can you tell her that it's about her granddaughter, Tanya Coppelli? I'm, er...a friend of hers."

The doorman nodded as she closed the door. "I'll see she gets the message." She padded away to another doorway and then spoke quietly to someone inside.

Riki looked around. The entrance hall alone was bigger than the entire ground floor of Jan's house. The overall impression was of light and good taste. An ornate stairway led up to a second-floor balcony. A round stained glass window above the door cast blurs of pastel color across the floor tiles. Paintings hung on paneled walls and porcelain statues stood in alcoves.

Riki was surprised that a stranger, dressed like herself, would so readily be granted admission. Yet something in the doorman's attitude made her think maybe people of disreputable appearance were not infrequent guests of the Coppellis and that it was unwise to give such people offense until you knew more about them.

A new figure appeared at the top of the staircase. This was an older, smaller woman, with the air of a personal attendant. She trotted to Riki's side.

"You were the person seeking to speak with Madam Coppelli, on the matter of her granddaughter?"

"Yes."

"Please, follow me."

Riki was led through the house to a small upstairs study. Books lined the walls and a solid wooden desk stood in the middle of the room. An elderly woman was seated there. Papers lay on the desk, although she showed no sign of having been reading. At a wave of dismissal, the attendant bowed out of the room, shutting the door as she went.

The seated woman's face held an expression of shrewd calculation. Riki met her gaze as steadily as she could. She sensed that she was being weighed up by someone who had no difficulty spotting a fool or a fraudster, and no qualms about dealing ruthlessly with either.

"You wished to see me."

"Yes, if you're Madam Isabel Coppelli."

The woman nodded in acknowledgment. "I am."

"I'm Rikako Sadiq. I know my name means nothing to you, but it will to your granddaughter."

"Ah yes, my granddaughter." Isabel Coppelli steepled her fingers, thoughtfully. "I know rumors are flying around certain sections of Landfall at the moment. But as far as I'm aware, none of these rumors contain the name you gave to my doorman. And I'm wondering how you came to hear it."

Riki licked her lips. This was the crucial point. Was Isabel Coppelli truly interested in her granddaughter's well-being, or was it just a political game?

"I know because I'm Private Rikako Sadiq of the Westernfort Rangers, and Tanya Coppelli is my patrol corporal. I was under her command when she was captured."

"Ah. I did wonder. But how do I know you're really who you claim to be, rather than an Intelligence Corps agent, here to stir up trouble?"

"Have you spoken with Tanya yet?"

"I have."

"Tanya's gene mother is Katryn Nagata. She has three sisters: Amy, Del, and Kay. Her twenty-third birthday was on March 26. We celebrated it while out on patrol. She doesn't have a steady partner or children. Kay's the oldest after Tanya, and she's a baker. Amy's the youngest and says she wants to be a Ranger as well when she grows up. Del's at that age where she doesn't know what she wants to do, and wouldn't tell anyone if she did." Riki paused. "I doubt the Corps interrogators have even asked for any of this, but I suspect a grandmother wouldn't have talked about much else, once you got past the opening formalities."

Isabel Coppelli leaned forward chuckling. "Oh, my dear. I don't know how long it is since someone last second-guessed me so well. Although maybe it isn't such a hard call." She raised her eyes again to Riki. "So. Why are you here?"

"I want to help Tanya escape and get her back to Westernfort. I'm hoping you share my aim."

"Supposing I did. Do you have any idea how difficult it would be?"

"I'm new to Landfall, so probably not. But I know you've got her out of the Corps dungeon and into the temple. It's a start."

"And an end too. I have a degree of influence with the Chief Consultant. But I've already pushed it to its limit."

"I think you could do just about anything you set your mind to."

"The Coppellis are a wealthy, powerful family, but if we blatantly break the law, the Sisterhood will crush us. We cannot defy them."

Despite what the words said, Riki sensed undercurrents. The old matriarch was thinking, scheming, and calculating. She would not give up, and there was no more imaginative or capable force in Landfall.

Riki paused while she considered what she knew and what conjectures she could draw. "So we need to get the Sisterhood to set Tanya free, without them knowing what they've done."

Isabel Coppelli did not bat an eyelid. "Do you have any idea how to do that?"

"No. But I suspect you do. Maybe not the full plan, but you're working on it. I'm here to offer my services, for whatever help I can give."

CHAPTER NINE—THE GAME BEGINS

The biggest problem Tanya had in reading *The Book of the Elder-Ones* was in not laughing out loud at some of the unintentionally funny sections. However, the Sisters would not take it well. They might even stop her from reading the book altogether, and while it was not exactly enthralling, she had nothing else in the way of entertainment. Also, while she was reading, whatever Sister was on duty would make no other attempt to convert her to the true faith. The dogmatic sermons were far less amusing than the book.

Tanya was sitting cross-legged on her bed. Her room was on the southwest side of the temple. The strong afternoon light directly hitting white paper was too dazzling for reading at the table, although the breeze through the window was pleasant. It carried memories of hot summer days, roaming through the fields and forests around Westernfort, with nothing over her head but green leaves and blue sky.

Tanya kept the book open on her lap but let her eyes slip out of focus. Could she act out such a convincing conversion to the worship of Celaeno that the Sisters would let her go? She glanced toward the white-robed figure by the door. Alas, it did not appear very likely. For women who were so uncritical in accepting a manifestly fabricated work of fiction, the Sisters were surprisingly distrustful when it came to their fellow human beings.

The sound of voices in the corridor outside made Tanya flinch. Always, in the back of her mind, she was braced for Guards to burst in and drag her back to their dungeon. Letting her think she was safe in the temple could be a ploy, designed to break her spirit. The woman claiming to be her grandmother might be one of their agents and the scene with the Imprinter a trick. The Intelligence Corps interrogators had to know that pain alone could not guarantee she was telling the truth. They had to destroy her will to resist before they could place any trust in what information they wrung from her.

Tanya looked up just in time to see the door opening. Isabel Coppelli swept into the room, her arms outstretched in greeting. A second, shorter woman hung back behind her, partially shielded from view. Tanya barely had time to put her book aside before her grandmother was upon her, taking her hands, pulling her to her feet, kissing her cheek and steering her toward the table beneath the window.

With her arm around Tanya's shoulder, Isabel murmured quietly, "I've brought a friend to see you. Don't look at her now. Wait until you're sitting down and have time to compose your face. And don't show that you recognize her or are in any way surprised. You also shouldn't talk to her directly. She's pretending to be one of my employees."

Tanya was glad that she had her back to the Sister as she digested the instructions. Who did she know in Landfall at all, let alone call a friend? She slipped into a seat at the table and fixed her attention on her grandmother sitting opposite. The other woman took up position, slightly back and to one side. Out of the corner of her eye, all Tanya could see was the view to chest height. The woman was of small build and wearing a loose cream shirt and dark green trousers, suitable clothes for an upper-class employee. Nothing put Tanya in mind of anyone she knew.

Tanya took a deep breath, composed her lips in what she hoped was a firm but natural-looking line, concentrated on keeping her eyes, forehead, and cheeks steady, and let her gaze flick up to the unknown woman's face. The warning to prepare her features had been wise. Without it, Tanya would have been manifestly dumbstruck at the sight of Private Rikako Sadiq standing placidly at Isabel's shoulder like a servant. Tanya's eyes returned to her grandmother, who smiled.

"I take it that you recognize my companion."

"Uh...yes. I...er, do."

Tanya swallowed and took another deep breath, fighting the urge to glance at the Sister by the door to see if she had spotted anything unusual. It would do no good if the Sister had, and might only raise suspicions if she had not.

Her grandmother continued talking evenly. "I considered coming alone to tell you about Rikako, but it would only waste time, and timing is crucial today. I'd also hope that any granddaughter of mine would be capable of holding a straight face when necessary."

"I did my best, but I wasn't expecting her."

"We rather thought you might not."

Tanya took a few seconds to collect herself, amazed by her own reactions as much as anything else. Whoever would have thought that seeing Rikako Sadiq would give so much pleasure? Yet Tanya could have happily stared at her for hours. Riki was the first familiar face Tanya had seen for months. She was a comrade-in-arms and she was from home—which surely was where she still ought to be.

"Why is she here?"

"Specifically as to why in this room with me now? Rikako and I have been working on plans to get you out of here and back to Westernfort."

"You're serious?"

"Oh yes. As for why Rikako is in Landfall at all, that's something you could talk about later. You'll be seeing quite a bit of each other. As a start to our plans, I'll be distancing myself from you. I'll announce that I don't have the time or the desire to visit you often. Not when I have so many other virtuous granddaughters who are more deserving of my favor. Rikako will be the one who visits you every day and passes any information between us. I'm supposedly introducing you to each other at the moment. The Intelligence Corps will read into this the message that I have limited affection for my heretic granddaughter, but I'm still keeping a watchful eye on her, out of family pride."

Tanya made sure that she had her face and breathing under control before asking, "Do you really think you can help me escape from here?"

"I wouldn't have said it otherwise."

"Won't you get blamed? You wouldn't destroy the whole family for me."

"You're quite right. I wouldn't. But we have a scheme, and the first step is to drive a wedge between Chief Consultant Bakara and Colonel Zelenski of the Intelligence Corps."

"How?"

"I possess some information about Bakara that should do the trick if we use it properly."

"Information you can use against her?"

"I'd be careful with the word 'against.' The Sisters are very dangerous to toy with. You can only push them so far. Remember, we could all be imprisoned and executed on the Chief Consultant's word, without trial or hope of appeal. If we threaten her, she'll crush us."

"You have some sort of hold on her."

"Not that secure."

"But I saw how you got her to overrule Colonel Zelenski."

"I have influence. Nothing more. And in order to have influence with the Sisters, you need to be useful. I've been useful to Bakara in the past. What influence I have is based on the hope that I might be useful again in the future." While she spoke, Isabel Coppelli's face was as placid as if she were discussing nothing more serious then the weather.

"Bakara was elected as Chief Consultant just three years ago, but she was somebody I'd been watching for some time. When the last Chief Consultant died, there were two main candidates in the election. Bakara was one and Joannou, who was the Consultant up at the Fairfield temple, was the other. Joannou found me less useful than Bakara did. Hence my choice was clear. I had an employee at the time, Jean Azid, who was an extremely resourceful woman. She manufactured some false evidence against Consultant Joannou and planted it in her room. When it was discovered, it rather spoiled Joannou's chances in the election."

"In her room? Azid broke into the temple?"

"As I said, she was extremely resourceful."

"Was?"

"Yes, alas. She was murdered just under a year ago, which is, I fear, a professional hazard for women in her line of work. A great shame. We could have done with her help now. However, I have records of her actions regarding Consultant Joannou."

"Did Bakara know what Jean Azid did?"

"Yes, and I even have proof that she knew."

"You're going to blackmail her?"

"Oh no. As I said before, that would be most unwise. Bakara would fight back and our long-term prospects wouldn't look good. We need to be altogether more creative in how we use what we have." Isabel Coppelli glanced at the sun's position and then turned to Riki. "And so. Shall we commence? It's about time for you to set things off." She raised her voice so the watching Sister could hear. "Leave us for a while. I wish to talk to my granddaughter in private."

"Yes, my lady." Riki give a small formal bow and left.

❖

Riki closed the door of Tanya's room behind her and walked away, past the Guards on duty outside. The spiral stairway was close by. At the bottom, she turned onto a long corridor that ended in hanging drapes over the exit from the outer sanctum. Riki stepped through, into the main hall of the temple. Again there were Guards, standing crisply to attention on either side. Their eyes flicked in Riki's direction, but they made no move to stop her or call her to account for being there.

All temples were composed of various sections. At the center was the main hall, where the faithful could pray, invoking the aid of whichever Elder-Ones they felt most appropriate. Close by would be the Guards' garrison, where the devout warriors had their barracks. The sanctum was the area where the Sisters and Imprinters lived. No one other than the priestesses and vessels of the Goddess could set foot on the holy ground, except for a few select Guards, when circumstances made it necessary. Most temples therefore had a small sub-region, the outer sanctum, where the consultant could hold private meetings with the secular officials of the town or city.

Landfall was the executive hub of the Homelands and had greater and wider need of such space. Hence the outer sanctum in the temple at Landfall was more than just a couple of audience chambers. It contained offices, archives, private shrines, and accommodation, including the room where Tanya was being held. It was also somewhere that Isabel had a permanent warrant for, allowing her to enter whenever she wished. Nothing said more about just how useful Chief Consultant Bakara had found the elderly matriarch.

Riki strolled away from the outer sanctum, trying hard to appear like any other devout visitor. However, her thoughts were seething. She could not get over her shock at the state Tanya was in. Not merely the ragged, bloodstained uniform, but more the haunted reserve in her eyes. How long had Tanya spent in the hands of the Intelligence Corps?

The sums did not add up favorably. Riki's route to Landfall had been diverted via Westernfort. Tanya might have spent well over a month in the Corps dungeon. What had happened to her? Riki stopped before a small shrine to an Elder-One—she could not concentrate enough to tell who—and tried to compose herself.

Riki would happily lie, dupe, and steal, but she had never let anyone else take the blame for what she had done, or suffer in her stead. Breaking the rules was a game, and if she lost, then she lost. She never tried to duck out when payback time arrived. When she thought of Loke, contempt formed a hard lump in her throat. Loke had screwed up, and rather than face the consequences, she had thrown Tanya to the Guards to save her own skin.

Riki closed her eyes and concentrated on calming her expression. Soon, she had a role to act out and could not afford to let her emotions get out of hand. When she and Tanya returned to Westernfort, then would be the time to deal with the bitch. Riki would put her anger on hold until then. She turned away from the shrine and began to walk.

The huge dome of the main hall arched high above her, fading into the dimness. The air was heavy with candle smoke and incense. Riki passed a row of statues, supposedly images of the Elder-Ones. For the faithful, these were semi-divine spirits whom the Goddess Celaeno had sent to prepare the world for the arrival of her mortal daughters. The Elder-Ones had stayed to instruct and guide the children of Celaeno, but eventually, their work complete, they had ascended to be with the Goddess. Yet they still watched over their protégés and would intercede with the Goddess on behalf of the deserving, if suitable offerings were made.

Riki's lip curled in a cynical smile. It was amazing how those offerings needed to take the form of payment to the Sisterhood, and the greatest offering of all was the imprinting fees. Riki reached the entrance to the imprinting chapels. Anyone who wanted a child had to come here to the Sisterhood and pay them whatever was asked.

The healer sense was the ability to manipulate bodies, using only the power of the mind. Supposedly all women had it to some extent, but in Riki's case, it was so weak that she could make no use of it at all. She was not even sure if the occasional flashes of heightened awareness when touching someone were real or imagined.

At the age of twelve, all girls were tested for their ability, and any who had the potential to become Imprinters were taken from their families and kept in the temples, thus ensuring the Sisters' control of human reproduction. Only Lynn in Westernfort had escaped their grasp, and allowed the heretics to found their growing community.

Riki passed by the imprinting chapels and continued her circuit of the great hall. In the middle was Himoti's sacred flame, burning on the altar. She was supposedly the greatest of the Elder-Ones, the patron of Imprinters and Cloners, the one who had first created the healer sense in women, by the strength and sanctity of her prayers.

Riki stopped in front of the flame, staring into it. Somewhere in the temple was the library where Gina Renamed, the founder of the heretics, claimed to have found proof that the beliefs of the Sisterhood were no more than misremembered folk myths. According to her, the Elder-Ones were ordinary mortals, travelers from another planet, who had been stranded and had needed to make the best they could of the new world.

Riki chewed her lip. What did she believe? She had clung to belief in the Goddess to annoy her mother. Now she felt a need to deny it, as an act of contrition. Yet this was equally flawed reasoning. She turned from the flame and continued walking. At the base of a nearby column was a statue of an Elder-One with white skin and scarlet hair. Another stood facing her across the aisle. This figure had green skin, although only her hands were visible; her face was hidden beneath a coat of blue fur. The representation was taken from a quote in *The Book of the Elder-Ones:*

> *Their skins were diverse in tone, and their hair was yellow and red and black, and all the shades between. And some were tall, and hair grew on their faces.*

Riki looked down at her own hands. Like all mortal women, her skin was soft brown, and her hair was a few shades lighter than black. The heretics claimed that the Elder-Ones were lost colonists, ordinary human beings, whose skin tones varied just a little more than usual— from light cream to dark brown. Riki looked back at the multicolored Elder-Ones, and realized that she did not believe a word of the Sisters' teaching.

So that's it. I really am a heretic, Riki said to herself. She raised her eyes to the domed roof above her head. What better place to come to the self-knowledge?

While walking the hall, Riki had not totally given her attention to the statues and architecture. Now her thoughts were interrupted by the sight of a tall woman in Guards' uniform marching into the temple. The excessive amount of gold braid adorning her tunic indicated someone of high rank. This was what Riki had been waiting for. She set off on an intercept course, soon closing the gap between them until she was close enough to spot the four gold stars on the Guard's shoulder badge.

The colonel was heading in the direction of the outer sanctum but stopped on the way to pray at the military shrine. Riki casually wandered by and arrived at the hanging curtains shrouding the entrance. The sentries had let her out without question, but their instructions were clearly different for anyone entering. A Guard with a sergeant's badge stepped forward.

"May I see your warrant to enter?"

"I was in here earlier. I'd just popped out, but I'm due back now," Riki protested.

"I still need to see your warrant."

"But you must have seen me leave. I was in here with Madam Isabel Coppelli."

"I need to see your warrant." The Guard sergeant was getting surly.

"But—"

"Now."

Riki sighed and dug through her pockets. On her previous arrival, she had been let through on Isabel Coppelli's warrant. Now she would have to produce one of her own. She pulled out the document she had been given at the Coppelli mansion and handed it over.

The Guard sergeant gave her a final belligerent glare and unfolded the sheet of paper with the official red stamp on the outside. As she studied it, her expression changed slowly from irritation to confusion, and she moved closer to the row of candles, angling the paper to the light for a better view. She looked at Riki, back at the paper, and then at Riki again.

"Where did you get this?"

Riki licked her lips nervously. "Um...It was sent to the Coppelli residence for me to use."

"When?"

"I don't know."

At a nod from the sergeant, the other Guards moved to form a ring around Riki. The faces under the gold helmets were hostile and suspicious.

"What's going on here?" A new voice rang out. The colonel had finished her prayers and was ready to continue.

"Ma'am." The sergeant snapped to attention. "This person is seeking entry to the outer sanctum and has presented this warrant. But it's a forgery."

❖

"I don't understand what your employee was doing with this forged warrant to start with." Colonel Zelenski returned to the point like a dog returning to a well-gnawed bone.

"It was a simple mistake."

"Simple?"

"An oversight on my part." Isabel Coppelli's tone was conciliatory. It had no effect on the Intelligence Corps colonel.

Riki kept back and said nothing. Initially, it had looked as if she would be dragged off to the Guards' compound, but it changed once Zelenski learned that Riki not only worked for the Coppellis but had initially gained access to the outer sanctum in the company of Isabel Coppelli herself, who was still in the temple. The colonel had decided to go straight to the top to sort out the matter. A degree of personal venom made it clear that she was nursing a grudge over the departure of Tanya from her dungeon.

"What could—"

Zelenski was interrupted by the door opening and the arrival of Chief Consultant Bakara.

"I understand there has been some problem."

"Yes, my lady." Zelenski pointed toward Riki. "This member of the Coppelli household was trying to gain entrance to the outer sanctum using a forged warrant."

Bakara methodically scanned everyone in the room, finishing with Isabel. "Madam Coppelli, do you have some explanation for this?"

"Thank you for coming. I'm sorry you've been bothered by all this nonsense." Isabel smiled at the Chief Consultant. "And yes, I do. I've decided that it's not fitting for me to be closely associating with a heretic. I've far too many demands on my time as it is. I'll therefore be curtailing my visits to my granddaughter. However, I wish for someone from my household to visit every day and ensure my granddaughter has all she needs in the way of clothes and other requirements. My employee here, Marlena, will be the one charged with this duty." Isabel paused briefly. "As you might remember, I requested a warrant on her behalf. I can only assume Marlena picked up the wrong document before we left."

The mask over the Chief Consultant's face made her expression hard to read, but the narrowing of her eyes indicated that this was the first she had heard of the request for a warrant. She looked at Isabel with something that might have been confusion, but said nothing.

Colonel Zelenski was not so inhibited. "That does not begin to explain what you were doing with a forged warrant to start with."

"I expect it was one of my great-granddaughters, playing games. You know what children can be like."

"This was not a—"

Isabel interrupted the Colonel, beckoning Riki forward to stand before Chief Consultant Bakara. "Please. Allow me to introduce my assistant. This is Marlena Azid. Maybe you remember her aunt, Jean Azid, who also used to work for me, before she had her unfortunate accident. Marlena will be taking on many of her aunt's roles for me."

The furrows on Bakara's forehead vanished. "Ah, yes. Of course."

"No child could—"

This time the Chief Consultant interrupted Zelenski. "It's all right, Colonel. I understand where the mix-up was. There's no problem."

Zelenski stepped back, clearly stunned into silence by the instant acceptance of Isabel's ludicrously weak explanation.

Bakara went on. "And before you leave today, Madam Coppelli, I'll give you a new warrant for Marlena. Just in case you...er...have difficulty finding the original warrant when you return home."

Isabel gave a gracious nod. "Thank you. That's most kind. I'm sorry about the mistake. I should have introduced Marlena to you earlier."

"It's no problem." Chief Consultant Bakara looked across the room at the furious Intelligence Corps colonel. "Thank you for bringing this to my notice, Colonel Zelenski. But everything is under control. If you could wait outside, we'll have our weekly briefing session, just as soon as I've sorted out the warrant for Marlena Azid."

Colonel Zelenski glared around in frustrated disbelief, then gave a sharp formal salute to Bakara, a scowl to Isabel Coppelli, and stomped out of the room.

❖

From the window of her room, Landfall was at a safe enough distance for Tanya not to feel overwhelmed by it. She leaned against the wall and stared through the bars. The sheer scale of the city was astounding. That women's hands could build something so vast, brick upon brick, was incredible. That anybody would want to live in the result after it was finished was incomprehensible.

The sound of the door made Tanya look round. Riki sauntered past the Sister on duty. At the sight of her, Tanya felt her insides kick in a rush of contrasting emotions, too raw and overwhelming to separate and identify. The intensity of the response confused her. She had not realized quite how desperate she was to see Riki again, to reassure herself that she had not imagined their meeting the day before. But after her experience in the Corps dungeon, was it surprising if she was a little volatile emotionally?

Tanya pulled out a chair and dropped into it, trying to mask her eagerness, and waited until Riki was also seated before speaking.

"How did it go yesterday?" Tanya had heard nothing after her grandmother had been summoned away by a surly Guard.

"Completely to script. Your grandmother's amazing. She knew Zelenski's routine to the second, and she knew just how everyone was going to react. She was pulling all the strings without them knowing it."

"I shouldn't have doubted her. Mom always said she was the most manipulative bitch under the sun."

"Did she mean that as a compliment?"

"I shouldn't think so. They didn't have a good relationship. Grandma's been fine with me, though. Maybe she's mellowed with age."

"Or maybe you're not as sharp-tempered as your mother."

"I can lose my temper. I thought I'd proved that to you."

"I'm a special case. I can infuriate anyone." Riki gave an ironic laugh. "And I'm hard to get rid of. I bet you thought you were safe from me here."

"No, believe me, I'm very pleased to see you." Tanya looked down, feeling suddenly very awkward.

Tanya still had no idea why Riki was in Landfall, but she had to be genuine. There was no way she could be part of an Intelligence Corps trick. Riki proved that Isabel really was her grandmother and that the Chief Consultant really had ordered the Corps to hand her over. Riki's presence was what allowed Tanya to believe that she truly had escaped from the Corps torture room and would not be going back. And Riki alone gave her hope that maybe, just maybe, she would see Westernfort again.

Tanya wanted to reach out and touch her, to reassure herself that Riki was real. Yet, of all the women from Westernfort, surely Riki was the one least amenable to being grabbed by her. Asking for a hug was out of the question. Tanya clasped her hands together under the table to stop them from moving of their own accord.

They were not friends. Tanya had to remember that. She knew her reactions were purely a result of what she had been through. The woman sitting opposite had not experienced the same nightmare and would not be feeling anything close to the same emotions. Tanya had to keep a grip on herself. She had no idea why Riki was in Landfall working to free her, but she was absolutely certain that it owed nothing to any concern for her welfare.

She needed some answers. "What are you doing here?"

"I've brought you some clean clothes, but the Sisters are inspecting them before they let you have them. I'm not sure whether it's to look for files sewn in the hem or to check that nobody has embroidered slogans like *Screw Celaeno* on the collar."

The new clothes would be welcome. Tanya was still wearing the uniform she had been captured in. The humor was even more welcome. Already, Riki had got under her guard. Tanya leaned forward over the desk, stifling a laugh, even as she wondered if this was the first time they had shared a joke. "I meant, why aren't you back in Westernfort?"

"Your mother was going to kill me."

Tanya grinned, thinking that Riki was joking again. "What did you do to upset her?"

"I meant it literally. I was going to be hanged. She thought I was the one who handed you over to the Guards."

Tanya's smile faded. She looked at Riki in shock. "But it wasn't you. It was Loke Stevenson."

"Yeah, I've worked that one out. But I wasn't able to convince anyone else. Loke did a good job of framing me."

"You were sentenced to death? Did they hold a trial?"

"I escaped the night before. But there was no way I wasn't going to hang. Everyone was convinced I was guilty. Loke switched cloaks with me, so I was wearing the one that had been dragged through the bramble by where you were ambushed."

"Just that?"

"Pretty much."

"Mom wouldn't convict you on such weak evidence."

"She was leading the lynch mob."

"She wouldn't—"

"Oh, she would. We had a private talk before I escaped. She kicked the shit out of me. I'm being a bit less literal there, but not much. The bruises have only just gone, else I could show you." Riki tipped her head toward the watching Sister. "Although I'm not sure what our chaperone would make of it if I started stripping off my clothes."

Tanya slipped down in her chair, feeling appalled, and unsure what to say. "I...I'm sorry. I know Mom...but she shouldn't have. It—"

"It's okay. If I'd done what she thought I'd done, I'd have deserved it and more. In the circumstances, she was quite restrained. It's Loke I want to get even with, not you or your mother."

Tanya stared in surprise. She would have thought Riki was the sort of person to hold a grudge. "It's good of you to look at it that way. I don't know if I would, in your place."

"It's not completely forgive and forget on my part. I'm looking forward to hearing your mother say she's sorry when we get back. Maybe grovel a bit. But that's why I've got to have you with me, to tell everyone the truth about Loke."

Of course. Tanya had known Riki's motives would not spring from altruism. "You could stay here in Landfall. It would be easier than trying to free me."

If Riki detected the bitter edge to Tanya's voice, she showed no sign. Her eyes were locked on the table, as if she were trying to stare through it. "I must go back. There's something I have to do."

"What?"

Riki pouted and twitched her head in a sharp movement, indicating that she was not willing to answer.

"What's so important?" Tanya pressed.

"Nothing much."

Tanya raised her eyes to the ceiling. Nothing much, but it was worth Riki risking her life over. Tanya felt a surge of anger. If Riki was refusing to answer, then it was probably something illegal or immoral—maybe both. It was all part of some stupid game.

"I guess I'm just lucky, then."

At last the sarcastic tone got through. Riki looked up, frowning. "For what?"

"That you stand to benefit in some way from me going home. I'd wondered why you were risking your neck to get me out. It's not the sort of thing I'd expect from someone like you."

Riki's expression flitted through a series of reactions before settling on a taunting grin. "You didn't think I was doing it for your sake, did you?"

"No. I never thought that for a moment."

"Good. We understand each other." Riki stood up. "And I've stayed long enough. It's your tough luck that you'll have to see me again tomorrow."

Riki turned and marched out through the doorway. Tanya watched her go, fighting the impulse to call her back. Riki's presence was stirring up a whirlpool of emotions. The woman was a complete pain in the ass, but Tanya just wanted to cling on to her and not let go.

CHAPTER TEN—DEALING OUT MISTRUST

The junior Sister announced Madam Coppelli and withdrew. Isabel advanced a few steps into the room. The surroundings were familiar. It was where the Chief Consultant generally conducted private meetings with secular visitors. Clear glass windows on one side commanded an impressive view over Landfall. The floor was lacquered wood. The walls were plain white plaster, hung with images from *The Book of the Elder-Ones*. The desk and chair were unadorned, but large and well made. Everything projected the sense of firm austerity, of power without self-indulgence.

The only other item of furniture was the small candlelit shrine at the rear, where Bakara was currently kneeling, hands clasped piously together. The musky tang of incense drifted down the room. While waiting patiently for Bakara to conclude her prayers, Isabel reviewed her opinion of the leader of the Sisterhood.

Chief Consultant Bakara was not stupid. She would not have risen to her present position if she were. The Sisters' hierarchy was as vicious and unforgiving as any other power game in Landfall. Yet she was far too linearly minded, which made her easy to outmaneuver. On a personal level, Isabel rather liked Bakara and was happy that the current plotting would not harm her beyond the loss of a few nights' sleep. Although for the sake of the family, Isabel would not have held back, whatever the consequences for the Sisterhood.

After a few more stanzas of prayer, Bakara rose and came to greet her visitor. "Madam Coppelli, you wished to see me?"

"Yes, I..." Isabel let her voice tail away while her forehead creased in a worried frown.

Bakara picked up on the expression at once. "What is it?"

"I'm not sure. But it might be very bad news. I came to see you as soon as I heard."

"What?"

Isabel stared at the floor as if marshalling her thoughts. She drew a breath and then began speaking cautiously. "Last night, someone broke into Jean Azid's family home and made off with some of her papers."

"Which papers?"

"That's just it. We don't know for certain, because they aren't there anymore."

"Have you any idea what they might be about?"

"Unfortunately, yes. From a few other clues, I suspect they relate to Consultant Joannou's fall from grace."

"What! Why was Azid hanging on to such material? I thought they were supposed to be destroyed."

"They were." Isabel let a hint of irritation creep into her voice. "Jean Azid was a trustworthy employee, but I guess all women in her line of work like to hedge their bets. It's against their nature to let go of any potential weapon, regardless of whether they have any intention of using it."

Bakara lifted her hand to rub her forehead. She stared straight ahead without focusing, her thought clearly moving on. "Do you have any idea who might have taken it?"

"One name tops my list." Isabel spoke tersely.

"Who?"

"You're not going to like it."

"Who?"

"Jean Azid had lots of enemies and emulators. But she died nearly a year ago. Why wait all this time? If there was anything in her rooms that someone wanted, they'd have stolen it months ago."

"So?"

"I don't think it's a coincidence that this robbery was a mere three days after Colonel Zelenski first heard Azid's name mentioned."

"You think it was the Intelligence Corps?" Bakara sounded incredulous.

"Yes."

"Trying to find out about me?"

Isabel shook her head. "No. About me. We both know Zelenski is furious over my granddaughter. With that awkward incident over the warrant she heard me talk about Azid. I suspect she did some digging. Maybe looked into Marlena as well. She found out what Jean Azid used to do for me and sent her agents to see if they could find any incriminating documents. Maybe she was hoping she could blackmail me into letting her take Tanya back. And instead, what they got was..." Isabel shrugged irritably.

"But this is guesswork?"

"Yes. It's a question of how much you want to trust my guesses. But one thing I would suggest is"—Isabel paused, chewing her lip— "keep an eye on Zelenski. Watch to see if her manner changes. She may drop hints, or even threats."

"You think she'd dare threaten me?"

"It depends what she has in her hand."

"She's true to the faith."

"I'd never question it. And that can make her more dangerous. If she thinks your righteousness is in question, she might feel she's carrying out the will of the Goddess in working against you. She'd feel justified in whatever actions she took. She might even try to arrange your removal."

"I don't know..." Bakara sounded anxious and unsure.

"And I could be wrong." Isabel made her tone conciliatory rather than convincing. "There may have been no papers left in Azid's possession to start with. All I'm saying is, keep an eye on Zelenski."

❖

Riki walked past the blank-faced Guards and entered Tanya's room. The Sister on duty had Tanya cornered near the window and was haranguing her earnestly. "Do you not feel the emptiness in your life? Denying the love of the Goddess is like—"

The Sister looked around at the sound of the door. Only her eyes were visible, so it was hard to judge her expression. Tanya however, looked relieved. A wide, welcoming smile flashed across her face, before settling into something more subdued.

Not speaking another word, the Sister toddled back to her seat by the door. Tanya collapsed onto a chair at the table with a sigh. Riki sat opposite and laid out the sheets of paper, pen and ink that she had brought.

"Your grandmother has arranged permission for you to write to her."

Tanya pulled a wry grin. "Do you mind if I take a long time? I need a break from Sister Patel."

"Take as long as you want." Riki leaned forward and dropped her voice slightly. "There's something else you have to do, though. On the third sheet are two faint boxes at the bottom of the page. You need to put prints from your index fingers in them, and don't make any other mark on the paper. When you're ready, let me know and I'll distract the Sister. But there's no rush."

Tanya gave a nod to show she understood and picked up the pen. Riki watched her open the bottle of ink and start writing. Tanya's expression was one of studious concentration. Light from the window accentuated the clean lines of her cheek and jaw. She was looking better, Riki thought. The new clothes had helped, but beyond that, her manner was more relaxed. Unlike the first time Riki had seen her in the temple, she no longer gave the impression of consciously working to keep panic at bay.

Compared to how she had been at Westernfort, Tanya somehow seemed both stronger and more vulnerable. Was it surprising, given what she had been through? Tanya was still the captain's daughter, an offshoot of a powerful family, and everyone's darling, but she was also in a tough spot and needed help. Furthermore, she was not bleating like a pathetic waste of space. Riki appreciated her composure, and that she did not need to be told anything more than once, as with the fingerprints.

Although Tanya had accused Riki of being the sort of woman who would abandon a comrade to rot in a dungeon, Riki knew, were their positions reversed, she would be able to count on Tanya. She had guts and she was not stupid. All things considered, Tanya was not such a bad choice for corporal. It was a shame that she clearly still thought of Riki as a first-class bitch.

Tanya reached the bottom of the page and moved the paper aside to start a new pile. She flipped through the remaining blank sheets pensively and then slipped the top one up to reveal the faint outlines on the page beneath. When next she dipped her pen in the bottle, a slight flick of the nib sent a single drop of ink landing on the tabletop.

Tanya raised her eyes to Riki's. "I'm ready whenever you are."

Riki pushed away from the table and strolled over to the Sister at the door. "Excuse me, Sister, but when I leave here, I was hoping to pray to the Elder-One Richard Turner, but I've been unable to find her statue. Where is she in the temple?"

"She's on the left, behind the northernmost column on the inner ring. She often gets overlooked."

"So if I was facing the eternal flame, she'd be..." Riki turned roughly north and gestured vaguely to her left.

"Oh, no, no. You need to..."

The Sister spent the next five minutes giving directions to Richard Turner, as well as several more Elder-Ones whom she clearly felt did not get their fair share of worshippers. The list kept growing, but at last Riki was able to thank her and escape.

"She does go on a bit," Riki said as she sat back at the table.

"You've noticed."

Tanya was at the top of a new page. Riki saw that the finished pile had three sheets in it and that the ink drop on the table was smeared.

"You did your fingerprints okay?"

"Yup. They're in the pile." Tanya answered without looking up.

"Great."

"It's a good thing grandma rescued me when she did, else my fingers might not have been in a fit state to make prints."

Tanya's tone was light, but Riki felt a kick of outrage in her guts. She drew a breath, hesitated, changed her mind, and then decided to ask anyway. "In the prison, were you questioned by the Corps?"

"Yes."

"I'm sorry. I saw the bloodstains on your clothes."

"That was from a nosebleed when I was captured. And Loke was the one who did it, punching me in the face." Tanya looked up. "The Corps did have a go at me, and it wasn't fun. But like I said, Grandma got me out before things got too serious." For a moment her expression faltered. "I'd just rather not go back there again."

Tanya returned to writing. Riki slipped down in her chair and turned her head to look through the window. However, her thoughts were not on the view of Landfall. She was surprised by the rush of anger she felt, and the surge of protectiveness on Tanya's behalf. Riki wanted to kill Loke, and whoever it was in the Corps who had hurt Tanya.

Would anyone believe that she was capable of getting so upset on someone else's behalf? Certainly not Tanya. Riki remembered the conversation of two days before. Tanya clearly took it for granted that

Riki would not help anyone without some personal gain. Riki clenched her jaw, trying to stifle any show of annoyance, but the exchange had irritated her beyond belief. Did Tanya really think she was so callous and cowardly that she would leave a comrade to be tortured to death? What sort of asshole did Tanya have her marked down as?

And was Tanya justified in holding her opinion? Not that she was right, but that Riki's behavior had given reasonable support for the belief.

The question dug uncomfortably into Riki's thoughts. Meeting her sister had set off a barrage of upsetting memories, and not just to do with her mothers. As a child, Riki used to have friends. She had been in more than her fair share of trouble, but nobody had hated her, as far as she could remember. Yet since joining the heretics, she had set herself against everyone. She had succeeded in hurting her mother, at a cost of complete isolation. Her loneliness had become obvious to her only when sitting in Jan's house, surrounded by her nieces and their playmates.

Riki looked back at Tanya, who was now on the fourth sheet. Despite skepticism over her motives, presumably Tanya was feeling moderately well disposed toward her at the moment. Maybe it was too late to change her image among the heretics, but there was no reason to keep annoying everyone for the fun of it.

"Tanya, I..."

Tanya glanced up. "What?"

"I really am sorry about what happened to you. I wish I could have stopped Loke somehow. I know I said I wanted revenge on the bitch, but you get first crack when we get back." Riki gave a lopsided grin. "I'll hold your jacket if you want."

"You honestly think Mom will stand back long enough to give either of us a chance to take a swing at her?"

A grin lit Tanya's face and her eyes locked briefly with Riki's before returning to her letter. Riki leaned back in her chair and studied the ceiling, while wondering why her stomach suddenly felt so strange.

❖

Riki walked down the temple steps and into the daylight outside. The sky was gray and the paving underfoot was wet and slick, but the cooler weather was a welcome break from the heat of the previous few days. A broad path led through gardens to the gates out. Beyond the railings, the streets of Landfall were seething with afternoon activity, undiminished by the light drizzle falling.

Riki paused at the exit from the temple complex. Guards also stood on duty here, swords drawn and at attention, seemingly aloof from the chaos around them. Their eyes were unfocused, dead to the streams of women passing in and out of the gates. Riki briefly considered the women in pristine red and gold uniforms, and then walked on.

She wanted to talk to some Guards, but not these ones and not so publicly. The sentries would be normal Guards, supposed soldiers who did nothing more adventurous than stand very still at conspicuous points around the temple, apart from the odd occasions when their officers decided that they needed experience in getting lost in the Wildlands. The Guards Riki wanted were those in the Intelligence Corps, and she had instructions on how best to make contact.

Riki turned right and strolled along the bustling pavement, dodging carts, horses, and fellow pedestrians. After a hundred meters, she passed the main entrance to the Guards' compound, again sparing the sentries no more than a glance in passing. Soon she reached a junction and turned onto a smaller side road, and then a narrow passage between two blank brick walls.

By now, she was alone. The sound of traffic on the main street had softened to a distant drone. Then she heard voices. For a second Riki hesitated before ducking back into the shadows. Farther along the alley, two women were deep in conversation. To Riki's relief, they soon moved away, having showed no sign of noticing her. Most likely they were innocently passing through, but Riki did not want to be waylaid before she reached her destination. She had reached an area where it would be easy to arouse suspicion, and she wanted her arrival to come as a surprise.

Once her route was clear, Riki completed the last hundred meters, to an unremarkable side door at the end of a blind alley. No sign hung on the building. It might have been unoccupied, were it not for the absence of litter in the door recess, proof that it was in regular use. Riki opened it without knocking and stepped through.

The interior gave the impression of being a half-abandoned storeroom. Empty crates were stacked at one side. Two women in scruffy civilian dress were lounging casually, using old barrels as seats. They broke off their conversation at Riki's entrance and got to their feet. Their expressions were hard and distrusting.

"What are you doing here?"

Riki tipped her head to one side. "I'd like to talk to Colonel Zelenski."

The older of the women gave her a long, appraising stare. "Who are you?"

"Someone Zelenski will want to talk to."

"You'll have to introduce yourself better than that."

"Why don't you send a message to Colonel Zelenski, then, and say Marlena Azid is here to share some information about her employer."

The woman hesitated, weighing up the words, and then jerked her head to her companion, who disappeared through another doorway at the back. She continued to study Riki.

"How did you know about us?"

"I have good sources."

"Care to share their names?"

"No."

The woman gave a snort of humorless laughter. "You better pray Zelenski does want to talk to you. Else you won't be leaving again."

Fortunately, it took less than a quarter hour to discover that Colonel Zelenski very much did want to speak to Marlena Azid. Riki was escorted through the rear doorway and down steps. A long underground passage ended in another flight of stairs up.

Riki and her guide emerged into an enclosed courtyard. An archway opened onto the parade ground in the middle of the Guards' compound, with a view across to Celaeno's temple rising on the far side. However, Riki did not have long to get her bearings. She was ushered through a doorway and into a small office.

From the layout and position of the building, Riki knew this was the Intelligence Corps Headquarters. She was struck by the thought that if they knew who she really was, she would have been kept underground. Riki glanced at the floor. Beneath her feet was the Intelligence Corps dungeon—somewhere she might yet end up if things went badly wrong.

Riki had to work to control her grin. The stakes were high, but the game was so much fun. She tried to clamp down on the excitement bubbling inside her, intoxicating like wine. She dared not let it blunt her judgment. The following scene would be crucial, and she was playing on her own, without Isabel Coppelli in support.

After a few minutes' wait, Colonel Zelenski stomped into the room. She sat on the desk, rather than behind it, and studied Riki thoughtfully.

"I understand you wish to talk to me about Madam Coppelli."

"Yes. I do."

"So talk."

"My aunt, Jean. Do you know who she was and what she used to do for the Coppellis?"

"I've found out a bit about her. She was a thief, among other things." Zelenski's disapproval was clear.

"It's the *other things* that are important. She was good at jobs that weren't totally legal. And for a price, she'd do anything."

"I can only express regret that she was killed before the law caught up with her."

"The law couldn't have done nothing. Not while the Coppellis have all the judges in their pocket."

Zelenski brushed some imaginary dust off her uniform. "While this is interesting, I don't see why you want to tell me."

"Aunt Jean was murdered."

"I know."

"But did you know it was on Isabel Coppelli's orders?"

"No." Zelenski looked at Riki more intently. "I assume you're not happy about that."

"Too fucking right, I'm not. I've been working for Isabel Coppelli for a few months, but it was only a week ago I found out. I don't think she knows that I know. In fact, I'm sure she doesn't, else I wouldn't be here. I want the old bitch to pay for what she did to my aunt. But the problem is that Coppelli has the Chief Consultant in her pocket. Bakara will protect her, so she has to be got out of the way first."

Zelenski's expression hardened. "That's a very serious accusation, and threat. Chief Consultant Bakara is the Goddess's representative on earth."

Riki paused, but she had noted that the Colonel did not sound as outraged as a devout Guard should. Clearly, Zelenski's loyalty to Bakara was already under strain.

Riki gave a one-shoulder shrug, half defiant, half cajoling. "Oh, come on. You must have noticed how Bakara jumps whenever Coppelli tells her to. Like that crap about Coppelli's grandkids forging the warrant. Making you hand over the granddaughter. Have you never wondered why?"

Zelenski opened her mouth but said nothing.

Riki continued. "Back when the last Chief Consultant died. There were two front-runners in the election. Remember?"

"Yes."

"Bakara and Consultant Joannou from up at Fairfield. And there was that scandal about Joannou, all hushed up, but it ruined her chances." Riki paused.

"Go on."

"How much of the story do you know?"

"Assume I know nothing. Enlighten me," Zelenski challenged.

"Okay." Riki paused. "A few months before the election, a young Sister hightailed it from the Fairfield temple. I guess it happens now and again, when a Sister discovers she isn't cut out for celibacy. Nobody acted surprised. I don't know if they tried to find her, but they didn't succeed. When the election was announced, and Bakara knew who her main rival was, her and Coppelli got my aunt Jean to track down the runaway."

"I assume that she managed it?"

"Oh yes. Aunt Jean was good at things like that. The ex-Sister had got herself a lover and didn't want to go back to the temple. My aunt promised not to tell anyone where she was if she'd write some letters to Joannou, making like they'd been having an affair, but putting a twist, as if Joannou had forced the young Sister into it. Then Aunt Jean got her to write a formal letter for the temple authorities, accusing Joannou of making her break her vow of celibacy. Saying that was why she'd run away, because Joannou had been abusing her, and she was speaking up now 'cause she didn't think Joannou should be allowed to become Chief Consultant. Aunt Jean took the letters along with a couple of trinkets. She went to the Fairfield temple, broke into the Consultant's bedroom, and planted the stuff. Then she sent the denouncing letter to the authorities at Landfall. When they got it, they ordered a search of Joannou's room, found the planted letters, and that was Joannou sunk."

Riki had finished speaking.

Zelenski got to her feet and walked slowly to the window, clearly thinking the story over. Without turning round, she asked, "Can you prove any of this?"

"Yes."

"Did Bakara know about it?"

"Yes."

"And can you prove that?"

"Yes. My aunt hung on to some stuff, and Coppelli kept other letters from Bakara. That's why she's got a hold on her. She's been blackmailing Bakara ever since she was elected."

"What proof could you get for me?"

Riki rubbed her nose. "Let's see. There's the letter from my aunt when she found the runaway, giving a breakdown on what was happening. There's the letter signed by Coppelli telling her to sort it out. And then there's a map of the sanctum at Fairfield, drawn by Bakara, with notes in her handwriting, saying things like *Joannou's bedroom*. I could also get the note from Bakara about the Sister's robes Aunt Jean wore to get into the sanctum. And there's the Coppelli accounts, showing regular payments from the temple funds. How much of that do you want?"

"All of it."

"It will cost. And I'll need some money up front."

Zelenski shook her head. "I'm not that gullible."

"I'll need to pay some people to keep quiet and to hand over the stuff."

"I want proof you're not lying first."

"That's easy. If you want proof you can get it today, though it won't stand up in court or anything. Next time you're with the Chief Consultant, mention my aunt, and then mention Joannou, and then mention how lucky it was that the letters were discovered before the election. Then say something about blackmail, and watch Bakara's reaction. I'm guessing you don't become head of the Corps without learning to spot a guilty conscience. And that's what you'll see in Bakara. Once you're happy she's guilty, leave a message for me. I'm at the temple every day. Then we can discuss the price."

"I thought you were doing this for revenge."

"I am. But if I'm selling out the Coppellis, I want the money to run a good long way."

❖

Zahina Brown sat in her usual seat at the back of the Three Bells Tavern, surveying the barroom though half-closed eyes. Most of the patrons were familiar to her, as she was to them, although they knew her by the nickname of Dicey. She was aware that she had the reputation of being a Corps informant, but she was confident that nobody realized she did more than inform. In fact, she held the rank of sergeant, with twelve years' service in the Intelligence Corps.

She certainly did not fit the public image of a member of the Temple Guard. Her clothes had been repaired so often they were more patch than original cloth. Dirt was engrained in the lines on her face. Her lank hair had not seen a comb for weeks. A half-empty tankard sat on the table in front of her. Brown wondered if anyone noticed that she never drank from it, but after all, Guards were sworn to abstain from alcohol. She would drink only when it was essential to maintain her disguise, and prayed to the Goddess afterward for forgiveness.

A woman sidled close to the table, keeping to the shadows. A deep hood further concealed her face from view. Sergeant Brown had been watching her since the moment she entered the tavern and was not surprised to see her approach. She could always spot the ones who had come to the Three Bells to speak with her. Some would approach her straight off. Some would skitter around for hours before edging close. Some would stare at her, and some would not glance in her direction, but Brown could spot them from the second they walked in.

The woman slipped into the chair opposite. "Is your name Dicey?"

"Why do you want to know?"

"I hear you buy information."

"Who told you that?"

"Just someone. So do you?"

"Maybe. Depends on the information."

The women leaned closer, and light from a candle touched her chin. From the absence of lines around her mouth, Brown could tell that she was young. Brown had already noted that she was short and lightly built.

"It's about Old Lady Coppelli."

"And supposing I was interested. What would you have to sell?"

"Some sheets from her accounts. Not the current ones, 'cause they'd get noticed quick. But from a couple of years ago."

Sergeant Brown scratched her chin thoughtfully. "What interest would I have in the financial dealings of an honest businessman?"

"Honest?"

"There are few who dare say otherwise."

"Yeah, well. What these pages show is that Chief Consultant Bakara has been regularly paying large sums from the temple funds into the old lady's pocket. Does that interest you?"

"Maybe."

"Yes or no?"

Brown looked at the other woman. "How do I know they're genuine? How did you get them?"

"They've got the Coppelli stamp on the bottom. And I got them by... Well, let's say that I work in the place. Somebody hinted that they'd pay me if I passed the pages over. She said the Intelligence Corps was interested. She offered to cut the money with me. But I'm wondering if I can get more if I sell them myself."

"How much do you want?"

"A hundred dollars."

Brown laughed. "I was thinking more about ten."

"Azid said she'd give me thirty."

Brown kept a stone face, but the woman was clearly an amateur, who revealed her hand far too easily. "Really? How about I make it forty?"

"Eighty."

"Sixty. Take it or leave it."

The woman ducked her head. "I'll take it." She scrabbled around inside her jacket and produced a wad of folded sheets, which she laid on the table.

Brown reached for them. The woman slapped her hand down on top. "I want to see your money first."

Sergeant Brown pulled a heavy purse from her boot and counted out the coins. The woman released the papers. Brown put them inside her own jacket without bothering to glance at the contents. Others could do the job better than she.

"They better be what you claim. Otherwise I reckon I know enough to find you, and you wouldn't want me angry at you. After all, you're going to have enough enemies with Azid pissed at you."

❖

Chief Consultant Bakara sat alone in her austere bedroom. Soon she would have to lead the evening prayers, but first she needed to compose herself. The meeting she had just had with Colonel Zelenski had left her shaken.

Madam Coppelli's guesswork had been right—of course. The old woman had not gained her reputation by chance. Bakara felt her features twisting in a bitter grimace.

Zelenski knew all about the plot against Joannou and had wanted Bakara to know that she knew. The significant look in the Colonel's eye when she had mentioned the incident left no doubt. Nor could it be coincidence that she had tied together Jean Azid, Consultant Joannou, and the discovery of the letters.

Bakara wanted to pray. Would the Goddess hear her? Yet Bakara knew that what she had done had been right.

Consultant Joannou had been a divisive figure, a hard-line zealot who would have embarked on a radical program, without thought of the cost. If she had become Chief Consultant it would have been a catastrophe. The Sisterhood, the whole world even, would have been torn apart.

As the time for the election had approached, Madam Coppelli had suggested a solution, and she had agreed to it. Bakara chewed her lip. Even though the plot had not required her personally to do anything very immoral, she could not claim innocence. She had prayed for forgiveness and done penance ever since, but now it seemed as if the past might wreak its revenge.

Removing Joannou's challenge, by whatever means, had been the pious thing to do. Bakara had not been motivated by thought of her own gain, but by love of the Goddess. Yet how many would believe her?

Regardless of what Colonel Zelenski might believe, she was clearly intending to use the information to push forward her own agenda. She had finished with an unmistakable threat of blackmail. Zelenski would not take such risks unless she was very sure of her position. Bakara raised her hand to her forehead. The questions now were, what could she do about Zelenski, and what would Zelenski try to do about her?

❖

Although night had fallen outside, Colonel Zelenski had no candles lit in her office. Often she thought best in the dark and she had already committed to memory everything she needed from the pages lying on her desk. They were the accounts sheets passed to Sergeant Brown, detailing payments from the temple funds to Isabel Coppelli. Chief Consultant Bakara was being blackmailed. The Azid girl's story was looking more and more likely by the day.

For herself, Zelenski needed no further evidence. Even Chief Consultant Bakara's mask had not hidden her guilty reaction when the subject of the letters found in Joannou's room was casually dropped into the conversation. Yet it was not proof Zelenski could present to others.

She pursed her lips, thinking of the unknown woman who had sold the accounts sheets. It was always the way, once news spread that the Corps were pursuing a suspect. Informers would emerge from the woodwork, each with their own bit of the story to sell. The evidence would mount, but Zelenski knew that she had to move quickly, before the word got back to Madam Coppelli as well.

The elderly matriarch was too dangerous an enemy to be left loose. Zelenski would not make the mistake of underestimating her. As soon as the Corps had the evidence, Isabel Coppelli would be secure in the dungeon below. Without its head, the Coppelli family would be far less of a threat.

But what to do about the corrupt Chief Consultant? Bakara was the Goddess's representative on earth. No court had the power to try her. Yet there was a precedent. Ninety-three years earlier, Chief Consultant Foster had suffered a lapse into insanity.

The secret temple library at Landfall contained books that had belonged to the Elder-Ones themselves. They had been left behind when the Elder-Ones ascended to join with Celaeno. Clearly the library had been to aid the Elder-Ones in their divinely appointed task, and left as a symbol of their wisdom. However, Foster had taken to reading the books, despite warnings that the library was for use by the Elder-Ones alone and contained knowledge not meant for mortal eyes.

Foster had gone mad and started ranting nonsense, similar to the blasphemous lies of the heretics. Was the similarity surprising? Reading the books had also sent the accursed Gina Renamed mad. Unfortunately, she had been able to escape and infect others with her insanity, which was why the world was now plagued with heresy. Small comfort that it would not happen again. When the source of Renamed's madness was revealed, the Chief Consultant of the day had ordered the library sealed, so that none might enter it again. The doors were all bricked up. Yet the harm had been done.

In Chief Consultant Foster's case, the madness had been contained. The town of Southwater was in the middle of a bleak salt marsh at the mouth of the Liffy River. The port was the town's only reason to exist and the temple was small and disregarded. In origin it was a hermitage, and its Sisters were known more for meditation than political ambition. Secure private quarters had been constructed in the temple, a place where Foster could live out her natural life in solitary confinement, thus ensuring her insanity did not spread.

On three occasions since, the secure quarters had been used, although never again for a Chief Consultant. It was a place where someone could vanish without a trace. No word or sign of the inmates had been heard since the day they entered the Southwater temple. Presumably the Sisters who cared for them knew more, if only the date of their deaths, but they maintained strict silence. Once in the secure quarters, the inmate might have ceased to exist. Maybe it would provide a solution for Chief Consultant Bakara. Better for her to disappear completely than have the scandal made public.

Colonel Zelenski nodded thoughtfully. Yes. Southwater temple would again swallow a chief consultant.

CHAPTER ELEVEN—RAISING THE STAKES

The window in Tanya's room gave a view mainly of the temple roof, with a selection of other roofs behind. However, if she hunched over the table and pressed her face on the glass, Tanya could also see a short section of the street in front of the temple.

Riki had just gone. Currently she would be exiting the sanctum, on her way to a meeting with Zelenski in the Corps headquarters. Tanya felt nauseous at the thought, but Riki clearly saw it as one big game. Her flippant attitude ought to be irritating—it always was in Westernfort. Yet now Tanya was finding it a source of comfort, and not just for humor. Riki did not have the first idea what fear was. She made incredibly reassuring company.

Even so, Tanya wondered why she was bothering to peer down at the road. The chances of spotting Riki were too small to consider. Tanya frowned. Just what did she think she would gain by it? Yet she remained in place, looking.

❖

The room Riki was shown into was the same as before, but this time Colonel Zelenski was already there waiting, seated at the desk. Riki felt a hard knot of tension in her stomach and an uncomfortable prickling at her nerve endings. Taking risks for herself was fun, but this was different. The game was moving into its next phase, which involved Tanya's position becoming a lot more precarious. So far, Isabel Coppelli had been spot-on accurate in predicting how everyone would react. Riki prayed that she continued to be right.

Riki stared at the floor, almost as if hoping to see through to the cells and interrogation rooms beneath her feet. Riki remembered the catch in Tanya's voice as she said that she did not want to go back. Yet Tanya was not chickening out or whining for sympathy. Riki just wished there was some way she could be more support, or even swap places. She would happily face the risks on Tanya's behalf.

The colonel's chair creaked as she leaned back. "You got my message."

Riki hardened her expression and looked up. This was not the time to let her performance waver. "Yup. And I guess you got the guilty reaction from the Chief Consultant, like I said you would. So. You ready to strike a deal now?"

"I am. For the information you outlined before, I'm willing to offer one hundred dollars."

Riki shook her head, laughing. "Oh no. I'm not handing it over that cheaply." She drifted a few steps closer to the desk. "Look. We can do it one of two ways. I want a thousand dollars. Now, you can say one hundred, I can say five thousand, and we can spend the next half hour haggling it down to a thousand. Or I can say one thousand, you can say yes, and we can go and do something useful in that half hour. Which way do you want it? Because I'm not handing the papers over for a dollar less."

"Don't be ridiculous. I'm not paying that much."

"Then you're not getting the documents."

Colonel Zelenski fixed a hard stare on Riki. "You're overplaying your hand. We'll get the documents, with or without your help."

"Some of them, maybe."

"We already have."

Riki gave a cynical laugh. "Yeah, I know. That little shit has already sold you the accounts sheets, hasn't she? You could have saved yourself whatever you paid her. Because my price is the same, regardless of how much stuff is there."

"My point is that we don't need your documents."

"Yes, you do. The accounts aren't enough to nail either Bakara or Coppelli, and you know it. You need something definite, in their handwriting, linking them to the frame-up of Joannou. And there ain't no one but me who can give it to you. There's no point searching, because I'm not stupid enough to leave them anywhere they might get found."

"There's more than one way you might be enticed to hand them over." Zelenski paused, significantly. "Our interrogators are very good at extracting information. I'm sure they can get the location of the documents from you without too much trouble."

Riki acted unimpressed. "If you want to take the chance. But you haven't got a lot of time, you know."

"We've got as much time as we want, and far more than you'd like."

"Not if you want to get the old lady's granddaughter back you haven't."

"Why not?"

"Because the old lady is planning on springing her granddaughter from the temple. She's not going to let her stay locked up forever. She's going to rig it to make it look like the heretics rescued her."

"I think she'll have trouble getting her granddaughter past the Guards on duty."

"Ah, but that's just it. Bakara is in Coppelli's pocket. The old lady will make Bakara send the Guards away and set up anything else she wants."

"Bakara wouldn't be so rash or so blatant."

"She's under Coppelli's thumb, and she hasn't got the guts to say no."

"How do you know about this?"

"I'm in the Coppelli household, and I'm good at hearing things."

"When did you find out?"

"A couple of days ago."

"Why didn't you tell me before?"

"Because I couldn't care less about the granddaughter. She's done nothing to hurt me. It's the old lady I want nailed. But I reckon you might be a bit more interested. From what I've heard, you've got four days at most to stop Coppelli and Bakara. And you can't do a thing to them until you've got my proof in your hands." Riki grinned. "So. It's up to you. Do you want to take the gamble that your girls can get the information out of me in time to stop the granddaughter from legging it?"

"Supposing I say you're bluffing?"

"You'd be wrong."

Colonel Zelenski sat silently for a long time, staring at her desk, but at last she looked up. "One thousand dollars?"

"Yes."

"All right. If the information is what you say it is."

"It is. And I want you to swear, on the name of Celaeno, that you'll give me the money and let me have free passage out of Landfall."

"In the name of Celaeno, on my honor as a Guard and by Hoy's sword, I swear that if you hand over documents proving criminal misconduct by Madam Isabel Coppelli and Chief Consultant Bakara, then I will pay you one thousand dollars and allow you to depart this place without hindrance or fear of arrest. Does that do you?"

"It does me fine. I'll be back tomorrow morning for a quarter of the money up front, and as long as you give me that, you can have your proof the day after."

Riki did not let her expression drop until she was back on the street and far from the Guards' compound. Once again, the meeting had gone exactly as Isabel Coppelli had predicted. Yet Riki could not stop feeling worried on Tanya's behalf. Regardless of her trust in Isabel, she could not bear the thought of Tanya returning to the Corps dungeon.

Riki came to a stop and looked around blankly at the houses around her, trying to sort out what was going on in her head. This was not just comradely solidarity. She felt fiercely protective. The more she thought about it, the more Riki wished she could go back to the temple, talk with Tanya, and hear her laugh.

Okay. I like her. The words bounced through Riki's thoughts. *A lot.* She sighed and carried on walking. If only the feeling were mutual.

❖

Isabel Coppelli was showing all the signs of being a grandmother in a mellow family mood. Tanya answered the questions as fully as she could, about her sisters, parents, home, ex-girlfriends, interests, and ambitions. Talking about her family with somebody who genuinely wanted to hear made her feel less homesick. It was the first time her grandmother had visited since Riki had arrived, and it was also going to be the last.

Eventually, Isabel bowed her head regretfully and sighed. "I'm afraid I've been here long enough, or at least as long as I can without somebody thinking it odd."

"I'm pleased you visited."

"But not as pleased as I am. It's always nice to meet a new granddaughter. Thirty-two just wasn't enough." The elderly woman smiled, looking like any other sentimental, doting grandmother. "When you get back, tell your mother how happy I am that she's given me four more and that I had this chance to meet one of them."

"I will."

"Your mother and I...I think you know how much I've regretted what happened between us. Tell her I'm sorry. And that's something I've said to precious few people in my life. It's good to hear she's doing well, and I'm not at all surprised that she's the captain. You rarely find a Coppelli at the bottom of the heap. You're a Coppelli too. Don't think you're going to get away with lounging around as a mere corporal for long."

"Oh, that's, um...we'll see."

Her grandmother laughed. "Don't play the shy, blushing bit. There's far too much of your mother in you to carry it off."

Tanya looked up in surprise. "I'm not sure if I see that."

"You didn't know your mother when she was young. Admittedly you're a bit less prickly than she was. That'll be due to growing up with a mother who's willing to let you be yourself, without making a battle about it every day." Isabel sighed. "But I really must go. We won't meet again, unless it all goes terribly wrong and we end up in the same cell. The timer is burning down. Your comrade has nearly finished winding up Colonel Zelenski." She paused. "That Rikako, she's a useful woman to have around."

"Yes. She's, um..." Tanya broke off, staring at the tabletop. "It's a shame we don't get on too well."

"Don't you?"

"She was always a troublemaker back at Westernfort."

Isabel looked thoughtful. "Yes, you're quite right. I know the sort. She is a troublemaker, and she'll always be making trouble for someone. The trick is to offer the right inducement so the someone is your enemy."

"I think she counts me as an enemy."

"Oh no. I'm sure she doesn't."

"I know we're working together now, but I don't know if we..." Tanya's voiced faded away. She was not sure how she felt about Riki and had no idea how Riki felt about her—or more disturbingly and truthfully, she was starting to get a good idea of how she felt about Riki and was quite certain that Riki did not feel the same way.

"Don't worry. I'm sure you'll sort it out between you on the way home. You'll see." Isabel pushed back from the table and stood up. "Good-bye, Tanya. It's been a great pleasure meeting you"

"And for me. Good-bye, Grandma Izzy."

Isabel Coppelli smiled and tottered to the door, moving like the old woman she was. Tanya remained at the table long after she had gone, thinking and watching the sun set over Landfall.

❖

Between the main doors of the temple and the entrance to the outer sanctum lay the military shrine. Statues of three Elder-Ones stood at the back of an alcove, one each for the Guards, the Rangers, and the Militia, in colors mirroring their protégé's uniforms. As befitting the patron of the oldest branch of the military, Natasha Krowe of the Rangers was in the middle, with her green skin and gray hair. On the right was the yellow-skinned and red-haired Guards' patron, Su Li Hoy, and on the left was David Croft. In her case, both skin and hair were plain black, like the Militia uniform. However, since David Croft was one of the Elder-Ones traditionally represented with fur on her face, little skin was visible.

The sight of soldiers praying at the shrine was common enough. Senior Sister Watkins spared only a glance for the kneeling woman in red and gold, until a soft voice hailed her.

"If you please, Sister."

Sister Watkins was on her way to an early morning meeting with the Chief Consultant, but she had a few moments to spare. She backtracked a few steps to the entrance of the alcove. "What is it?"

The Guard got quickly to her feet, but then hesitated, shifting her weight from foot to foot. She was clearly a young recruit, with a blank badge of rank. Her red tunic was devoid of braided ornamentation. The cheek guards of her helmet hid much of her face, but from what could be seen, her expression was deeply troubled. Her eyes flitted uneasily, not fixing on anything.

"What is it?" Sister Watkins repeated.

"Sister I...I want to..." The Guard caught her lip in her teeth. "May I ask your advice on something?"

"You may."

"Supposing a Guard was given orders to kill a prisoner, in cold blood, without a trial. Would it be murder to obey those orders?"

Sister Watkins paused, quite sure that she was not being asked a hypothetical question. This did not cause her concern. Watkins could think of several circumstances that might result in such an order being given, although it was unusual to select such a young, naïve Guard to carry it out. More typically, these deeds were entrusted to experienced members of the Intelligence Corps. However, reassurance was being asked for, and that she could give.

"Not all trials can be held in public. Sometimes even the report of a crime can result in the sickness spreading among weak minds. Even though there's no record, rest assured that the criminal has been duly tried, convicted, and sentenced. The Guards are in the forefront of our war against the heretics, and are sometimes called on to go beyond the bounds set for other women. In your service, you may be asked to do things, without question, that would normally be a sin. You must have faith in your officers. They are carrying out the will of the Goddess."

"But supposing..."

"Yes?"

"Supposing it wasn't one of your direct officers who gave the order. Just someone who had a much higher rank than you, but outside your chain of command."

Sister Watkins' surprise increased. Something was definitely not right. "I can't see that it would be likely, but even so, no senior officer would give such orders without the blessing of the Chief Consultant."

"But suppose something made you think maybe...they didn't..."

"They didn't what?"

"Maybe she was giving you the order so her own women wouldn't get in trouble. You weren't sure. But something you overheard...and perhaps it was...the Chief Consultant didn't want her to...so they..."

Sister Watkins stared sharply. The Guard was drifting into incoherence, but a clear thread was emerging. "Are you saying that this has happened to you?"

"I...no, Sister. No. I was just wondering. I..." The Guard broke off her denials, breathing heavily. "I must go. I'm due back on duty. I'm sorry for taking up your time."

The Guard sidestepped and hurried away across the floor of the temple. Sister Watkins drew a breath, about to call her back, but already she had gone. Anyway, Watkins had heard enough. This was definitely something she should discuss with Chief Consultant Bakara. Behind her mask, a grim smile settled on her lips. Just as well that she was on her way to a meeting. Sister Watkins turned and headed toward the entrance of the sanctum.

❖

"It's odd walking around in a Guard's uniform, how everyone jumps out of your way." Grinning at the memory, Riki leaned over her crossed arms on the tabletop. "It would be really useful if you wanted to get across town in a hurry. And I liked the boots that made me a few centimeters taller."

"Where did Grandma get the uniform for you?" Tanya asked.

"I don't know. Maybe the same place she gets the list of who's due to visit the Chief Consultant, and when."

"Do you think Sister Watkins will have passed the message on to Bakara?"

"Your grandmother does. And she's pretty good at saying what people are going to do before they know themselves."

"I know, and I trust her, but..."

The wobble in Tanya's voice made Riki look up. Tanya was staring at something outside the window, but Riki was sure that she was not seeing whatever it was. The muscles in her jaw were working, in a manifest battle to keep her expression steady. Without thinking, Riki reached out and laid her hand over Tanya's on the table.

"It won't be for long. Your grandmother has it all covered."

Tanya's head snapped back, facing Riki. Her eyes widened in evident surprise. Her hand flinched as if about to pull away, but then relaxed, staying in contact.

Riki felt her insides kick as her eyes locked with Tanya's and stayed there. A feeling of utter self-consciousness swept over her. All she could think about was how Tanya's hand felt, lying under hers. What should she do? Ignore her hand? Move it? Leave it where it was and wait for Tanya to move?

"About now, your grandmother is going to be..." Riki stopped. Trying to act as though she were not staring into Tanya's eyes and holding her hand was not going to work. "Look. I know you think I'm a total pain in the ass. Most of the time you're right. And you think I'm a selfish bitch who's only helping because it's in my own best interest, else I'd leave you to die in the Corps dungeon. But you're wrong there. I don't walk out on my comrades. I'm on your side."

"Yes. I'm getting to realize that." Tanya's hand twisted over, so their palms were together. Her thumb and little finger wrapped around the sides of Riki's hand. "And I'm sorry I punched you outside the stores, after the fire."

"You've already said that once."

"Yeah, well. This time I mean it."

The Sister on duty coughed, reminding them of her presence. Both Riki and Tanya jerked their hands away. Riki turned her face to the window while her insides again flipped over. It was ridiculous. She had heard people going on about how it felt when they were falling for someone, but she had always thought they were exaggerating. Yet her heart was pounding as if she had run ten kilometers and her hand was aching through to the bone.

Outside the window, the sun was dropping toward the roofs of Landfall. Time was moving on. Riki dragged her thoughts on track.

"Your grandmother is going to call on the Chief Consultant in a few minutes. I must go. I need to be with Zelenski when she hears the news."

"Yes. Right. I'll, um..." Tanya sounded as if she was suffering from the same turmoil.

Riki stood up and brushed her hands nervously through her hair. Her eyes again met briefly with Tanya's. "It'll be fine. Don't worry." She took a step back and mouthed the words, "I'll see you on the docks."

❖

From the window of the Chief Consultant's audience room, Isabel Coppelli could look right across Landfall, as far as the downstream docks on the Liffy River. The sight recalled old memories. She had been seventeen when her own grandmother put her in charge of the Coppelli warehouses there. It had been a hard test, cross-checking everyone who might double-cross her, bribing and bullying, haggling and hassling, while all the time keeping her paperwork clean, but she had met the challenge, as she had every other one over the intervening seventy years.

Only once had she seriously miscalculated in her judgment, and that had been with her own daughter, Piety. Isabel smiled at her reflection in the window glass. Perhaps, in a spirit of reconciliation, she should try to think of her daughter by the name she preferred. After all, it did suit her better. With hindsight, she should have known better than to try dominating Chip. She was too much her own woman—Isabel's smile broadened—and her mother's daughter.

Isabel's musings were interrupted by the rustle of cloth and the sound of the door closing. She composed her face into an angry frown and turned around.

Chief Consultant Bakara had entered the room. "You wanted to speak with me?"

"Yes. I've just received some serious news."

"What is it?"

"Colonel Zelenski. She's arranging to have my granddaughter murdered. Of course, I've got no proof, but my sources have picked up on it. Zelenski hasn't got her own women on duty outside Tanya's room, but she's pulling strings. She's fixing the sentry rota so there'll be a squad of young simpletons on together. Gullible enough to think they have to obey an order from a colonel without referring it to their own officers."

Bakara turned away, rubbing her forehead, as if to soothe a headache. "I...I think you may be right. I've heard—"

"You knew already?"

"Vague reports. I wasn't sure of the target. Or who the officer was. But yes. It could be. I just can't see why she'd do it."

"Because she can."

"That's not a reason."

"How about, because she wants to show you that she can."

"I don't see..."

"Zelenski has a hold over you. She wants to send the message that she can do whatever she wants and you dare not stand in her way."

"But why have your granddaughter killed?"

"She's furious we removed Tanya from her prison. She wants to hit back and make her point by showing how she'll deal with any attempt to overrule her in the future. You could arrest the Guards who do the killing, but you won't dare use their testimony against Zelenski. She'll force you to cover for her. And then she'll really have you in her grip."

"What do we do?" Bakara sounded despairing.

"The situation isn't hopeless. I've got my people working on it. Given a couple more days, I should be able to dig some skeletons out of Zelenski's own cupboard. But I need more time, and I need to know Tanya is safe while I do it. Which is where you can help."

"How?"

"Take the Guards away from Tanya's room and keep her door locked."

"Colonel Zelenski won't agree to that."

"And I won't agree to my granddaughter being murdered. Zelenski will be angry, but it will take her a few days to make a new plan and that's all I need. In the meantime it doesn't matter what she will or won't agree to. The sentries outside Tanya's door are ordinary Guards, not Intelligence Corps. That's why I've heard about what she's planning. Her own women would have followed orders without a fuss. If you go to the Guards on duty and tell them to leave, they won't disobey a command from the Chief Consultant."

Riki dropped the papers on the desk. "There you go. As promised."

Colonel Zelenski picked up the top one thoughtfully and sloped it to the lantern behind her. From the light shining through, Riki could tell that it was the map of the sanctum at Fairfield. Zelenski pursed her lips and took up the next sheet. Riki waited patiently while each document was examined in turn.

At last, Zelenski put the papers aside and looked at Riki. "Very good."

"I told you it would be. So. Where's my money?"

Zelenski continued to stare coldly across the desk.

Riki sneered. "You're wasting your time, trying to intimidate me. You swore on Celaeno's name, and a Guard never breaks an oath like that. It's your honor at stake."

"Indeed." Zelenski sighed and got out of her chair. She pulled open the door of a nearby cupboard and reached inside. "Here's your money."

The purse landed on the desk with a heavy thud. Riki grabbed it, tugged open the drawstring, and peered in. "I guess you'd be insulted if I counted it out."

"You can if you want."

"Nah. I'll trust you." Riki grinned and turned to the door. "Thank you. And good-bye."

"Before you go."

Riki looked back. "What?"

"I was wondering, if I ever had use for your talents again, whether I'd be able to contact you."

"I'd have to tell you where I was. And I'm not sure I want to."

"I'd make it worth your while. People who know how to get information are always useful."

"I'll think about it. Maybe when the money runs out."

"It would—" The sound of running stopped Zelenski. Urgent knocking followed.

"Enter."

"Ma'am." The door opened and a Guard appeared, an Intelligence Corps member judging by the less-than-immaculate condition of her uniform.

"What is it?"

"The heretic in the temple, ma'am, Coppelli's granddaughter. You wanted to know if the watch outside her room was changed. I've just heard. Ten minutes ago, Chief Consultant Bakara went along in person and ordered the Guards to leave. There's just the one Sister inside the room now, keeping an eye on her. The door's locked, but we know where the key is."

Riki grinned. "What did I tell you?"

"Yes. You were right—again." Zelenski stared first at Riki and then down at the papers on the desk. "But now I have what I need to act. Corporal." Her eyes returned to the soldier at the door.

"Yes, ma'am."

"I want a detachment of six Corps Guards. Armed, in uniform, and in the courtyard. Fifteen minutes."

"Yes, ma'am." The Guard vanished.

Zelenski drew a sharp breath. "You've been accurate and very useful. I hope our paths cross again. It might be beneficial to us both."

"We'll see." Riki tilted her head, listening to the shouted orders echoing around the courtyard and the sound of people running. She glanced once again at the colonel. "Good-bye. And have fun."

❖

Tanya jumped at the pounding of heavy feet in the corridor outside. The key rattled in the lock and then the door was flung open. The Sister on duty had been dozing. She scrambled unsteadily to her feet as seven armed women in Guards' uniforms stormed into the room. Tanya shrank back against the wall. It required no acting on her part. A raw panic seeped over her.

"What's going on?" the Sister piped up. She was ignored.

Colonel Zelenski stalked forward. "You're coming with us."

Tanya could not speak.

"You can't—"

Zelenski cut off the Sister's protest. "We're just making sure we know where she is."

"The Chief Consultant said—"

"There's been a change of plan. And there's a lot more changes to come."

Two Guards strode forward and grabbed Tanya's arms. They hauled her away from the wall. For three steps Tanya went placidly, but then she gave in to the panic. She pulled back and then threw her weight to the right, struggling frantically. More Guards surrounded her. More hands grabbed her. Tanya heard a squeal from the Sister who had gotten caught up in the mêlée. Then Tanya heard metal on metal, the sound of a sword being drawn.

"Stop this at once."

Colonel Zelenski's eyes blazed over the line of her sword. Tanya froze and then sagged in the grip of the Guards. The fight was hopeless. Through the Guard's legs, she caught sight of the Sister on her knees, holding her torn mask in place. From what Tanya could tell, the Sister was not hurt, apart from her dignity, but it said much about the Guards' state of mind that none were helping her rise. At the word of command, Tanya was marched from the room. Zelenski and two other Guards went ahead, and another pair kept close behind. Twice one of their boots caught on Tanya's heel.

The tight group emerged through the hangings at the sanctum entrance. The Guards standing watch were clearly startled, but despite the drawn sword, the sight of the Intelligence Corps Colonel was enough to reassure them that no action on their part was needed.

Zelenski led the way across the main hall. A gaggle of worshippers, dithering in the temple doorway, were roughly shoved aside, and then the party was outside. The last shreds of sunset lay orange on the western horizon, and a few stars were starting to show. Gardens surrounded the temple. The scent of flowers mingled with the dust of the city. Tanya gulped the warm evening air, trying to stay calm.

She was taken through the small side door that had been used on her way into the temple. A company of about thirty Guards were drilling in the middle of the parade ground, with an officer in charge, bellowing commands. The Intelligence Corps party skirted around the marching formation and then continued in a straight line for their headquarters. They passed under the archway.

Tanya had another brief glimpse of the interior courtyard before she was propelled through a doorway and down stairs. The underground prison was as she remembered it. The ill-lit corridor reeked with the stench of confinement. The damp stone walls closed around her like a tomb. Already, the Guard in front had the door open. Tanya was shoved into the cell. The door shut. The key turned. Footsteps marched away, and then there was silence.

Tanya fumbled around until she found the bunk. She sat and pulled her heels up, hugging her legs. She did not want to be there. Fear surged through her, drowning her senses. But she knew it was not the same as before. Now, she had hope. She had faith in her grandmother. So far, the elderly matriarch had been right at every step.

But supposing she failed now? Groaning, Tanya rested her head on her knees. Images of the interrogation room were trying to possess and overwhelm her. She needed something to distract her thoughts— anything. Abruptly, a memory dropped into her head from less than an hour before. Riki holding her hand.

Tanya opened her eyes and stared blindly into the darkness. Why had Riki done that? Was it just a friendly gesture of support? And what about the warmth in Riki's voice and the depth in her eyes? If it had been anyone else, Tanya would have had no doubts reading the signs. But from Riki?

Admittedly, Riki was no longer acting like a total jerk. They were united in fighting the Guards. When Riki said she would not desert a comrade, Tanya believed her. However, this did not mean that Riki felt any sort of affection for her.

Tanya knew she could not trust her ability to read Riki, because she was not an unbiased observer. She had let herself become fixated. It was understandable in the circumstances. But in conjuring up the sound of Riki's voice, and the expression on her face, was Tanya's memory being faithful to the facts? Or was it reflecting her own emotions and offering merely a desired fantasy?

Tanya let her head sink onto her knees. Regardless of the truth, she so desperately wished that Riki were still with her, holding her hand.

CHAPTER TWELVE—SELLING A DUMMY

Early morning sunlight flooded through the clear windows and splashed across the polished floor. Paintings of bygone Coppellis stared down sternly from paneled walls as Riki wandered past. She sighed. Her surroundings were luxurious, but nothing promised relief from her current mood. Normally the cabinets holding rows of books were a great source of entertainment. Not at the moment. The only thing with any appeal was the brandy bottle standing on the inlaid table in the middle of the room.

Riki had been staying in the Coppelli mansion ever since embarking on the scheme to free Tanya. The protected accommodation meant she had been shielded from close scrutiny by the Corps agents. Also, when the game was done, the Intelligence Corps would be out looking for her blood. Riki did not want a trail leading back to her sister's home. Isabel was sure that, in a year or so, it would be safe to return to Landfall. Once Zelenski was out of the way, Riki was determined to pay an extended visit to Jan, as well as seeing her other sisters.

In the meantime, living in the Coppelli mansion had been an introduction to a new world for Riki. The amenities of Landfall far exceeded what could be found in the heretic strongholds, and the Coppellis had the best of whatever was available. Riki's gaze skimmed along the row of cabinets. Printed books were an example. As children, the heretics were taught to read and write, but the small population could not support a printing press. A few books had been taken to Westernfort and Ginasberg by heretics, but when fleeing for their lives, women generally concentrated on clothing and food, rather than fiction and poetry.

Fine brandy was also unavailable outside the homelands. The tavern in Westernfort served only home-brewed beer and wine. Riki considered the bottle and cut crystal glasses, but then turned away. From a purely material point of view, Riki was sure her host would not mind her drinking, but this was not the time to blunt her mind. Riki wanted all her wits for the day ahead.

Riki forced herself to take a book from the shelves and sit with it open on her lap. However, five minutes passed before she noticed that the book was open on a blank page. Riki flipped forward to the start of the text and tried to focus.

Tanya had been taken to the Corps dungeon at sunset the previous day. It was now well past sunrise. If the Corps' interrogators had gotten straight back to their questions, those ten hours might have been an awfully long time. Her grandmother was sure that Tanya would not be harmed until Zelenski had finished dealing with the Chief Consultant. But what if she was wrong?

Riki closed her eyes and slumped in her chair. When had she started to care so much about Tanya? This went beyond reasonable concern for a comrade in danger. And why was it so hard to let go of the memory of holding her hand? Had Tanya meant anything by it? She had not pulled away—quite the opposite. Was it just because she was nervous? The circumstances hardly counted as normal. Could anything she did serve as a reliable guide to what she was thinking?

The sound of the door made Riki leap from the chair, dropping the book. Isabel Coppelli had entered, dressed in outdoor clothes.

"Is it news?" Riki asked.

"Yes. I thought you might like to know that Chief Consultant Bakara has sent a message, asking me to visit as soon as possible."

"Why has she waited so long?"

Isabel laughed. "It's about when I expected. I imagine she isn't looking forward to breaking the news to me that my granddaughter is back in the Corps dungeon. She'll have prayed to Celaeno before accepting that only earthly intervention would help. She also probably waited for a letter from Zelenski."

"Will Tanya be all right?"

"I'm sure she is. The Corps prefer taking their time over questioning people and they won't think they have any reason to rush." Isabel considered Riki thoughtfully for a few seconds. "You'll need to change into your disguise fairly soon. You're about to become dangerously unpopular with Colonel Zelenski."

"Right. I'll find Dev."

"I should see you again before you leave, but if not, I'd like to say that I've found it a pleasure working with you. Should you ever decide to return to the Homelands, I can guarantee you a job. You have skills I'd find most useful. Maybe not in Landfall, while Zelenski is around, but I don't think she has a long career ahead of her. While waiting for her to go, another town would be safer. The Coppellis have interests across the Homelands."

"I'll think about it. Although..."

"Although you have reasons to stay in Westernfort? I understand, and regardless, I wish you well in the future."

"Thank you."

"If we don't meet again, then good-bye and safe journey." Isabel smiled and went.

Riki picked up the dropped book and brushed dust off the cover. She was still not going to be able to read but was feeling less on edge. Things were moving forward. Riki returned the book to the shelf and also left the room, in search of Devishi Tang.

❖

The Chief Consultant was praying again when Isabel arrived. It said much about her state of anxiety that she broke off immediately, clearly placing more importance on conversation with the Coppelli matriarch than with the Goddess. Bakara hoisted herself off her knees and stood with her hands clasped together over her chest.

"I...I'm afraid I have bad news," she began hesitantly.

"About?"

"Your granddaughter."

Isabel took two paces forward. "How? You said you'd remove the Guards from outside her room."

"I did. And she hasn't been killed, I don't think, but..."

"What has Zelenski done?"

"She came over last night with a squad of her women. They got the key, burst into your granddaughter's room, and took her back to their prison. I'm sorry. Zelenski caught us by surprise. We weren't expecting her to be so direct. They even assaulted the Sister in the room."

"Assaulted?"

"She was knocked over. I think it was mostly by accident, but even so..." Bakara was clearly shocked by what had happened.

"Has Zelenski said anything? Sent a letter?"

"Yes. Not long ago."

"And you waited for it before sending for me."

"Er... yes." Judging by the blush above the gauze mask, the implied criticism in Isabel's tone had gotten through.

"What did Zelenski say in her letter?"

"She knows all about Joannou, and what your woman did. And she has proof, the map I drew for Azid, other things. She's talking about having me removed. I—" Bakara's head sank. "I don't know what to do."

"Have you answered her letter?"

"No. I wanted to talk to you first."

"That was sensible." Isabel made no attempt to keep her tone respectful. Bakara was too worried to take offense.

"What can I do?"

"Let me talk to her."

"What can you say?"

"I've been doing my own digging. I think I've found a weapon to use against Zelenski. Something she won't want to become general knowledge."

"What?"

"To reveal the information would compromise my sources."

"But will it be enough? Will she hand over the documents?"

"Hopefully." Isabel compressed her lips in a firm line. "I'd like more. And if I'd had more time I'd have gotten it. But I know the dirt is there, and if I play it right, I might make her think that her position is weaker than it really is."

Bakara returned to the shrine, as if seeking comfort. Isabel heard her start to speak a few times, but stop. She was clearly too frightened to stay silent, but unwilling to say too much. Eventually, she said, "Zelenski. She was talking about putting me in...in secure confinement... and..."

"The old Chief Consultant's quarters at Southwater?"

Bakara turned to face Isabel. "How do you know about them?"

Isabel gave a humorless laugh. "There's not a lot that goes on in the Homelands that I don't know about. I've been aware for decades that the Sisterhood has a place to put people when you want them to disappear. Southwater was the most likely location."

"I don't want to go there."

"No. I imagine you don't. Although I believe the accommodation is very comfortable, if a little on the quiet side." Isabel paused for a second. "And as it happens, they've been in my thoughts recently."

"Why? What about them?"

"To be blunt, I want somebody put there. My granddaughter."

"Your granddaughter?"

"Yes. She's a heretic, and to be honest, I don't think she's about to recant. However, she's my flesh and blood, and I want her somewhere safe, so she can never again be used as a pawn against me. Also, my family's name would be better served by having her well out of sight. The Southwater quarters seem a good place. She'll be secure, well provided for, and not mistreated. And Zelenski shouldn't put up too much fight against sending her there."

"You're going to suggest it to her?"

"More like tell her it's what's going to happen. I don't like overplaying a weak hand, but I don't have much choice in this case."

"So? You're going to say...?" Bakara was struggling to keep up.

"I'm going to talk to Zelenski as soon as I leave here. I'm going to tell her about the information I've dug up on her, imply I have more, and see if I can bluff her into giving up the documents and my granddaughter. I want you to have a river barge waiting on the downstream docks after sundown tonight, ready to go to Southwater. Have some Sisters on it, briefed that they will be taking a new resident for the Southwater temple, and enough ordinary Guards to prevent any accidents on the way. I'll send another of my granddaughters to keep an eye on things for me. If I can get Zelenski to agree, I'll have her deliver Tanya to the docks tonight." Isabel looked up. "Is all of this satisfactory with you?"

"Yes." The relief in Bakara's voice was unmistakable. "If you can persuade Zelenski to give up the documents...anything. I'll sort out the river barge. It'll be waiting. If you really think you can..."

Isabel smiled grimly. "Yes, I do."

❖

Isabel was shown into Zelenski's office as soon as she arrived at the Intelligence Corps headquarters. She glanced around, noting that the room was furnished for functionality rather than to impress. The Corps had other venues for people they wanted to intimidate. The colonel was sitting behind her desk, with two other officers in attendance.

Zelenski leaned back and considered her visitor patronizingly. "Have you come with a message from the Chief Consultant?"

"Not exactly." Isabel looked disdainfully at the other officers. "I think you might want to listen to what I have to say in private."

"I don't th—"

"Believe me. You don't want anyone else to hear what I have to tell you."

Zelenski's brows drew together angrily, but then she gestured to her subordinates. "Wait outside."

Once the door had shut, Isabel pulled a chair around and sat uninvited, then stared coldly at Zelenski. "I understand that, last night, you invaded the temple sanctum with a group of armed soldiers, stole the key to my granddaughter's room, and took her away, in defiance of the Chief Consultant's command."

"You understand correctly. And you know why I did it."

"Not precisely. I'm unsure on some details."

"There's no point playing games."

"I'm not playing. This is far too serious."

Zelenski sighed in exasperation. "You were going to arrange for your granddaughter to escape. I wanted to be sure she's still in custody when this entire matter is resolved."

"Ah, was that it?" Isabel nodded. "What I meant when I referred to not knowing the details was, I suspected you'd done it because someone had told you lies. The exact nature of the lies was what I didn't know."

"I have proof."

"I doubt it."

"I know all about your scheme to discredit the other candidate for Chief Consultant during the last election."

"Yes. You said in your letter, and in a very threatening fashion, I might add. Which was what baffled Bakara. She'd put off telling me about you abducting Tanya, waiting for more information, thinking maybe you'd had a good reason. But when she got your letter this morning she formed the opinion that you're suffering from a type of insanity. That was when she sent for me. To let me know my granddaughter was in the hands of a madwoman."

"This isn't going to—"

Isabel brushed aside Zelenski's objections. "However, I was able to put a different interpretation on events, because I know something Bakara doesn't." She met Zelenski's eyes. "How much did you pay Marlena Azid?"

"Enough."

"Enough for her to run away and make a new start somewhere?"

Zelenski nodded.

"I thought so. We discovered her quarters empty this morning. And a few clues as to what she's been up to."

"She's sold you out."

Isabel shook her head. "No. Not me."

Zelenski sighed and stood up. She unclipped a key from her belt and opened a cupboard. After slapping the extracted wad of papers onto the desk, Zelenski dropped into her chair and sat, smiling triumphantly.

Isabel pointed at the papers. "May I?"

"Feel free to look at them for as long as you like."

For the next five minutes, Isabel studied each document in turn, paying particular attention to the pages cut from an accounting ledger, but eventually she placed the last sheet back on the desk and sat back.

"Well?" Zelenski asked. "Anything you want to say?"

"You mean apart from observing that although Marlena is an accomplished actress, she's a complete novice at forgery?"

"What do you mean?"

Isabel paused thoughtfully. "Have you cross-checked any of the documents to see if they're genuine?"

"There wasn't time last night. But we've checked the stamp on the accounting sheets. It's one of yours, all right."

"Yes. Those are genuine. But she was rather selective in which sheets she gave you."

"We didn't get them from Marlena Azid."

"Yes, you did. She was capable of playing more than one role."

Zelenski frowned in confusion, but then her expression hardened again. "It doesn't matter. They prove the Chief Consultant was paying you money."

"Yes."

"You were blackmailing her."

"No."

"So why was she paying you?"

"That's what I meant about being selective. Marlena missed some important sheets at the beginning and the end. A few years ago, I loaned the temple some money for urgent repairs to the roof of the main hall. Interest free of course, and as a further act of piety, I wrote off the last tenth. That's what the money was. Repayment of a loan, and if you'd had the beginning and end sheets it all would have been quite clear. I can arrange for the books to be sent to an auditor if you wish."

Zelenski glared at her. "Maybe you can worm your way out of that one, but not the rest."

"Except they're all blatantly counterfeit. That's what we found in Marlena's room. Evidence that she'd been playing around at forgery." Isabel picked up the map. "I can't reveal how I know, but I assure you, not only is this not Bakara's handwriting, but the interior of the Fairfield sanctum looks nothing like this. And that's not a matter of opinion." She waved the sheet at Zelenski. "Send someone to Fairfield with this and see if it bears any similarity to the place. The external outline is about right. But anyone navigating by it would end up trying to walk through walls."

"But..." Zelenski looked stunned.

Isabel picked up another sheet. "And this. It's not my handwriting. Marlena was trying to copy it, but the angle of the downstrokes is wrong. The loops are too narrow, and her hand was moving slowly when she traced my signature. Look at the quiver. But don't take my word. Go and check. I've signed enough documents in my life."

"I..." Zelenski picked up a sheet and examined the signature closely.

Isabel returned the paper to the desk and smiled grimly at Zelenski. "So. How much did Marlena sting you for this load of rubbish?"

The disbelief on Zelenski's face switched in an instant to fury. "I'll get her."

"I'd say good luck in trying, but I'm not sure you'll have the chance."

"My agents will—"

"How much longer do you think they'll be your agents?"

"What do you mean?"

"You seem to have forgotten that last night, you led an armed party into the very sanctum of the temple, in direct defiance of the Chief Consultant. You drew your sword, stole a key, attacked a holy Sister, and abducted someone the Chief Consultant had ordered you to leave alone. And then this morning you sent the Chief Consultant a threatening and abusive letter." Isabel fixed a hard stare on the Colonel. "What happens to a Guard who breaks her oath of obedience to the Chief Consultant?"

"But—"

"I could list the offenses you've committed, starting with unfitting behavior for an officer and ending with blasphemy and treason. I'd say you're looking at a court-martial, dishonorable discharge, and possibly a death sentence."

The blood drained from Zelenski's face. "I wasn't..."

"Admittedly, the forged letters might stand as a mitigating factor, but you acted against the Goddess's representative on earth on such a flimsy basis without checking first."

"But, I know...she..."

Isabel waited for the spluttering to stop. "However, you have something I want. My granddaughter. Which is why I'm prepared to do a deal with you."

"What?"

"I want you to hand over my granddaughter, unharmed, at the downstream docks tonight. There'll be a river barge waiting."

"Taking her where?"

"That's none of your business, and I'd have thought a very minor concern to you, given your current situation. If you do this, I'll plead your case with Bakara. As you've doubtless observed, I have influence with her. If we can resolve this with no harm done to anyone, then I think I can guarantee you won't be court-martialed."

"Influence?"

"Yes. Much the same as I now have influence over you."

Zelenski sank back in her chair, eyes closed. Isabel watched. The Intelligence Corps commander had reached her position by schemes, tricks, and double-dealing. Years sitting behind a desk had blunted her nose for a trap and let her rely on bullying rather than subtlety, but now that she was on the trail, it would not take long to reach her conclusions.

Zelenski opened her eyes. "You set me up."

"Me?"

"Yes. Marlena Azid couldn't have run all this on her own."

"You're welcome to your opinion. But my advice is not to think too much about it, because you won't like where you end up."

"I know where I've ended up. Right where you wanted me. Okay. I'll hand over your granddaughter at the docks. I don't have a choice, do I?"

"Not if you don't want to be in a cell within the next hour."

Isabel stood up and reached onto the desk. "I'll take my accounts sheets, if you don't mind. I might need them for the tax auditor. But it would be as well for you to burn all the rest."

As the door opened, Zelenski spoke again. "The story about Joannou, was any of it true?"

"Of course not. Do you think I'd let you anywhere near the truth?" Isabel smiled at the Intelligence Corps Colonel, still seated at her desk. "And do I need to tell you that it would be better never to mention any of this again?"

"No."

❖

Riki tied the laces on her boots and stood up, again viewing the world from a clear four centimeters higher than usual. She clasped her hands around her expanded waist and shifted the padding slightly, getting it to sit more naturally. The other woman in the room, Devishi Tang, took a step back, examined her critically, and then handed over a long braided wig. Riki slipped it carefully on her head, pushing any stray locks from sight. After a final prod with her tongue at the pads inside her cheeks, everything was complete. Devishi stood beside her and the pair studied their reflections in a full-length mirror.

"So, Dev? What do you think?" Riki asked.

"You don't look a lot like me. But I guess you look more like me than like yourself, which should be good enough. There isn't going to be anyone on the barge who knows me by sight."

"Except Steph."

"She doesn't count."

Riki grimaced and lifted the long hair off her neck. "August isn't a good time to be walking around with all this padding strapped around me."

"I'm sorry. I'd have put more effort into losing a few kilos, if I'd known the problems it would cause you." Devishi laughed as she spoke. She was one of Isabel's granddaughters, an easygoing young woman with a sharp sense of humor, who had been summoned from her usual base in Eastford to assist in the scheme.

Riki grinned. "I think it's one of the reasons you were picked. Padding is an easy disguise to make me look like you from a distance."

"And if I thought losing weight would make me look like you, from a distance or anywhere else, I'd give it a go. Even though I'm a Tang, I think I got most of my genes from the Coppelli side of the family, and they've never had the reputation for turning out beauties."

"Tanya is..." Riki stopped herself and covered by adjusting her wig. "Tanya is going to be so pleased to get out of prison."

"I'll bet. I should think you'll both be happy to see the back of Landfall."

"I've enjoyed being here. It's been fun."

Devishi laughed. "You ought to watch that attitude. Playing games with Grandma Izzy is addictive, and you don't want to know the sort of trouble she can get you into. Trust me, I speak from experience."

❖

The Chief Consultant's prayers were getting more desperate, judging by the fervent muttering. The heavy scent of incense was choking. Bakara knelt by the shrine, but she was on her feet before Isabel was halfway into the room, although she waited until the door was closed before speaking.

"What did she say? Have you got the documents?"

Isabel smiled. "Yes. It worked."

"Praise the Goddess." Bakara turned back to the shrine and raised her clasped hand to her forehead, clearly giving thanks for her reprieve.

Isabel waited until she had the Chief Consultant's attention before continuing. She pulled a wad of papers from inside her shirt. "Here they are. The map you drew for Azid. Some regrettably indiscreet letters. Not one is much in itself, but together they add up to a complete picture."

"And this is all of them?"

"Zelenski assures me these were all she had."

"She swore an oath?"

"Yes."

Nodding, Bakara took the offered documents and leafed through them, stopping at her own hand-drawn map. "What should we do with these?"

"I'd recommend burning them as soon as possible."

"Yes. Of course." Bakara looked at the shrine, where a row of small candles was lit. "A suitable offering. Though I'll be giving more to the Goddess later."

"As will I."

Isabel watched the Chief Consultant burn the documents, one by one, in the small gold offering bowl beneath the shrine. The thought shot through Isabel's head that, at the very same moment, Colonel Zelenski was probably in the process of burning her forged copies of the very same documents. It was neatly symmetrical and ironic.

And of course, the sheets Bakara was burning were not the originals—those were still safe inside the Coppelli mansion—but they were not deliberately clumsy and inaccurate, like the copies sold to Zelenski. Isabel had considered handing over the originals to Bakara, but the Chief Consultant's eyesight was weakening, and it would take far more than a ten-second scan to spot the work of a skilled forger, such as the one Isabel employed. With an ever-uncertain future, the original documents might yet find a use.

When the last sheet had been turned to blackened ash, Bakara again faced Isabel. "Thank you. As ever, you've been most helpful, and you will find me suitably grateful."

"I'll consider myself adequately repaid by the safe delivery of my granddaughter into your secure accommodation." Isabel let her face reveal a hint of distress. "Her mother and I had family issues, from when she was a child. I've always felt I was partly to blame for what happened...her joining the heretics. If we'd worked out our relationship better, maybe..." Isabel sighed. "The past cannot be changed. But I feel I owe it to her to make sure her daughter is safe and unharmed for the rest of her natural life. The repayment of debts. Does that make sense to you?"

"Yes. I think so. I've made the arrangements you asked for. A barge will be waiting at the downstream docks after sunset. Three Sisters and a squad of Guards will be on board."

"Thank you. My granddaughter, Devishi Tang, will also be on the barge, with an attendant, but I hold you responsible for ensuring Tanya is handed over safely at Southwater."

"Of course."

Isabel smiled. "Once my heretic granddaughter has disappeared from the eyes of the world, I think it would be better if we never mention any of this again."

❖

Riki stepped from the carriage, accompanied by her attendant, Steph, who was carrying their baggage. The river barge was moored a few meters away. Behind her, the driver flicked the horses' reins, and the carriage rumbled across the cobblestones, returning to the Coppelli mansion. Apart from activity around the barge, the downstream docks were deserted, lit only by the rising moons.

After the heat of the day, the cool dockside was pleasant. The sound of water slopping against the stone quay was scarcely louder than the whispering from the three Sisters huddled by the foot of the gangplank. Uniformed Guards stood to attention in a line along the waterfront. The crew were dark figures on the barge, acquiring detail only when they entered the circles of light given by the lanterns, mounted bow and stern.

At Riki's approach, the Sisters broke off their quiet conversation and turned to her. Their white robes were luminous in the moonlight. One took a half step forward. "Good evening."

Riki bowed her head. "Good evening, holy Sisters. I'm Devishi Tang. I have a letter from my grandmother, introducing me and my attendant, and one from the Chief Consultant, but you'll need better light to read them."

"That's not necessary. We've been informed of who you are."

"And has"—Riki paused—"my cousin arrived yet?"

"No. We're still waiting for her, but—"

The Sister broke off at the sound of more wheels, rattling over the uneven stones. An enclosed prison wagon appeared around the side of the nearest warehouse. The plain-clothed driver reined the horses to a stop close by where the Sisters and Riki were standing, and then she and her second jumped down and went to the rear of the wagon. The door was unlocked and three more women emerged. In the middle was Tanya.

Riki felt her insides kick. Had Tanya been mistreated, despite Isabel's assurances? The light was too poor to tell. Riki wished there was a lantern close by, though she could do nothing with the information, whatever state Tanya was in, and it was no bad thing if the darkness prevented the Corps agents from identifying Marlena Azid, should any have seen her visiting Zelenski.

Tanya's body language shouted bewilderment and fear, but this told Riki nothing. It was the role she was supposed to be playing.

"This is the one?" the lead Sister asked.

"Yup. Here's your heretic."

"Thank you."

The Sister gestured to the uniformed Guards, who formed up around Tanya and rapidly bundled her up the gangplank. Throughout this, Riki hung back, as if disinterested. Only after Tanya was out of sight below deck did she also mount the gangplank, followed by Steph and the three Sisters.

While the crew made ready to depart, Riki stood in the middle of the barge, well away from the lanterns, and watched the four Intelligence Agents around the prison wagon. They in turn were looking at the barge and showing no sign of leaving. Riki pursed her lips. If they had hurt Tanya, Riki wanted to come back to Landfall, hunt them down, and do something equally nasty to them. But it was a childish impulse and missed the point. Riki's expression eased into a smile.

Isabel Coppelli had won. She had beaten the Corps. Tanya was out of the dungeon and on her way home. That was the real score.

❖

The four agents watched in silence as the crew cast off and the river barge drifted into the night. They then clambered back on their wagon, but still made no attempt to move from the dockside. After a few minutes' wait, the sound of hooves announced the arrival of a lone horsewoman.

The rider paused by the wagon. "The heretic left on the barge?"

"Yes. With her escort."

Another agent pointed at a speck of light on the water. "There you can just see the stern lantern."

"Right. I'm on it." The horsewoman, Lieutenant Maz Turan, waved an informal salute and urged her horse onward, following the barge downriver and away from the city of Landfall.

CHAPTER THIRTEEN—
THE OLD THREE-CARD SHUFFLE

The barge was three days out of Landfall, traveling with the current, and halfway to Southwater. The river had widened and was now twice the size as when it had flowed through the city. Earlier that morning they had passed the spot where the Liffy joined with the Wade, flowing down from Fairfield.

Fields, woods, and villages drifted by on the riverbank. The pace and mood of the journey were lazy beneath the scorching sun. The cool breeze off the water was welcome. Riki sat on the foredeck, in the shade of an awning, with a book open on her lap. The ragged fringe on the canvas fluttered, sending dancing shadows across the page. Riki considered moving slightly, so it would be less distracting, but it was not as if she was actually reading, merely turning the pages at a methodical rate.

Piercing squeals made her look up. The barge was passing a sandy spot on the bank, where five small girls were splashing naked in the water. They were the ones screeching. Beyond them lay planted fields, a collection of farm buildings, and a dirt track fading away into the distance.

Riki smiled at the girls and was about to return to her book when she heard someone approaching. The oldest of the three Sisters was coming to join her under the awning. Riki shifted to make room.

"Good morning, holy Sister."

"Good morning, Devishi Tang." The elderly woman eased herself onto the bench.

"It's a pleasant day the Goddess has sent us."

"Indeed. Though I fear, a little hot below deck. I've come to cool down for a moment."

"And I'm very pleased to have your company." Riki kept her tone just on the believable side of obsequious.

"I note you haven't visited your cousin."

Riki made a dismissive noise and held up her book, a battered, well-thumbed copy of *The Book of the Elder-Ones*. "Not because of the heat. I'm a faithful daughter of the Goddess. I'm here on my grandmother's orders. But were it up to me, I'd have left the family shame in the Intelligence Corps dungeon where she belongs. I certainly have no wish to socialize with her."

The Sister nodded. "Your piety does you credit. And, to be honest, your cousin isn't pleasant company."

"I don't doubt it."

"She has a crude turn of phrase and she"—the Sister hesitated—"she doesn't seem fully in her right mind. She's forever asking what's going on and insisting her name isn't Tanya. Do you know if she suffers from mental problems?"

"She's a heretic and believes their foul lies. She must have mental problems. No sane woman would credit any of it for a second."

"Maybe. But you'd think she'd know what her name was."

Riki shrugged. "Perhaps they have some depraved naming ceremony, when they renounce their old life along with the Goddess and enter the cult. She might want you to call her by some blasphemous title. If I were you, I'd ignore everything she says and certainly not ask what she wants to be called."

Again the Sister nodded. "Yes. It must be something like that." She sounded happier, as if Riki's suggestion had eased her doubts.

They sat in silence for a while longer, but then the Sister stood. "I'd better return to my watch." She started to leave.

"Holy Sister."

"Yes?"

"I'm truly sorry for the trouble you've been put to, for the sake of this stain upon my family. I feel soiled just knowing that she's so close by."

The Sister put a hand on Riki's head in blessing. "My child. No blame attaches to you. Your faith marks you as pure. Good day." She wandered back to the hatch.

Riki picked up her book. Her eyes returned to the riverbank. The playing girls were now far out of sight. Riki stared into the distance.

Several times over the previous days, she thought she had seen a horsewoman shadowing the boat. It was not unexpected. Their plans allowed for the Intelligence Corps tracking the boat, and so far, their plans were working perfectly.

❖

The town of Southwater consisted of a busy port, a small temple, and not much else. It lay in the middle of an expanse of salt marsh at the mouth of the Liffy River, on a rocky islet—the highest point for kilometers around. The only way to reach it was by boat. To the south another kilometer of tidal mud, quicksand, and brackish water separated the town from the ocean. A dredged channel allowed seagoing vessels to reach the port, where produce bound for Landfall was transferred to river barges.

The town existed only to support the docks. It consisted of inns for travelers, taverns for sailors, warehouses for goods, homes for dockworkers, and a Militia station to ensure that the law was upheld. With limited space on the islet, the buildings were densely packed. None of the roads were wide enough for a horse-drawn wagon or carriage. Handcarts were the way goods were moved. Feet were the only method of transport.

The temple was positioned at the apex of the hill, overhanging the docks. In midafternoon, Riki stood on the busy quay, staring up at it. The location seemed an unlikely one for a temple—surely the town was too small to justify it. Yet it was a very good place to keep a prisoner secure. Lock down the docks, and no one could enter or leave the island, and searching the entire town would not take long.

A noise made Riki glance back. Tanya was being brought on deck. It was the first time Riki had seen her since they boarded the barge, and her first chance to assess her state in daylight. To Riki's relief, although Tanya was filthy and disheveled, she appeared unharmed. Thoughts of what the Corps might have done had been preying on Riki's mind.

Soon, the party were assembled on the quay. The Sisters set off in the lead, climbing the streets to the temple. Behind them were the Guards surrounding Tanya in tight formation, with Riki and Steph tagging along at the rear.

"Why are we here? My mom'll—" Tanya's voice rose in a whine

that was quickly silenced by a slap from a Guard.

Riki kept her eyes averted, trying to appear unconcerned, although she felt a flare of anger. She had to maintain her act for a little while longer. Soon the charade would be over, and then she could flatten the next person to mistreat Tanya.

A brief period of standing around ensued at the temple gates, while the letter of introduction and explanation from Chief Consultant Bakara was dispatched to the Consultant in charge of the Southwater temple, and then they were ushered through to a small audience chamber that undoubtedly fulfilled the entire role of outer sanctum for the minor temple.

The Guards from the barge had been left in the main hall and their place taken by four members of the Southwater Company. These now stood at the rear of the room, two on either side of the doorway. Steph had also remained outside, so only Riki, Tanya, and the three Sisters were present when a short, round woman in white robes entered.

She bustled forward to greet them. "In the name of the Goddess, welcome to Southwater. I am Consultant Sharif. I understand you have someone for me to care for."

The eldest of the three Landfall Sisters nodded respectfully in acknowledgement. "Celaeno's blessing on you too, Consultant. Yes. Allow me to present Tanya, whose family would prefer if her last name was not mentioned. She has, regretfully, become ensnared in the wickedness of the heretics' lies."

Tanya broke in. "Look. How many fucking times do I have to tell you? I ain't this Tanya. And I ain't no frigging heretic. But you—"

The Sister ignored the outburst. "She is, I'm afraid, somewhat confused and argumentative."

Riki however, stared at Tanya, screwing her face in a deep frown and eventually taking a step forward to look more closely. "Um..."

"What is it, my child?"

"Are you sure this is my cousin?"

"Pardon?"

Riki turned to the Sisters from Landfall. "I admit I've never met her before, but she was described to me."

One of the other Sisters spoke up. "I did a few turns in her room, keeping watch. I must admit, she isn't acting the same. But it certainly looks like her...I think," she ended weakly.

"My grandmother said she had a faint scar on her cheek. Here." Riki brushed the side of her own face indecisively and then looked at the Sister expectantly, as if hoping to have her words confirmed.

"Oh, I um...don't remember."

"That's what I've been sayi—" Tanya was interrupted this time by Consultant Sharif.

"Do I understand there's some doubt as to this woman's identity?"

Riki gave a polite half bow. "Yes, revered Consultant. She's supposed to be a cousin of mine. But although she mostly matches the description, there's the matter of the scar. And she's possibly a centimeter or so too tall."

"This is easy to check." Sharif looked at one of the Guards by the door. "Go and find Sister McKay and ask her to escort the Imprinter in here as soon as possible. Or, if she is currently engaged in her duties, to let us know when she'll be free." Sharif turned back to the others. "We have limited requirements for an Imprinter in Southwater, so hopefully she'll be available. But if not, I'll arrange suitable facilities while we wait."

Fortunately, the Southwater Imprinter was not otherwise occupied, and soon a woman in blue entered the audience room in the company of two more Sisters. The Imprinter was a very old woman who hobbled forward unsteadily, leaning on a supportive arm. Riki guessed she had been sent to Southwater as a semi-retirement from another, busier temple. After all, how many women in the small town would want to get pregnant in any given year? However, as long as age had not damaged the Imprinter's mind, she would still be capable of reading DNA.

"You have need of me, Consultant?" the Imprinter asked once she had reached the group in the middle of the room.

"Yes. Do you see these two young women? I wonder if you could tell us how closely they're related."

"Of course, Consultant."

Riki held out her hand for the Imprinter. The ancient fingers felt loose and light, wrapping around hers. No strength remained in the grip. The mottled skin had a rough, dry texture. For three minutes, the Imprinter shut her eyes and held Riki's hand, then moved to Tanya. Her forehead furrowed, enhancing the lacework of wrinkles. After more consideration she returned to Riki and then back to Tanya again.

While this went on, the Sisters waited patiently. However, when the Imprinter returned to Riki for a third time, Consultant Sharif spoke up. "Can you tell us anything, Imprinter?"

The old woman opened her eyes. "It's very hard to be sure. I think they may have had a common ancestor, nine or ten generations ago. But I'd need more time."

"They couldn't share grandmothers?"

The Imprinter's expression eased. "Oh no. Not anywhere near that close. The two lines have been completely separate for at least eight generations."

Consultant Sharif bowed her head in gratitude. "Thank you, Imprinter. That's all we need to know. You may go."

Once the Imprinter and her two helpers had left, Sharif turned to Tanya. "So. Who are you?"

"Hoo-fucking-ray. At last. This is wh—"

"And I'd advise you to keep your tone respectful."

The implied threat stopped Tanya short. Her eyes darted around shiftily, and then she began again in calmer tones. "Sorry, Sister."

"Consultant."

"Oh yeah. Sorry, Consultant. My name's Pat Oduro."

"And why were you on the barge?"

"It was all the Corps' doing, weren't it?"

Riki looked on, impressed. She had wondered at Tanya's ability to act out the part, but so far the upright corporal was doing a good job of playing a lowlife thug. The dirt smeared across her face and the spikes of unkempt hair gave her the right appearance. When added to the surly leer, she looked surprisingly unlike herself. No wonder that the Sister who had sat watch in Landfall had been unwilling to confirm her identity.

Consultant Sharif frowned. "What did the Corps do?"

"They got me out of the lockup."

"Which lockup?"

"In Landfall. Me and my mates had been in the tavern. We weren't causing no trouble, but this other gang came on all mouthy. They started it...honest. The landlady called the Militia. And yeah, I was kicking the bitch, but she—"

"I don't think we're interested in details of how you came to be in the lockup. You can save those for the magistrate. What did the Intelligence Corps do?"

"Uh, right, Sis...Consultant." Tanya licked her lips. "I thought I'd be up in court in the morning. But I'd only been in the lockup a short while when some women turned up. They didn't say who they were, but the Militia were shit-scared of them. You could see it in their eyes, and there ain't no one who scares the frigging Militia apart from the Corps. They checked out everyone, and when they saw me, they laughed and said I'd do fine."

"Nothing else?"

"No. Just that. The Militia looked the other way when they took me out of the lockup. They dumped me in the wagon for an hour, then took me down to the docks. The agents said if I knew what was good for me I'd not say a word. So I didn't. I'm not fucking stupid. I'm not crossing the Corps. But I never thought I was going to be brought down here. My mom'll kill me when I get home. I was supposed to be—"

"I think that's enough." Consultant Sharif terminated the tale.

"I did try to say, once we were—"

"I said, that's enough."

"Oh, yeah. Right, Consultant." Tanya ducked her head sheepishly.

Consultant Sharif faced Riki. "There's clearly been some confusion. As to how to proceed, if you don't mind, I'd like a few minutes to pray for guidance. Would you be so kind as to wait for me here?"

Riki bowed. "Of course, Consultant."

Sharif's gaze shifted back to Tanya, the wrinkling around her eyes making her distaste clear. "Guards. Can you take this woman to a quiet place and make sure she stays put and doesn't cause any disturbance?"

"Hey. Ain't you going to send me back to Landfall?"

Tanya's protests were ignored, and she was bundled away. Consultant Sharif and the Landfall Sisters followed more sedately.

Alone in the room, Riki drew a deep breath. One more step complete. Soon, very soon, she and Tanya would be on the way home to Westernfort.

❖

"I've reread Chief Consultant Bakara's letter and spoken to the Sisters who accompanied you from Landfall, and I now think I understand what has happened." Consultant Sharif spoke deliberately, clearly choosing her words with care. "I'm afraid the Intelligence Corps, for some reason, have declined to hand over your cousin as agreed. We must draw the conclusion that she is still in their hands."

"Some might say it was the best place for her." Riki and Consultant Sharif were the only ones in the audience room.

"Yes, Sister Rochel said you had little sympathy with your cousin."

"I'm a faithful daughter of the Goddess and a devout supporter of the holy Sisters. This heretic and I may share genes, but she's no kin of mine. Unfortunately, my grandmother doesn't see things in quite the same way."

"But you agreed to do this task for her."

"She's both my grandmother and my employer. If I wish to continue working in the family business, I had no choice."

"What were you intending to tell your grandmother when you returned to Landfall?"

Riki pursed her lips. "What can I tell her? The Intelligence Corps still have my cousin."

Consultant Sharif lifted her clasped hands to where her mouth would be, behind the mask, and bowed her head, either praying or thinking. With a decision clearly reached, her eyes returned to Riki. "I won't ask you to default in your duty to your grandmother, but as a faithful daughter of Celaeno, I'd ask you not tell anyone about this, including your grandmother or your servant, until you've first spoken to the Chief Consultant. If you're agreeable, I'll give you a letter to take to her, explaining the matter."

Riki hesitated, but then nodded sharply. "All right."

"Thank you. I believe the river barge is due to return to Landfall this evening."

"I'll not be on it. The upriver journey against the current is slow, and I've business matters to attend to. I've already sent my servant ahead to reserve rooms in the Pig and Whistle for tonight. Tomorrow, we'll take the ferry to Salsport and hire a fast carriage there."

"Very good. I'll have my letter delivered to the Pig and Whistle before sunset."

Riki gave a polite bow of acknowledgment. "What are you going to do with the look-alike the Corps gave us?"

"To be honest. I haven't given the matter much thought. She doesn't seem a suitable candidate for our facilities. The quarters were intended for a rather better class of person." The Consultant's tone made it plain that she did not relish the idea of looking after the ill-mannered lout for the rest of her life. "But if we release her, I'm worried she might talk."

"Who'd pay attention to a lowlife like her? And what could she say? Someone mistook her for someone else. I'm sure she comes out with far wilder stories when she's drunk. And if she has any sense, she'll keep quiet, what with the Intelligence Corps' involvement."

"There is that."

"If you want, I'll take her back to Landfall with me. I think the holy Sisters put up with her quite enough on the way here. I imagine they were looking forward to a calm return journey, without the foul-mouthed obscenities."

"It's considerate of you to offer."

Riki smiled. "But if you want my best advice, I think she's already had far more attention than she warrants. Dump her with the town Militia. I'm sure there's room in the lockup. It's where she belongs. If the local magistrate can't sort the case out, she'll have her sent back to Landfall."

"Yes." Sharif drew out the word, thoughtfully. "Yes, I think you're right. An easy solution. The town lockup."

❖

The Pig and Whistle was the most expensive inn at Southwater, but seeing that it was owned by the Coppellis, room rates were even less of an issue than normal, and members of the wealthy family were rarely bothered by cost. The entrance hall of the inn was lined with dark wood paneling and smelled of spice, but Riki did not have long to admire it. Noting the good cut and material of her clothes, a member of the staff descended on her almost before she was inside the door.

"May I help you, madam?" A sickly sweet smile split the porter's face.

"If you could. I sent my woman along earlier to reserve rooms. My name is Devishi Tang."

"Ah, yes. Please follow me."

"You could just give directions."

"No, no. Let me show you the way." The woman bobbed and nodded all the while she was speaking, with the inane smile plastered across her lips.

Riki followed after, thinking about the recent display of sycophantic groveling that she had put on for the Sisters and Consultant. Maybe it had not been as exaggerated as she had thought. The porter was taking the act into a completely new realm. Riki wondered how rich, stupid, and arrogant the inn customers had to be before they took it all at face value.

The porter soon stopped outside a door on the second floor. "Here you are, madam. And if there is anything at all I may do, please, there's a bell inside that you can ring."

"Thank you."

The porter opened the door and then ducked back out of the way for Riki to enter. "There you go, madam."

"Thank you."

"It will be my privilege to help in any way I can."

"Thank you."

"And if—"

"Yes. Thank you." Riki shut the door firmly.

Soft laughter came from the other side of the room. "What's wrong? Don't you like having your ass kissed?"

Riki turned around, grinning. "No. At least, not by strangers."

"I'll make a note of that."

Devishi Tang was sitting in an overstuffed chair. Her clothes were of everyday appearance and mud stained from travel, making her somewhat out of keeping with the rest of the room, which was luxurious to the point of opulence. Clear glass windows offered views over the port. Thick rugs covered the floor. The furniture was well crafted and clearly made to last for generations. The Coppelli employee, Steph, was also present, hovering in the background.

Riki dropped into an empty chair.

"How did it go at the temple?" Devishi asked.

"Completely to script. Tanya should be dumped in the Militia lockup any time now. You're going to get a letter tonight, to hand-deliver to the Chief Consultant before you tell your grandmother that the Sisters lost Tanya."

"Great."

"Yup. And do you know what's even greater?"

"No."

"I can take all this off." Riki stood up again and stripped off first her wig, then the embroidered burgundy jacket and blue silk shirt, before starting to untie laces on the padding. Steph hurried over to assist.

"I've brought some unexciting clothes for you and Tanya to wear. They're in the bag over there." Devishi pointed to a worn holdall in the corner.

"Thanks. When did you get here?"

"Just before midday. I left the carriage at Salsport." Devishi stretched out her legs, yawning. "Anything else I need to know?"

"I think we've got a Corps agent as a tail."

"They're nosy little buggers, aren't they?"

"She might follow you back. Is she likely to hear that you drove down if she starts asking questions in Salsport?"

"No. The carriage and horses are in a family stable. No one will spill anything."

Riki glanced at Steph, who was currently loosening ties in a businesslike fashion. She was typical of the Coppelli employees Riki had met in Landfall, competent, loyal, and silent, unless she had something important to say. But of course, Isabel Coppelli would not surround herself with unreliable, loose-mouthed fools.

In a few more seconds, Riki was down to her underwear. She grinned her thanks to Steph and then knelt to rummage through the bag Devishi had brought. Suitably sized plain cotton shirt, trousers, and lightweight boots, all in neutral colors, were folded at the top. Meanwhile, Devishi had also started undressing and replacing her clothes with the far more costly outfit that Riki had just removed.

"I've booked you a room at the Old Tin Dog, down at the east end of the harbor. Give them the name of Babs Dunning," Devishi said once both women were seated again.

"Okay."

"But I think you might want to stay here and eat in this room with me and Steph. I can guarantee the food will be better. And there'll be less chance of you being spotted if you wait until after dark to slip out."

"You've talked me into it."

"And while I remember." Devishi went to another bag. "Here's a Militia release warrant for a Patricia Oduro."

Riki took the offered sheet. The last time she had seen it, the paper had been blank, except for Tanya's two fingerprints in faint boxes at the bottom. Now an official signed and stamped release warrant had been filled in around them, asserting full payment of all fines owning. Yet another example of penmanship from Isabel's skilled forger.

"Now for dinner." Devishi looked down at herself and sighed. "I guess since I'm the one wearing the clothes, it's my turn to be groveled over."

❖

Tanya kept up her litany of complaints as the four Guards hauled her through the doorway of the Militia station. "I can't stay here. My mom'll frigging—"

"Shut up." One of the Guards slapped the side of her head.

Tanya flinched away, ducking her ears below shoulder level. The repeated blows would have been annoying, except they proved she was not dreaming. Grandma Izzy's plans had worked. In just a few more minutes she would be out of the Guards' custody. Not by escaping, but by duping them into relinquishing her. Not yet free, but one huge step closer.

The militiawoman on duty at the station sat up straight. Judging by her bleary eyes, she had been sleeping. "What's up?"

"We've got a customer for your lockup."

"What's she done?"

"Drunk, abusive, and fighting."

"In the temple?" The militiawoman sounded astonished.

"Nah. Back in Landfall."

"So what's she doing down here?"

"The Consultant wanted to talk to her."

"Why?"

The Guard sergeant leaned over the seated militiawoman. "Her holiness didn't tell me. And I didn't ask. Now are you going to open your lockup so we can put her inside? Or are you going to sit here asking pointless questions all day?"

"But what are we going to do with her?"

"Hang on to her until your magistrate next calls by. Or until someone comes to claim her. Assuming anyone wants her."

"The magistrate ain't due for three weeks." However, the militiawoman had given in to the pressure and was on her feet, slipping the key to the lockup off the chain on her belt.

"Then you're going to have plenty of time to get to know her well."

The door swung open and Tanya was shoved inside. She landed on a pile of damp straw that was, presumably, her bed. The door thudded shut and the key turned in the lock. The sound was one that Tanya was getting to know well.

She looked around at her new quarters. The lockup was three meters wide and maybe four long. A piss bucket stood in the corner, though judging by the smell, most occupants had made other arrangements. Tanya's gaze drifted up. At the top of the wall was a small barred window, twenty centimeters square. Through it she could see a patch of blue sky. Tanya smiled. If nothing else, it was an improvement on the Corps dungeon.

Even at sunrise at the start of a perfect summer's day, the salt marshes presented a bleak, cold picture. Intelligence Corps Lieutenant Maz Turan stared across the expanse of reed beds, mud, and oily water. The breeze carried the smells of salt, rotting plants, and tar. She shivered and turned her attention to the dockside.

Various craft were making ready to depart, long, flat river barges and tall-masted cargo ships. Porters were trundling back and forth with their handcarts. However, the boat that interested her was the small rowing skiff that ferried foot passengers to Salsport. At three kilometers away, the village marked the nearest point on the mainland.

Several passengers were already seated, including the Coppelli grandchild, Devishi Tang, in her distinctive burgundy jacket. The servant was beside her. Maz Turan climbed down into the boat and took her place in the stern. This was the first time she had seen Devishi Tang up close. It was only by checking the log at the Pig and Whistle that she had found out her name.

Once the barge had passed the last town on the Liffy and Turan had known for sure that her quarry was going on to Southwater, she had ridden ahead and arrived several hours before the barge. She had followed the party to the temple gates and seen the Sisters and their Guards return to the docks. She had then followed the servant to the Pig and Whistle and got back to the temple gates in time to tail Devishi Tang also going to the inn. And now she was going to sit in the ferryboat back to Salsport with Tang and her servant.

One of the oarswomen dropped into the skiff, making it rock wildly. Her colleague loosened the moorings and threw the ropes to her before following. They took their seats and pushed off from the quay.

Lieutenant Turan leaned back, as if enjoying the sun on her face. Her eyes drifted to the temple above the town. She was pleased to be on her way back to Landfall, able to make a full report.

The heretic had been taken into the temple and left in the custody of the Sisters there. Asking questions would be a waste of time. On past experience, the Sisters would deny all knowledge. Colonel Zelenski would not be happy with the news. There was no hope of reclaiming the heretic for the Corps to question, although on the plus side, there was no chance of her ever escaping. It was a mixed result, but one thing was for certain—Tanya Coppelli would never be seen or heard of again.

CHAPTER FOURTEEN—THE FINAL TALLY

Five mornings later, Lieutenant Turan stood to attention in Zelenski's office in Landfall, or as close to attention as senior Intelligence Corps agents could be bothered with.

"Tanya Coppelli was deposited there?" Zelenski asked.

"Yes, ma'am. She was with them when they went into the Southwater temple, and they all left without her."

"You didn't make further inquiries at the temple?"

"I didn't think there'd be any point. And my instructions were not to make myself known."

"No. You're right. The Sisters will never as much as acknowledge the quarters are occupied." Zelenski sighed. "Do you know if Devishi Tang is back in Landfall yet?"

"No, ma'am. But I'd guess she's a ways behind. I was on the ferry from Southwater with her. She hired a carriage from the stables at Salsport, which are another Coppelli business. I watched her go, then picked up my horse and came on as quickly as I could, using relay posts. I passed her a few kilometers along the road out of Salsport, but didn't see her again."

"You did a good job."

"Thank you."

"You can go."

"Yes, ma'am."

Once the door was shut, Zelenski rubbed her forehead, considering the news. She had ordered the tail on the barge mainly out of curiosity. Zelenski knew she had lost in that particular game. There had been only a weak chance of the agent turning up proof that Coppelli and Bakara had conspired to set the heretic free. Even if the evidence had been forthcoming, Zelenski doubted that she would have been able to make use of it.

And the heretic had not been freed—quite the opposite. Some comfort could be had from knowing that she would never be able to infect anyone else with her poison. The Southwater quarters were nothing if not secure, but Zelenski would rather have had Tanya Coppelli in the cells below her, and the opportunity to extract every last scrap of information the woman knew.

The Southwater quarters were a bit of a surprise. Surely they were far too valuable a resource to be wasted on the unrepentant heretic. Why had Bakara agreed to it? What was the hold Isabel Coppelli had over her? Because there had to be something.

With all the lies and double-crossing, Zelenski was still very sure of one thing. Bakara had some secret crime on her conscience, and Isabel Coppelli knew what it was. Zelenski thought back to Bakara's guilty reaction when she had mentioned Consultant Joannou.

Zelenski groaned at the memory. That had been the bait in the trap, and she had swallowed it whole. The woman calling herself Marlena Azid had told the truth about Bakara having something to hide. It might be the only true thing she had said. She certainly was not who she claimed to be. Rather too late, Zelenski's agents had found out that Jean Azid had no nieces of the right age, and none she did have were named Marlena.

Isabel Coppelli was the one behind it all. But maybe Marlena Azid had revealed one other truth. There was no point going after the old rogue while she had the Chief Consultant in her pocket. First Bakara had to go, and then Coppelli would be without her defender.

But how?

Zelenski knew her position was precarious. She had been maneuvered into thinking her hand was stronger than it was, and then caught out, dangerously exposed, when she overplayed it. She was going to have to bide her time, go slowly, and be very sure before she moved against the Chief Consultant again. The first thing was to find out just what Bakara's guilty secret was.

Bakara was not at all like her predecessor, Chief Consultant Pereira. Pereira had been an unwavering enemy to the heretics. She had understood that the Corps was the only force who could stop the spread of foul lies, and that mercy was not a virtue when the soul of the planet was at stake. Better to cut out the cancer than to let the whole body die.

Zelenski's face furrowed in thought. Bakara was soft on heresy. She and Zelenski had fought many times on the issue. Was that the clue to Bakara's secret? Surely Bakara was not a sympathizer. No. Zelenski shook her head. That was beyond what she could bring herself to believe. However, some clue lay there. She knew it. Joannou had been set in the same mold as Pereira.

The Goddess would be better served when Bakara was gone and a true defender of the faith was put in her place. Getting rid of the weak, flawed Chief Consultant was her duty to the Goddess, and no matter how long it took, she would not fail. Zelenski smiled grimly. After all, she had the resources and she had the time.

Chief Consultant Bakara read the letter once more, then folded it and placed it in the middle of her desk. With her fingertips, she aligned the bottom edge with the grain in the wood, as if by making it lie straight, she could straighten her thoughts. The outside looked so innocuous, clear except for her name in Consultant Sharif's bold script. The contents were problematic, both in what they said and in the implications that followed.

Colonel Zelenski had double-crossed her and had not handed over Isabel Coppelli's granddaughter. But had Zelenski wanted the switch to be discovered, or had she been hoping that it might go unnoticed? From the letter, it was clear that only Consultant Sharif's prudence in checking with an Imprinter had exposed the deception.

Bakara tried to think it through logically. Whatever scandal Isabel Coppelli had uncovered, obviously it genuinely scared Zelenski, otherwise the colonel would not have given up the letters and map. Yet, regardless of whether Zelenski thought the swap with the look-alike would be spotted, she had been prepared to take the risk.

Bakara rubbed her forehead. The problem was that she had no idea what threats had been used on Zelenski. What if it was something that would incriminate her as well? Isabel Coppelli had been very careful not to reveal the details.

When Isabel heard about her granddaughter she would be furious, and Zelenski would surely be her first target. But who else might be brought down by the infighting? Isabel had charged the Sisterhood with keeping her granddaughter safe. Would she feel that she had been let down?

Bakara sighed and leaned back in her chair. The plotting and second-guessing was sending her head into a whirl. Yet one thing was clear. Colonel Zelenski had become a major problem, but she was a problem that could be dealt with far more easily if she was off guard. If she thought she had gotten away with her ruse. Whichever way Bakara looked at it, events would be better controlled if Isabel Coppelli did not find out what had happened to her granddaughter, and to this end, Consultant Sharif had made one practical suggestion.

Bakara lifted the small bell off her desk and rang it.

A white-robed Sister opened the door. "Yes, Chief Consultant?"

"Send the Coppelli representative in."

"Yes, Chief Consultant."

Devishi Tang appeared shortly. The young woman, in her rich burgundy jacket, marched to a spot a respectful distance from the desk and bowed. "You wanted to see me, Chief Consultant?"

"Yes. I've read this letter from my beloved Sister in Southwater. She informs me that the arrangements made for your cousin didn't work out as planned."

Devishi Tang looked politely attentive, but said nothing.

"Have you told anyone of this?"

"No, Chief Consultant. I arrived back in Landfall only an hour ago."

"And what are your plans?"

"I'll report to my grandmother this evening before returning to my home in Eastford tomorrow."

Bakara nodded thoughtfully. "Consultant Sharif informs me that you have little sympathy with your cousin."

"She's a heretic. What more need be said?"

"You're not distressed by her disappearance?"

"No, Chief Consultant, not personally."

"Even though your cousin might already be dead, and if not, then she soon will be?"

"I won't be wasting tears over her."

"But your grandmother might."

"I fear my grandmother has given in to misguided sentimentality.

Old women can become overindulgent with their grandchildren and blind to their faults."

Bakara took a breath, wanting to pick her words carefully. "So I ask myself, what good would be achieved by letting your grandmother know of what happened?"

"Chief Consultant?"

"At best, your grandmother will suffer needless grief on behalf of someone who doesn't deserve it. At worst, she'll be drawn into direct conflict with the Intelligence Corps. Even if your cousin isn't dead yet, and your grandmother secures her release, it will only bring more ignominy to the Coppelli name."

"But my grandmother..."

"I think we're agreed that your grandmother's judgment is lacking in this matter. Rest assured I won't let it drop, but I'll act prudently and in accordance with the will of the Goddess. I only ask you to leave this to me and don't involve your grandmother. You needn't tell a direct lie. Say that the affair has concluded satisfactorily, and your cousin is where she should be. A small distortion, for your grandmother's peace of mind as much as anything."

Devishi Tang's eyes fixed on the floor and her forehead furrowed. "I'm...not sure."

"I would offer prayers on your behalf, for a compassionate and dutiful granddaughter."

"The prayers of the Chief Consultant are a blessing I don't deserve, but..."

"And give you a gift of two hundred dollars..."

Devishi Tang looked half persuaded.

"...now, and a further two hundred after you return home."

"You're most generous. And you're right. Why upset my grandmother, when nothing can be gained by it?"

"That is most obliging of you, my child."

"I'm pleased to be of help, Chief Consultant."

Bakara relaxed. The first issue was resolved. After a few more rounds of polite exchanges, Devishi Tang was escorted from the room in the company of a Sister who had been given instructions concerning the money.

Alone again, Bakara left her desk and went to stare through the window. The Guards' parade ground was immediately below. The hard-packed earth shimmered in the heat of the afternoon sun. Directly opposite stood the Intelligence Corps headquarters. Bakara's eyes narrowed. She could only assume that Tanya Coppelli was still in the cells beneath it—if she was still alive.

Bakara's eyes moved on. Beyond the compound lay the roofs of the city, and beyond them lay the rest of the world—the world that the one true Goddess, Celaeno, had chosen for her daughters. Behind her mask, Bakara grimaced. Guiding this world was her sacred duty, and Bakara knew she was the only one who could ensure that the will of the Goddess prevailed.

Bakara thought of her predecessor, Chief Consultant Pereira. She had been a devout woman, resolute in her commitment to wipe out the heretics. In Bakara's opinion, far too resolute and dogmatic. Pereira was the one who had allowed the Intelligence Corps to break free from the Guards' command structure, so the Corps colonel reported directly to the Chief Consultant. She had allowed them the license to act outside the rule of the law, and the Corps had taken full advantage.

Yet, with hindsight, many of the Corps' actions proved counterproductive. Rather than crushing opposition, indiscriminate brutality had won sympathy for the heretics. Faithful daughters of the Goddess, who had no interest in the blasphemous lies, would sing songs glorifying the heretics' leaders and turn a blind eye to their agents. To have any hope of defeating the heretics, the Sisterhood must keep the support of the ordinary citizens. This would mean reining in the Intelligence Corps.

Colonel Zelenski had been a protégée of Chief Consultant Pereira. Even before the current train of events, she and Bakara had been on a collision course. The fanatical colonel could not see that her ruthless methods were the heretics' best recruitment tool. Zelenski clearly thought she should act more and more aggressively until the heretics were destroyed, and refused to believe that the common mass of citizens would revolt against the Sisterhood long before that point was reached.

If the Sisterhood were to remain as guardians to the souls of Celaeno's daughters, then Zelenski had to go—permanently. Bakara closed her eyes in regret. The battle between them was now too personal for any other solution, and she must move quickly and decisively. Yet not to a public court-martial. The situation required something quieter, using the power invested in her as the earthly representative of the Goddess. All that was then needed was to pick the right officer to carry out the orders, before Zelenski had a chance to make her next move.

Bakara went to the candlelit shrine and knelt to ask forgiveness for what she must do.

❖

Militia Corporal Jay Delores was enjoying a quiet snooze when she was awakened by pounding on the street door. She lumbered to her feet and swung the hatch open. A small, lightly built woman was standing on the cobbles outside. Her face was screwed into an angry scowl. Her body was swaying as if she was too wound up to keep still.

"What do you want?"

"Have you got my frigging sister in there?"

"I don't know. What's your sister's name?"

"Pat Oduro. Patricia. 'Cause if she ain't here after I've come all this way, I'm going to fucking kill someone."

"Yes. Calm down. She's here."

The news did not make Oduro's sister look any happier. "Hoo-fucking-ray."

"You want to talk to her?"

"I want to kick her frigging ass."

"I'll have to let her out before you can do that. And at the moment, she stays put until the magistrate deals with her."

"Yeah, yeah, it's already been seen to back in Landfall. I've got the warrant for her release." The angry woman pulled a sheet from her pocket and waved it in Delores's face through the hatch.

The Militiawoman grabbed the paper. "Why didn't you say sooner?"

"You didn't think I'd come all the way from frigging Landfall just to shout at her through the keyhole, did you?"

Corporal Delores ignored the woman and tilted the paper to catch the evening sunlight. The official stamp and magistrate's signature were at the top, and two fingerprints, taken at the time of arrest, were at the bottom left. Everything else was in order, detailing the payment of all outstanding fines. Delores stepped back and opened the door.

"Come in. I'll get her out of the lockup for you."

As soon as she was inside, the short woman raised her voice. "Oi, Pat. You there?"

"Yeah." A voice answered indistinctly from the lockup.

"What the fucking hell you doing down here?"

"Weren't my fault."

"It never is. Hey, Officer?"

Corporal Delores had the key off her belt and was inserting it in the lock. "Yeah?"

"Why was she bought all the way down here? What sort of fucking game was it? I thought someone was having a laugh when they told me."

"Somebody wanted to talk to her."

"What frigging nutter was that?"

Delores faced the short woman. "It was the Consultant at the temple. And if you don't want to join your sister in the lockup you should watch your mouth."

"Oh. Sorry. Didn't know."

Corporal Delores stood in the open doorway. Currently the cell held two occupants. The sailor who had been carried in after a heavy lunchtime drinking session was still sleeping, curled in a corner. Her rasping snores continued unbroken. The Militiawoman glanced at her. She was the usual run of patron for the Southwater lockup. Most likely the drunken sailor would stay there until the ship's captain bailed her out in time to depart.

Oduro was a different matter. Something about her did not fit, and that worried Delores. She had no idea why the Consultant had wanted to talk to the woman, and she did not want to know. Oduro acted and spoke like a common thug, yet her eyes moved with a sharp intelligence. In the six days she had been in the lockup, she had given no information about her family, friends, or job, and that was unusual. Most women of her type talked nonstop. Some needed threats to make them shut up. Delores sensed nasty secrets lurking, and the sooner the woman was gone, the better.

"Okay, Oduro. You can come out."

The prisoner emerged, blinking in the light of the main room.

"By the Goddess, look at you. What a fucking state. Did you go out in your best clothes?" the sister crowed.

"Sort of."

"Well they ain't anything to talk about now."

"Weren't my fault. The lockup's a pig sty."

"You're the stupid pig."

An argument was clearly about to break out. Corporal Delores cut in. "You can squabble about clothes all the way back to Landfall if you want. I need your prints on this and then you can both get out of my station."

Oduro grunted sullenly and stumbled to the desk in the corner. Delores laid the paper and the inkpad before her and watched her put her release fingerprints in the bottom right hand boxes. By the rules, the releasing officer was supposed to check the match using an eyeglass. Delores settled for squinting in the last of the fading sunlight. The match looked close enough. In fact, she did not care whether it was or not. She wanted the two sisters gone before a fight started.

"Can she go now?" the small sister asked. Oduro just stood, scowling.

"Yeah. The pair of you. Shove off."

"Come on, Pat."

The sisters disappeared into the street, but their voices could still be heard.

"I don't know why I frigging bother with you."

"Weren't my fault."

Corporal Delores shut the door and returned to her chair. Things were back to normal and already she was feeling happier. The peace of the Southwater Militia station was broken only by snores from the drunken sailor in the lockup. Smiling, Jay Delores lifted her feet onto the desk and closed her eyes.

❖

Devishi Tang lifted her brandy glass and swirled the amber liquid around. The rich, sweet aroma was nearly as satisfying as the taste, but not quite. She took a sip and sighed with contentment. It was good to be off the road and back to the comforts of the Coppelli mansion.

The sun was now low in the sky, and the enclosed courtyard was in shade, pleasant after the heat of the day. The air was full of the scent of flowers and the sound of splashing water from the fountain. Devishi hooked her ankle around the leg of another chair and pulled it forward to use as a footstool. She took a second sip of brandy and smiled at her grandmother.

"I was amazed Bakara went as far as paying me money to keep quiet."

"Yes. That was a pleasant surprise. To tell the truth, I wasn't sure she would even decide to hide the story from me. On one level, it wouldn't have made too much difference. But I'm pleased with how it's turned out. It means she's making her own plans to deal with Zelenski."

"Any idea what those plans are likely to be?"

"She's going to have the colonel killed, of course."

Devishi pursed her lips thoughtfully. She was surprised not by the casual way her grandmother treated the topic of violent death—such things were hardly a rare occurrence in the unforgiving world of Landfall politics—but that the Chief Consultant should be the one employing the tactic.

"You're sure of that?"

"Oh yes. Bakara believes Zelenski stole incriminating documents, used them to bully and blackmail her, deliberately defied her orders, and then double-crossed her. She's going to think Zelenski is totally out of control. And Bakara's going to want her out of the way before she causes more trouble. Remember, they didn't even start out as allies."

"Killing Zelenski seems a bit extreme. Although it will cheer a lot of people up." Devishi knew her words were an understatement. The head of the Intelligence Corps was hated across the Homelands.

"It's the best way to make sure that nobody else ever gets to hear what Bakara thinks Zelenski has found out. It's just Zelenski's tough luck that Bakara is blaming her for all sorts of things that she hasn't done"—Isabel paused, frowning—"yet."

"Yet? You think she will?"

"Zelenski is shrewd enough to unravel our plot, given time, and she doesn't give up. She'll dig down to the truth. And once she gets there, she could be very dangerous. Fortunately for us, she isn't going to get the time." Isabel turned her face to the fountain in the middle of the courtyard. Her expression showed no trace of concern or regret.

"You're sure?"

"Very. If Bakara was planning some other fate for Zelenski, she'd have brought me in to help. Whether she's consciously aware of it or not, the reason she paid you to keep quiet was so it would be a private matter between her and the Goddess."

"I was expecting the Chief Consultant to be a bit more"—Devishi waved her free hand, hunting for the word she wanted—"forgiving, unworldly."

"Don't be misled by all their talk of love. If there's one lesson you should take from this, it's that the Sisterhood and the Guards are the most dangerous enemies you can have, because they can always convince themselves the Goddess wants them to do whatever it is they're doing. They see compromise as a betrayal of their faith."

"An all-or-nothing game?"

"Indeed." Isabel reached out and plucked a bloom from a nearby bush. "If someday you come to sit in my place and play games with the Sisterhood, make sure you have every step charted and know exactly where you're going to end up. If you can't guarantee being on the winning side, then throw in your hand before the stakes get too high."

"At the moment, I'm still taking lessons from the best player in Landfall." Devishi smiled at her grandmother. "You worked it all out very neatly. Tanya is free, but the Sisters think the Corps have got her, the Corps think the Sisters have, and Zelenski will be gone before anyone gets the chance to swap notes. The Chief Consultant is further indebted to the family. And between them, they've paid us one thousand four hundred and sixty dollars."

Isabel Coppelli raised the flower to her nose and inhaled the scent, while her eyes danced in amusement. "Oh yes. It never hurts to turn in a profit."

❖

High tide was covering the marshland. Only the tips of reeds and the tallest sand banks broke the surface of the water. The sun was setting behind the temple, casting a golden glow over the waves. Thin bands of purple cloud lined the horizon. From the activity on the decks of two seagoing ships, it was plain that they were preparing to set sail on the high water.

Tanya trekked down to the harbor beside Riki, savoring the simple action of walking under the open sky without Guards around her or her hands bound. She was out of prison. She was free. She could relax—almost.

Tanya knew Riki would have arranged passage for them and had deliberately left getting her out of the lockup until the last possible moment. The Intelligence Corps had assuredly followed them to Southwater. Colonel Zelenski would not have given up on her so easily. Grandma Izzy had thought the Corps would not hang around for long, once the Sisters and Devishi left, but there was always a risk they had left an agent in place.

Even though the lengthy stay in the lockup had not been pleasant, the less time she was on the streets of Southwater, the less chance of being spotted. Who thinks of reporting someone already in a lockup? If she and Riki could just get onto the ship and have it cast off, she could feel truly safe, but not until then. Tanya clamped her jaw as the fears resurfaced. Surely she would not fail now. Her eyes drifted to the reed beds. If anything went wrong, she would throw herself in the water. She would rather drown in quicksand than return to the Corps dungeon.

Tanya's gaze touched briefly on Riki, strolling next to her. Abruptly, Tanya's pulse rate soared and it had nothing to do with fear. Riki was all spark and audacity. Tanya could feel the energy radiating off her. Riki's head and shoulders were back, her bearing nine-tenths swagger. Her grin showed an utter lack of concern for the Guards, the Corps, the Sisters, or the rest of the world. It was not just a façade of bravado. Tanya had come to realize it went far deeper. Yet surely Riki's heart was not untouchable. If the devil-may-care rebel could be made to care, what expression would Riki's face hold in the heat of passion?

Tanya caught her breath even as a crooked flagstone made her stumble. She had to concentrate. Falling over would be an idiotic blunder when she was trying to avoid attention.

They reached the gangplank to one ship readying for departure. A sailor on deck waved to Riki. "You found her, then."

"Propping up a bar, like I said," Riki called back.

The sailor laughed and returned to coiling her rope. Riki strolled up the gangplank. Tanya followed, reaching the deck, leaving Southwater.

"I stored our stuff over there." Riki pointed to a couple of bags. "Do you want to grab a clean shirt?"

Tanya considered what she was wearing. Grandma Izzy had provided new clothes in Landfall. The outfit selected for the evening the Corps reclaimed her had been chosen to look suitably costly for a

Coppelli scion when clean in the temple, and suitably inconspicuous after two weeks in a cell when on the Southwater docks.

"I think I'm okay. What do you think?"

Riki gave her a serious appraisal. "You're right. You'll attract less attention as you are, rather than if you start stripping off."

Tanya's pulse leapt again as Riki's eyes swept up and down her. Her knees felt wobbly. She pointed to a low crate on the seaward side. "I'm going to sit down."

"Okay."

Tanya staggered over and collapsed. Even before she was settled, she heard a wooden clattering as the gangplank was hauled in. Either Riki's timing was perfect, or the crew had been waiting for them.

Tanya raised her eyes. Sailors were climbing through rigging overhead, loosening sails. She felt the ship sway. Steadily the movement became more pronounced. The ship rode a soft wind, carrying them out to sea. Tanya looked back. Already ten meters of water separated the ship from the harbor wall.

They had left Southwater.

She was free.

The ship drifted on, slow and sedate, down the channel between sandbanks, moving into deeper water. Tanya looked back. The temple crouched atop the rocky island, overshadowing the town like the Sisterhood overshadowed the Homelands. Yet already it was fading into the dusk.

She was free.

Tanya's gaze moved back to the boat. On the other side of the deck, Riki was laughing with a sailor. Tanya remembered her grandmother's words. *She is a troublemaker, and she'll always be making trouble for someone.*

Riki was making trouble for her at the moment—the most pleasant type of trouble. Yet Tanya knew it could lead her into making a complete fool of herself. They had been enemies in Westernfort. Tanya no longer felt that way, but how did Riki feel about her? Despite their daily meetings, they had never shared a private conversation. Always the Sister on duty had been watching, an inhibiting presence, even if she could not overhear what was said.

Supposing Riki got bored on the journey and wanted to stir things up. Without Guards as a target, there would be no one else to annoy.

Was Riki about to revert to being a pain in the ass? Riki had said she was on Tanya's side. Did that still apply? Would she want to hold hands again?

Tanya groaned and closed her eyes. *I've got to get a grip,* she told herself. Her head and heart were all over the place. They had a long trip ahead together, without anyone else as distraction. Tanya took a deep breath, unsure whether the ripples inside her were due to worry or expectation.

Unexpectedly, a laugh bubbled up inside her. Oh yes. She was certainly free, if such trivial matters were the main thing on her mind. Tanya opened her eyes and looked from Riki to the temple, fading into the dark, and then back to Riki.

She was free.

Part Three

Homecoming

CHAPTER FIFTEEN—INTO THE WILDLANDS

The coastline was an undulating red band of striated sandstone cliffs, laced with a ragged tracery of trees at the top and a white fringe of surf at the bottom. Riki leaned against the ship's railing, watching kilometer after kilometer slip by. Overhead, a stiff breeze was filling the sails. The prow sliced through blue-green waves, sending up plumes of salt spray that glittered in the sunlight.

The marshy lowlands around Southwater were four days behind as they reached the midway point on the journey to Coldmouth. The ship's route had rarely strayed more than ten kilometers from the shore, and never out of sight of it, except for the morning they had awoken to a dense sea fog. The sailors had taken in the sails until the sun had burnt off the mist and they could again see where they were going. The captain had maps, as well as star charts for guidance, but the coast was the surest navigational aid.

Riki turned and rested her back against the rail. On the other side of the ship was nothing but sea. How far did it go? What land would you reach if you kept sailing due south? Nobody knew, but someday, someone would go to find out. Riki smiled. The thought of adventure was exciting, discovering places no woman had ever seen before, but she would not be the one who sailed off over the horizon. Her discoveries would be made on foot. She was a Ranger, not a sailor.

Riki's smile faded. Was she still a Ranger? If she had stayed in Westernfort for the trial, a dishonorable discharge would hardly have been necessary, although Captain Coppelli might have insisted on it for administrative reasons. Had she been formally discharged in her absence? Not that it mattered. Once Tanya told her story, a full reinstatement would be a certainty. Riki chewed her lip. Should she accept it? Was that what she wanted?

With hindsight, joining the Rangers had not been a wise move. She was never going to fit in with obeying orders—not when breaking rules was so much more fun. Isabel Coppelli had offered her a job. The idea was tempting. Riki had loved every second of outmaneuvering Colonel Zelenski. Perhaps she could really take over the role once fulfilled by Jean Azid.

Riki's plans went as far as getting to Ginasberg, speaking with her mother, telling what she had learned from Jan, and then apologizing for all the years of being an utter little shit. Once she had done that, what reason would she have to stay with the heretics? Yet if she went, would she miss the wilderness unbearably? What did she want to do with her life? Riki sighed. Half-worked-out schemes bounced around in her head, but she was nowhere close to reaching any conclusion.

The sound of laughter drew Riki's attention back to the ship. Tanya was on the aft deck, chatting with the other passengers. The conversation was obviously amusing and friendly. Tanya was sprawled casually, propped on one elbow, with a smile lighting her face. Riki felt a sudden tense knot squeeze her stomach. She wished she knew what Tanya thought of her. Even more than plans for the future, this had been scrambling Riki's head.

The ship was small, less than twenty meters long, with a crew of five and two other passengers on board. All space below deck was taken up with cargo. The crew and passengers slept on deck, with only the awning for shelter. In the hot summer nights and the absence of rain, this was no hardship. However, it meant that she and Tanya were unable to talk without risk of being overheard, nor would they, until they disembarked.

Once they reached Coldmouth, acquired ponies and supplies, and headed off into the Wildlands, then there would be just the two of them together for thirty to forty days. They would be able to talk all they wanted. What was she going to say to Tanya? And what would Tanya say to her?

The tension in Riki's guts tightened. For the first time since she and her mother had fled the Homelands, she would be spending time in close contact with someone her own age who just conceivably thought that she was okayish. Riki fixed her eyes on the horizon. Could she remember how to conduct a normal, pleasant conversation?

And of course, it was not merely a conversation she wanted from

Tanya—or maybe it was. Riki winced, exasperated with herself. Her emotions were taking her into unknown territory. Her reputation as the town's bad girl had ensured that. Fewer than a dozen girls within three years of her age had lived at Ginasberg, and all were either too frightened or too disapproving to associate with her. Riki had been the outsider, taunted, demonized, or ignored.

She had been living in Ginasberg for three months when Beth asked her for a kiss. The proposal had been more challenging than seductive, and had not been helped by Beth following it up with, "Pam Collins has dared me to." Even so, with hindsight Riki wondered if she ought to have said yes, since it was the only offer she had ever received.

What chance was there of things changing now? Was it really just her reputation that had scared people off? Exactly how did Tanya feel? What clues should she look for? Supposing Tanya was interested, what then? Was it better to bluff things out, or admit a total lack of experience? It would be easier if Tanya ignored her, like everyone else had done. Riki's palms were getting sweaty. She wiped them on her legs and then looked at Tanya, lounging on deck.

The other passengers were still talking, but Tanya's attention had drifted away and she was staring in Riki's direction. For a moment, their eyes locked and Riki felt a physical jolt. The deck beneath her feet bucked. Had the ship hit a rock? Riki grasped the railing to stop herself from stumbling. Abruptly Tanya turned back to her companions.

Riki looked out to sea, trying to act relaxed, trying to act like her heart had not just jumped up her throat, but every doubt and fear resurged through her head. *Oh shit, girl. You are going to make such a fool of yourself.*

❖

Tanya stood on the head of the gangplank and viewed the scene. Coldmouth was a small town at the mouth of the Coldwater River. The farms and towns along the river formed the western edge of the Homelands. At its nearest, Landfall was over six hundred kilometers east. The overland journey by cart took a month in good weather, far longer in bad. Produce bound for the city could get there quicker and cheaper if shipped down the Coldwater, along the coast, and up the

Liffy. The port at Coldmouth was thus the counterpoint of the one at Southwater, and like Southwater, its environs were uninviting, but rather than marsh, the region around Coldmouth was dry.

Rolling sand dunes stretched along the coast on either side and extended inland for as far as Tanya could see. The town looked to be fighting an unending battle with windblown sand. The Coldwater River snaked wide and languid through the red landscape. Its delta was over a dozen kilometers wide, sliced with sandbars. The town was built beside one of the deeper channels that allowed seagoing vessels to dock. At the far end of the quay stood a tall tower, where a beacon burned at night. The shifting sandbanks were a serious shipping hazard and no captain wanted to get too close during the hours of darkness.

The harbor was swarming with activity, as was the large adjacent market, crammed with traders' booths. Solid warehouses lined the surrounding streets and beyond them, the roofs of houses ended in an irregular line where the dunes began. A row of pollarded trees ran around the perimeter of the market. Their twisted branches formed a loose web, providing some shade for those beneath, although most of the market was exposed to the harsh August sunlight.

The ship had docked on the morning tide. Despite the early hour, the temperature was climbing. Tanya could taste sand and salt in the air. Riki had already disembarked and was weaving her way between the crates, sacks, barrels, sailors, porters, and carts that crowded the quay. Tanya waved good-bye to the crew and hurried to catch up.

Coldwater was smaller than Westernfort, yet still it felt alien to Tanya, a town of strangers where she recognized no faces. The screaming babble of voices matched the frenetic pace. Everyone was in a hurry and nobody was willing to wait their turn. The only order was that the quickest and strongest went first. However, Riki sauntered along with a happy grin, dodging obstacles without breaking stride.

Riki moved as if dancing, carefree, her body always perfectly balanced, adjusting smoothly to the swirl of activity around her. Hearing anything over the uproar was impossible, but Tanya was sure, even were there utter silence, Riki's footfall would make no sound. It was the way she slipped through the forest, silent and swift, leaving no trace of her passing. Tanya dropped back a step so she could study Riki—her shape and the way she flowed. Tanya's eyes started at Riki's shoulders and slowly sank lower.

Without warning, Riki pulled up beside a porter who was loading a cart with sacks. Tanya barely managed to avoid running into the pair. She took a small step back.

"Where's the Coppelli offices?" Riki shouted to be heard.

"Over on Southside." The porter jerked with her thumb.

"Thanks."

After more hectic minutes of battling through the scrum of bodies, they arrived at their destination. Riki pushed open the door and stepped through. Tanya followed, pleased to escape the noise and chaos. Yet, even here, three women were having a loud argument about a delivery of wine. At last, an agreement on "first thing tomorrow" was reached and two women left.

The other turned to face them. "What do you want?"

"Are you the forewoman?" Riki asked.

"Yes. So what do you want?" The forewoman was clearly still riled after her battle over the wine. Her tone was combative.

Riki pulled a note from her pocket and handed it over. As she read it, the forewoman's expression went from irate to respectful. She looked up.

"Ah, yes. Right. How can I help you?"

Riki smiled. "We need three ponies. Two saddled, one as pack. Sound and healthy, but nothing that will attract attention when we ride out on them. And enough supplies for forty days. Trail kits. Blankets, waterproof canvas, flint and tinder."

"Weapons?"

Riki glanced at Tanya. "What do you think? Will trail knives be enough, or do you want a bow?"

"A small bow wouldn't hurt, and a sheaf of arrows."

The warehouse forewoman nodded. "Very good. When do you need it by?"

"The sooner the better."

"Will two hours be okay?"

"That'll do fine."

"And would you like to wait somewhere more comfortable?"

Riki grinned. "Why not?"

The forewoman lead them to another room clearly intended to impress business contacts. Sounds of the market were a muted background drone. Brightly colored rugs covered the floor in reds and blues. The furniture was elegant and arranged for effect. Open windows overlooked a tiny courtyard garden. Wine, water, and sweet brandy stood ready at the side.

"Help yourself to whatever you want. I'll have food sent in." The forewoman ducked out of the room.

Riki poured herself a glass of wine and sank into a pile of silk cushions on a wicker chair. "Your grandmother certainly knows how to write a note to her employees."

Tanya dithered between the wine and water before also selecting wine and settling in another chair. "She's had a lot of practice."

Tanya took a sip and then stared at the ripples on the surface, unsure what to say next. She and Riki had been together for eight days on the boat and had met a dozen times in the temple, but never before had they spoken without anyone to overhear or observe.

So what should she say to Riki? Make a dry observation about the irony that Riki's breezy disregard for authority, which made her so infuriating in Westernfort, was so attractive when the authority took the form of the Sisterhood and the Guards? Maybe point out that the difference between an insolent smirk and a friendly grin was a matter of perspective, and with her current perspective, Riki's grin made her knees go weak?

Should she talk about the nights in the temple, when she had lain awake, wishing that Riki was beside her? Tanya took another sip of wine. It was all far too blatant. She might as well come straight out with, *Tonight, when we make camp, how about we share blankets?*

Tanya swallowed the wine. She could always just talk about the weather. Or she could start off mumbling vaguely and see where it got her. Tanya licked her lips and leaned forward, but at that moment, the door opened and a girl came in carrying a large platter of fruit, bread, cheese, and sliced meats.

"Please, ma'ams. Rodgers told me to bring this in to you."

"Thank you."

The girl deposited the food and left. Tanya sighed and sank back in her chair. There was no rush. A long journey lay ahead. She did not have to say anything now—much easier to wait until they had relaxed and were sure of no interruptions. She did not want to risk saying the wrong thing.

❖

From Coldmouth, a trail led north through the dunes, marked by tall posts. The shifting sands would soon cover any trace of a road, but by following the line of posts, a traveler could take a direct route across the changing landscape, without becoming lost and running in circles. The route was shorter and safer than the riverbank, with its loops and mud sinks.

Sounds of town and port had faded long before they forded the last narrow distributary of the Coldwater delta, but the breeze off the sea still whispered over the sand. The dunes ahead had a patchy cover of long grass and low, clinging vines. Overhead the sun was approaching its zenith. Shadows were foreshortened, falling directly under the horses' hooves.

Riki glanced at Tanya, riding beside her. She had been subdued since leaving the boat, scarcely saying a word. Was it due to anxiety? Was she worried they might get stopped at the point of leaving the Homelands?

Riki opened her mouth, then closed it again. In truth, they had not spoken much on the ship either, mainly socializing with the other passengers and crew. Was it that Tanya did not like her company, and now that it was just the two of them, she had nothing to say?

The top of the next dune gave a view ahead. A few kilometers away the first scattered trees clawed a hold on the land, twisted dawn firs, the same species as in the marketplace, although here growing to their natural height. A huge loop in the river glittered to the west.

Riki cleared her throat. "Your grandmother and I discussed the route to Westernfort."

"And?"

"There were two options. Normally, people go for the shortest distance through the Wildlands. We could go upriver, until we're due east of Westernfort, but I think we'd do better heading off from here and skirting around the bottom of the Longstop range. It'll be quicker. I didn't mention it before in case we were overheard."

"Do you know the region?"

"No. But I won't get lost. Is that okay with you?"

Tanya nodded. "Sure."

"This trail fords the river ten kilometers north of here. Once we've crossed, we can turn west."

"Okay."

"We'll also be way south of anywhere the Guards go. So there's no risk of running into them."

"Yep."

"You're not still worried about the Guards, are you?"

"No. Like you said, they won't be down here."

"Right."

As conversations went, it was far from scintillating. Riki clenched her jaw. If the silence was not due to worry about the Guards, the only other option was that Tanya simply did not want to talk. Presumably this in turn meant Tanya's thoughts about her went along the lines of, *Thanks for rescuing me. I no longer think of you as a pain in the ass, merely a dull ache. Now let's rush back to Westernfort so I can meet my mothers and you can start calling me ma'am again.* But Riki knew she was being unfair. Just because they were no longer enemies did not mean Tanya had to count her as a bosom buddy, or anything else.

Riki averted her face, while working to keep her expression unconcerned. She wanted to hold Tanya's hand again—or she thought that maybe she did. Regardless, it was quite obvious that Tanya would not want to hold hers. Beneath the regret, Riki was not surprised to feel an inkling of relief. Nothing else made her quite so nervous as the thought that Tanya might want to be more than friendly.

And nervous was not too strong a word. *It's absurd. I'm more scared of Tanya than I was of Colonel Zelenski.* Riki derided herself. *Maybe I should deliberately do something stupid tonight, then she can put me back on her list of people she'd like to throttle, and we'll be on familiar ground again.*

The idea was ridiculous but tempting.

❖

The sand dunes were eventually lost under a thicker covering of trees. The terrain started to rise and the underlying bedrock broke through in places, revealing more of the striated red sandstone. The soil was darker and richer. Dawn firs were interspersed with broadleaf trees, mainly tiger oak and hillash. Dover fern formed most of the ground cover. Tanya grinned, remembering claims it was named that because you came across it over and over and over again.

They had seen no one since leaving Coldmouth, apart from the crew of a passing barge, when they forded the river. This region was so sparsely populated it could hardly count as the Homelands. The town of Coldmouth was an isolated outpost, required only because deep-drafted ships could not sail upriver to the regions where farming was a practical proposition.

Tanya took a deep breath of woodland air. She was back in the Wildlands, where she belonged. She had seen Landfall, admittedly not under the best of circumstances, but enough. She had no wish to see more. Meeting Grandma Izzy had been the best part. She would have liked to have spent more time with her elderly relative, but even were it safe, she would not want to face the noise, crowds, and alienation of the city again. Tanya had not realized how much she would miss ordinary things like trees and open sky.

A bird perched, head height on a dawn fir, too concerned with the berries held in its wingclaws to break off chewing as they passed. Tanya twisted in her saddle.

"Is that a chippit?"

Riki glanced back. "Looks a bit like it, but its tail is too short. And it hasn't got the yellow bars under its eyes."

"That's what I thought. I wonder what it is."

"When we get to Ginasberg, we can ask Ash O'Neil. She'll know, if anyone does."

"If she doesn't, do I get to name it?"

Riki laughed. "If you want."

Tanya straightened and looked forward, intrigued by thoughts of the journey ahead. The route would take them across the Wildlands, seeing places nobody had ever been before. Who knew what they would find? And there was nobody better to travel with. Tanya had complete faith in Riki's wilderness skills. When Riki said she would not get lost, she had not been boasting.

Tanya glanced at her companion. Riki was even more at home in the Wildlands than she was. Yet Riki was not out of place in the Homelands. She could play the Ranger or the city hustler with equal ease. Tanya's eyes were caught by the sight of Riki's hands, noting their precise grip on the reins. Her fingers were like the rest of her—small and agile, in constant motion, yet appearing relaxed by virtue of always being in the right spot. Tanya felt a blush rise on her cheeks as she realized where her thoughts were heading. She looked away.

They had not spoken much on the trail. The debate about the chippit had been the first words they had exchanged in ages. When they made camp would be the time to talk. Tanya felt tense. What would Riki want to say? And how would she respond if Tanya said what she wanted?

How much of Riki's behavior in Landfall had been an act? Riki had worked to free her, but admitted she had personal reasons. She claimed she was on Tanya's side, but was that only because the Guards were a common enemy? Would she want to be friends? Even if she did, would she be interested in anything more?

The sinking sun shone directly in Tanya's face. They would be making camp in another hour or so. Then would come the answers. Tanya caught her lip in her teeth. She was going to be so disappointed if Riki said no, but what reason did she have to expect any other answer?

They had made a small campfire to cook over, but in the warm night, it was not needed for heat and they had let it burn down to glowing embers. Stars were splashed across the black sky. The hard edge of their brightness was softened by Hardie, rising near to full in the east. Riki rested her arms across her raised knees and stared over the landscape. A light wind ruffled the trees, making the world ripple in a blue haze under the moonlight. No other lights shone out. They were alone in the Wildlands.

The ponies were grazing on the banks of a stream. The running water and the huffing of their breath were the only sounds nearby, though night birds screeched farther off. Tanya lay on her back at the other side of the campfire. She appeared to be staring at the stars, but then she sat up and shifted closer.

"I wish there was some way I could thank you properly for helping free me."

The emotion in Tanya's voice drew a modest shrug from Riki. "Your grandmother would have done it anyway, with or without me. She's the one to thank. I was just on hand."

"But you were the one who gave me hope. When I was with the Corps it...I told you it got nasty for a while. Even when Grandma got me out of their hands, I couldn't let myself think I was safe, in case it was a trick. It wasn't until you appeared that I could believe. I don't think you realize just how much you meant to me."

Riki ducked her head, confused and awkward. "If you help me get even with Loke, we can call it quits."

"Revenge? Is that your sole motivation in this?"

"No, of course not."

"So what are your other reasons?"

Tanya was clearly probing. Riki felt an answering flash of annoyance. She had already said she would never abandon a comrade. Presumably this was not enough. Riki glared at the embers. She did not want to mention her gene mother's treachery, or her guilt over her birth mother. Those subjects were too raw.

"Everyone in Westernfort and Ginasberg hates me. Mostly it's fair, but not this time. Is it so strange to want to clear my name?"

"I don't hate you."

"You used to."

"And you weren't too keen on me."

Riki frowned. The conversation was ricocheting around and she had the uncomfortable feeling that she was missing half the steps. "I was jealous of your rank. You being a corporal when I'd just been busted. I thought you only got it because of your mother."

"You might be right."

Tanya's bleak tone surprised Riki. "No, you're fine as a corporal. It's me who's the lousy soldier."

"You've got a lot of skills a Ranger needs. You're just lousy at doing what you're told."

"Yeah. But isn't that most of what being a soldier is about?"

"Sometimes. Not always." Tanya paused. She looked as if she was struggling to say something, but then curiosity took over. "That time when Gerry Baptiste told us to prepare our kit, and you vanished off. Where did you go?"

"The moggies by the kitchen had just had a litter of kittens. I wanted to say good-bye to them before we left."

"The sergeant gave us an order and you wandered off to play with moggies?" Tanya sounded half amused, half disbelieving.

"I knew my kit was good. If you hadn't gone over it three times as hard as for anyone else, it would have passed muster." Riki heard the bitterness in her own voice, more than she had intended.

"I'm sorry. You're right, I did. I wanted to find something wrong."

Riki's anger died in amazement that Tanya so readily conceded the point. Obviously she did not want to get into an argument.

"It's okay. You don't have to apologize just because I helped save your life." Riki tried to turn it into a joke.

"I might have ulterior motives." Tanya's voice was softer than before, underlain with meaning.

Riki looked up from the ashes of the fire. Tanya had shifted closer and was staring at her intently. Riki's heart pounded and a clammy sweat sprang up on her palms. She knew that she had just moved way out of her area of experience. Fighting a surge of panic, she hunched her shoulders and stared at the ground between her feet. Her mouth went dry, too dry to speak—not that she could think of anything safe to say.

Tanya leaned still closer. "I'm pleased we've got this chance to get to know each other better."

"Don't worry. You won't feel that way for long."

Tanya drew back. Riki did not need to see her face to know that the attempt at humor had fallen flat. Riki wanted to reach out to Tanya, but her body would not obey her. She stared at her own fingers locked around her knees. Despite all attempts to loosen them, they stayed bound together in a death grip. Her brain had turned to petrified mush.

"You don't want to get to know me any better?"

"Any reason why I should?" Riki cursed herself. She had not meant the words to sound confrontational, but that was clearly how Tanya interpreted them. She shifted back to her original position on the other side of the fire.

"Nope. None at all."

"I didn't mean I..." Riki swallowed. She could not work out what to say. *See, I said you wouldn't feel that way for long,* did not seem like a good idea.

Tanya was fumbling with the pack on the ground behind her. With her face averted she mumbled something Riki did not catch.

"Pardon?"

Tanya did not repeat it.

Riki watched in despair. "Do you want me to tell you more about the moggies?"

"No. That's okay. I'm going to sleep." Tanya pulled out her blanket and shook it free. The ends snapped like a whip.

"Right."

Riki retrieved her own blanket and wrapped herself in it beside the remains of the fire, but she could not sleep. Had Tanya just been hitting on her? Had she completely blown it? Or had she had a couple of minor fits and missed chunks of the conversation? Because it had gone from amiable to disaster without any of the normal intervening steps.

Riki licked her lips, trying to force herself to speak aloud. To say something along the lines of, *Tanya, I didn't mean that I don't want to know you better. In fact, I'd like to get to know you incredibly well. But you surprised me, and I panicked, because nobody has ever hit on me before. That is, if that's what you were doing. And I didn't mean what I said to sound the way it did. So can we please try the conversation again and see if I can do better the second time around?*

She could not bring herself to say it. Riki rolled onto her side. She remembered her idea from earlier that day. *Maybe I should deliberately do something stupid tonight, then she can put me back on her list of people she'd like to throttle, and we'll be on familiar ground again.* It looked as if she had succeeded on that one after all.

Chapter Sixteen—Spadehorns In The Marsh

The journey across the region of sandstone hills lasted for three days and then their route descended into a wide basin filled with swampland, reminiscent of the area around Southwater. However, the plant and animal life were noticeably different, due to the water being fresh rather than salt. The scenery was not shown to its best by the weather, which had turned to rain the evening before. A network of low islands stood bleak and forlorn amidst the reed beds, crowned with clumps of drooping trees. Gray clouds blanketed the sky and the temperature was cold for late August.

Fortunately, the rain was holding off, no more than the occasional splatter of light drizzle. Tanya looked around, shivering in ankle-deep water, while waiting for Riki to wave her forward. They had considered detouring around the marsh, but Riki had been sure she could find a way across, and there was no saying where they would be taken if they tried to go around.

So far, Riki was doing well, although progress was slow and Tanya was fed up with wet feet. She considered the rising ground at the other side of the swamp. At their current rate, they would reach it well before nightfall. Tanya tried to cheer herself up with thoughts of building a fire, warming up, and drying off.

Riki was four meters ahead, testing the ground cautiously with a long stick. Tanya came behind, leading the ponies. The risk of getting trapped in mud made riding too dangerous. For their part, the ponies were clearly very happy for the chance to take it easy and chomp on any water plants they liked the look of. One species of floating blackweed was a particular favorite. As well as the wet feet, Tanya was getting fed up with having her arm wrenched every time a pony spotted another clump.

"This way," Riki called, pointing to her right.

Tanya advanced another dozen meters. The water now reached mid-calf. A larger island, maybe a quarter kilometer in length, lay just off their course. At its peak, it stood a dozen meters above the water level. The trees on it formed a modest wood.

"Riki!" Tanya called out.

"Yes?"

"Do you think we could head there for lunch?" Tanya pointed to the island.

"Sure." Riki returned to her scouting.

Tanya studied her back. In the three days since their conversation by the campfire, Tanya had not been fair, and she knew it. To say that she had been cold-shouldering Riki was an understatement, and Tanya was well aware that her behavior was unjustified, petty, and immature. Riki was perfectly entitled to reject any unwanted advance, and she was not interested. That much she had made clear by the way she had responded, as much as what she had said. Her body language had screamed *back off and don't touch.* She had clammed herself shut, head down, refusing eye contact, arms clasped defensively in front of her.

Tanya derided herself. Had she really expected anything else? The enmity between them had faded, but this did not mean Riki had to be interested in anything other than friendship. Tanya was not arrogant enough to think that every woman in the world was going to want her. Clearly she was not Riki's type. But just what sort of woman did Riki go for? She had never given any clue.

Maybe Riki had been a tad curt in her brush-off, but from then on she had been making a manifest effort to be friendly, although nothing even faintly suggested a sexual overture. Tanya had been the one who responded coolly, keeping a distance and blocking all conversation beyond the mundane. She could not help herself. She wanted Riki.

Tanya knew she had to accept that it was not going to happen. The knowledge hurt. Tanya realized just how much she had allowed herself to become fixated on Riki. Even now, cold, miserable, and soaked to the knees, Tanya knew she was ogling, watching Riki's head tilt as she studied the marsh, her arms held out for balance, the way her clothes tightened across her hips and shoulders as she moved. Unless Tanya could pull back and get her emotions under control, she was going to carry on hurting.

The pack pony lunged for another wreath of blackweed, almost jerking Tanya off her feet. She moved her foot sharply into a wide straddle for balance and the resulting splash sent cold water as high as her waist. It trickled down unpleasantly under her belt. Tanya yanked on the reins, venting her ill temper. The pony looked at her reproachfully and continued chewing.

Riki called out and waved her forward again. Tanya looked at the island, now less than half a kilometer away. With luck, another ten minutes would see them there. She wanted a break.

❖

Riki barged her way through the band of reeds and stepped from muddy water onto watery mud. However, in a few more paces, the ground had firmed up. This swamp was not tidal like a salt marsh, but seasonal flooding meant the lower areas spent months submerged, which killed most seedlings. Hence, an uneven band of knee-high grass, a dozen meters wide, ran the length of the island between the reeds and the trees.

The top of the hillock was densely wooded, mainly by spindly bogash. Coils of stinger vine filled the spaces between the trunks, sending tendrils spilling across the grass. Riki grimaced. Just touching the vine leaves resulted in serious acid burns that could even be fatal in extreme cases. Fortunately it was no more resilient to full immersion than the bogash, and the grass was clear of it, apart from the shoots that had crept out since the last spring rains.

Riki walked up the incline, feeling the water in her boots squelch with each step. An old tree had fallen across the grass, forming a functional bench. Riki trudged over to it and sat. She considered taking off her wet boot, but there was not much point. The grass was soaked from the morning rain. A fire would be needed to get anything dry, and without boiling water, they could not prepare the dried food.

Tanya was a couple of meters behind, leading the ponies.

Riki waited for her. "Do you want to stop here long enough to get a fire going? I don't mind doing it."

Tanya's shake of the head looked more like an irritated twitch. "No. I just wanted a break from standing around in water."

"Okay. I'll see what we've got to eat." Riki tried to sound as upbeat as possible.

"Do that."

"The ponies will like the chance to graze."

"If they eat any more they'll burst." Tanya was definitely angry at something.

Riki thought it wiser to say nothing more. She undid the bag where fresh food was stored. A little rooting around produced flat bread, cooked on the campfire the previous night, cheese and dried fruit, also a water flask. She refastened the bag before giving the pony a shove on its flank, sending it to join the others grazing by the waterside.

Riki sat on the fallen tree and handed a half share of the food to Tanya, who received it with a grunt of acknowledgement, and then ate quickly in silence. Riki was still only halfway through her lunch when Tanya had finished.

Tanya stood and flexed her arms, as if trying to rid herself of an ache. "I want to unwind. I'm going to practice my archery for a few minutes." She kept her back to Riki and threw the remark over her shoulder.

"Sure."

Riki watched her stomp to her pony and yank the bow from its pack. Tanya was clearly in a bad mood. She had been in one for three days. Riki flipped her thoughts to the conversation that had set it off. Had Tanya been hitting on her by the campfire? Or had Tanya been after something completely different? If so, Riki had completely failed to pick up on it.

Riki even wondered if she had suffered a minor brainstorm, announced *I wouldn't piss on you if you were on fire,* and then forgotten she had said it, because it was hard to think of any other justification for the way Tanya was acting.

In the distance, the air was streaked brown with rain. Riki fixed her eyes unseeing on the line of hills. Was it her fault? Maybe she really had lost the ability to get along with anyone. Or maybe it was nothing to do with what she had or had not said. Maybe Tanya had never stopped disliking her, and now that they were away from the Guards, the need for pretense had gone. Since leaving Southwater, Riki had done her best to be friendly and Tanya had flung it all back in her face.

A burst of huffing recalled Riki's attention to her surroundings.

Something had excited the ponies. Their foraging had taken them farther down the island, but they would not stray far. Riki's gaze moved on. Beyond the ponies, an extended family of coppons were rooting through the mud offshore, their white ear tufts flashing semaphore messages. Overhead, a gissard hovered, on the lookout for reedmice. A female spadehorn was wading through the water a hundred meters from the island.

Riki's focus settled on Tanya, who had her bow strung and was using an isolated tree stump as a target. Tanya's body was athletic and well proportioned. Her face in profile was finely chiseled. The bogash stump, a clear thirty meters away, already bristled with a tight ring of arrows. Riki sighed. The woman was good-looking, capable, brave, and as much fun to have around as a hangover. And Riki had taken enough. If Tanya wanted to be antisocial, Riki could play the same game. She'd had plenty of practice.

Riki considered the reeds bending in the wind. Rain was on the way. Riki tried to judge when it would reach them, hoping they would be out of the marsh before then and settled under canvas—ideally with a nice fire going as well.

Her eyes moved back to Tanya and her head flipped around completely. Maybe the situation could be resolved. Perhaps she should talk to Tanya, ask what was wrong, and see if there was a way to sort things out. What did she have to lose by trying? Riki sighed. More to the point, why was she unable to put Tanya out of her mind for longer than five seconds?

A loud snort made Riki look back to the marsh. The female spadehorn had changed direction and was wandering closer. It was a fully grown adult, two meters high at the shoulder. The huge herbivore was in its summer pelt, though the heavier fur would come through soon. Its rump was bulky, showing the accumulation of summer fat that would see it through winter. The flat, shovel-like protrusion on its nose was half a meter long. In cold weather, the spadehorn used it for digging through snow. Currently it was proving just as effective in loosening roots in the soft mud.

Riki was unworried by the animal's approach. Spadehorns were placid animals, too large to fear predators. Furthermore, they had weak eyesight. Ears and nose were their keenest senses. Since this one had certainly never smelled a human or a pony before, even if it caught their scent, "strange and inedible" would be the only message it would take, and for any animal that translated into, "Leave it alone."

Riki returned to the archery display. Tanya had shot all twenty-four arrows, and from what Riki could see, not missed once. However, the exercise did not appear to have cheered her up. Tanya had been staring in Riki's direction, but as soon as Riki looked over, she turned away sharply and marched off to reclaim the arrows. From the body language, Riki wondered whether Tanya had been toying with the idea of using her as the next target.

Tanya reached the stump and started pulling arrows from the rotten wood. Watching her, Riki again battled to understand how she could find anyone so infuriating and upsetting, yet still want them to spend as much time together as possible. Riki closed her eyes and sank her head into her hands. What was going on with her head, and how was she going to sort it out?

With her eyes shut, the quieter marshland noises rippled through Riki's thoughts, attracting her attention for the first time. Under the whisper of grass and hiss of waves among the reeds, Riki noticed a soft, breathy sound. It came from the wood behind her, half chirp, half grunt, and had been there for some time, Riki realized, just below the level of notice. Her mind had been so preoccupied she had failed to pick up on it before, but now she did.

Riki leapt to her feet, shocked by her lapse. Of all oversights a Ranger could make in the wilderness, ignoring the murmur of a young spadehorn was one of the most suicidally stupid.

Riki looked around frantically. Tanya was at the tree stump, the adult female was in the marsh, and the baby was in the wood. The mother spadehorn must have left it while she went foraging. Regardless of the youngster's exact position, she and Tanya were between mother and baby, and that was a bad place to be.

Riki moved down the slope, waving her arms, in the hope of catching Tanya's attention. They needed to back away quietly. She did not want to call out—the mother spadehorn would hear and respond, yet Tanya was not in any hurry to turn around. Riki looked at the female spadehorn. It was no more than twenty meters from land and unmistakably wading in Tanya's direction, coming back to reclaim its offspring.

Still Tanya would not look around. What was wrong with her?

Surely she was not so intent on reclaiming arrows that she could not hear the approaching spadehorn. Despite the risk of making noise, Riki had to do something. She opened her mouth to shout when she saw a movement between the trees. The baby spadehorn appeared, directly above where Tanya was standing. The youngster was under a meter high, one of that year's births. The horn on its nose was merely a bump.

"Tanya. Spadehorns. You're between a mother and baby."

Riki kept her voice as low as possible, but it did no good. The young spadehorn had seen Tanya. It might have no idea what she was, but for a young spadehorn anything unknown was frightening when its mother was not nearby. The baby gave a warble of alarm. Immediately, the mother responded, bellowing and breaking from a peaceful shuffle into a charge.

Tanya had jerked around at Riki's call. Now she took off, leaving the way clear between the two spadehorns. However, the mother was close enough to see her, and the angry animal had clearly identified her as a threat to its young. The adult spadehorn veered around, changing course, and still pursuing Tanya.

Riki looked on in horror. Tanya could not outrun the spadehorn, either on the grass or in the water. Nor could she take refuge among the trees. The spadehorn's thick fur would shield it from the stinger vine, but Tanya's clothes would not give the same degree of protection. She was young and healthy, and unlikely to be killed by vine stings alone, but running through it would be impossible. The pain would have her collapsed on the ground within seconds.

Riki raced forward. She had no clear idea what she could do to help, but she could not let Tanya face the spadehorn alone. A fist-sized stone caught her attention. Riki scooped it up and flung it at the young spadehorn. The rock bounced of its shoulder and the animal squealed, more surprised than hurt. Even at a few months, it was too big and thick-skinned to be injured by one thrown stone.

Riki looked for a second missile, but it was unnecessary. The youngster's cry had produced the desired effect on the mother. The female spadehorn was lumbering around in a wide loop, crashing through reed beds and charging at the new threat to its baby.

Riki's feet skidded in wet grass as she stopped and turned. Already, the furious adult was bearing down fast. Riki fled before it, but she could no more outrun the spadehorn than Tanya could. This left only one option. A bogash tree, larger and sturdier than most others, stood at the edge of the wood, relatively clear of stinger vine at its base. But could she get to it? The thunder of immense hooves was gaining.

Before Riki was halfway to the tree she knew she stood no chance. With each step, the sound of the spadehorn got louder, the pounding hooves, the tearing grass and the snorted breath. At the last moment, Riki hurled herself aside.

A thump hit her in midair, a glancing blow strong enough to send her spinning. She hit the ground hard, still rolling. The spadehorn thundered past. Riki levered herself up, hauled her feet under her, and continued running. She did not have time to find out whether she was badly hurt.

The adult spadehorn's charge had carried it on several meters, but it swung its rump around in a tight circle, tearing up clumps of mud and grass with its feet, and again hurled itself at Riki. However, the bogash tree Riki was aiming for was now just a few steps away. She launched herself over the coils of stinger vine, hit the trunk with one foot, and grabbed hold of an overhead bough. She swung herself up. Her legs locked around the branch as the spadehorn crashed into the trunk. The entire tree shook. Leaves and dead twigs rained down.

The spadehorn bellowed and stamped back three paces. Riki hauled herself higher into the tree and wedged her body in firmly. She wrapped her arms around the main trunk. Again the mother spadehorn cannoned into the bogash. Riki felt the shock rattle her bones. An ominous crack came from the base of the tree, but it stayed upright.

The mother spadehorn pawed the ground with its front feet, tearing grooves in the soft mud. Its breath hissed and roared like water hitting fire. Then it advanced again, more slowly, and pressed its huge shoulder against the trunk. Riki clung on as the tree swayed under the force. She could hear roots snapping, but the tree did not fall, and at last the spadehorn turned away and trampled up and down the grass, bellowing its fury. The youngster trotted to its mother's side, still warbling unhappily. The sound did nothing to calm the mother.

Riki looked up and down the island. The ponies had trotted farther away. This might have been to avoid the spadehorn, or to find better food. Either way, they had returned to grazing. Tanya had also retreated to a safe distance, too far to judge her expression. She was looking around and kicking through the grass, as if searching for something to use, but there was nothing she could do to help. Nor was there any need. Eventually the spadehorn would get tired and go.

Riki would have liked to wave, to let Tanya know that she was okay, but now that she had stopped moving, the pain from where she had been struck was building into throbbing fire, engulfing her side. It took all her willpower to remain clinging on. Riki closed her eyes, thankful the spadehorn had given up the attempt to knock over the tree. She rested her head on the bark, trying to block everything out.

A half hour passed before the mother spadehorn left. Twice it started to trot away, raising Riki's hopes, only to remember its anger and come bellowing back. Riki was at the end of her endurance when the mother finally waded off through the swamp with its offspring at its side. Once it had definitely gone, Tanya advanced to the tree.

"Riki. Are you okay?"

"I will be." Riki braced herself to jump down.

While wedged in the bogash, her injured side had stiffened. She hurt badly enough just sitting still. Moving was going to be hell, but she could not stay where she was. Riki grabbed hold of a branch with both hands, hoping to swing clear of the stinger vine. As she moved, fire erupted down her side. Her left hand lost its grip and she dropped too soon. Luckily, she still avoided the vine, but landed awkwardly, twisting her ankle and ending up curled on the grass.

"Riki!" Tanya sounded frightened.

Riki tried to roll onto her feet. She got as far as her knees on the third attempt, and then Tanya was at her side, holding her steady with an arm around her shoulders.

"Riki, are you okay?"

"I'll survive. I got a belt from the spadehorn. But I don't think anything's broken." Riki clenched her teeth and stood up. Her head swam, and the world shifted out of focus, but then it settled.

"Sit down. We'll camp here."

Riki shook her head. "This is probably where the spadehorns sleep each night. The mother will have calmed down by then, but I'd rather not be here when they return."

"Are you okay to walk?"

"Of course."

Riki hobbled a few steps, and then looked back. Tanya was

watching with a deeply troubled expression. Riki tried to smile. "I'd count it as a favor, though, if you rounded up the ponies."

"If you're sure."

Riki made her way to the waterside, trying to take bigger steps. She could almost persuade herself that her side was loosening up with the movement.

Tanya arrived with the three ponies. Riki glanced at the saddle packs.

"Have you got your bow?"

Tanya shook her head. "No point. I dropped it when I ran, and the spadehorn trod on it."

"Is it no longer usable?"

"Only as firewood."

Riki stepped into the water.

"Riki?"

She looked back. "What?"

"Anything I can do...I...just let me know." Tanya looked and sounded as if she was struggling to find the words she wanted.

Riki nodded and managed a tight smile, to show she appreciated the concern. She looked across the marsh. The edge of the swamp was only five kilometers away. With luck, they would be there in a couple of hours. Then she could lie down and rest.

The hills on the far side of the marsh were carved from more of the red sandstone. The soil was well drained and mercifully clear of stinger vine. Tiger oaks formed an unbroken canopy, restricting undergrowth to a few clumps of dover fern. An abundance of fallen branches littered the ground. Collecting wood for the campfire would not take long.

The rain clouds had passed over and the sky was clearing. Light was improving, and an hour remained before dusk, but they would be going no farther that day. As soon as they reached dry land, Tanya hurried forward. Riki had been swaying noticeably as they covered the last kilometer of swamp. She was clearly suffering and unfit to go anywhere else, but she still plodded on, doggedly putting one foot in front of the other.

Tanya placed her hand on Riki's shoulder. "Hey. Hold up. We're making camp."

"Where?"

Riki's face was bloodless and her eyes were dazed. The sight increased Tanya's determination to stop for the day. Riki was clearly far more hurt than she had implied. Tanya glanced around. Everywhere on the hillside was pretty much the same. She pointed to a nearby spot between the trunks of three large tiger oaks that would be sheltered should the rain return.

"There."

Riki nodded and staggered to the site, then leaned against one of the trees, breathing in shallow gasps.

"Sit down. I'll sort out the ponies," Tanya said.

"I'll help."

"Don't be stupid. Sit down and rest."

"I'm all right."

"You're lying."

Riki glared at Tanya but then slid to the ground. The fact she had given in so quickly worried Tanya more than anything else. Quickly, Tanya unsaddled the ponies. From the packs, she pulled blankets, canvas, water bags, and tinderbox. Within minutes, a fire was going and Tanya had rigged a waterproof canvas as a shelter, arranged the packs where they would be dry, and laid out the blankets.

Throughout this, Riki sat with her eyes closed. Tanya knelt by her side. "Come and lie down."

Riki opened her eyes and started to move, but stopped, wincing.

"Stay still. Where are you hurt?"

Riki's hand indicated her left side, under her arm. Tanya put her hand onto Riki's forehead and exerted her senses.

"You've got the healer sense?" Riki's voice was a whisper.

"Don't get excited. Not enough to talk about, but maybe better than nothing."

Tanya closed her eyes, trying to feel her way into Riki. She knew her ability with the healer sense was limited, but she so desperately wanted to help and ease the pain she saw in Riki's contorted features.

Tanya slipped into the light trance. Beyond the confines of her own body, she became aware of warm flesh, flowing blood, and electric pulses in nerves. She sank deeper in. A mass of ruptured veins bloated in her sight, offending her with their wrongness. Nerve endings were afire, signaling damage as pain, but she found no broken bones or crushed organs.

Gently, Tanya tried to ease away dead blood, knit together flesh, and dull the flaring nerves. She knew she lacked fine control. Her efforts were clumsy and imprecise, like an idiot wrestling with fog. She could only hope she was doing more good than harm and speeding Riki's recovery. She certainly had not reversed the injury, as a skilled healer might have done in minutes.

Tanya opened her eyes. Riki was staring at her face, but then immediately dropped her gaze, flushing softly.

"Thanks," Riki said quietly.

"Did that help?"

"Yes. A lot."

"Do you think you can move now?"

"I'll try."

This time, with a little assistance, Riki levered herself from the tree trunk and shuffled the short distance to the bivouac. She lay face down on the blanket. Tanya wanted to reach out and stroke her head, kiss her cheek, and tell her it would all be okay. She restrained the impulse and instead turned to the fire.

Soon, boots, wet socks, and cloaks were at one side, drying in the heat, and rice, dried meat, and beans were in a pot, bubbling over the flames. The food would be soft and edible in a half hour. While waiting for it to cook, Tanya went back to the waterside, and searched the reed beds in the fading light. Finding the plant she was after did not take long. Deadwort sap had no medicinal use, other than to induce numbness, but that would ease Riki's pain and allow her a decent night's sleep. Tanya returned to the camp.

"I've found some deadwort." She held up the dripping roots. "Do you want it?"

"After we've eaten."

"Okay. Dinner's about ready."

Tanya helped Riki sit and passed her a bowl. They ate in silence. Riki probably needed all her concentration to deal with the food. For herself, Tanya stared into her bowl because she dared not look at Riki.

She could not escape the twin images—the horror she had felt, seeing the charging spadehorn toss Riki aside, and the tactile memory of Riki's body, alive under her hand. This journey was about to get even more awkward and stressful. She cared about Riki, and now that Riki was injured and needing help, keeping a distance between them was going to be impossible.

CHAPTER SEVENTEEN—UNKNOWN TERRITORY

Riki put down her bowl gingerly. She was not finding it easy to predict which movements her left arm could perform with safety. The smallest, most innocuous action could trigger explosions of fire, while larger, more expansive gestures might cause nothing more than a twinge. More generally, the ache in her side was building again, although Tanya's intervention had taken the savage edge off the pain.

However, the fire and food were comforting, she was warm and dry, and it was a relief to be sitting quietly. Riki looked up. Firelight danced on the leaves overhead in gold and green, and above them the sky was darkening to black. No stars broke through the clouds. The world outside the firelight was disappearing into the night. Riki hunched forward, closer to the flames.

"How do you feel?" Tanya asked from the other side of the fire.

"Like I've been kicked by an angry spadehorn."

"Surprising, that."

Riki smiled at the dry, humorous tone. Perhaps drawing the spadehorn's attack had not been such a stupid idea, if it got Tanya talking in a friendly fashion again.

Tanya held up the deadwort she had gathered before dinner. "Are you ready for this?"

"I guess so."

"Do you need my help?"

Riki nodded. She could feel the bruise stretching from under her side around to the middle of her back. Even if her left arm could move freely, she would not be able to reach the whole area.

Tanya pulled the knife from her belt and sliced the root open. Thick green sap oozed out. Tanya's nose wrinkled. The odor of rotten eggs soon wafted across to Riki. Deadwort was undeniably effective at numbing pain, but it was never going to be first choice for anyone with access to a proper healer. Riki was pleased she had decided to finish her dinner first.

Tanya moved closer. "Do you need help getting your shirt off?"

"Yes." Even with help, Riki suspected that the maneuver was going to be tricky.

Tanya's hands moved to the buttons on Riki's shirt. Her eyes were fixed rigidly on the task, staring at each button in turn. Riki found her own attention locked on Tanya's face, a few centimeters away. If Tanya looked up, their eyes would meet. Riki felt a pulse kick in her gut. Suddenly, she was not so sure whether Tanya's help in applying the sap was a good idea. Riki concentrated on the stench of deadwort, surely the least erotic scent in existence.

The last button slipped free. Tanya carefully rolled Riki's open shirt over her shoulders and down her arms. Riki winced as a line of agony ripped up her side.

"Sorry."

"You're doing okay. I'm just very stiff."

Riki eased her right hand from her shirt sleeve. Tanya assisted with the other arm and then shifted around. Riki leaned forward, resting her elbows on her knees. Warmth from the fire flowed over the exposed skin on her stomach and breasts. Behind her, Tanya sucked a sharp breath in through her teeth.

"Does it look bad?"

"Like you said. As if you've been kicked by a spadehorn."

Riki felt Tanya's hands lightly press against her back and up her side. The touch shot through her. In an instant, the pain and the reek of rotten eggs were as nothing. Riki gasped.

"Did that hurt?"

"It's all right. Carry on."

Riki was pleased Tanya could not see her face. Tanya's hands felt warm, strong, and sure, and so very good. Riki let her head drop forward. Her fists tightened in her lap, and abruptly, tears formed in her eyes. She wanted Tanya to touch her, but this felt like cheating. Was it wrong to enjoy the sensation so much?

❖

Tanya spread the last of the deadwort sap over Riki's back. The mass of black blotches looked awful, especially with the yellow and purple stains around the edges. However, Tanya felt satisfaction that the bruise had come out so quickly. It showed that her work with the healer sense had achieved some good, speeding the body's natural processes. She suspected Riki would not be ready to travel tomorrow, but within a few days she should be healed.

Riki was hunched over her knees. Tanya had tried to be gentle, yet she had felt Riki flinch and heard her gasp frequently. Of course, Tanya had needed to work at keeping her own breath steady, although she suspected, for quite different reasons.

"That's it. I'm finished. How does it feel?"

"Tingling. I think it's starting to work."

"Do you want to put your shirt back on?"

Riki shook her head. "I don't want to wrench anything. Could you just drop it over my shoulders?"

Tanya picked up the discarded shirt and draped it around Riki. The amber firelight was flowing over Riki's skin, softening the tight curve of muscle and adding a warm flush, but Tanya noticed Riki's nipples were hard and erect.

"Are you cold?" The words were out of Tanya's mouth before she had taken time to think. She bit her tongue. *Why not be completely honest and admit you were ogling?*

"A little." If Riki realized the prompting behind the question, her tone gave nothing away.

Tanya carefully added a blanket and then returned to her previous spot at the fireside. She considered her hands forlornly. The stench of deadwort was going to be with her for days.

"Thanks."

Tanya looked across the campfire. Riki's elbows were on her knees and her head was down in a posture of dejection. Tanya resisted the temptation to shuffle back beside her. "I'm the one who owes thanks."

Riki glanced up through her fringe of dark hair. "What did I do?"

"How about, saved me from being killed by the spadehorn?"

"I didn't do much."

"That's not the way I remember it."

"We were both in equal danger."

"I was the one the mother chased until you lured it away. And that was what you wanted, wasn't it? You wanted it to go for you rather than me."

"I was too angry at myself about not hearing the baby earlier. I couldn't think straight. It wasn't a thought-out plan."

Tanya hesitated, staring into the fire, but then her eyes retuned to Riki. "I don't believe that. You deliberately put your life on the line to save mine."

Riki shrugged. "Well. You're the important one, aren't you?"

A flare of anger sparked inside Tanya and then died. Riki's voice was sincere. Her words had not been meant as a jibe. "You're just as important as me."

"Except there's no point in me going back to Westernfort without you. I'll just get strung up. You're the important one, because even if you go back alone, you can tell people it wasn't me who handed you to the Guards."

"Is that really so important to you?"

"Wouldn't you want to clear your name?"

"Yes. But I'm not sure I'd be so quick to die for it." Tanya smiled, trying to show her good intent. "I think you're selling yourself short. I think you're the sort of Ranger who'll risk her life for her comrades. And I wanted to say thank you."

"It's..." Riki clenched her fists, clearly battling some emotion. "Promise me something?"

"I'll try."

"If anything does happen to me. Promise you'll go and see my mother in Ginasberg, Kavita Sadiq. Tell her everything. I didn't betray you and I helped you in Landfall. Tell her she doesn't need to be quite so ashamed of me."

"Your mother? Surely she's the one person I wouldn't need to tell. She must know you wouldn't have done it."

"No. She's the reason I have to go back. I've got to say I'm sorry to her. I've been...I've..." Riki was struggling.

Tanya frowned, trying to put herself in Riki's position—not easy, since she knew that neither of her own mothers would have doubted her for an instant. Was Kavita Sadiq really so mistrustful and hard-hearted when it came to her daughter?

"Why do you need to say you're sorry to her? What have you done?"

"Everything."

"Such as?"

"I've tried to hurt her. I was angry. I thought it was her fault our family got split up. But it wasn't. In Landfall, my sister told me—" Riki broke off and raised a hand, shielding her eyes.

"Riki?"

"My gene mother. She was the one who informed to the Guards. She wanted my birth mother caught and executed, so she'd get custody of me. One of my mothers tried to get the other one killed, over me."

Riki's fingers tightened over her eyes and her shoulders were shaking. Feeling shocked and confused, Tanya scooted to Riki's side and put a supportive arm around her. "That's awful. But it isn't your fault. I don't see you're the one who needs to apologize."

"I do. I've been nothing but a bitch to her. That was why I used to steal and smash things, and fight. Because I knew it hurt her. And when I got in trouble and got a beating for it, I never used to care, because she'd cry more than me." Riki's words were coming between sobs. "When she heard about you and the Guards. And they blamed me. It would sound like I'd finally gone to the limit. Done something really bad, just to hurt her. And she nearly got killed because of me."

Not knowing what to say, Tanya stroked Riki's back. To her surprise, Riki turned and burrowed into her, crying. Tanya held her gently, remembering the bruise, but Riki seemed beyond noticing such minor issues.

"I've made a fucking mess of everything. But if I do just one thing right in my life, I've got to go back. I've got to tell Mom how sorry I am."

"Hush. It's all right. We'll get back. You'll see her. And I'm sure she knows. She's your mother."

Tanya was unsure what she was saying, but it had a calming effect. She rubbed the back of Riki's head while the sobs faded to intermittent shudders. The tension slipped from Riki's body, although her face remained buried in Tanya's neck.

Tanya stared over Riki's shoulder, into the dark forest. The nearest trunks were painted orange by the firelight, but night had claimed the rest of the world. Tanya knew Riki's disclosure was because of feeling emotional and weak from her injury, rather than anything to do with personal trust. However, Tanya was pleased that she was the one Riki had unburdened her heart to, even if due purely to circumstance. More about Riki now made sense. And of course, it was nice to have the excuse to sit by a warm campfire, holding her.

❖

A gissard was screeching its morning challenge to the world. Riki opened her eyes. Dappled dawn sunlight fell obliquely through the trees, making dust shimmer in the air. Already the night chill was fading. It was going to be a warm day.

Riki crawled from her blankets, then stood and stretched. The bruise on her left side made only the faintest complaint. In just five days it was almost fully healed, thanks to Tanya's help. Tanya had been modest about her ability. She might not have enough control to count as a healer, but she certainly belonged in the section of the population who could put the skill to some practical use.

Riki's eyes settled on Tanya, who was still sleeping. Maybe the encounter with the spadehorns had not been a bad thing. It had got them back on friendly terms. Riki still felt awkward when she remembered breaking down on the evening after the attack, but telling someone about her mothers had been cathartic. Finally saying it aloud had helped Riki put her mistakes into perspective. She felt more positive about her future. She was still unsure where she wanted to go, but understanding where she had been made a good starting point.

Tanya had also responded supportively. A solid level of trust now existed between them. As they rode, they chatted and joked easily—apart from Riki being hampered by awareness of just how attractive Tanya was. Even now, watching her sleep, Riki felt her insides melt into goo.

Riki could not restrain a grimace. She was worried that, before long, she would say something and wreck their friendship. After all, she had screwed up every other personal relationship in her life. What made her think she would not do it again? Riki was certain that revealing just how much she liked Tanya would be a major mistake.

Or would it? Tanya had been happy to hold her hand back in the temple. Was that just due to fear about returning to the Intelligence Corps dungeon? And what had Tanya been getting at that first night in the Wildlands? Riki chewed her lip nervously. Perhaps she should say something. Test Tanya's response. Even if she was uninterested, she might still feel flattered. Maybe it would not be a disaster.

Riki's stomach turned to ice. She knew there was no way she would have the courage to face a rejection. She was fairly sure she would not have the courage to deal with an acceptance. Saying nothing was safer all round.

Tanya's eyes flickered open. Riki realized she was staring and quickly shifted her gaze to an innocuous patch of ground.

"Morning," Tanya spoke through a yawn.

"Morning."

"Been awake long?"

"No. I've only just crawled out of bed."

Tanya rubbed her face and sat up. "Whose turn is it to sort out breakfast?"

Riki grinned. "Yours."

❖

By midday the temperature was soaring. Tanya felt sweat trickling down her sides and sticking her clothes to her body. They were riding through mature woodland, mainly yellow cedars. Skirrales were leaping around in the branches overhead. The ponies' hooves sounded hollow on the open forest floor.

Their route descended into a steep valley where boulders protruded from the hillside in buttresses. A break in the trees afforded views over the lowlands to the west. At the valley bottom, a river cascaded through a series of rock pools. The banks were lined with grass and the clear water looked better than inviting.

Tanya turned to Riki. "How about we stop for lunch? The ponies can graze, and we can have a swim to cool off."

"Yeah. Okay." Despite her words, Riki sounded uncertain.

Tanya swung her leg over her pony's rump and jumped down, then strolled to the waterside. "I want to swim first. I'll enjoy my food more if I'm not so sticky."

She glanced over her shoulder. Riki had also dismounted and was standing a few steps away. She looked apprehensive but nodded an agreement when she saw Tanya watching.

Tanya turned back to the water and began undoing the buttons on her shirt, while her thoughts trotted along a line of speculation. Riki was decidedly ill at ease. If the wilderness expert had spotted anything dangerous, she would say, so it had to be something she did not want to discuss. Was it that Riki could not swim? Or was it a general reluctance to take her clothes off?

Tanya caught her lip between her teeth, trying to think dispassionately, although with the way her emotions were running, the subject was not one she could be impartial about. However, as she recalled their journey, apart from when she was applying the deadwort, she had never seen Riki wearing anything less than a full set of clothes. Tanya knew she would have remembered if she had.

Tanya bent and untied her boots. Had Riki always been so coy? She tried to remember back to when they had been with the other members of the patrol. Rangers in the Wildlands were living on top of each other for months on end. Just in the daily run of things, people would wander around in varying states of undress. How had Riki been then? Excessive prudery or exhibitionism would have drawn comment. The fact Tanya could remember nothing implied that Riki had behaved like everyone else.

So what had changed? The obvious answer was that there were just the two of them, and she and Riki were no longer enemies. Why should this make a difference? Riki was clearly nervous. Was she frightened that Tanya was going to jump her? To be honest, such a concern would not be totally unwarranted.

Tanya slipped off her boots, stood, and unbuckled her belt. The last of her clothing landed on the grass around her ankles. Tanya stepped out of them, took three running steps, and jumped into the water.

The shock of the cold punched through her thoughts, driving all else away. Tanya surfaced and turned onto her back, staring up at the perfect blue sky. After the heat and stickiness of the ride, the water was wonderful. For a while, she simply enjoyed the sensation of floating and watching black dots of birds wheel overhead, but then her gaze drifted down.

Riki was standing motionless, waist deep at the edge of the pool. Her eyes were transfixed on the spot where Tanya's breasts and stomach were breaking the water, seeming oblivious to all else, but abruptly her gaze shifted and their eyes met. Immediately, Riki dived underwater, but not before Tanya had seen the hot blush sweep over her face.

Tanya kicked out toward the far side of the pool. Conjectures, hopes, and questions again dominated her thoughts. But she had gotten one answer—Riki could swim. And it was the second time that day she had caught Riki watching her. The first had been that morning, when she woke. Through slit eyelids she had seen Riki staring at her.

Riki's feelings about her had clearly changed, just as her feelings for Riki had changed. But had they changed in the same way? Riki seemed to like her. But how much and in what way? If Tanya had caught anyone else looking at her as Riki had just been doing, she would have had no trouble answering that last question. It did not make sense. Tanya remembered the response when she tried to sound Riki out before. However, the message she was getting now was that trying again might be worth the attempt.

Tanya stopped swimming and started treading water, wondering if she had really reached the decision that she thought she had. She sighed; her head was in a state. Closing her eyes, Tanya let herself sink underwater. Maybe the cold would bring her to her senses. Or maybe she would go ahead and risk alienating Riki again.

Why did life have to be so complex?

❖

The first stars pierced the darkening sky. Tiny Laurel was rising full, while the larger half-crescent of Hardie was sinking in the west. Riki rested back on her elbows and stared at the moons, then turned her gaze to the campfire they had built to cook dinner over. The temperature was dropping with nightfall, although the air was still pleasantly warm. Should she let the fire go out? An hour might pass before they wanted its heat, and by then she and Tanya would be asleep, wrapped in their separate blankets.

Riki stared at the dying flames, but she no longer saw them. Weaving through the fire came the vision of Tanya, swimming at lunchtime. Riki felt her body loosen as another tactile image swept over her, this one imagination, not memory—the image of what it would be like having Tanya's body close beside her and sharing her blanket. The flames engulfed Riki's eyes as the fantasy drew her in.

"How far do you think we've gone?" Tanya's voice broke into Riki's daydreams.

"Pardon?"

"I asked how far we'd gone, in terms of getting back to Westernfort. But by your face, I've dragged you away from somewhere really nice, so if you want to go back there, just ignore me."

Riki swiveled around and sat upright, cross-legged. She struggled to pull herself into the real world. "No. It's okay, um...I'd say we were doing all right. We're, er..."

Tanya laughed. "And now you've gone red. Dare I ask what you were thinking about? Or should I just guess?"

Riki ducked her head, feeling her cheeks burn, even though Tanya had said what, rather than who. She mumbled, "You'd probably guess right."

"It's okay. My own thoughts go there from time to time. Although thinking is nowhere near as much fun as doing."

Tanya's eyes were fixed on her. Riki knew it without looking. Did the statement count as flirting? Riki's pulse leapt and a coil of alarm knotted her stomach, but this time she refused to let it paralyze her. She forced her back to straighten and lift her head. Yet, despite her determination, she could not make herself face Tanya.

"No. I suppose not."

"Suppose? Aren't you sure?"

"No."

"What are you unsure about?" Tanya's tone had changed. No longer teasing, she sounded soft and earnest, gently probing.

Summoning her resolve, Riki turned her head. Her eyes locked with Tanya's, less than a meter away. The shock ripped through Riki as the rest of the world vanished. The intensity on Tanya's face left no room for doubt. This was it. This was serious, and there was no backing away. Tanya was making a play for her, and Riki's only options were to accept or to run—and how would she live with herself if she ran?

Riki fought to control her voice. "At the moment? What to say next."

"Why?"

"Because I don't want to say the wrong thing."

Tanya slid closer. Riki uncrossed her legs, straightening them, so they would not get in the way. Tanya continued staring deep into her eyes. Riki's heart hammered against her ribs. She had never realized that breathing could be such a difficult activity. Something was not right with her lungs, but she could not free enough attention to work out what the problem was.

"What sort of wrong thing are you worried about?"

"Some stupid comment that would make you back away."

"You don't want me to?"

"No."

"Then do you want some good news?"

"What?"

"You don't have to say anything."

Tanya was close enough for her hand to slip around the back of Riki's neck, a soft contact that triggered shock waves down Riki's spine. Panic made a final attempt to freeze Riki, but her muscles were no longer capable of resistance. Her eyes closed. She flowed under the pressure of Tanya's hand, coaxing her forward until their lips met.

Tanya's mouth molded against hers. Riki heard herself moan. Her body rippled and dissolved. She clung to Tanya, an anchor in the chaos. The tip of Tanya's tongue teased Riki, pressing between her lips and running along her teeth, prying them open. Riki responded, opening her mouth and letting Tanya's tongue enter—a taste/non-taste that was nothing, and yet overwhelmed all other senses.

Riki's head was swimming. She was not surprised when her back touched the ground. Tanya had lowered her to the grass, their kiss unbroken. Riki's body was helpless, clumsy, but she could no longer fall. Her grip on Tanya's shoulders loosened, freeing her hands to explore the warm contours of bone and muscle. Riki was amazed. She had known how much she wanted to touch Tanya, but had not realized how much she needed to.

In turn, Riki was aware of Tanya's hands, sliding down her side, pulling up her shirt and burrowing beneath. Tanya's fingers were firm and sure. The touch on Riki's skin flared through her, redefining her body. Tanya's hand advanced, sliding over Riki's stomach and cupping her breast.

Panic erupted. In alarm, Riki grabbed Tanya's wrist through the cloth of her shirt. Tanya broke from the kiss and raised her head. At first, her expression was dazed, but surprise hardened it.

"Is something wrong?"

"I just wanted to say I..." Riki gasped. "I was always in trouble as a kid, at Ginasberg. The other kids. Their parents. They wouldn't have anything to do with me."

Tanya frowned, plainly bewildered. "What?"

"I never had any friends or..." Riki knew she sounded like an idiot. "I've just never..."

Tanya's face knotted in confusion and then cleared. Her eyes narrowed. "You're saying you've never done this before?"

"No."

"Never?"

"You're the first person I've kissed, apart from my mothers and sisters."

Tanya dipped her head. Her mouth joined with Riki's, moving slowly, deliberately. Her tongue slipped between Riki's lips, caressing, teasing, arousing. She raised her head again. "You've kissed your mother like that?"

"No."

"Then it doesn't count."

"I know. That's what I mean. I don't want you to think, or expect... or..." Riki ran out of words.

"What I'd expect from a bad—" Tanya broke off. Her eyes met Riki's. Her expression changed from humor to affection, and then to something like wonder. "Don't worry. I'll go slowly. And any time you want, we can stop."

"You're okay with that?"

"I think it will kill me. Even so, I promise I'll stop whenever you want."

Riki placed her hand on Tanya's face, stroking her thumb along the line of cheekbone. The gesture was partly tender and partly to give herself a few more seconds. She was still nervous, but need overwhelmed any fears. More than this, staring into Tanya's eyes, Riki felt safe. She trusted Tanya. She ran her fingers into Tanya's hair and drew her into another kiss.

For a while, they lay on the grass, until Tanya pulled away. Her hand moved to Riki's shirt. One by one, Riki watched the buttons loosened. Her shirt fell open, exposing her breasts to the moonlight and Tanya's gaze. The eyes on her felt like a physical caress.

Slowly, very slowly, Tanya lowered her head. Her lips brushed Riki's skin and then opened, taking in Riki's nipple, sucking hard with a faint touch of teeth. Riki's stomach kicked. Spikes of desire shot through her. Arousal surged over her skin.

Tanya's hand was at her waist, fumbling with her belt. Soon Riki would be naked. Anticipation battled with apprehension. Her body yearned for the contact, but she would feel so vulnerable as the only one unclothed.

Riki picked at Tanya's shirt. "You too."

Tanya sat up, smiling. Not bothering to unbutton her shirt, she pulled it over her head, and then undid her belt. Within seconds, Tanya was naked. Riki's eyes took control of her soul, paralyzing her. The breath stopped in her lungs. She scarcely noticed when Tanya completed the task of stripping her.

Carefully, Tanya stretched out over Riki, straddling her thighs and pinning her to the ground, covering her, holding her, protecting her. Tanya's elbows planted on either side of Riki's shoulders. Her mouth traveled over eyes, ears, and throat, before returning to Riki's lips.

Riki was lost in passion. Tanya's body filled her arms and overloaded her senses. Her breath was ragged with desire. The weight of Tanya, the touch of skin on skin, inflamed the ache between her legs. Uncontrollable tremors run through her.

"Tanya, please."

"I'm not going too quickly, am I?"

"No." Riki struggled to find the words. Her body was drowning out all else, making thought impossible. "I need..."

Tanya's expression changed to a knowing smile. "Ah."

Riki was not certain what she was asking for, and was disappointed when Tanya shifted off her. She wanted their bodies in hard contact, but then Tanya's hand slid down, over ribs, stomach, and into the junction of her legs.

"Like this?"

Riki could not have answered. She did not need to. Tanya gently eased her thighs apart. A touch, a finger sliding slowly, and then returning more deliberately. Riki cried out. Her body arched, out of control. Tanya's fingers continued their advance, opening and entering her. The movement of Tanya's hand was the central pivot of Riki's existence. Her whole body contracted around the fingers filling her.

She was helpless with the need for release.

Riki's orgasm exploded, erupting from each muscle, each bone, with every throb of her pulse. And then she fell back to earth, gasping.

"Okay?"

Riki opened her eyes. Tanya's face was centimeters away, staring into her, affection and desire manifest. Riki's heart melted in the heat.

"Yes."

Riki expected Tanya to remove her hand, but she kept it in place, comforting, filling Riki beyond the merely physical. Tanya's thumb still stroked her, matched to the ebbing pulse of pleasure as they lay, held by each other's eyes. Then Riki felt the tension rebuild. Needing no word, Tanya caught the rhythm, molded the surge, and again took Riki over the edge.

The last ripples faded away. Tanya wrapped her in an embrace, holding Riki close as she sucked air into her lungs. Tanya's lips brushed across her cheek.

Riki's breathing stilled. The world was back in place and yet different. Riki pulled back slightly so she could see Tanya's face—her lover's face.

"How do you feel?" Tanya asked.

No words could answer the question. Riki just smiled and pushed Tanya's shoulder, rolling her onto her back. Now, for the first time, Riki was the one looking down.

Tanya was beautiful. Every square centimeter of her was beautiful. Riki placed her hand over Tanya's right breast. The weight, the warmth, and the softness filled her fingers. And Tanya gasped. Riki hesitated, surprised at herself for being surprised. Of course the things she did would draw a response. Inexperienced did not mean ineffectual.

Tanya was waiting. Carefully, Riki began to experiment, all the while keeping her eyes on Tanya's face, watching her actions mirrored there, seeing what worked and learning what was needed. Riki's hand slid between Tanya's legs, into the warmth and wetness. Tanya bucked, a convulsive, whole-body contraction.

She gripped Riki's shoulder, fingers digging in. Her face contorted. Her body shook. Tanya had surrendered all self-control. The knowledge was daunting yet exciting, and Riki felt both commanding and controlled. She was guiding Tanya's arousal, but her actions were dictated by the rhythm of Tanya's breath. Riki could not stop.

Tanya hit climax. Watching her body arch, her face twist in ecstasy, Riki was consumed by a wild array of emotions. She felt triumphant, loving, smug, humble, powerful, and awed. She brought Tanya to another climax, and then again. She could have carried on forever.

Eventually Tanya caught Riki's wrist and tugged weakly, laughing with her eyes closed. "Enough. Stop. I just want to hold you."

Tanya flung her arm around Riki's shoulders and pulled her close. They lay side by side, wrapped in each other's arms as their lips again joined in a series of soft kisses. Riki felt happy and sated. Eventually, she rolled away and looked at the sky. Her body was heavy, her muscles pliant and relaxed.

Tanya kissed her ear and then raised herself on an elbow. "You didn't want to say stop, then?"

"Would you really have stopped?"

"Of course."

The blankets were lying beside the red embers of the fire. Tanya slipped onto one, pulling Riki after her, and lay on her back. Riki snuggled close into the curve of Tanya's arm. With her free hand, Tanya pulled a single blanket to cover them.

Riki laid her head on Tanya's shoulder. It felt a very safe place to rest, but she was unsure what to do with her hand. At first she draped it across Tanya's stomach, and then in the center of her chest. Neither felt right. Hesitantly, she slid it across, so her palm cupped Tanya's breast. A sigh sounded between Tanya's lips, and over Riki's hand she fastened her own, holding it in place.

Tiredness washed over Riki. For the first time since she was twelve years old, she drifted off to sleep feeling completely at peace with the world.

CHAPTER EIGHTEEN—THE RANGER POST

It was going to be another hot day. Above the hills, the sky was pale yellow, turning to deepest blue overhead, without a wisp of cloud. A heat haze shimmered in the distance. The breeze blew warm and dry.

Riki knelt by the saddlebags, nominally packing the supplies for another day of travel. However, she was aware that she was being very uneconomical in her actions. The big problem was her cheeks. She was grinning so much her face ached.

Admittedly, the ache was not severe enough to directly hamper her folding the blankets or sealing the tinderbox in its waterproof wrapper, but every time Riki thought about her face, she was reminded of why she was grinning. This was what distracted her. She would drift away in a daze and eventually the blanket, bag, or wrapping would slip from her hand, putting her back at step one. She was also finding even the simplest decisions difficult—decisions such as, should she fold the blanket top to bottom first, or side to side?

Riki glanced up, estimating the time from the sun's position. Sunrise was long past. She and Tanya had overslept. Remembering why they had overslept made the grin on Riki's face stretch still wider. She gazed happily at the blanket in her hand until she remembered she was supposed to be folding it. Riki sighed and shook the blanket out flat. Yet already her attention was wandering.

A few meters away, Tanya was standing with her back to Riki, looking down at the saddles by her feet—the saddles that she was supposed to be putting on the ponies. Riki studied her thoughtfully. She suspected that Tanya's productivity was no better than her own.

Riki's appraisal started at Tanya's head and then slid lower. Riki felt her stomach flip a somersault. The cloth of Tanya's trousers was pulled tight enough to reveal her outline and loose enough to hint at more. Riki's pulse accelerated. Her hands thrummed with the tactile memory of running down Tanya's back and over those hips, touching warm, naked skin.

While Riki watched, Tanya twisted slightly to one side, pulling the cloth tighter. Riki's eyes were riveted to the sight. She then realized that the movement had been because Tanya was now looking back over her shoulder. Riki glanced up guiltily and met Tanya's eyes. She felt a blush darken her face. However, Tanya only smiled before walking over and crouching behind Riki. Her arms slid around Riki's waist for support.

"Enjoying the view?"

"Um...yes. I was." Denying it was pointless.

Tanya's breath was warm on Riki's neck, followed by her lips, kissing behind Riki's ear and nibbling on the lobe. Her tongue teased and inflamed.

Riki closed her eyes. The soft touch of Tanya's mouth was sending electric flares down her spine. It was all Riki could do to continue breathing. Eventually, Tanya ceased nuzzling but kept her lips close to Riki's ear.

"So, you enjoyed last night?"

"Yes."

"Do you think you might want to do it again sometime?"

"Maybe." Riki tried to match the light, playful tone.

Tanya's hands released their grip on Riki's waist and moved to the buttons of her shirt. The first one slipped free.

"How about now?"

❖

The upland area was etched with eroded canyons and buttes. The ground was hard and rocky. Most topsoil had been washed away by wind and rain. Stunted firs sprouted wherever they could attach their roots, while elsewhere, low alpine perennials clung to the bare rocks. Only in sheltered valleys was significant vegetation found.

The weather was still good for the start of October, although the heat had gone from the sun. The nights were drawing in. As they rode along the bottom of a sheer-sided canyon, Tanya considered the lengthening shadows. She estimated that two hours of decent daylight remained.

At the end of the canyon, they reached a deeper basin, a couple of kilometers wide, where a moderate covering of trees and bushes was interspersed with swaths of knee-high grass. Tanya urged her pony down the incline before noticing that Riki had stopped and was looking around.

"What is it?"

"I recognize this. I know where we are."

"So where are we?"

Riki grinned. "Two days south of Ginasberg."

"You've patrolled out here?"

"A few times." Riki pointed to the cliff rising on the opposite side of the basin. "There's a Ranger post over there."

Tanya smiled at her affectionately. Riki had done well at finding a route through the wilderness. Tanya had never doubted that she would. "Nearly home."

Riki smiled back and geed her pony on.

A ring of Ranger posts existed around both Westernfort and Ginasberg. Tanya knew the location of the posts around Westernfort, but she had never been assigned to Ginasberg and had rarely traveled out this way. Riki was far more familiar with the terrain.

Ranger posts were concealed bases used for overnight stops. All the posts were well hidden and easily defendable. Should the Guards ever mount an expedition against the heretics' strongholds, the posts were intended to offer a safe retreat between skirmishes. They were also invaluable to anyone caught out by harsh weather, and were kept stocked with emergency supplies.

Riki led the way to the other side of the basin. The trees, mainly hagwood firs, grew denser here. Between them were thickets of rock holly and sugarleaf, shrouding the base of the cliff. Not until they were right on top of it did Tanya spot the dark crack splitting the rock face. Riki slipped from her pony's saddle and walked toward it. Tanya did likewise.

The crack turned out to be the entrance to a winding cave, wide enough to admit a pony. Like all the posts, if you did not know where it was, you could have passed within a dozen meters and not spotted it.

Leaving the ponies to graze, Tanya and Riki entered the cave. After a few turns, the sides fell away and the roof opened to the sky. They were at the bottom of a wide sinkhole in the rocks. A small cabin leaned against one side, and a shallow pool provided fresh water. There was enough space for the ponies to come in, although for the moment, they were better off outside.

Tanya pushed open the cabin door and peered in. The floor of the single room was hard-packed earth; the walls were rough timber on three sides and natural rock on the other. The only contents were a couple of straw-stuffed mattresses and a wooden chest for supplies. A stone hearth with a chimney was built against the rock face. Tanya had already spotted the stack of cut logs outside. She grinned. The nights had been getting cold. The thought of an evening snuggled up in front of a fire with Riki was definitely pleasant.

❖

The Ranger urged her horse on at a sharp pace. She had not made as much progress as she had hoped that day. Lack of familiarity with the terrain was partly the cause. It was several years since she had last patrolled the region. The light was now fading and she wanted to reach the Ranger post before nightfall to give herself a chance to feed her horse, settle in, and get the fire going.

The summer had been chaotic. Captain Coppelli had thrown all her resources into recapturing Private Sadiq. Not surprising, yet the captain's judgment had surely been compromised by her personal involvement. Every available Ranger had been sent after Sadiq, including many who had more important things to do. They had also been kept on the hunt long after any hope of success remained, while vital jobs had been postponed.

Thinking about it, the Ranger grimaced. The year was not one she would like to repeat. Life was finally quieting down and getting back to normal, although people were still being shunted out of their routine, filling in where needed. Her current mission was an example, making an inventory of emergency supplies in the Ranger posts before winter arrived.

The sun had set and darkness was thickening under the hagwood firs. The Ranger hunched her shoulders against the chill wind. Fortunately, her destination was at hand. She had just a few hundred meters to go when she heard a horse snort.

Startled, the Ranger pulled her own mount to a halt. Who could be here at this time of year? She glanced around apprehensively. Surely a detachment of Guards could not have gotten so close to Ginasberg without being noticed. And yet, with all the turmoil, maybe the watch had slipped.

The Ranger pursed her lips and then slipped from her saddle. The most likely explanation was that the horse belonged to another Ranger—someone like herself, frantically making up for lost time with an unscheduled journey, but it never hurt to be too careful.

She tied her horse's reins to a hagwood, pulled her bow from the pack, strung it, and then stuck three arrows in her belt. Fortunately, the undergrowth here provided better cover than for most of the region. She crept between the trees, keeping her movements as silent as possible. From the shelter of a bushy rock holly, she peered at the grassy area in front of the Ranger post.

Three ponies were grazing. Only two had saddles; the other was clearly a pack animal. Although there was no sign of who they belonged to, the Ranger relaxed. A party of two was very unlikely for the Guards—they preferred to travel in number. Almost, the Ranger left her hiding place, but a niggling doubt, a seventh sense, made her wait.

She heard footsteps. Someone was leaving the cave. The Ranger ducked further behind the rock holly and peered between the leaves, trusting to the encroaching darkness to aid her concealment.

A figure strolled into view. Although the day was nearly done, the light was still sufficient for the watching Ranger to identify Rikako Sadiq, sauntering into the open. Sadiq was wearing civilian clothes, and her hair was longer than the last time the Ranger had seen her, but she was unmistakable, from her brazen swagger to the arrogant smirk on her face.

Sadiq had been tried in her absence. Captain Coppelli's orders were clear. The renegade was to be shot on sight. The Ranger pulled an arrow from her belt and nocked it on her bowstring. She placed her fingers at either side of the shaft. But before she could draw, she heard someone else.

The presence of Rikako Sadiq, so close to Ginasberg, had been a huge surprise, but this was nothing compared to seeing Tanya Coppelli also emerge from the cave mouth.

The Ranger lowered her bow, her head reeling. What was going on? How had Tanya escaped from the Guards? And what was she doing here, in the company of Rikako? Stunned, the Ranger remained frozen as the two women claimed the ponies and led them into the cave.

Only once the scene was deserted did she retreat. She had no idea how the two women had come to be at the post together, and she was not about to ask. Apart from easing her curiosity, the information was unnecessary. The obvious conclusion was that Rikako Sadiq and Tanya Coppelli were on their way back to Westernfort, and they had to be stopped.

Leading Ranger Loke Stevenson slipped away through the darkening woodland, back to her horse. She had plans to make.

❖

Midnight was close. Loke pressed herself against the rocks of the cave entrance and peered in. Laurel was rising behind her, but the weak moonbeams could not pierce the blackness. Loke concentrated on her ears. Faintly she could hear hefty breathing from the ponies, and nothing else. She slipped into the cave and inched her way forward, testing each footfall.

At the point where the cave opened into the sinkhole she paused, studying the scene. She did not need to rush. Moreover, she must not rush. She would have just one chance and could not afford a mistake. Weak moonlight fell on the rock face on the far side. The three ponies were standing motionless around the pool. Their tails twitched intermittently from side to side, but they were clearly sleeping.

Loke strained her eyes. The door of the cabin was outlined in dull red. By the look of it, a fire was burning down inside, but no lanterns or candles were lit. Loke cautiously advanced. As she passed, one of the ponies shuffled its feet; the hooves clattered loudly on rock. Loke froze and waited, but no other sound or motion disturbed the silence. She reached the cabin door and slowly drew her sword.

Again Loke paused, listening, while weighing up her plans for the last time. She had to kill them both. Loke felt her jaw tighten in an involuntary grimace. She did not like the idea, but she had no choice. Tanya had the more damaging testimony to deliver, but Rikako returning to Westernfort alone would be nearly as bad. They must have been together for some time. Who knew what they had told each other? The mere fact Rikako had chosen to return would ensure that she got a hearing. She might even be carrying letters.

Loke hoped she would be able to kill both in their sleep; a quick stab through the throat, that would prevent the one she struck first from crying out and waking the other. However, Loke knew nothing was certain. She had to allow for some disturbance, and possibly a struggle with her second victim.

Rikako Sadiq was the one to dispose of first. In Loke's estimation, she was the more dangerous and less predictable of the two. Undoubtedly, Tanya Coppelli was a competent Ranger, intelligent and skilled with a bow. Yet she was no match for her mother, Captain Chip Coppelli. She lacked aggression and fire. She could put a dozen arrows into the heart of a target, but Loke did not think she would be so quick to put one into the heart of a woman. Tanya had never killed, never been in a fight with deadly intent. If it came to one on one, Loke counted on having the advantage, because Tanya would freeze, just for that split second, before striking the fatal thrust.

Loke edged the door open, a millimeter at a time, and slipped inside. As she had thought, the remains of a fire in the hearth were sinking into glowing embers. The soft red glow flowed over the room. Loke waited for her eyes to adjust before moving.

She looked for the two sleeping bodies. One blanket-covered form was immediately apparent, but there was no sign of a second. Loke's forehead furrowed in confusion and her eyes returned to the first shape. This time she studied the outline in closer detail and realized that two women lay under the same blanket, fitted close together, like spoons. Loke could not restrain her wry smile. So that was how it was.

Loke stood over the sleeping figures. The frown deepened on her face. Rikako was closer to the wall. Tanya lay behind, with her right arm over her lover's shoulders, holding her close. Her hand was in front of Rikako's face. Although unintentional, the positioning effectively shielded Rikako. Tanya's throat was in turn equally well protected by Rikako's head.

Loke held her sword out experimentally, judging angles and swings, and then stepped back, chewing her lip. The wall was too close to let her put a forceful blow into Rikako's chest. The only guaranteed quick killing strike on either woman was to Tanya's back, between her ribs and piercing her heart.

Loke stepped forward again, tightening her grip on the hilt of her sword. She drew back her arm, and then stopped. She would kill Tanya, but it would leave her with Rikako to confront, awake and forewarned. Even so, she would have the advantage. She ought to win. Yet Rikako was quick and far too good in the wilderness. If she chose to flee rather than fight and made it to the woods, the odds did not look good at all.

Loke stared at the two figures. What was her best option? What other opportunities to kill them would she have? An ambush on the trail was not a good idea. If she picked her position, she would be able to put an arrow through one, but the other would then be a fast-moving target, and far harder to hit.

Loke's thoughts churned through plans and conjectures. They had to be heading for Westernfort, but they would undoubtedly stop at Ginasberg on the way. Their next night would be spent at the Ranger post below Turner's Lookout. Loke's frown faded as a new plan seeded itself. It should work, and even if not, she would have lost nothing. The chance would still be there to stab them in their sleep, and maybe tomorrow night they would be a little farther from the wall.

Slowly, she backed toward the cabin door and left. With a little effort she would arrive at the next post several hours before Tanya Coppelli and Rikako Sadiq, which would give her plenty of time to prepare a surprise for them.

❖

Sunset was more than an hour away as they rode along the ridge toward the next Ranger post. The exposed location meant that few trees grew to obscure the panoramic view over the land below. This was the last of the high hills. The terrain ahead leveled out into softer contours, and forests of firs replaced the dry, barren uplands.

Riki fixed her eyes on the horizon, following the direction of her thoughts. Ginasberg was a mere forty kilometers due north, a day's journey. In her heart she was both eager and worried. Would she be able to find the words she wanted? How would they be received? Would her mother forgive her?

Tanya rode beside her in silence. Was she also thinking ahead to being reunited with her mothers? Although for her, the occasion was guaranteed a good outcome.

At the end of the ridge, they descended into a depression in the hillside that turned into a steep-sided ravine. The route was traveled often enough to leave a visible trail along the bottom. They rounded a sheer escarpment as the valley walls fell away. Before them lay an area of bleached grass, scattered bushes, and spindly trees. A ring of limestone fists punched up through the thin upland soil, between cracked fissures.

Riki pointed to the largest stone bastion and reined her horse to a standstill. "The Ranger post is in there. And I think someone's already home."

"Why?"

"Do you see that wooden bridge over the crevice in front?"

"Yes."

"It's the only way in that doesn't involve a climb. But normally we don't advertise the post's location by leaving the bridge out. It gets hidden under those bushes." Riki nodded at the ones she meant. "Either somebody's been lazy and not put it away when she left, or she's still here."

"No sign of horses."

"They get put to graze a little farther down the hillside where there's a stream and the grass is better."

Tanya raised her voice to a shout. "Hello? Anyone here?"

They waited while the echoes faded over the hillside.

"Maybe she's down seeing to her horse," Tanya suggested.

"Should still be in earshot."

Riki hopped down from her pony and walked the short distance to the bridge. The fissure it spanned was less than four meters across and of a similar depth. The outcrop on the other side rose in a flat wall, except for the small cleft the bridge led to. The fissure ran for a dozen meters in either direction before more cliffs sealed it off. As far as could be seen, the floor was flat, but it was hidden beneath a covering of dover ferns. Windblown soil could accumulate at the bottom, and it was sheltered from direct sunlight. Footprints marked the ground around the bridge, scuffed in places, but definitely caused by a Ranger's boots.

"These prints are fresh. Two hours at most. The wind would have blown them away if they were any older."

Tanya had remained seated on her pony. She stood in the stirrups and scanned the surroundings before also dismounting. "Must have had to go and do something. There's still an hour before dark. She might come back."

Riki shrugged and walked onto the bridge. The structure was light enough to be put out by one woman, yet robust enough to take the weight of several. However, as she approached the middle, Riki felt it bouncing under her feet more than she remembered. She glanced back. Tanya was a few meters behind her and had not yet set foot on the bridge.

"You better wait there. I think the bridge is in need of—"

Suddenly, the planks under Riki's feet gave way with a loud snap. Her knees flexed in an automatic but pointless attempt to keep her balance. The bridge cracked in two and Riki tumbled to the bottom of the ravine.

She had no time to think, but fortunately her instincts kicked in. Her arms shot out for balance. Her knees bent, ready to take the impact. Her feet hit the ground and she pitched forward into a roll. Fire erupted in her ankle, but faded almost as quickly—nothing worse than a sprain. Fortunately, the thick plant cover cushioned her from worse bruising, and the falling timbers landed away from her. Riki rolled once more and ending up sitting among the crushed ferns and broken wood, more surprised than hurt.

"Riki!" Tanya shouted.

Even before Riki could draw breath to reply, Tanya's head appeared at the top of the crevice.

"I'm okay."

"You're sure?"

"Yes." Riki took a deep breath. "Just a bit shook up."

"What happened?"

"The bridge broke when I was standing on it."

The fear on Tanya's face faded to an amused pout. "I guess if you can come out with smartass answers you must be okay."

"You asked the question."

"Wait there. I'll get a rope to help you out."

Riki grinned and looked at the remains of the bridge. The largest section had fallen against the side of the ravine and now stood propped beside her at an angle. She could see where the under-strut had cracked. To a first glance, the wood appeared weathered but sound. Then her eyes caught a glimpse of clean white wood. Riki pulled away the shrouding ferns to take a better look.

"Tanya!"

"What is it?" Tanya's head reappeared. Her expression showed rekindled alarm.

"The bridge was sabotaged."

"What!"

"Here. Somebody has hacked at the strut to weaken it." Riki looked up. "It's a trap."

"Who would—" Tanya met Riki's eyes. "I'm not going to leave you here."

"They'll be watching. You're exposed. You can't help me by being a target."

"I—"

Abruptly, Tanya broke off and ducked out of sight. Riki heard her run away, and then the unmistakable twang of a distant bowstring.

"Tanya!" Riki could not stop herself from shouting, although she did not expect an answer. Her only comfort was that she had heard no cry and no thud of a body hitting the ground.

Leather creaked. A pony snorted, followed by rapid hoofbeats echoing between the rocks, and then fading into silence.

Riki got uneasily to her feet. Who had sabotaged the bridge? It was not a likely tactic for Guards, even if a company was in the region and had discovered the post. Had she and Tanya been the targets? Or had they stumbled unwittingly into a trap intended for another victim? In which case, who and where was she? But if the trap had been for Tanya and her, who might have seen them approaching and wanted to stop them? Who would shoot at Tanya?

At that point, Riki's thoughts lurched to an uncomfortable stop as one plausible answer presented itself. She peered around the fissure. Was there any point in hiding? The saboteur would have seen her fall and would know where she was. Lying down and playing dead was not a good idea. Even if her words to Tanya had not been overheard, anyone with a modicum of caution would put a few arrows into an easy target, just to be sure.

Riki looked up at the sound of footsteps. She was about to find out the saboteur's identity—not that she felt much doubt. Riki was unsurprised when Loke Stevenson appeared at the rim above her, holding a strung bow with an arrow nocked on the string. It took Riki a split second to realize that there was a point in hiding after all. She dived into the space behind the solid timber remains of the bridge. An arrow hit the rocks by where she had been standing.

Five seconds of silence followed.

"Tanya," Loke shouted at the top of her voice.

The silence continued.

"Tanya Coppelli. If you don't come back, I'm going to kill your girlfriend."

Use of the term *girlfriend* made Riki frown. When had Loke spotted them, and what had they been doing? It was decidedly unpleasant to think they had been spied on.

"Come on, Tanya. I know you. Even if you weren't fucking her, you wouldn't run off and desert a comrade. I know you're still here, listening."

Riki heard Loke as she stamped up and down the length of the ravine. Riki shifted from side to side behind the bridge panel, to keep herself covered.

"You better come out. Now. Or you'll regret it." Loke was sounding increasingly desperate.

Riki decided that she might as well get the answer she wanted, rather than listen to the inane threats. "Why did you call me her girlfriend?"

"I saw you last night."

"Ah."

"I crept into the Ranger post. I was going to stab you, but you were all wrapped up in each other's arms. I couldn't get a clean stroke."

"Oh. You saw us asleep." Riki felt a sense of relief that was completely disproportionate, giving the situation.

"Yes." Loke's tone was terse and distracted. She raised her voice again. "Tanya. I know you're close by. This is your fucking last chance."

"Last chance or what?"

Loke ignored Riki and carried on shouting. "If you don't come out, I'm going to get some lamp oil from the supplies in the post. Then I'm going to toss it down into the ravine, with a torch. The ferns will go up nicely. Do you want to hear your girlfriend scream as she burns?"

Riki looked at the dover ferns. They were starting to wilt with the end of summer and would burn well enough. She leaned her head back on the rocks and caught her lip in her teeth. She was sure she knew the game that Tanya was playing, and wanted to give her every last second.

"I'm going to get the oil."

"You've left yourself a jump," Riki pointed out.

Loke merely snarled and stomped along to where the ravine narrowed to little more than a meter. She slipped her bow over her shoulder and stared at the rock face where she would land. Riki peered between the wooden slats, watching her. Loke backed off a few steps, clearly preparing to take a running jump, but then stopped and looked around, shifting her weight. She took an indecisive half step away from the crevice.

Riki spoke again. "You know she's gone, don't you?"

"You think she'd run off and leave you?"

"It depends on how you look at it."

"She's too damned noble to ditch a comrade."

"What would you know about being noble?"

Loke spun away from the ravine. Her head jerked left and right. "Tanya."

"She's not stupid, you know."

Abruptly, Loke pulled her bow off her shoulder and set off at a run, away from the ravine.

"Loke, before you go. There's something you need to know. Something I found out about Tanya when I was in Landfall." Riki shouted, unsure whether her words would get any response, but through the gaps in the timber, she saw Loke reappear on the brink.

"What?"

"The Coppellis. They run half of Landfall. Tanya's grandmother, Isabel Coppelli, she's sharp. She's the shrewdest woman I've ever met in my life, but the whole family are the same. And Tanya's a Coppelli."

"Where's this going?" Loke was fidgeting, impatience manifest in every muscle of her body.

"When you started shouting threats, Tanya would have still been quite close, so she'd have heard your voice and recognized you. And what you were saying. All that 'Come out or I'll kill your girlfriend' rubbish. She knew that if she did what you said, you'd have killed us both for sure. It wouldn't make my life one iota more secure. You need us both dead, else you're sunk. You were bluffing with a completely empty hand. And I can tell you that any Coppelli would have spotted it in an instant."

"This is fucking pointless." Loke turned away.

"No. Wait. What I want to say is that Tanya would have known that the only way to keep me safe was for her to run away. She knew when you eventually realized that she'd gone you weren't going to hang around, wasting time, trying to kill me. Because even though you'd be safer with us both dead, she's the one you really have to stop from getting to Ginasberg and talking to people. And she's got a big head start. She took two seconds to work out what's taken you twenty minutes. Because she's smart and you're not. Like you've just wasted another two minutes, listening to me tell you something you'd finally work out for yourself."

"Fuck you." Loke darted out of Riki's sight. The sound of her running footsteps pounded away.

"No, thanks. I'm already claimed." Riki pulled a wry smile. She had no hope of getting Loke to waste more time listening to her. She could only pray that Tanya had enough of a lead for what she had to do.

Riki heard distant hoofbeats that faded almost immediately. She crawled from behind the planks of the bridge and examined the fissure wall. The rock face was vertical, but covered with cracks and nodules. It ought to be readily climbable.

Riki flexed her ankle experimentally, testing where she had sprained it when she fell. A few twangs darted up her leg, and it was going to be stiff when she woke the next morning, but it would not stop her from climbing out. Riki reached up, seeking her first handhold. She wanted to get on Loke's trail as soon as possible. Unfortunately, she was unlikely to do it quickly enough to be of any help to Tanya.

CHAPTER NINETEEN—THE OLD BLOCK

B y the time Tanya reached the wooded lowlands, the sun had sunk close to the horizon. Tall fir trees grew on either side of the trail, towering over her and blocking what little daylight was left. Despite the gloom, Tanya pressed ahead hard, but in another half hour true night would fall and she would not be able to maintain her wild gallop.

Yet, even if it were not for the fading light, Tanya knew she could not keep up the pace much longer. The pony's flanks were heaving. The animal was nearing its limits. She had no hope of outrunning Loke. The pony was a solid, reliable beast that had carried her without complaint. Yet it had been chosen for its commonplace quality. Loke, however, was mounted on one of Westernfort's finest horses.

Loke would also have a sword, a trail knife, and a bow. The only weapon Tanya had was a long knife—pointless to regret the spadehorn trampling her own bow. Waiting until she was overtaken was a bad idea, but she had another plan. Already, Tanya had reached into her saddlebag and got what she needed. Now she had to find the right spot. The encroaching forest was promising, and before long a suitable configuration appeared. As soon as she was past, Tanya reined her pony to a stop and leapt off, then rushed back to where two trees stood like sentinels on either side of the trail.

How much time did she have? How long had Loke waited before coming in pursuit? Tanya clenched her jaw, trying not to think of the most worrying question of all. Was Riki all right?

Tanya shook her head to clear her thoughts. Concentration was vital. The item she had taken from the saddlebag was a long length of cord. Normally it had been strung up to make a bivouac on rainy days.

Again Tanya would tie it between two trees, but for a very different reason.

Tanya grabbed a low branch and hauled herself up. The urge to rush was overwhelming, but she forced herself to stop and think clearly. The job had to be done right. She looked carefully at the trail, and then the space above it, estimating the height of a horse, and then the height of a rider on its back. Once the cord was knotted securely around the tree trunk, she jumped down and repeated the process on the other side. The closeness of the trees meant not only was the cord long enough to stretch between, but the spot was so dark that the trip line was invisible.

All Tanya's instincts were to run, wasting not a second more, but from the middle of the trail, she made herself stop and examine her handiwork one last time, rechecking her estimate of height. She would get no second chance. If the cord was too high, it might as well not be there. If it was too low, it would hit the horse's head—painful for the horse, but possibly having no debilitating effect on the rider.

Tanya was satisfied. The trip line was as good as she was going to get it. She spun away and ran to where her pony was standing, head sagging and with labored breath. Now that the pony had been allowed to stop, getting it to move again required several slaps on its rump and a hard yank on the reins. Thereafter it clumped along, refusing to rush. Nerves inflamed Tanya's impatience. She was not helped by the sparse undergrowth beneath the firs that meant she had to drag the pony well clear of the trail before she was sure it was out of sight. Loke might be along any moment.

At last, the pony was far enough from the trail. Tanya grabbed the knife from her pack and rushed back. A mixed patch of dover fern and lemon vine grew ten meters from the spot where the trip line trap was set. Tanya dived into cover behind it. Now all she could do was wait, and worry.

Tanya closed her eyes, listening for hoofbeats. The wind rustled over the treetops. A chippit was making its distinctive clicks on a nearby branch, but nothing else. Loke had not raced quickly into pursuit. Tanya desperately hoped this did not mean she had stayed at the Ranger post long enough to harm Riki.

Seconds trickled by. The light ebbed. Through a gap in the trees,

Tanya saw the first star glinting in the deep blue sky. Her right hand ached from clenching the knife hilt and her palm was sweating. Forcing herself to relax, she laid the knife on the ground. When she heard Loke's approach would be quite soon enough to pick it up. She stretched her fingers one at a time and rubbed her palm dry on her trouser leg. The last thing she wanted was the knife slipping in her grasp at the critical moment.

She was going to kill Loke. Tanya knew it. Even if the renegade Ranger was thrown from her horse and knocked unconscious, Tanya dared not take the time to untie the cord from the trees and secure Loke as a prisoner. She dared not get into a fight. Not just for her own sake, even though it would be her knife against Loke's sword. Fairness was not the issue, nor was playing the odds.

Loke was a traitor. Major Kaur had threatened to reveal the truth about Tanya's capture if Loke did not cooperate. Would Loke try to bluff it out and hope that Kaur was not believed? Or would Loke open the gates of Westernfort for the Guards? Would she really sacrifice the entire town to save her own skin? Tanya shook her head. The stakes were too high to gamble with.

When Tanya enlisted in the Rangers she had sworn to protect Westernfort. Killing Loke was not about revenge, or justice, or anger, or saving her own life. It was about doing what she had to do, because if she failed, then the citizens of Westernfort would be in danger. Regardless of what she felt, she was honor bound not to take risks with their safety.

Both of Tanya's mothers had killed. The topic had rarely been discussed, but she had grown up with the knowledge, accepting it unthinkingly. However, Tanya was thinking about it now. The night before she had enlisted in the Rangers, Mama Chip had sat with her, talking about all the things that becoming a Ranger would mean. They both had to be aware of the need to keep the roles of mother and commanding officer separate, but more than this, Mama Chip had spoken of the duties, the responsibilities, and the risks of a Ranger's life.

Mama Chip had also talked of the first time she had killed a woman, in a battle with a gang of thieves, back when she had been a new recruit in the regular Homelands Rangers. She had spoken of what it was like when she had stood over the bandit's body and realized she had taken the woman's life—the guilt and doubts that had replayed themselves for years in her dreams.

Tanya thought she had listened carefully and understood. Now she knew that she had understood nothing, and the current situation only made it harder. She had thought that, if ever she killed, it would be some anonymous Guard, one of the evil enemies of her childhood games, not someone who had been a friend. She had thought she would have comrades at her side. She had thought it would be in the thick of battle with no time to think. Yet, alone and dispassionately, she was preparing to kill a woman she had known all her life.

The faint sound of hooves beat in the distance. Tanya bowed her head, eyes closed, and then reached for her knife. The time of waiting was over.

The pounding hooves got louder, the rhythm of a horse in full gallop. Tanya peered between the ferns and saw Loke emerge from the thick dusk that had swallowed the distance. The renegade Ranger was pressing on furiously, hunched off center in the saddle, head ducked, searching the ground. Clearly she was looking for signs of her quarry leaving the trail. Loke had seen the pony and would know her horse had the speed to overtake it, as long as Tanya was not able to slip away from the trail and hide in the forest.

Tanya looked at where she knew the cord was. Loke's lopsided posture meant her head was far lower than normal. Was she low enough to miss the cord altogether? The horse was now only fifty meters away, hurtling along the path. Only seconds remained. Tanya waited until the animal was just a few strides from the cord, and then she whistled.

The horse barely flinched; the rhythm of its hooves did not falter. However, the effect on Loke was immediate. She jerked upright and around, staring into the forest. Her hands on the reins tightened, but she had no time to do more. An instant later, Loke hit the cord. The contact flipped her backward, ripping her from the saddle. The horse raced on. Even before Loke crashed to the ground, Tanya was on her feet charging forward, knife in hand.

Loke groaned. Her limbs twitched, and she rolled onto her back.

Tanya skidded to her knees beside the woman on the ground. Her eyes were fixed on the point she was aiming for, her target. Her arm was pulled back, ready to strike. Her hand was clenched around the hilt.

She thrust forward, driving the knife point into Loke's chest, using the classic clean killing blow taught to all new recruits, between the ribs and into the heart.

Tanya was surprised at how the knife sliced into flesh, exactly the same as a practice dummy. Why had she thought a woman would be special? That the knife would make a different sound, or perform differently? And since it felt no different, why was her hand seized with cramps?

Tanya's focus shifted, away from the red stain seeping around the embedded knife and onto the dying woman's face.

Loke's eyes were open, staring at Tanya. "You didn't have to...I would have..." She gasped the words.

"I had no choice. I'm sorry." Tanya heard the catch in her own voice and was amazed at how sincere her apology was.

"You didn't give me...not a...chance. I..."

"It was what I had to do."

Loke's eyes closed, her head sagged to the side. The last breath whispered between her lips. "Coward."

"It's not that. I didn't have the—" Tanya stopped speaking. Lokelani Stevenson could no longer hear her.

❖

Riki rode along at a canter, leading the pack pony. The last orange glow of sunset was fading in the west. The farther she went, the more her fears intensified. Surely she would find Tanya before nightfall. Riki could not bear the thought of a night alone, worrying. How far had Tanya gone? Had Tanya hidden? Or had she tackled Loke by herself?

Riki hoped it was the first option. If she could find Tanya, they could deal with Loke together. Riki knew that her wilderness skills would give them more than enough edge. They would be two against one. They could make a sensible plan. But would Tanya see it like that? Would she have tried to tackle Loke alone? And if so, had she succeeded?

The forest was disappearing into the night. Riki bit her lip anxiously. She did not want to stop before she found Tanya, but equally, she did not want to ride into Loke. Tall fir trees now overshadowed the trail. Even when the moons rose, the light would not be enough to ride by. Riki was just about to concede that she would have to call a halt when she saw a dark shape on the trail ahead—a riderless horse grazing at the roadside. As she got closer, Riki spotted other shapes. A figure lay sprawled on the ground and another sat beside it, hugging her knees.

Riki jumped down from her pony. Tanya looked up but made no other move. Her face was drawn. The dim light was still sufficient for Riki to tell that she was crying. Riki knelt by Tanya's side and put an arm around her shoulders.

"Are you all right?"

Tanya merely nodded in reply.

"You're sure?"

"Yes."

Riki glanced at the body on the ground. "You dealt with Loke." She bit her lip. Why state anything so crassly obvious?

"I had to."

"Of course."

"But it wasn't—"

Riki felt Tanya shaking and hugged her tight. "It's okay. It's okay. Don't cry. She's not worth it."

"She called me a coward."

"Why?"

"Because I stabbed her without giving her a chance to draw her weapon."

"She didn't mean the sort of coward who'll hand a comrade over to be tortured to death to save her own skin?"

Tanya buried her face in Riki's shoulder. "I know you're right. It's what I've been telling myself. But I killed her. It's so final. She might have surrendered."

"Not likely."

"Maybe I could have done something else."

"You didn't have any option."

"Mom would have..." Tanya's words ended in a sob.

"Your mother would have done exactly the same thing. Your grandmother, on the other hand, wouldn't have trusted Loke from the start. She'd have made a better offer to the Guards, tricked them into killing Loke, and then got them to pay her for the privilege of pretending they hadn't."

Tanya's shoulders again shook, but this time in weak laughter. "I'm not sure even Grandma would pull that off."

"I wouldn't bet against her." Riki pulled back and stared into Tanya's face. "I know you're upset. I admit I've never killed anyone, so I don't know how I'd feel. But I know you did what was necessary, nothing more. And I know your mother will be proud of you. You're like her. An upstanding, responsible sort of Coppelli. It's a different style from your grandmother, but they don't make mediocre Coppellis. You're a chip off the old block."

Tanya ducked her head with a sad smile. "That's not where Mom's nickname comes from."

"It doesn't matter. You're still like her."

Tanya still looked unhappy, but she was more resolute than when Riki arrived. Riki stood and pulled her to her feet. "You can't sit here all night. We need to eat and sleep. There's an open space by the trail a hundred meters back. We'll make camp there."

"What about Loke?"

"She can stay here tonight. We'll take her to Ginasberg with us tomorrow."

"My pony's in the woods over there."

"I'll get it. You take my pony and the pack back up the trail. Wait for me. You don't need to sort out anything."

"I'll do my share."

"You already have."

Riki watched Tanya lurch away unsteadily, leading the two ponies. Then, for the first time, she studied the body at her feet. Riki crouched and pulled the knife from Loke's chest. It had been a strike straight to the heart. Altogether too quick and easy, in Riki's opinion, for what Loke Stevenson's crimes had deserved. But of course, Tanya had done what was necessary, and nothing more.

Ginasberg was set in a huge natural cavern, hollowed by nature in the walls of a deep canyon. The overhang meant it could not be entered by ropes from above, and the height meant it could not be reached by ladders from below. The only way into the town was along a wooden walkway suspended from a gantry on the cliff above, which could be withdrawn or even burned, should the Guards mount an attack.

The defensive attributes of the site were why it had been chosen for the second heretic stronghold. The land above Ginasberg had been cleared of firs to make farmland to support the population. The discovery of a rich seam of iron ore in the cliffs had been an unexpected bonus that had accelerated the town's expansion.

When Riki and her mother arrived at Ginasberg, only fifty people lived there. Now the population numbered over three hundred. However, only one person was in view when Riki and Tanya emerged from the forest in the late afternoon. Half a kilometer away, the fields ended abruptly at the brink of the chasm, splitting the ground. A well-worn trail led to the head of the gantry, where a lone figure stood in the middle of the track. Even at the distance, Riki had no problem identifying Lieutenant Ash O'Neil.

Obviously their approach had been spotted and word taken to Ginasberg. Riki wondered what the message had said. Any local Ranger would recognize her, but possibly not the woman she was with. O'Neil would have no doubts, though. She had known Tanya since the day she was born, and had been a friend of her parents long before that.

Riki and Tanya rode calmly through the deserted farmland, leading the pack pony and Loke's horse behind them. O'Neil waited with folded arms and a pensive expression. She neither moved nor spoke until they had dismounted and walked the last few meters to stand before her.

O'Neil's eyes darted between them, but fixed in the end on Riki. "I guess it won't come as too much of a surprise that I have orders to shoot you on sight?"

Riki shrugged. "It's pretty much what I expected. I'm pleased you've decided to disobey orders."

"I thought it wiser, considering who you've got for company." O'Neil's eyes turned to Tanya. Finally, the stony expression crumpled and a broad smile broke through. "You won't believe how pleased I am to see you, girl. But nothing like as pleased as your mothers are going to be."

"I'm pretty happy about it as well," Tanya said. "And Riki wasn't the one who handed me over to the Guards."

"I guessed, since you're riding with her. Who was?"

Tanya jerked her thumb at the body draped across the horse. "Her. Loke Stevenson."

"I see you've taken care of the matter already."

"She didn't leave us any choice. She spotted us riding in and tried to ambush us."

"We heard the Guards had captured you. That you'd been taken to Landfall. We didn't think to see you again."

"Riki rescued me from the Corps dungeon."

"She..."

Riki grinned. O'Neil looked so uncharacteristically dumbstruck. "I had to. I knew Tanya was the only person who'd be able to convince Captain Coppelli that I was innocent."

"But how?"

"I had help."

O'Neil shook her head, still looking dazed. "Okay. There's obviously a good story here, but we don't need to stand around outside while you tell it." Her eyes fastened on Riki. "As I said, I've orders to kill you. I'm going to assume it's a formality that those orders are revoked. In the meantime, consider yourself on parole."

"I promise I'll be on my best behavior."

"I want something better than that." However, O'Neil smiled as she spoke. She turned and made a beckoning gesture.

Within seconds, Riki heard footsteps on the wooden walkway and three Rangers appeared over the cliff top. Riki felt her grin broaden in response to the serious expressions on their faces. Their fists were clenched and their eyes jumped between O'Neil and herself, clearly expecting instructions to take her prisoner. Instead, O'Neil pointed to the ponies and Loke's horse.

"Take care of the animals and their cargo. You can bury the body anywhere you like. I can't imagine many will be wanting to visit the grave to pay their respects."

"And Sadiq?" one asked.

"She's currently on parole. And while it will require official confirmation from Captain Coppelli, in the meantime, I think it would be appropriate to treat her and Corporal Tanya Coppelli as returning heroes."

Riki knew that the expression on her face was now an insufferable smirk, but she could not help it and would not have changed even if she could. The three Rangers looked so completely astounded. They tottered toward the ponies like sleepwalkers. Maybe they assumed they were dreaming and wanted to act the part.

Riki and Tanya followed O'Neil to the gantry. Ginasberg was not a suitable home for anyone afraid of heights. The walkway was a solid enough construction, wide enough for two women to walk abreast, with a secure handrail the entire length. However, it was still suspended in midair and the cliff below descended sheer for three hundred meters. Even after living at the town for years, some women preferred not to look down when walking on it.

The sight of Ginasberg, carved from the rock, made Riki's grin fade. Soon she would be meeting her mother. This was the moment that had been driving her ever since she had spoken to her sister in Landfall. It was the thing she had to do, but that did not mean she was looking forward to it.

O'Neil continued talking. "If you've just come across the Wildlands, I guess you'd like a few days to rest before heading on to Westernfort."

Tanya answered. "Just a day or two. I want to see my family as soon as possible. I know my mothers will have been worried about me."

"Worried doesn't begin to cover it. I'd propose sending a messenger immediately to tell them."

"Yes. Do."

"It means you won't get to see their happy faces when they hear the news."

"I suspect they'll still look happy when I get there."

Riki played no part in the conversation. The Ginasberg end of the walkway was getting close and she could see people congregating, doubtless expecting the town's bad girl to be making her final appearance before being carted off to Westernfort. They were going to be so disappointed. Riki tried to amuse herself with the thought, but her growing nervousness got in the way.

O'Neil stepped off the walkway, onto the solid rock of Ginasberg. The crowd looked on expectantly. O'Neil drew a breath, preparing to address the gathering, but a disturbance made heads turn. Kavita Sadiq pushed through the ranks and stepped clear, a few meters away.

The fear and misery on her mother's face hit Riki with a hammer blow. She opened her mouth, but no words would come.

Kavita Sadiq took a stumbling step, as if her knees were about to give way. Ignoring the rest of the crowd, Ash O'Neil moved forward, placing a supportive hand under Kavita's arm, steadying her and claiming her attention. She then spoke, loudly enough for the onlookers to hear.

"I'm pleased to tell you that, for the first time ever, your daughter isn't in trouble and hasn't done anything wrong." O'Neil paused, clearly considering her words, then added, "That I know of. She's technically on parole until I get word from Westernfort to confirm it, but I think you can be assured that all charges against her will be dropped."

Riki stepped forward and cleared her throat. "Mom, I've got to tell you I—"

She got no further. Her mother grabbed her in a crushing embrace, squeezing the air from her lungs. Riki felt her mother shaking, sobbing, and tears falling on her neck. Suddenly, her own eyes flooded and it was all she could do to cling on. She was aware of noise in the background, but she did not care who or what it was. At least three minutes passed before her mother relaxed her grip enough for Riki to pull back.

"Mom, I've got to tell you. I spoke to Jan in Landfall, and she—"

Tears were rolling down Kavita's face, but her smile was pure delight. "Jan! How is she? Have—"

"She's fine. And Fia. And the kids. I've got letters for you. But what she told me—" Riki broke off, marshalling her thoughts. The revelations could wait. She knew what she had to say. "Mom, I'm so sorry for all the trouble I've caused you. When you heard about Tanya, I know you must have thought I'd turned someone over to the Guards, just for a petty argument, but I—"

Her mother interrupted the flow of words, with a hand pressed softly to the side of Riki's face. "Oh no. I knew you were innocent. You were always a little wild, but you were never evil."

Riki closed her eyes. Was this the final thing to feel guilty about—that she could have doubted her mother's love for her? At the same time she was carried away by a surge of happiness. She would have the chance to put everything right. The past could not be undone, but the future was hers, to make what she would of it. No avenues had been lost. No doors were closed.

Kavita again pulled her close, stroking the back of her head. Old memories overwhelmed Riki. She surrendered all self-control, letting herself be as a small child once more, sheltered from the world in the safety of her mother's arms.

❖

Rain was falling on Westernfort and dusk was advancing. Tanya stood at a window overlooking the main square, in her parents' house. A few people were scurrying across, dodging puddles, with their heads down and shoulders hunched. The open space was less than a hundred meters across, unpaved and surrounded by solid, one-story stone buildings. Compared to Landfall it was quiet, rustic, and safe.

Warm firelight filled the room behind Tanya and reflected off the thick green window glass. As the light outside faded, less and less could be seen. It was time to close the shutters, but she hesitated. The scene outside was so very familiar, and one she had thought never to see again.

The last few hours had been hectic. Tanya felt as if she had been hugged, congratulated, and cried on by the entire population of Westernfort. At last things were calming down. Mama Kat was helping her youngest sister with schoolwork; her middle sisters were off with their friends, no doubt telling them all about the daring escape from the Intelligence Corps dungeon; and Mama Chip was having a formal meeting with Riki in the Rangers' headquarters.

Tanya pursed her lips, wondering how the discussion was going. All things considered, she thought it better if whatever issues lay between them were sorted out that evening. Otherwise, it might be awkward at breakfast tomorrow morning. Tanya was planning on spending the night in her room in her parents' home, rather than the barracks. She was also planning on having Riki stay with her. A smile slipped onto Tanya's face at the thought.

A new figure appeared at the far side of the square, running toward the house—Riki. Tanya opened the window, pulled the shutters closed, and was sitting waiting by the fire when the door opened.

Riki shook the rain off her hair and glanced around somewhat hesitantly. She looked relieved to see only Tanya waiting. On their arrival in Westernfort, Riki also had received her share of hugs and backslaps, and had clearly not known how to deal with the unaccustomed attention.

After stripping off her cloak, Riki trotted over to the fire, planted a quick kiss on Tanya's lips, and then sat down close beside her, holding her hands out to the flames. Wisps of steam came off her sleeves. Tanya put her arm around Riki's waist.

For a while, they sat happily together, but Tanya could not restrain her curiosity. "How did the meeting with Mom go?"

"Fine."

"And?"

"She apologized lots for kicking me and for wanting to hang me. She thanked me for bringing you back and then apologized some more. She said she was canceling my demotion to private, so I'd get back pay at the higher rank for all the time I was away. Then she apologized again."

"So you're a leading ranger."

"No."

Tanya turned her head to stare. "Why not?"

The corners of Riki's mouth pulled down in a wry grimace. "I thought I'd use her apologetic mood to ask a favor. I've asked for an unconditional discharge from the Rangers."

"Why?"

"Because I'm a lousy soldier. If I stay on, it won't be long before I'm in trouble again. And your mother will really feel bad about demoting me then."

Tanya needed a few seconds to adjust to the news. Surely Riki could have said what she was planning beforehand—if it had been planned. "So, what will you do?"

Riki reached into her pocket and pulled out a small stone, which she handed over. Tanya looked at it. The rock consisted of rust-colored nodules, with a few flakes of scratched glass embedded in it. "What is it?"

"Mostly, it's iron ore. I picked it up from Mom in Ginasberg. It's what they mine there. But do you see the crystals it in?"

"Yes."

"They're diamonds. Tiny ones, but still diamonds. They aren't very common, but over a year, the miners dig out maybe a kilo or so, along with the tons of iron ore." Riki took the sample back. "But I'm partly guessing, because they don't bother chipping them out of the ore. They go into the furnace and get burnt off."

"The diamonds?"

"Why not? They're useless out here. We need the iron for knives and plows and nails. But there are no jewelers to cut and polish the stones, and nobody with a fortune to spend buying them after it's done."

"What are you going to do with them?"

"When I was in Landfall, staying at your grandmother's mansion, I got to see all the things they have in the Homelands that we just don't have the people or the resources to make. Like books and brandy and silk shirts. And I was thinking that if I made it worth the miners' while, they could put any gemstones they find aside, and I can take them to the Homelands and trade them for some of the luxury items that folk in Westernfort would want and could afford to buy."

"The Homelands? Won't it be dangerous?"

Riki grinned cheerfully. "Yup."

"You can't just take them to a shop. Who'd trade with you?"

"There's a profit to be made. I'm sure your grandmother would be interested. And she'll be able to sort out how to get the details lost in the paperwork, so the Sisters and the Guards don't find out. I'm no good as a Ranger, but I know I'll make a great smuggler."

Tanya's surprise was giving way to irritation. It would have been nice if Riki had given her the chance to discuss it, rather than springing the whole scheme all on her as a fait accompli. It was not as if they had been short of time for talking on the journey. "You've been planning this. Why didn't you talk it over with me first?"

"It was just vague ideas. I hadn't totally made up my mind until I was with your mother, standing to attention, and I knew that being a Ranger was never going to work for me. So I asked to be let out."

"But what about us? You don't want to run off to the Homelands and finish with me, do you?"

Immediately, Riki grabbed Tanya's hand and pressed it to her lips. "Of course not. But if we're involved with each other, we wouldn't be allowed to stay in the same patrol anyway."

"So? At least we'd be able to spend our off duty time together."

"We still will. We'll probably have even more time. You'll be out with your patrol for four or five months a year, playing with the Guards in the Wildlands. That's when I'll do my round trip to the Homelands. If I was in another patrol, I might get sent out when you return. Whereas this way, we know I'll be waiting for you, ready to make your life miserable when you get back here."

Tanya sighed. How could anyone be so exasperating in such an endearing way? Riki was impulsive, unpredictable, and trouble. She was not going to change. In her heart, Tanya knew she would not have it any other way.

She leaned forward and kissed Riki slowly and thoroughly before putting her lips close to Riki's ear. "You obviously don't have the first idea about what makes me miserable."

About the Author

Jane Fletcher is a GCLS award winning writer and has also been short-listed for the Gaylactic Spectrum and Lambda awards. She is author of two fantasy/romance series: the Lyremouth Chronicles—*The Exile and The Sorcerer*, *The Traitor and The Chalice*, and *The Empress and The Acolyte* and the Celaeno series—*The Walls of Westernfort*, *Rangers at Roadsend*, *The Temple at Landfall,* and *Dynasty of Rogues*.

Her love of fantasy began at the age of seven when she encountered Greek Mythology. This was compounded by a childhood spent clambering over every example of ancient masonry she could find (medieval castles, megalithic monuments, Roman villas). Her resolute ambition was to become an archaeologist when she grew up, so it was something of a surprise when she became a software engineer instead.

Born in Greenwich, London, in 1956, she now lives in southwest England, where she keeps herself busy writing both computer software and fiction, although generally not at the same time.

Books Available From Bold Strokes Books

Blind Curves by Diane and Jacob Anderson-Minshall. Private eye Yoshi Yakamota comes to the aid of her ex-lover Velvet Erickson in the first Blind Eye mystery. (978-1-933110-72-1)

Dynasty of Rogues by Jane Fletcher. It's hate at first sight for Ranger Riki Sadiq and her new patrol corporal, Tanya Coppelli—except for their undeniable attraction. (978-1-933110-71-4)

Running With the Wind by Nell Stark. Sailing instructor Corrie Marsten has signed off on love until she meets Quinn Davies—one woman she can't ignore. (978-1-933110-70-7)

More than Paradise by Jennifer Fulton. Two women battle danger, risk all, and find in one another an unexpected ally and an unforgettable love. (978-1-933110-69-1)

Flight Risk by Kim Baldwin. For Blayne Keller, being in the wrong place at the wrong time just might turn out to be the best thing that ever happened to her. (978-1-933110-68-4)

Rebel's Quest, Supreme Constellations Book Two by Gun Brooke. On a world torn by war, two women discover a love that defies all boundaries. (978-1-933110-67-7)

Punk and Zen by JD Glass. Angst, sex, love, rock. Trace, Candace, Francesca...Samantha. Losing control—and finding the truth within. BSB Victory Editions. (1-933110-66-X)

Stellium in Scorpio by Andrews & Austin. The passionate reuniting of two powerful women on the glitzy Las Vegas Strip where everything is an illusion and love is a gamble. (1-933110-65-1)

When Dreams Tremble by Radclyffe. Two women whose lives turned out far differently than they'd once imagined discover that sometimes the shape of the future can only be found in the past. (1-933110-64-3)

The Devil Unleashed by Ali Vali. As the heat of violence rises, so does the passion. A Casey Family crime saga. (1-933110-61-9)

Burning Dreams by Susan Smith. The chronicle of the challenges faced by a young drag king and an older woman who share a love "outside the bounds." (1-933110-62-7)

Fresh Tracks by Georgia Beers. Seven women, seven days. A lot can happen when old friends, lovers, and a new girl in town get together in the mountains. (1-933110-63-5)

The Empress and the Acolyte by Jane Fletcher. Jemeryl and Tevi fight to protect the very fabric of their world: time. Lyremouth Chronicles Book Three. (1-933110-60-0)

First Instinct by JLee Meyer. When high-stakes security fraud leads to murder, one woman flees for her life while another risks her heart to protect her. (1-933110-59-7)

Erotic Interludes 4: Extreme Passions. Thirty of today's hottest erotica writers set the pages aflame with love, lust, and steamy liaisons. (1-933110-58-9)

Storms of Change by Radclyffe. In the continuing saga of the Provincetown Tales, duty and love are at odds as Reese and Tory face their greatest challenge. (1-933110-57-0)

Unexpected Ties by Gina L. Dartt. With death before dessert, Kate Shannon and Nikki Harris are swept up in another tale of danger and romance. (1-933110-56-2)

Sleep of Reason by Rose Beecham. While Detective Jude Devine searches for a lost boy, her rocky relationship with Dr. Mercy Westmoreland gets a lot harder. (1-933110-53-8)

Passion's Bright Fury by Radclyffe. Passion strikes without warning when a trauma surgeon and a filmmaker become reluctant allies. (1-933110-54-6)

Broken Wings by L-J Baker. When Rye Woods meets beautiful dryad Flora Withe, her libido, as hidden as her wings, reawakens along with her heart. (1-933110-55-4)

Combust the Sun by Andrews & Austin. A Richfield and Rivers mystery set in L.A. Murder among the stars. (1-933110-52-X)

Of Drag Kings and the Wheel of Fate by Susan Smith. A blind date in a drag club leads to an unlikely romance. (1-933110-51-1)

Tristaine Rises by Cate Culpepper. Brenna, Jesstin, and the Amazons of Tristaine face their greatest challenge for survival. (1-933110-50-3)

Too Close to Touch by Georgia Beers. Kylie O'Brien believes in true love and is willing to wait for it, even though Gretchen, her new boss, is off-limits. (1-933110-47-3)

100ᵗʰ Generation by Justine Saracen. Ancient curses, modern-day villains, and an intriguing woman lead archeologist Valerie Foret on the adventure of her life. (1-933110-48-1)

Battle for Tristaine by Cate Culpepper. While Brenna struggles to find her place in the clan, Tristaine is threatened with destruction. Second in the Tristaine series. (1-933110-49-X)

The Traitor and the Chalice by Jane Fletcher. Tevi and Jemeryl risk all in the race to uncover a traitor. The Lyremouth Chronicles Book Two. (1-933110-43-0)

Promising Hearts by Radclyffe. Dr. Vance Phelps arrives in New Hope, Montana, with no hope of happiness—until she meets Mae. (1-933110-44-9)

Carly's Sound by Ali Vali. Poppy Valente and Julia Johnson form a bond of friendship that becomes something far more. A poignant romance about love and renewal. (1-933110-45-7)

Unexpected Sparks by Gina L. Dartt. Kate Shannon's attraction to much younger Nikki Harris is complication enough without a fatal fire that Kate can't ignore. (1-933110-46-5)

Whitewater Rendezvous by Kim Baldwin. Two women on a wilderness kayak adventure discover that true love may be nothing at all like they imagined. (1-933110-38-4)

Erotic Interludes 3: Lessons in Love ed. by Radclyffe and Stacia Seaman. Sign on for a class in love…the best lesbian erotica writers take us to "school." (1-9331100-39-2)

Punk Like Me by JD Glass. Twenty-one-year-old Nina has a way with the girls, and she doesn't always play by the rules. (1-933110-40-6)

Coffee Sonata by Gun Brooke. Four women whose lives unexpectedly intersect in a small town by the sea share one thing in common—they all have secrets. (1-933110-41-4)

The Clinic: Tristaine Book One by Cate Culpepper. Brenna, a prison medic, finds herself drawn to Jesstin, a warrior reputed to be descended from ancient Amazons. (1-933110-42-2)

Forever Found by JLee Meyer. Can time, tragedy, and shattered trust destroy a love that seemed destined? Chance reunites childhood friends separated by tragedy. (1-933110-37-6)

Sword of the Guardian by Merry Shannon. Princess Shasta's bold new bodyguard has a secret that could change both of their lives: *He* is actually a *she*. (1-933110-36-8)

Wild Abandon by Ronica Black. Dr. Chandler Brogan and Officer Sarah Monroe are drawn together by their common obsessions—sex, speed, and danger. (1-933110-35-X)

Turn Back Time by Radclyffe. Pearce Rifkin and Wynter Thompson have nothing in common but a shared passion for surgery—and unexpected attraction. (1-933110-34-1)

Chance by Grace Lennox. A sexy, funny, touching story of two women who, in finding themselves, also find one another. (1-933110-31-7)

The Exile and the Sorcerer by Jane Fletcher. First in the Lyremouth Chronicles. Tevi and a shy young sorcerer face monsters, magic, and the challenge of loving. (1-933110-32-5)

A Matter of Trust by Radclyffe. When what should be just business turns into much more, two women struggle to trust the unexpected. (1-933110-33-3)

Sweet Creek by Lee Lynch. A celebration of the enduring nature of love, friendship, and community in the heart-warming lesbian community of Waterfall Falls. (1-933110-29-5)

The Devil Inside by Ali Vali. The head of a New Orleans crime organization falls for a woman who turns her world upside down. (1-933110-30-9)

Grave Silence by Rose Beecham. Detective Jude Devine's investigation of ritual murders is complicated by her torrid affair with pathologist Dr. Mercy Westmoreland. (1-933110-25-2)

Honor Reclaimed by Radclyffe. Secret Service Agent Cameron Roberts and Blair Powell close ranks to find the would-be assassins who nearly claimed Blair's life. (1-933110-18-X)

Honor Bound by Radclyffe. Secret Service Agent Cameron Roberts and Blair Powell face political intrigue, a clandestine threat to Blair's safety, and the seemingly irreconcilable differences that force them ever farther apart. (1-933110-20-1)

Innocent Hearts by Radclyffe. In a wild and unforgiving land, two women learn about love, passion, and the wonders of the heart. (1-933110-21-X)

The Temple at Landfall by Jane Fletcher. An imprinter, one of Celaeno's most revered servants of the Goddess, is also a prisoner to the faith—until a Ranger frees her by claiming her heart. The Celaeno series. (1-933110-27-9)

Protector of the Realm, Supreme Constellations Book One by Gun Brooke. A space adventure filled with suspense and a daring intergalactic romance. (1-933110-26-0)

Force of Nature by Kim Baldwin. From tornados to forest fires, the forces of nature conspire to bring Gable McCoy and Erin Richards close to danger, and closer to each other. (1-933110-23-6)

In Too Deep by Ronica Black. Undercover homicide cop Erin McKenzie tracks a femme fatale who just might be a real killer…with love and danger hot on her heels. (1-933110-17-1)

Stolen Moments: Erotic Interludes 2 by Stacia Seaman and Radclyffe, eds. Love on the run, in the office, in the shadows…Fast, furious, and almost too hot to handle. (1-933110-16-3)

Course of Action by Gun Brooke. Actress Carolyn Black desperately wants the starring role in an upcoming film produced by Annelie Peterson. Just how far will she go for the dream part of a lifetime? (1-933110-22-8)

Rangers at Roadsend by Jane Fletcher. Sergeant Chip Coppelli has learned to spot trouble coming, and that is exactly what she sees in her new recruit, Katryn Nagata. The Celaeno series. (1-933110-28-7)

Justice Served by Radclyffe. Lieutenant Rebecca Frye and her lover, Dr. Catherine Rawlings, embark on a deadly game of hide-and-seek with an underworld kingpin who traffics in human souls. (1-933110-15-5)

Distant Shores, Silent Thunder by Radclyffe. Dr. Tory King—along with the women who love her—is forced to examine the boundaries of love, friendship, and the ties that transcend time. (1-933110-08-2)

Hunter's Pursuit by Kim Baldwin. A raging blizzard, a mountain hideaway, and a killer-for-hire set a scene for disaster—or desire—when Katarzyna Demetrious rescues a beautiful stranger. (1-933110-09-0)

The Walls of Westernfort by Jane Fletcher. All Temple Guard Natasha Ionadis wants is to serve the Goddess—until she falls in love with one of the rebels she is sworn to destroy. The Celaeno series. (1-933110-24-4)

Change Of Pace: *Erotic Interludes* by Radclyffe. Twenty-five hot-wired encounters guaranteed to spark more than just your imagination. Erotica as you've always dreamed of it. (1-933110-07-4)

Honor Guards by Radclyffe. In a wild flight for their lives, the president's daughter and those who are sworn to protect her wage a desperate struggle for survival. (1-933110-01-5)

Fated Love by Radclyffe. Amidst the chaos and drama of a busy emergency room, two women must contend not only with the fragile nature of life, but also with the irresistible forces of fate. (1-933110-05-8)

Justice in the Shadows by Radclyffe. In a shadow world of secrets and lies, Detective Sergeant Rebecca Frye and her lover, Dr. Catherine Rawlings, join forces in the elusive search for justice. (1-933110-03-1)

shadowland by Radclyffe. In a world on the far edge of desire, two women are drawn together by power, passion, and dark pleasures. An erotic romance. (1-933110-11-2)

Love's Masquerade by Radclyffe. Plunged into the indistinguishable realms of fiction, fantasy, and hidden desires, Auden Frost is forced to question all she believes about the nature of love. (1-933110-14-7)

Love & Honor by Radclyffe. The president's daughter and her lover are faced with difficult choices as they battle a tangled web of Washington intrigue for...love and honor. (1-933110-10-4)

Beyond the Breakwater by Radclyffe. One Provincetown summer, three women learn the true meaning of love, friendship, and family. (1-933110-06-6)

Tomorrow's Promise by Radclyffe. One timeless summer, two very different women discover the power of passion to heal and the promise of hope that only love can bestow. (1-933110-12-0)

Love's Tender Warriors by Radclyffe. Two women who have accepted loneliness as a way of life learn that love is worth fighting for and a battle they cannot afford to lose. (1-933110-02-3)

Love's Melody Lost by Radclyffe. A secretive artist with a haunted past and a young woman escaping a life that has proved to be a lie find their destinies entwined. (1-933110-00-7)

Safe Harbor by Radclyffe. A mysterious newcomer, a reclusive doctor, and a troubled gay teenager learn about love, friendship, and trust during one tumultuous summer in Provincetown. (1-933110-13-9)

Above All, Honor by Radclyffe. Secret Service Agent Cameron Roberts fights her desire for the one woman she can't have—Blair Powell, the daughter of the president of the United States. (1-933110-04-X)